DO645377

RING OF
LIES

RING OF LIES

RONI DUNEVICH

Translated from the Hebrew by Sara Kitai

HARPER

NEW YORK • LONDON • TORONTO • SYDNEY

HARPER

HarperCollins books may be purchased for educational, business, or sales promotional use. For information please email the Special Markets Department at SPsales@harpercollins.com.

Originally published as *Amok Mebifnim* in Israel in 2011 by Kinneret, Zmora-Bitan.

First Harper Paperback edition published 2016.

Designed by Leydiana Rodriguez

Library of Congress Cataloging-in-Publication Data has been applied for.

ISBN 978-0-06-227978-1 (pbk.)

16 17 18 19 20   RRD   10 9 8 7 6 5 4 3 2 1

For my mother

"History is a symptom of our disease."

—MAO TSE-TUNG

"Forget about Istanbul."

"He's late?"

"Dead."

"How?"

"Not now. You have to go back."

Galia lets out a long breath. "We're an hour away from Bolu."

"Go back," the man orders. "There's a leak."

"From the Nibelungs?" she asks.

"Probably from our side, too. Take two guys, go back to the warehouse, do what has to be done, change faces, and fly out through Ankara."

"And the others?"

"They go as planned, through Istanbul," the man says.

"Istanbul squealed?"

"Let's assume he did."

"How did he die?"

"Not now."

"Where's the pit?"

"On the top of Mount Bolu. Under the snow."

"Where on the top?"

"We're checking on it."

"We won't have time to dig a new one."

---

1   All hours are given in local time.

"I know. We're checking on it."

"There's no acid," Galia says.

"Do without it."

"And the electric burns?"

"Get rid of the plastic sheets, pails, rags, towels. Wipe everything down. Outside, too."

"If they were on to Istanbul, they're on to us, too," she says.

"Where are you exactly?"

"Approaching Körfez. Ninety miles east of Istanbul."

The man examines the map on the huge monitor. "Turn back where the highway meets Route 100. There should be a reserve gallon of diesel fuel in the trunk."

"Diesel fuel?"

"Burn him."

"We have no weapons, nothing. They took everything. All the stuff must be back in Ankara by now . . ."

He's silent.

"Give me a minute to get organized," Galia says.

Her breathing quickens.

"You'll be fine."

She snaps out rapid-fire orders into another phone, trying to keep cool.

He hears a siren approaching on her end. "What's that?"

"An ambulance. Two and Six are going back with me," she says.

"Not Six. His wife's nine months pregnant."

"So Seven. Two and Seven."

"Give Seven the fuel. He's good at that."

He gives her the coordinates of the pit Istanbul dug two days ago on the snowy summit of Mount Bolu.

They have to make it to Ankara in time for the morning flight. A hundred and twenty miles. The Turkish soil is burning. Their intelligence agency is on the hunt for General Farzan Karabashi, a key figure in the Iranian Revolutionary Guards. The man vanished from the streets of Ankara two days ago, and Turkey wants to prove to Mahmoud Ahmadinejad that it isn't just a friend but a genuine ally.

Acid rises in his throat. He snaps into the microphone, "I need a thermal satellite over Bolu. Anatolian Plateau. Turkey. Now."

"One hour and forty-two minutes from now. Confirm?" a young woman reports from the operations center.

He feels like smashing one of the monitors.

"Confirm?" she repeats.

"No. That's too late."

There's no video. It's as though the blackout has stretched all the way to their location.

It's cold on Mount Bolu. Minus three. And there's no time.

He scans the giant monitors on the wall. His eyes linger on the three-dimensional image of the spice warehouse, a window-less, one-story concrete structure. Two thousand square feet. Walls insulated against cold and heat. An autonomous climate-control system to preserve the freshness of the valuables inside.

He zooms in for a closer view. Behind the last row of shelves, a yellow *X* is painted on the warehouse floor in a rectangle the size of an average living room. There, bound to a chair, sprawls a lifeless, naked body.

He switches back to the frontal view. On a faded sign, the name FALACCI BAHARAT is written in white letters against a red background. A lone forklift is parked beside the entrance, casting a long shadow.

He looks at the satellite image from the afternoon. The area is densely forested. The mountaintops are snowcapped. There's a sharp curve in the nearby highway, followed by enormous tunnels. The warehouse is situated on the sharp slope of the mountain, far from the houses of the town. There's only one access road.

A separate monitor is filled with a photo of the squad leader. Her face is expressionless.

They shouldn't return to the scene of the operation. It's against regulations. Strictly forbidden. But that's exactly what he ordered her to do.

One by one the senior staff members file quietly into the underground war room, whispering, getting updates, voicing speculations. A chair squeaks. Someone's knee pops.

One chair, the one belonging to the chief of Mossad, has been empty since the start of the crisis. Everyone has taken note.

In the middle of the night, five stories underground, the operational nerve center on the other side of the double glass partition is buzzing with activity.

What happened to Istanbul? How could he have died minutes before he was supposed to go out on his mission?

The head of Internal Security enters the war room. He's wearing a black leather jacket; his expression is tense. His head is shaved. The crease of a blanket is still etched on his cheek. He takes his place. He's the one who has to hunt down the source of the leak before the night ends.

And he? He's been here since six yesterday morning. Where will he go when the night is over?

For the past three months, he's been personally commanding a large number of operations all over the world. Whispering has begun in the corridors. Something is happening to him.

He was supposed to be with Galia in Bolu, but she asked to go alone. He gave in.

He tries to push his acute anxiety for her out of his mind.

Silence in the situation room. No chirping phones. Except for the faint hum of the air conditioner, all is quiet. He has to rescue Galia tonight, or else she'll come back in an aluminum box.

Nineteen other men do not dare breathe.

But the responsibility is his alone. They're just the audience. They're watching him the way you watch a gladiator.

"We're at the observation post, about two hundred feet from the warehouse," Galia reports in a tense voice.

"Gut feeling?"

"It stinks."

"Sorry. Who's going in?"

"Me. Seven and Two will keep watch here."

"Send Seven in."

"I'll do it."

She'll manage. She always manages. She has nine lives.

"Has anything changed there?" he asks.

Nothing but breathing on the other end. A long minute goes by. "No. It's dark."

"Go slow."

"Fuck!" she hisses. "It's almost three thirty and we still have to bury him . . . We won't make it to Ankara before seven."

He hears her breathing quicken as she moves forward, taking silent steps.

"Okay." She takes a deep breath. "I'm going in."

He stares at the image of the warehouse on the monitor, trying to picture what she's seeing.

The iron door opens noisily.

He holds his breath.

"It's dark. I'm turning on my flashlight."

Now steps echo in the high-ceilinged space.

"Oh my God!"

"What happened?"

"He's not here!"

In the dark situation room, everyone freezes.

"Get the hell out of there!"

A terrifying barrage of gunfire.

A choked moan of pain.

A faint thud.

Rapid breathing.

"I'm hit . . ."

Everything stops.

The sound of men shouting comes through his wireless headset.

Then the line goes dead.

It was because of Reuven Hetz, sitting behind his desk, that he was forced to live a life he didn't want.

Hetz, the head of Mossad, had to raise his head to meet Alex Bartal's glance, which, for the last three months, he'd been avoiding religiously. They shared a long history as volatile as a minefield.

Reuven didn't stand up to greet him, and Alex didn't sit down. He just stared at the chief, his clenched fists turning white at either side of his worn jeans.

The oppressive silence dragged on. The space between them crackled with tension.

Reuven focused his close-set eyes on Alex's chest and finally said, "We're forced to have this meeting because of what happened tonight in Bolu." He licked his lips with his pale tongue, separating the paragraphs.

"You know them as the Nibelung Ring. They help us with the most dangerous operations in Europe, but apart from that, you and the other Mossad operatives don't know a thing about them." Another lick of his lips.

"The Nibelungs are sleeper agents who live in major European capitals, local citizens with reliable covers. Some of them have families. They assassinate, sabotage, burglarize, and keep suspects under surveillance as skillfully as we do. They work alone. Nibelungs can lie dormant for years, wake up, kill two people in a few seconds, and then go back to sleep for another long period."

Lick.

"We don't know them, and they don't know us; the separation is absolute. They are an external defensive ring around us," Reuven said. "An immune system."

Reuven's desk was empty, his computer screen dark.

Alex moved back.

Reuven leaned forward and rested his elbows on the empty desktop. *If he rolled up his sleeves, you'd see a layer of Teflon instead of skin*, Alex thought.

"The day I stepped into this job," Reuven said, "there was an envelope waiting for me in the safe. It contained the name of the man who heads the Nibelung Ring. The prime minister is only letting me tell you the name now because of tonight's disaster. The information is at the very heart of this country's covert operations. If you share his name with anyone without the proper authorization, you'll spend the rest of your life in prison."

Reuven seemed to relish this information that defined his superiority. Lowering his glance, he said quietly, "His name is Justus."

"That's it?"

Reuven pursed his lips, took a deep breath. "He's German, Christian, fifty-three years old. He lives in Berlin and runs dozens of Nibelung agents throughout Europe. The Nibelungs don't know one another. They are trained for critical one-man missions in friendly countries. If one is lost, we can't launch any dangerous operations in that country because under no circumstances can we leave traces that lead back to Israel. Wherever we lose a Nibelung, we have no local backup force.

"A good Nibelung is the difference between a lethargic police investigation and a diplomatic incident. They're classic 'cleaners.' They stay behind, dispose of evidence, and remove all traces. Are you beginning to understand the extent of the damage?"

Reuven moistened the tips of his index fingers with his tongue and smoothed down his bushy eyebrows.

"Justus and the Ring report directly to the prime minister. Everything's coordinated without any intermediaries. Nothing is in writing."

In Wagner's opera cycle, which Hitler was so fond of, the Nibelungs are dwarves struggling to keep a gold ring out of the hands of the gods.

"Has Istanbul's body been found?" Alex asked.

"No."

"He might be alive."

"Istanbul's dead, Alex." Reuven blinked like a crocodile.

"Says who?"

"He has three-week-old twins waiting for him at home. He comes from a prominent, wealthy Jewish family in Istanbul. He has no reason to disappear."

Lick.

On his only visit to Reuven's home, Alex had found bare walls and not a single personal item. For a moment, he'd suspected that the man's house had a false bottom.

"One day we're going to miss these times, Alex. In another year or two, a vacation in Bodrum will seem as plausible as a vacation in Tehran," Reuven said, sipping what was left of his black coffee.

There was a momentary oppressive silence.

Then Reuven said, "From the initial debriefing of the operatives, we know that they were ambushed at the spice warehouse by soldiers wearing black combat overalls and armored vests. It sounds like Özel Tim. There was an ambulance waiting nearby—it arrived less than a minute after the shooting."

"The leak didn't come from us," Alex cut in. "We didn't know Istanbul's identity. The Turks must've gotten hold of him, and he gave up the warehouse."

"So why didn't they attack when the whole team was inside?" Reuven asked, examining the burnished mahogany surface of his desk.

"Maybe Özel Tim didn't have time to get ready. Is there anything new from our sources in Ankara?"

"Politicians are usually asleep at six in the morning. When they finally get up, they run straight to the newspaper and look for any mention of their names."

Reuven turned to look out at the coastal road. "You've been in this business long enough to know that sometimes the price is painful. We'll thank God if this whole thing ends with only two losses."

Alex approached, pressed both palms on the barricade-like desk, and bent toward Reuven. "You're not planning to fight for Galia?"

Reuven looked at Alex's hands as if he were looking at a dead cat.

"Definitely not right away, and it would depend on the cost. She has a Dutch passport."

Alex straightened up and strode back to the far end of the office. "Her Dutch identity won't hold up longer than a day," he said too loudly.

"No one wants Galia back more than I do," Reuven said hastily, "but don't forget, Mossad isn't supposed to serve its agents.

The agents are supposed to serve Mossad. If we have to give up Galia in order to avoid taking official responsibility for the screwup in Bolu, we'll do it—with a heavy heart, but we'll do it."

Alex closed the distance between himself and Reuven.

Reuven straightened up and tensed.

"You have no problem abandoning your best people?"

"Everyone can be replaced," Reuven hissed.

Even you, Reuven, Alex thought.

The head of Mossad nodded, as if reading his mind.

"Galia was going to be the first woman to head Operations," Alex said.

"You are not the one who's going to appoint the next chief of Operations," Reuven fired back. "I've heard that the two of you are close. People talk."

Reuven backed away from the desk, from Alex. The wheels of his desk chair spun soundlessly.

Sweat was forming on Alex's back. It was always too hot in the chief's office.

"You didn't bother to come down to the war room even once all night," Alex said.

"I was tied up in intense consultations with the prime minister and the head of the Ring," Reuven replied too quickly, as if he'd prepared his answer in advance. "I couldn't conduct those discussions in front of everyone."

A ping sounded. Reuven moved closer to the computer. His eyes darted across it. "Unit 8200 interception: The Turkish government is about to announce that they have found the body of General Farzan Karabashi. They are holding a female Mossad operative with Dutch citizenship who was involved in his abduction, torture, and murder. She's injured."

"How do they already know she's Mossad?" Alex asked.

"She must've talked. She's wounded and she needs treatment. Anyone would talk."

"Not Galia."

"Alex, you can't run the intelligence agency of a country like ours if you let your emotions get the best of you."

The chief swung his armchair around and bent over the safe, making sure to hide the digital pad with his shoulder as he entered the code. The cast-iron door opened with a sucking sound.

He rummaged through the cardboard folders inside, pulled out a thin green one, opened it, and handed it to Alex.

The first thing Alex saw was a picture of a man with a high, curved forehead, like a dolphin's. His light blue eyes sparkled.

"That's Justus. I want you to meet with him this afternoon. Keep your eyes open, sniff him out in your inimitable way. Justus runs all the Nibelungs personally. If there was a leak, it came from him. Don't hesitate to attack. Shake the tree and see what falls out."

"Maybe you should shake it yourself?" Alex suggested.

"I have to go on working with him," Reuven said. "I don't want to ruffle his feathers. Anyway, I already have urgent meetings scheduled with the PM, the Ministry of Foreign Affairs, the legal advisers. And we're expecting a full-out media blitz."

The course of action was predictable. For the next few days, the State of Israel would offer no response. The familiar evasion tactic—the safe haven for prime ministers and Mossad chiefs who screw up.

"I've put together an investigative team led by the head of Internal Security. They'll look into whether we had a leak here. They'll want to talk to you when you get back from Berlin," Reuven said.

The phone on the desk chirped.

Reuven grabbed the receiver. He listened in silence, closed his eyes, and finally nodded and said, "I understand."

Then he opened his eyes, stared into space, and announced, "The prime minister has ordered an immediate halt to all our European operations."

"And how are we supposed to understand what's going on, from Fox News?" Alex wondered.

They both felt that their ship was filling with water.

"Three months ago, I suggested that you take some time off. You have more than two hundred days saved up. You've been through things that would shake anyone up. Maybe after Berlin you'll take a little rest?"

A hopeless dawn rose outside the window. A flash from the depths of his memory, a picture that would never be erased: the hospital in Hampstead. His wife, Naomi, lying on the pale linoleum floor. Dark blood pooling around her. Her face growing pale.

A strange fluttering in the air. Silence. He heard himself say, "You didn't even come to *shivah*."

Reuven stared at the muted coastal road through the bulletproof window.

"And you were there when she died," Alex added.

"Don't blame me for the mistakes in your life," Reuven said quietly, not without rancor.

"You walked into the hospital waiting room with your gun drawn. You didn't wait to see who was there," Alex said.

"Enough! I don't want to hear it anymore."

"You haven't heard anything yet," Alex hissed, his ears burning. He spun around and headed for the door.

"How's Daniella?" Reuven called out behind him.

His back muscles tightened.

"Have you told her yet?" Reuven twisted the knife.

As he left the chief's office, Alex was seized by an intense urge to shower.

With a sense of urgency, Alex shoved warm clothes into a black duffel bag, almost forgetting gloves and a scarf.

The house was quiet. The windows were shut; everything was locked.

The fraction of a second between the time he turned off the lamp in the dining room and when he slammed the front door was enough for the dead Naomi, the black-framed photograph, to throw him a scolding look: *You can't escape. You won't be able to forget.*

Later, at Ben Gurion Airport, the Gulfstream raced madly down the runway, its engines screaming, the terminal and waiting planes blurred through the windows.

Alex took his first deep breath since leaving the war room that morning.

Text message: Meeting set for 16:00 in the Bebelplatz, Berlin.

He looked at his watch and did a few calculations, then got up and touched the pilot's shoulder. The pilot turned around and removed his headset, revealing two round monkey ears. His breath smelled of eggs.

"We're making a stop in Florence."

The pilot nodded. "How long?"

"Up to three hours."

The pilot nodded again and replaced his headset.

Alex walked back and sank into the tan leather seat. He looked up at the ceiling, at the approximate spot where two Glock 17s, bullet clips, stun grenades, first-aid supplies, and a sterile emergency surgery kit were hidden.

The malicious final moment of his meeting with Reuven echoed in his mind. He thought about his daughter, Daniella.

Last December, right after she finished basic combatant training, Daniella was sent to London on her first operational mission. She was abducted by the Quds Force, Iran's unit for secret extraterritorial operations. Alex had rushed to London to rescue her. Out of options, he contacted Jane Thompson, a British former Mossad agent. Together they launched a predawn raid on the Iranian house, and after a bloody gun battle Daniella was freed.

Daniella was wounded and had to undergo surgery in a nearby hospital. While he, Jane, and the male agent were sitting in the hospital waiting room, Naomi, Alex's wife, suddenly appeared.

Eventually Alex realized that the person responsible for Daniella's abduction was sitting right beside him.

The man pulled a gun.

Reuven arrived in the midst of the fight between Alex and the traitor. Reuven reached for his gun, shot the traitor, and killed him. A stray bullet from the traitor's gun hit Naomi. She died almost at once. Alex would never forget her last words to him.

Later, he found out that Daniella had been tortured and raped.

For the last six weeks, she'd been on a remote farm in eastern Tuscany. He made sure to call her regularly. She made sure to keep the conversations short.

He remembered Daniella in the recovery room, still woozy from the anesthesia, asking, "Where's Mom?"

For a moment, he couldn't speak.

"What happened, Dad?"

"What?"

"Tell me what happened."

"She was here . . ."

"When?"

"During the operation."

"So why'd she leave?"

"She didn't leave."

"Where's Mom?"

"She was shot."

"What . . ."

"Mom is gone."

The secure satphone buzzed.

Reuven Hetz. "The Turkish media is boiling mad. The Ankara police just announced that they found the body of the kidnapped Iranian general and arrested a female Mossad agent carrying a forged Dutch passport."

"That's it?" Alex asked.

"I wish. The Turkish prime minister said that Israel has flagrantly crossed all the red lines and violated Turkish sovereignty. The Turkish Ministry of Foreign Affairs announced that Erdoğan ordered his ambassador in Israel to return immediately to Ankara. Ahmadinejad was quoted as saying that Iran will avenge General Karabashi's death with blood and fire."

"As expected. Did the Turks say anything about Galia's injuries?"

"She suffered moderate injuries."

Should that make him happy or sad? "They didn't mention Istanbul's disappearance?"

"He didn't disappear, he's dead. And, no, they didn't say anything."

Alex was silent.

Reuven hung up.

Text message: Are you okay?

Sent by Jane Thompson. Her name on the screen awakened a small bird from its deep sleep.

He considered calling her, but he heard the pilot say, "Two minutes to touchdown!"

The Tuscan countryside appeared below between white clouds, followed by the centuries-old red-tiled roofs of Florence. The Gulfstream's landing gear dropped down with a thump. The pressure in his ears grew. Butterflies swirled in his stomach. Soon he would see Daniella. Fear gripped him. How would she react?

Just to hold her in his arms.

To feel that he belonged to someone.

Awaiting him at the end of the highway, past the string of semi-trailers crawling along like snails, was a terrible conversation with Daniella. He slammed the steering wheel with his open hand. He had to tell her that he was coming.

The road was wet, and the trucks' wheels sprayed mud onto his windshield. Then traffic began to flow, and the green road signs slid past in a blur.

He exited the highway at Valdarno. The rolling hills of Tuscany were a patchwork of bare vineyards and olive trees. The waters of the Ambra rushed by. Cars climbed the narrow winding road to Bucine.

He had a thick, rough espresso at a roadside snack bar at the entrance to the town. A dying neon light flickered on the red-and-white Kinder chocolate wrappings. A slot machine clattered somewhere. He put the small empty cup on the counter and left.

"Signore?" a woman called after him.

He looked for her, ready with an apology. A tiny woman, she was hidden behind the cash register, wrinkled and old, dressed in black, her thinning hair pulled back tightly in a bun. She smiled at him, rubbing her thumb and index finger together.

He hurried back and paid her, adding a one-euro tip. "*Mi dispiace.*"

After passing a row of village houses, he turned right into a wooded area. The winding, bumpy road was covered with morning fog. The road descended, then climbed again, revealing an elongated vineyard with blackened, ropey stems. The horizon was lined with snowcapped blue mountains.

He followed the road into a forest, where the sun glimmered through the sparse treetops. Silvery spiderwebs clung to spindly, brown, leafless trees, and the rotting ground was strewn with pine needles. He opened the window and slowed down, listening to the wind and the twittering of the birds.

The dense woods thinned out, and vestiges of frost glittered on wild grass. A large puddle reflected a mass of heavy clouds, close, threatening the sun.

A muffled shot rang out.

He braked and tensed.

A pair of birds flew off in alarm. The sky darkened, casting the woods into shadow.

Another shot, thick and blunted, from a hunting rifle.

Strange. Hunting was prohibited in early spring.

He continued down the dirt road. The acrid smell of smoke came in through the window. Orange flames rose from a pile of dry branches on the edge of the vineyard. The road to the farm was lined with olive trees.

This was where Daniella was supposed to be.

He pulled into the carport, his tires crushing gravel, and parked behind a jeep.

A lovely piece of land, rich and peaceful, that was not meant for him.

The stillness brushed his ears like soft down. He had come here from the midst of a terrible noise that enabled him to shut out the voices that had been drumming at his heart for the last few months.

Time passed slowly here. Dammit, the bombshell would have to wait. He would just see her, hug her, stroke her face, and say nothing for the time being.

His phone was already in his hand. What would he say?

Finally, he called.

A call-waiting beep went on and on.

"Yes?"

He choked up. That was how she always answered the phone.

"It's Dad . . . How are you, dear?"

"Hi, Dad. Where are you?"

"In Italy."

"Where?"

"Milan. I want to come see you." Coward. Pathetic liar.

"Where—here?"

"I want to see you."

"When?"

"Today."

"You're not busy?"

"I'm dying to see you."

He heard her deep breathing. "It's not such a good idea . . ."

His heart dropped.

"A quick visit, just to see you."

She took a deep breath. "I still need to be alone . . ."

Through the phone, he heard a door close and footsteps going down stairs.

The long silence was discomfiting. Suddenly he saw her, and his breath caught in his throat.

She was walking alongside a red mountain bike, the phone was at her ear, and her face was gaunt and sad. She didn't appear to have seen him.

"I love you, little girl . . ."

"I know . . ."

He wanted to cry but couldn't. He yearned to open the car door and run to her, but his body stayed glued to the seat.

She disappeared behind a wall of cypress trees.

"Later, Dad." She hung up.

"Yes, later," he said to the air, and leaned his head back.

With her uncompromising gentleness, she had driven a wedge between them.

He waited to be sure their paths wouldn't cross, and then he sped back down the winding road, his teeth clenched.

The weather along the short flight path from Florence to Berlin was turbulent. The plane bobbed like an empty bottle in a stormy sea.

Reuven called on the secure satphone. "Turkish Prime Minister Erdoğan called a press conference and demanded that Israel apologize to Turkey and Iran for its crimes. He announced that he's ordered the expulsion of our consular staff from Ankara. Are you in Berlin yet?"

"Soon."

"We found a lawyer to represent Galia, but the Turks won't let him see her in the hospital. He believes he's been hired by a Dutch human rights organization. The Turkish media reported that soldiers from the Turkish antiterrorism squad are guarding the hospital. We managed to get a photo of her medical report. It's blank. They didn't even record her temperature or blood pressure."

Alex felt as if someone was hammering a nail into his head.

"We're fucked, Reuven."

The chief was silent.

"I'll get whatever I can out of Justus," Alex said. "I'll see you in the office tonight and think about what to do."

Reuven still said nothing.

Keep silent, deny, ignore. In retrospect, sending a Mossad team into the heart of a country as problematic as Turkey had been a big mistake, even despite the valuable intel that General Karabashi had given them.

Reuven hung up.

Now the PM and Reuven were going to hide themselves behind the defensive shield known as "no comment." No admission of guilt—no responsibility. And with no responsibility, they could keep their jobs.

Though he was exhausted from the sleepless night, he was too upset to doze on the plane. His thoughts went to Galia, her isolation, her distress, her pain. He tried to remember whether Turkey had capital punishment.

The growing pressure in his ears interrupted the mounting anxiety of his thoughts. The pilot descended, landing at Tegel Airport.

He usually managed to avoid Berlin. He'd had to go there twice. First in the early '80s, on the hunting expedition where he met Jane. The second time was about two years ago, when he'd spent only a few hours there.

Alex disembarked from the plane on shaky legs.

A limousine whisked him to the modern terminal. A stone-cold voice announced the last call for a flight to Moscow. A chill went through his body. The guttural sound of German filled his mouth with a metallic taste.

The rubber stamp came down on his forged passport.

A taxi took him into the most scarred city in the world.

Here the Third Reich was born, and here Kristallnacht took place. Here blood-soaked World War II was launched, and the final solution to Europe's Jewish problem was plotted. Here an empire was created and then razed to the ground. Here Adolf Hitler flourished and then took his life. Here the dividing wall between the East and the West was erected, and the Cold War broke out. Here the Stasi unleashed its reign of terror, and here the Wall was torn down and the two Germanys were reunited.

Outside, an ominous winter day. Minus nine, said a billboard. The streets were covered in fresh snow and the sky was leaden. Just a faint bluish light.

He got out of the cab on Unter den Linden, and the cold lashed at his face like a curtain of needles. His feet crushed the coarse salt and pebbles that had been scattered on the ice.

He had fifteen minutes until the meeting. Germans wrapped in hats and scarves hurried past him. Bebelplatz was close. He recognized the impressive Humboldt University building. A sudden gust of wind sent a shiver through him. He made his way carefully along the icy path.

Bebelplatz was flat, rectangular, snowy, and empty. He looked for the monument buried in the cobblestones. He saw pale light coming from a bare, square window in the center of the ice-covered surface. He approached and looked down into the space. It was about fifteen feet square. Its walls were lined with empty bookshelves painted white.

Here, in 1933, the Nazis had burned twenty thousand books written by Jews, Communists, and liberals who refused to accept Nazi principles.

The whispering monument was bloodcurdling.

It was as if it were murmuring, *Your mother is dead.*

Alex's eyes were fixed on the empty bookshelves. The cold seared his mouth and windpipe.

Reflected in the glass floor beside him was a large image of someone else. He hadn't heard any steps approaching. Alex turned and examined him. The tall German had a large, strong build.

"You are the emissary," the man declared, the wind playing with his mane of white hair. Alex recognized the dolphinlike forehead and nodded.

"So the boss is too busy to see me," the German added, slightly offended. A moment later, he decided to smile and reached out to shake Alex's hand. His own hand was encased in a fine-quality glove. His grip was warm and strong, but his bottom lip drooped as if he'd just gotten bad news.

"How are you, Justus?"

"Spring does not arrive here until a month after it reaches Munich in the South," Justus said.

"What happened to your man in Istanbul?" Alex asked.

Justus smiled mischievously. "What's your rush?"

"In one hour last night we lost the Istanbul Nibelung, and the leader of our operational team was wounded and captured. Even if she's released, she's burned forever. Do you still insist on foreplay?"

The German's smile flew off, gone with the wind. He shook his head.

"Could Istanbul have betrayed us?" Alex asked.

"No chance," Justus said.

"So why are the Turks only talking about a female Mossad agent and not saying a word about him?"

"I do not know yet," Justus said. "But I know my people very well. I promise you, Istanbul was no traitor."

"Based on what?"

"I can read people like an open book."

"Really?"

Justus studied him. "You are too close to your operative to handle this matter with the good judgment it requires."

"Really?"

"You are a man of nearly endless patience who is at the end of his rope."

Another gust swept across the empty plaza. Alex felt as if he'd been stripped of his clothes. "Why did you want to meet here?"

"Why not?" Justus asked.

"Is this your favorite spot in Berlin?"

"One of them. I love books. For me, this place is like the mouth of a volcano. Lava seething with hatred flows under our feet, threatening to erupt. Here, you can actually see it. If you are looking for beauty, go to Paris. People come to Berlin for its scars. Do you read German?" Justus tightened the gray cashmere scarf around his neck.

Alex nodded.

"There is a quotation from the Jewish poet Heinrich Heine engraved in the bronze tablets buried in the snow right under the soles of your shoes." His face was enveloped by the white breath coming from his mouth. "'This has been just a prelude. Where they burn books, they will ultimately burn human beings, too.'"

A harsh wind was blowing in Bebelplatz.

"Let's walk. It is not so cold when you walk," the German said, beginning to move. He must have weighed at least two hundred pounds, but the snow didn't crunch under his shoes.

They walked west on Behrenstrasse in silence. A young man wearing a long black coat was walking on the other side of the street. A scarf covered his face, and a flat cap hid his head. He was wearing low, rough boots with rounded toes. He seemed to be looking at them.

Alex said nothing to Justus.

Was the man across the street a threat?

And again, the man shot him a glance.

Café Einstein on Friedrichstrasse was packed with defrosting Berliners, refugees from the bitter cold. The walls were light colored, but the dark furnishings made the cramped, heated space even more oppressive. They sat on barstools at the wooden counter that faced the street. The daylight was dwindling on the bustling street, and illuminated signs were already lit and glittering on the snow. Alex took off his coat, scarf, and gloves and said with a smile, "Do you also put your houseguests in the freezer first?" He was beginning to be able to feel his face again.

"I prefer short meetings," Justus said and stood up. "Espresso?"

"Cappuccino," Alex replied. "Strong." It would be interesting to see whether he could extract anything worthwhile in the short time the German allotted him.

Behind him, someone placed a stack of rattling saucers on a counter.

Justus returned and set down two cups.

"Tell me about Istanbul," Alex said and took a sip of his coffee. To his surprise, the cappuccino was decent.

Justus sat down slowly, then ran his hand over his face as if trying to erase an image from his mind. "If I had another two or three men like Istanbul in the Ring, we'd be in much better shape."

"What happened to him?"

"At 2:02 this morning, his heart stopped beating. Five weeks ago he had his annual checkup. He was given a clean bill of health, as usual." Justus downed his espresso in one long gulp. He put the empty cup down with the handle precisely parallel to the bar and the spoon lying on the saucer in front of the cup, also parallel to the edge of the bar. He wiped the corners of his mouth with a paper napkin, folded it diagonally, and placed the perfect triangle under the rim of the saucer. Alex felt like a voyeur at a private ritual. "How do you know that his heart stopped beating?"

"Every Nibelung has a chip in his or her body with a sensor that contains a satellite transceiver. If the pulse stops, I receive a signal."

"Maybe it's just a glitch?"

"That has only happened once, when the Vienna Nibelung was undergoing an MRI after a road accident. The chip interfered with the magnetic field. If it were just a glitch, he would have shown up in Bolu and carried out his mission. Istanbul is dead.

"He comes from a wealthy Jewish family. They are descended from Spanish Jews who fled to Italy during the Inquisition and arrived in Istanbul in the eighteenth century. The Falacci family."

Falacci . . . Falacci . . . the red sign on the front of the spice warehouse!

"Falacci Baharat?"

"Exactly."

"The warehouse in Bolu belonged to Istanbul?"

"You seem surprised," Justus said.

We're morons, Alex thought. *Hopeless morons.* "Who chose that warehouse for the operation?"

"Reuven asked his Jewish helpers in Turkey for a safe place close to the Istanbul–Ankara highway," Justus said. "Times are hard in Turkey now—that is what he told me. Everyone's afraid to help."

"You suggested Istanbul's warehouse to Reuven and he agreed?"

"He had no choice," Justus said. "Time was running out, and the location looked perfect. We knew that Karabashi had come for only twenty-four hours. So, yes, I suggested it to Reuven, and he agreed."

If Reuven had revealed that information at the start of the crisis last night, Alex would never have sent Galia into the trap. Reuven had brought about the disastrous contact between Mossad and the Nibelung Ring. Reuven had made a terrible mistake. And Reuven had lied.

Alex said, "Someone was on to Istanbul and got to the warehouse through him, and then from the warehouse to us."

"Or the other way around," Justus said with a sour smile.

"Where did Istanbul disappear from?"

"His office, on a street behind the Egyptian spice bazaar in Istanbul."

Reuven had chosen to endanger Galia because he figured that when the Turkish police discovered Istanbul's body, they'd go straight to the spice warehouse in Bolu and find Karabashi's body.

Reuven had chosen to keep that information from him.

Alex leaned closer to Justus. "How many people knew that Istanbul was a Nibelung?"

"Just Reuven and I."

Justus's left eyelid twitched.

"Have you spoken to Istanbul's family?"

"They thought they were talking to a journalist. They don't know that he was working for us. They have no idea where he is, and they are very worried. I checked with the Istanbul police and the hospitals . . ." His lower lip drooped again. "No body resembling him has been found in Istanbul in the last twenty-four hours."

"How do you explain that?"

Justus shook his head and smiled. "You are so anxious to find an answer that you have convinced yourself that it is hidden inside my head. As far as I know, it is not there."

"Are you willing to give me a frank answer to a question?" Alex asked.

Justus nodded reluctantly, running his fingers over one of his cashmere-lined black Pecari leather gloves. Their white stitching was raised. Two hundred euros a pair.

When their eyes met, Alex whispered, "What makes a Christian German like you run a dangerous ring of sleeper agents for the Jewish state?"

The tension that had gathered in the lines on the German's face

faded. "It is a long story," he said. "In the early sixties my father decided to aid Israel. He was invited to Jerusalem for some event and
met with David Ben-Gurion and Isser Harel there. He told them
about his vision of the Nibelung Ring. Harel was against it at first,
but after a long year of investigations and feasibility checks my father began to set up the Ring. I am second-generation."

So am I, Alex almost said. *But of something else entirely.*

Reuven hadn't even hinted at this.

The two men sat in silence.

"My father's name is Gunter," Justus added. A shadow crossed
his face.

"Another cappuccino?" the German asked, lowering himself
to his feet from the barstool.

Alex shook his head. "Is your father still alive?"

Justus nodded, sat down again, and played with the edge of
the folded napkin. "He no longer recognizes me."

"He's at home?"

"He is in the final stages of Alzheimer's and suffers from respiratory problems. He recently had a severe stroke. He is in a sanatorium in Davos. When he was diagnosed, he made me swear
that I would take him there, to the Zauberberg. As a young boy,
he read Thomas Mann's book and decided to end his life on the
mountain."

His blue eyes glowed like a winter sun.

Alex thought of his dead parents. They'd grown distant and
smaller in his memory. He ought to weed the grass around their
graves.

"If you are staying the night in Berlin, I thought you might
come to my home tonight. I live in Grunewald, just outside the
forest. Your parents—are they alive?"

"No."

Behind them, someone spread a newspaper.

"They are from here, from Europe?"

"You mean the Holocaust?"

Justus sipped air from his empty cup. Then he nodded hesitantly.

"My mother's from Poland. She was a Holocaust survivor." Alex smiled sorrowfully. "I'm second-generation, too."

"Something is causing you pain," Justus said.

He didn't respond.

"You hate Germans?"

"No," he replied too quickly.

"It is perfectly understandable." Justus smiled and shook his head. "But unjustified."

The German wouldn't drag him into a conversation about the Holocaust. He had his limits.

Alex said, "If an economic crisis should occur in Germany tomorrow and the stock market in Frankfurt collapsed, the extreme right wing would raise its head and suddenly prove to be a significant force in Germany. Maybe even the ruling power."

"As with all peoples, the Germans have their ugly side," Justus said. "But there is also another Germany that is thriving. There are wonderful, humane, and enlightened Germans. Berlin is a cosmopolitan city, a cultural cornucopia. The younger generation is healthy and conducts serious research into our dark history. But you refuse to see any of that. For you, a German is an armband. *Arbeit macht frei.*"

Bile rose in Alex's throat. He crossed his arms over his chest. He sipped the last few drops of his coffee. The remains of sugar at the bottom filled his mouth with comforting sweetness.

"Reuven told me that you had a tragedy," Justus said softly and folded his large fingers. "I know that you are going through a bad time."

Reuven the chatterbox. A man of his rank in intelligence should know how to keep his mouth shut. But Reuven Hetz was drawn to meddling and manipulation like a bee to pollen.

The coffee grinder stirred into life and whined persistently. The air was flooded with the rich aroma of ground beans.

"The daughter is well?" Justus whispered with hesitant empathy.

The daughter. Such a German construction. As if Daniella were a hanger, or an old suitcase.

Alex nodded reluctantly.

The German played with the napkin again, finally straightening it out. "We never had children. We tried."

A motorcycle roared past the street. Justus looked out, his eyes moist.

A waitress cleared the plates off a nearby table, careful to keep her eyes down. Justus gave her a long look. A small smile appeared on his lips. He straightened the teaspoon. "Reuven also told you to shake the tree?" the German asked quietly.

Alex smiled, then nodded. *Reuven the snake. He pitted us against each other as if we were fighting cocks with razors tied to our legs.*

Justus's BlackBerry vibrated. He glanced at it. His face darkened. His lower lip dropped, exposing his bottom teeth.

"What's wrong?" Alex asked.

"I don't believe it."

His face was white.

"We have lost another one."

"Where?"

"Lisbon."

Justus looked defeated. Sweat glistened above his upper lip. He put his face in his hands and sighed.

Alex touched his shoulder gently. The German seemed surprised by the gesture and mumbled something in German.

"Turkey was just the beginning," Alex said.

"How many Nibelungs are there in the Ring?" he then asked.

The German gave him a distant look. "As many as are needed."

"Has anything unusual happened recently? Has your house been broken into, or your car? Did you lose any documents? Feel like you were being followed?"

Justus gave him another distant look.

"Is someone following you?"

"Enough!" Justus snapped. He moved away and looked out onto the street.

"So what happened?"

"Guessing is for the foolish and the impatient," the German said.

"Apart from you, who has the list of Nibelungs?"

Justus turned his head, looked straight at Alex, and, after a slight hesitation, replied firmly, "No one."

"Where is it written down?" Alex fired.

Justus narrowed his eyes as if he were looking at an intrusive bug. "In my head."

"Dozens of people, hundreds of meetings, thousands of payments?"

"In my head."

The German walked to the back of the café.

The milk frother clattered noisily. A hoarse voice was singing in German.

Justus returned and sat down, his hands smelling strongly of lavender soap. He whispered, "Knowing Reuven, I assume he asked you to shake the tree, not cut it down."

"I'm going outside for a minute," Alex said and stood up.

A young Japanese woman sitting beside him gave him the once-over and then, behind her hand, giggled in embarrassment.

Justus gave him a look. Then he nodded, but his thoughts seemed far away.

Outside, needles of frost stabbed at his bare face.

He turned on the phone scrambler and punched in a number.

Reuven answered after the first ring.

"We just lost the Lisbon Nibelung," Alex said.

Reuven's breathing was tremulous. "Damn, what's going on there . . ."

"Reuven, we're at war."

Alex went back into the heated café. Justus's chin was resting on his fist, a worried expression on his face. "You reported to Reuven?"

Alex hesitated for a moment before nodding.

Justus whispered, "Someone is threatening the Nibelung Ring. Someone has infiltrated it."

Suddenly he tensed, and his face grew hard.

"What's wrong?"

"Outside, across the street, at the entrance of H&M."

Alex saw him right away. A man of about thirty, dark complexion, black hair, staring. "You know him?"

"Look to the left, next to the Montblanc window . . ." Justus said. "Another one."

Low, rough boots. Earlier, that guy had been wearing a long black coat. Now he had on a short blue ski jacket. The raised collar hid his chin.

He might already have been with them at Bebelplatz.

Alex turned around casually and scanned the patrons of the café.

"Let's leave, lead one of them to a quiet place. We'll interview him and find out who they are," Alex suggested.

"I cannot afford to get into trouble here," Justus replied. "This is Berlin. People know me. Let's shake them off so we can think quietly about what to do."

Alex nodded.

Justus looked at his watch. "Ten to five. Do you know Invalidenfriedhof?"

Alex shook his head no.

"You know Berlin?"

"Not in great detail."

"Invalidenstrasse, next to the Berlin–Spandau Canal, leads to Scharnhorststrasse. There is a military cemetery for fallen soldiers of the Prussian army—Invalidenfriedhof. Let's try to lose our tail and meet there in forty-five minutes."

Alex couldn't resist. "Another one of your favorite spots?"

Justus's face was tense. "It's quiet there now, and by the time we get there it will be dark. I know the place well. If anyone follows us in, we can overtake him without being discovered. Let's separate now. Go to the Friedrichstrasse station. I will go in the opposite direction."

Justus stood up.

"Where in the cemetery?" Alex asked.

"Go inside and turn right. You will see seven headstones crowded together. There."

DIARY

22 JUNE 1940

They hung the swastika flag from the pinnacle of the Eiffel Tower. Each day at noon they march in a parade to the beat of drums from the Arc de Triomphe, along the Champs-Élysées, to the Place de la Concorde.

The Nazis stomp on our land in their occupiers' jackboots.

Like a dog marking its territory with a yellow spurt of urine.

23 JUNE 1940

The Führer was here today.

The Führer arrived in Paris, and the commandant brought him to our café. My hands shook.

The Führer was here today and tasted my brioche, and for a moment he smiled, but then he sniffed the air and grimaced.

What is it, mein Führer, the commandant inquired.

The Führer put the brioche down and said: There is a smell of Jews here.

11 OCTOBER 1940

I cannot go to the synagogue or ask forgiveness from the Merciful One. It is Yom Kippur eve, but our forged papers say we are Christians.

The hall of the Friedrichstrasse station looked like the inside of a food processor in action. People flowed up and down the many staircases, packed together on the platforms, and poured out onto the busy street. Heavy smells of frying and reused oil rose from the fast-food stands.

Alex boarded the first train going west and then south, toward Wannsee.

Rough Boots boarded the car adjacent to his.

A beep announced the closing of the doors. Alex leaped off the train, but at the last moment grabbed the pole next to the door and swerved back into the car.

Rough Boots discovered his mistake too late and was stranded on the platform.

The doors closed with a whoosh. Rough Boots kicked a bench and pulled a phone out of his pocket. *Amateur.* Alex could have taken him easily, could have neutralized him and dragged him outside to the tracks, where he'd shove his face into the filthy snow and pull his secrets out of him. But it was rush hour, and security cameras were installed all over the station. Earlier, he'd spotted a couple of uniformed policemen.

The train gathered speed. The Germans kept their eyes lowered. He had time to think about recent events.

What did the murder of Lisbon mean? Did it exonerate the Turks?

Who'd decided to attack the Ring?

Justus's tree needed another, harder shaking.

He'd lost Rough Boots easily, but he'd been in the business long enough to know that every Rough Boots had a replacement. Now he himself was in their crosshairs.

A chilly voice announced in German: *Nächste Station—Hauptbahnhof.* People filed off and onto the train in perfect order. The doors closed. The train moved away from the platform. He got off at the Zoologischer Garten and crossed over to the opposite platform. Three minutes later, a train approached with a low whistle and a chilling gust of air. He boarded and got off at Hauptbahnhof. He walked toward the fast-food stands. He didn't see any suspicious reflections in the shop windows facing him.

Alex took the escalator down to the bottom floor. Then he turned around and went back up to the S-Bahn level and stood at the edge of one of the platforms. Dozens of people were waiting for the train.

A train arrived and stopped. They all got on.

Alex didn't.

He was alone.

The station clock showed 17:07. He took out his phone, located the cemetery on the map, and checked the distance: just over half a mile—a ten-minute walk on slippery ice.

He exited the station and turned right, onto Invalidenstrasse. His phone started vibrating.

Reuven said, "Turkish TV is showing a picture of the body of General Farzan Karabashi, including close-ups of his face and the burns. The Turkish lawyer tried again to see Galia. The Turks won't let him in. They claim she has a severe infection and her condition is deteriorating."

The nail that had been pounded into his head penetrated deeper; the pressure became more painful.

"How was the meeting with Justus?" Reuven asked.

"We only just started talking," Alex said. "Justus is being followed. I wanted to attack. Justus preferred to shake them off. We're going to meet somewhere quiet now. We have to warn the Nibelungs."

"If someone's sitting on Justus, warning the Nibelungs might expose them all," Reuven said in the distant tone of a Swiss pharmacist.

"Saving lives is more important," Alex said.

"I'll be in the office till late. I'll wait for your call," Reuven said, hanging up.

Alex checked the time. Fourteen minutes left. The temperature was plummeting.

He needed a taxi.

But traffic was snarled, and a river of taxis filled with lucky passengers was creeping past him. He began to walk.

He switched to running, slipped, and almost fell. Running would at least get his blood circulating and warm his body. On the other hand, everyone on the street would notice the six-foot-five man sprinting on the ice.

He slowed down to a quick walk, passing the Hamburger Bahnhof Museum and the Bundesministerium für Wirtschaft und Energie, then turned left onto Scharnhorststrasse.

The cemetery gate was open.

17:33.

Justus the pedant must certainly be here already.

The cemetery was dimly lit from the streetlights. He walked for a while on the snow-covered main path and then stopped and listened. His eyes were adjusting to the darkness. It seemed that no one was there.

He could make out the silhouettes of crowded headstones. The keys to his house and car were in his pocket. The keychain had a tiny flashlight on it. He pressed the button, and a pale white light poured onto the snow. Bare trees moaned in the wind.

Where was Justus?

He retreated, slipped on something wet, and fell flat on the frozen snow. The keys flew out of his hand. He was in total darkness. He felt around in the snow until he found them. He pressed the button. The white light came on.

His heart was pounding.

He was sitting in a pool of blood.

Alex's heart was thumping painfully. He stood up and shone the light on the backs of his legs. His jeans were covered in blood. So was his blue jacket.

Whose blood was it?

The time on his phone read 17:41. He called Justus's number.

The call was picked up on the second ring, but the person on the other end didn't utter a word.

"Hello?"

The call was disconnected.

Alex redialed.

Justus's phone had been shut off.

He passed his flashlight over the snow. The pool of blood was the size of a large washbasin. Big dark drops led to the far end of the cemetery, where it bordered the Spandau Canal. The small beam of light revealed freezing water and cracked ice.

Going back to the puddle of blood, he took out a fresh tissue and dipped it in.

That's when he noticed it. A black leather glove with raised white stitching.

He called Reuven.

"How do you know it's Justus's blood?" the chief asked.

"His glove is lying on the snow. I took a sample. I'll send it to you on the plane waiting at Tegel. I need a courier here to bring it to the plane."

Silence.

"Without Justus's BlackBerry, we have no way of warning the Nibelungs," Alex said.

"This is a disaster," Reuven said from far away, absorbed in his own thoughts.

Then he hung up.

Alex was left there, freezing under a bare tree.

Mossad's outer ring of defense had lost its head.

He had to get out of there. Whoever had attacked Justus might still be nearby, waiting for him.

The remains of the Berlin Wall cut through the cemetery. He was standing in what used to be the death zone.

If he dug in the ground under the snow beneath his feet he would be able to touch the bones of SS-Obergruppenführer Reinhard Heydrich, the head of the Gestapo and the Third Reich's Main Security Office, the commander of the SS, the SD, and the Einsatzgruppen, and the chief architect of the extermination of Europe's Jews. Heydrich had been assassinated. A temporary wooden marker resembling a totem pole with a swastika carved into the top had been erected over his grave. Hitler planned to construct a monumental tomb in his honor, but he never got the chance.

At the end of the war, the marker disappeared.

A passerby might notice the beam of the flashlight. He had to get out of the cemetery.

Alex took off his bloodstained jacket and rubbed at the synthetic fiber with a handful of snow. It did no more than blur the edges of the stain. He emptied the pockets and folded the jacket under his arm. Freezing, he hurried out of the gruesome cemetery.

This time luck was with him, and he managed to hail a taxi.

"Where to?" the cabbie asked in Turkish-accented German.

Alex struggled to remember the name of the main shopping center.

"Sir?" the cabbie prodded.

"KaDeWe," he said finally, surprising himself.

The driver gave him a dicey look in the rearview mirror.

In the dim light in the rear of the cab, he saw dried blood on his left glove.

It was a frustratingly slow drive through congested streets with blinding lights. The tires threatened to lose their grip on the icy surface. It had begun snowing again, the flakes catching in the headlights of the cars moving in the opposite direction.

"KaDeWe," the cabbie said under his black mustache as he rolled to a stop.

Alex paid the man and got out.

He twisted his jacket around his waist so that only the lining showed, and tied the sleeves together in the front.

He purchased black trousers, T-shirts, a sweater, a black jacket, thermal socks and underwear, and a black trolley bag. Then he went into the men's room and changed, folding his stained clothing neatly and taking it with him. He threw the dirty bundle into a trash can outside. After stocking up on basic toiletries at a drugstore in Europa-Center, he hailed another cab. The radio crackled noisily.

Alex texted Reuven: "Send courier to Abion Spreebogen Hotel. Visconti."

Done, Reuven texted back with surprising alacrity.

He didn't really need a lab test. The blood on the ice belonged to Justus. If only he'd made it to the cemetery a few minutes sooner . . .

Reuven called as he was about to enter the hotel, which was situated on a bend in the Spree River.

"I need people. Time isn't on our side."

"I can't send the team. The PM refuses to sign off on it. What else do you need?"

"A gun, ammo, money. Make that two guns."

He could sense that Reuven was about to burst from curiosity, but Alex kept his silence.

"Any news on Galia?" he asked instead.

"No."

Reuven hung up.

Alex checked the street before walking through the door.

The young lady behind the Abion Hotel reception desk was charming, but he found it hard to return her smile. Alex went up to his room. Two glass walls looked out over the frozen river.

Alone, he was powerless. He needed his people here, but they were off-limits to him. Whoever had brought down Istanbul and Lisbon was still out there. Other Nibelungs were in danger. Every second counted.

He couldn't do it alone.

He called the only Nibelung he knew.

"It's all over the news, Alex," Jane Thompson told him. "It's all they're talking about on TV reports, commentary. Are you all right?"

"You're in danger. The Ring is in danger," he said in a measured tone.

"What do you mean?"

"Two Nibelungs have been killed. Their bodies haven't been found."

"What?"

"Istanbul and Lisbon."

"How do you know?"

"I'm in Berlin. I met with your boss."

"You didn't!"

"Justus is dead." He was desperately thirsty. Opening the minibar, he took out a bottle of water.

"Justus?"

"I'm sorry." He drank from the cold bottle.

"He's really dead?" she said. He could hear the pain in her voice.

"I need you here. We fucked up."

"Where are you?"

"Alt-Moabit. Abion Spreebogen Hotel."

Silence on the other end.

He held his breath.

"Name?" she asked.

"Visconti. Be careful."

"I'm on my way."

He prayed that he wasn't making the worst mistake of his life.

Reuven called.

"We just heard from a reliable source in the Milli Istihbarat, the Turkish intelligence agency. They raided the home and office of Haroun Falacci in Istanbul. They found his pickup truck. There were large bloodstains on the backseat, and signs of a struggle."

"That's it?" Alex asked warily.

"I wish. In the back of the truck they found an eight-gallon tank of fluoroantimonic acid, along with an empty bathtub, a shovel, gloves, and a gas mask. They got the picture."

"What about Istanbul's body?"

"Nope. They took his wife and three brothers in for questioning. They've called a press conference for eight thirty, about half an hour from now. They'll probably release the information then."

Alex finished off the rest of the water in one long gulp.

"The Turks didn't find out about Bolu from interrogating Falacci, Reuven. If they'd nabbed him, they would have plastered his picture all over the news and now they'd be celebrating their coup. They'd be basking in the glory of having uncovered an Israeli spy ring. That's a much more dramatic story than Galia's arrest."

"You're saying it was the other way around? They found out about Falacci from the warehouse in Bolu?" Reuven asked.

"Not necessarily. But someone else iced Falacci. And the Turks only did it after the raid in Bolu. And that same someone also took out Lisbon."

"So you think the person who got to Falacci has no connection to the Turks or Bolu?"

"Exactly. Somebody has decided to take down the Nibelungs. He's already finished off two of them, and Justus. Without Justus's BlackBerry, we can't know whether he's gotten to any others. We're in the dark here."

Alex got the other bottle of water from the minibar.

"You're saying the discovery of the Bolu warehouse was just dumb luck?" Reuven asked.

"Maybe. Someone could have tossed them a crumb and it set the Middle East on fire. But whoever it was isn't targeting Mossad. They're only targeting the Nibelungs. I'll check out Justus's place tonight. What's his last name?"

"Erlichmann. Justus Erlichmann."

"I need the address," Alex said.

"I'll send someone ahead to disable the alarm. It's a job for a specialist."

"Why?"

"You'll see when you get inside."

"What do I tell his wife?" Alex asked.

"His wife died just over a year ago."

Alex undressed and got into the shower. His whole body ached from cold and tension. Under the soothing hot water, he was able to unwind a little. It was the best thing that had happened to him in the past twenty-four hours. He closed his eyes, attempting to suppress the thoughts racing through his head.

The water washed it all away. He lathered the soap and scrubbed his body vigorously with the suds.

When he was a child, he'd once sat down in his father's reading chair with a Time–Life picture album on his lap, as heavy as a gravestone. It contained shocking photographs from World War II that brought to life his mother's terrifying stories, about her as a young girl struggling to get free from the war's claws: the concentration camps she managed to escape from with his grandmother, the fear, being at the mercy of traitorous Poles, the loss of her childhood, of hope, of joy.

Those Germans—that's what her parents called them. *Those Germans*, they'd say, stressing the demonstrative with loathing.

The appalling pictures in the book had given shape to the stories in his mind. It was the first time he'd seen the face of death. One group of photographs in particular remained engraved in his memory.

It was a series of four photos taken in rapid succession during the battle for Leipzig. In the first, two American soldiers were firing a machine gun at German troops from the balcony of an apartment.

In the second picture, one of the soldiers was missing and the other was lying lifeless on the balcony floor, still wearing his helmet, with dozens of empty shells around his feet. Beside his head was a pool of blood that reflected the white clouds.

In the last two pictures, the pool of blood grew progressively larger.

He'd been forced to listen to his mother's horror stories about the war in Poland. He remembered how she'd described their desperate escape, hunger, fear, capture, escaping again and being captured again, torture, shots fired, being wounded.

After she had kissed his brow and tiptoed out of the room, the pictures of the machine gunner in Leipzig would rise up and haunt him.

He was six, and even the electric trains he got for his birthday couldn't restore his innocent happiness.

The bathroom had steamed up.

The water was boiling hot.

Alex felt cold.

Someone was knocking on the door.

He turned off the water and grabbed a thick towel. "Who is it?" he asked in English.

"A friend of a friend," a voice answered.

"Hold on a second."

Alex pulled his clothes on, his body still wet and shivering. He opened the door and saw a young face smiling at him.

He recognized the courier. He gave him the plastic bag with the blood sample. The man handed him a black toiletry bag and left.

Alex set the bag on the bed and opened it. Two Glock 17s, four full magazines, and a fifty-round ammo box. A long brown envelope contained twenty thousand euros in used bills held together with a rubber band. He took out the magazines, broke open the two pistols, checked the chambers, tested the triggers, and examined the top cartridge in each magazine. When he was done, his hands reeked of gun oil.

Jane was on her way. She was the only Nibelung he knew, the only person who could help him. Contact between them was strictly forbidden. But Justus had disappeared, Reuven was far away, and danger was looming.

He felt anxious about seeing her again so soon. It was premature. Their reunion in London three months ago, when she'd helped him rescue Daniella from her abductors, had clearly reignited old fantasies. But then the shots fired in the hospital had taken Naomi's life, and his world had been turned upside down. Ever since, he'd been walking on eggshells, trying to figure out what he could allow himself and what he couldn't; what was proper.

Reuven called. Alex tensed, readying himself for the blow.

"They released Galia's picture. It's better that you don't see it."

"Where is it?"

"They put on a thick layer of greasepaint, but you can see that her interrogation was brutal."

"What about that lawyer? Has he been allowed to talk to her?"

"They let him see her for a couple of minutes."

"What did she say?" Alex asked, his throat seizing up.

"She's unconscious. On life support."

Reuven was still on the line, breathing in his ear.

"The Turks knew from the start she was Mossad," Alex said. "Someone ratted her out. They don't need a confession. It's time we bite the bullet and get her out of there alive, while we still can."

"I discussed it with the PM. He's against it."

"Put the pressure on and he'll understand that he has sole responsibility for her life. He'll fold."

"I have to consider the big picture, Alex. The country's interests come first."

Alex took a deep breath. Reuven had known that Galia was going back to the warehouse, and he hadn't objected. And it was Reuven who'd told them to use Istanbul's warehouse in the first place, creating a crack in the wall between the Ring and Mossad. Now he was trying to dodge responsibility, opting to abandon her without batting an eye.

"You have to save her," Alex insisted.

The line went dead.

Alex splashed cold water over his face, praying that he would see her again.

The BBC was showing a photo of an ecstatic man wrapped in a tallis and holding two tiny infants. The anchorwoman kept repeating the name "Falacci." The Turkish security organization was conducting a manhunt for him. They believed he could lead them to members of an Israeli spy ring operating in their country, she reported. Cut.

The front pages of the Turkish papers. Cut.

The Turkish prime minister, Recep Tayyip Erdoğan, delivering a frenetic statement, his eyes blazing. The British interpreter translating: "Israel will soon pay for its crimes against the Turkish people." Cut.

A picture of Karabashi's dead body bound to the chair in the spice warehouse in Bolu. Cut.

The Iranian's lifeless face. Cut.

Back to the studio. The anchorwoman was talking about the United States, President Obama, the Sixth Fleet in the Mediterranean. Cut.

A pair of stealth bombers taking off at night from Whiteman Air Force Base in Missouri.

Good God, the situation was snowballing out of control. Alex turned off the television.

The Turkish media was champing at the bit. More fresh meat was being thrown into its gaping jaws by the hour. Reuven hadn't revealed the extent of the damage.

He called room service and ordered two large bottles of plain mineral water. They arrived almost immediately, brought by an amiable young German who bowed, smiled, and left.

Alex locked the door behind the waiter and went over to the window, looking out at the lights of Berlin. He stood there for quite some time.

Jane was on her way. He'd long ago forgotten how to woo a lady. He'd always been secretly in love with her. Tonight, if he wanted her, she would be his. There was a cold lump in the pit of his stomach. He moved closer to the window. The river below was frozen, the cracked ice lit by the streetlamps. A warm orange glow issued from the heated living rooms in the buildings on the opposite bank. Daniella was far away, Naomi was buried deep in the ground, and he was in a business hotel in a city he'd always shunned, his heart fluttering in anticipation of the arrival of the woman he loved. Was he still capable of satisfying a mature woman, a hungry woman who had yet to taste the monotonous fare of married life?

Love doesn't want you anymore at that age, like an employer who prefers only young blood.

Last December in London, after twenty-five years, he'd sensed that what they'd once felt for each other had been rekindled, but Naomi still stood between them. He didn't dare to cheat on her. Now that the barrier was gone and he could do as he pleased, the woman of his dreams was threatening to become a reality.

Alex sat down on the edge of the bed. A German flag lit by a projector was waving above the glass dome of the Reichstag. He closed his eyes and felt the sleepless night demanding its due.

He and Jane had been two of the four agents chosen for the squad. They met for the first time during the briefing in the safe house in Paris. The moment he caught sight of her, he fell dumb. Later, he was mostly befuddled. For seventeen months, along frozen highways, in nasty cheap hotels, running from one safe haven to the next under stolen identities, they chased after targets and eluded pursuers, strangled and stabbed, fired guns and planted bombs, the constant pressure telling on them. The prolonged isolation, the distance from home, the unrelieved tension—it all ate away at them. For the duration of the mission, they were allowed no contact with their families, save for one brief meeting he had with Naomi in a gloomy Swiss hotel. He managed to resist the temptation for a long time. Jane waited with exemplary patience.

When a bomb exploded in the safe house in Marseille, they knew for certain that their identities had been blown. They fled. That night, they could no longer keep their hands off each other.

It was the best and worst time of his life. He spent weeks planning how to tell Naomi he was leaving her.

Giving in to exhaustion, Alex lay down on the bed fully clothed and fell asleep instantly.

DIARY

---

23 FEBRUARY 1943

At the café this morning, someone tossed a two-word phrase into the air: *concentration camp*.

19 JUNE 1943

Drancy is not an internment camp but a concentration camp. A concentration of Jews. The new camp commandant came to the café this evening. He is German. He was sent here to increase the rate of transports to the East. His very aspect inspires terror.

22 JUNE 1943

Since the beginning of the occupation, Le Monde *has been steadily shrinking.*

In the boulangerie, where no one can see me, I have begun to read the Resistance paper, Combat. Combat *is steadily growing. When I finish reading it, I throw it into the wood-burning oven.*

23 JUNE 1943

When the smell of Wehrmacht oiled leather jackboots blends with the aroma of rising yeast dough, my soul seeks refuge from the devil.

Alex woke up with a start and opened his eyes. The light was on. His heart was pounding. Outside the glass walls, the lights of the hotel shone on thick snow falling silently.

He heard a gentle knock on the door.

He got up from the bed, grabbing one of the pistols and holding it behind his back as he moved toward the door.

His phone vibrated.

The phone could wait.

Another knock.

He opened the door and his jaw dropped.

She stood there, frozen in place. Then a smile spread across her face.

His mouth was dry. He seemed to have swallowed the words.

She came in, moving toward him without any hesitation, and he threw his arms around her. She slammed the door shut with her heel and dropped her bag on the floor, freeing her hands. With sparkling eyes, she studied the contours of his face and then wrapped him in a soft embrace. "Oh, Alex . . ."

A shudder went through him. Her first touch was new and familiar at the same time.

"I've been waiting so long . . ." she whispered.

He pressed his body to hers, and she brought her lips to his. Her kisses were endless and demanding, her lips silky, her mouth cool and fresh. He closed his eyes and sent his tongue in search of hers. She gathered his face in her hands and moved her lips away.

She gave him a gentle shove and he retreated, bumping into the bed and falling back with a happy laugh. She sat down on top of him and he could no longer speak. A wave of lust passed through his body, heating his flesh, the sweet feeling spreading through his loins. He shut his eyes and felt the warmth of her face on his.

Her lips flitted over his mouth and her breasts pressed into his chest as he stroked her slender back from shoulder to firm butt. He envisioned her young and naked, revealing all. Her scent was burned into his memory.

She stretched her body out beside him and closed her eyes, and they were both enveloped by a tender serenity. It had been ages since he'd lost all sense of time and place like this. Her breath brushed his neck, and a pleasant quiver ran down his spine. All the while, her sparkling eyes gazed at him from up close and her long fingers stroked his face. Closing his eyes, he surrendered, the terrible events of the past day melting away and draining out of his body.

They lay there for a long time, caressing each other and kissing.

A ping.

His body tensed. Her phone was on the desk.

"Don't move," she whispered. "I'll be right back." She got up, and he watched her tall, agile figure cross the room. She glanced at the screen and tossed the phone aside, then returned to the bed and settled herself on top of him again, her body giving off a pleasant warmth.

For a moment he forgot the madness going on outside, down there in freezing Berlin, in Istanbul, in Lisbon, and God only knew where else.

Her body was rubbing up against his. "We have to go," he mumbled.

"In a minute." She buried her face in the curve of his neck. It was hot.

Later they rose and got ready to leave. He gave her one of the Glocks and two magazines, and stuffed the envelope with the cash into the pocket of his new black North Face jacket.

The ashen-faced reception clerk kept asking whether something was wrong. He said no and paid the bill, and they walked out.

Jane drove them west in her rented Mercedes. Alex filled her in on the events of the past twenty-four hours, from Bolu to Invalidenfriedhof. She nodded, her jaw clenched.

"We have to turn Justus's house upside down until we find the list of Nibelungs."

"There may not be a list," she said.

"There has to be. No one could keep so many details in his head, no matter how phenomenal his memory."

"You don't get it. Justus is a genius. Are you sure it was his blood?"

"We'll know for certain in the morning."

"He deliberately stretched the limits of his memory. There was Alzheimer's in his family. He was afraid that one day he'd find out he had it, too," Jane said.

"Have you seen him lately?" Alex asked.

"I was supposed to meet him at the Tate Modern in London at the end of February. There was an exhibit he wanted to see. Marcel Duchamp, Man Ray, Francis Picabia. I waited more than an hour."

"He was late?"

"He didn't show."

"Had that ever happened before?"

"Never. Justus was more punctual than the Deutsche Bahn."

"Did you meet up eventually?"

"The next day. He was acting odd."

The phone in Alex's hand vibrated.

Reuven.

"Sorry, Alex," he said.

"What for?"

"Galia."

"What about Galia?" he asked, although his heart was already seizing in pain.

Reuven waited a moment before hanging up.

"What happened?" Jane asked.

His dry eyes burned.

"She's dead."

Justus Erlichmann had chosen to surround his house with a black wrought-iron fence whose bars were topped with pointed gilt finials as sharp as bayonets. The large two-story building stood in the snow, its zabaglione-colored walls and inviting facade conveying a deceptive innocence. Snow was still falling, piling up on the dark slate roof tiles.

Going in through the service entrance at the side of the house, they found themselves engulfed in a heavy silence. Jane was in the lead. She switched the light on. They were in a huge heated space with a high ceiling and bare brown brick walls, plastered and painted in white to half their height. A green light showed on the silent alarm panel. The "neurosurgeon" had been and gone without leaving a trace. Stifa Kadosh was Mossad's top expert at picking intricate locks and disabling sophisticated alarms.

A forty-foot glass wall in the living room looked out over a large backyard. The outside lights shone on the somber, majestic forest beyond.

Alex turned around and gaped in awe at the bookshelves along the whole length of the room.

If the list of Nibelungs was hidden among the books, it would be easier to find a lost sardine in the ocean.

On the wall facing the kitchen was a painting in the style of Mark Rothko as big as a king-size bed. The intensity of the rough color blocks was hypnotic.

Jane came closer and wrapped her arms around him, her body offering the warmth he so desperately needed. Her face lay in the crook of his neck. His eyes were wide open. When she kissed his neck, he shuddered and said, "Galia's mother will be devastated. She raised her on her own. Galia's father was a pilot. He was killed in the Yom Kippur War."

Jane released him and walked away. He heard her footsteps going up the stairs.

In the silence, his head was inundated with thoughts of Galia. He saw the part she had played in his life. Her life had been in his hands. He would never forget the sound of the moan that escaped her when she was hit.

He would do whatever it took to find the person responsible for her death.

He would find him, and he would plunge a dagger into his heart.

Jane went into the bedroom, on the upper floor. She bumped into one of the tall floor lamps whose linen shades cast the room in a gentle golden glow. From the wide bed there was a view of the forest, its bare trees visible in the garden lights.

She opened the drawer of the nightstand and then closed it immediately, ashamed to be invading the privacy of her handler. His spirit still hovered in the air of the room. She turned to leave.

On the wall near the door of the bedroom were three erotic etchings from Picasso's *Vollard Suite*. In the first, a stout, fleshy man was lifting the sheet off a sleeping woman. In the second, a bearded man lay on a couch, his head resting on his elbow, peering in obvious delight at three naked dancing girls. In the third, two men and two women encircled a giant male head. Their sexual organs were drawn crudely and prominently, conveying a sense of unbridled lust. She'd had the same impression the last time she was here.

Going down the stairs, Jane passed a dark drawing by Henry Moore from the series documenting Londoners' stoicism during the Blitz. She found Alex in Justus's study, sitting on the rug beside the antique tortoiseshell desk. He was scrutinizing a safe concealed in a cabinet. On the wall was a splatter painting of panoramic proportions. She sat down in the soft leather swivel chair and watched him while he concentrated on the safe. He got up using all fours, and his age told on his weary face. But the look in his eyes was so intense that she imagined he could drill into the safe with the force of his gaze alone.

"It's a Breitenbach. Made in East Germany," he said. "We're going to need help. Did you find anything?"

"I couldn't . . ."

She went to the living room to wait.

Alex went upstairs and walked past the bedroom without going in. He found a workroom, where a giant scale model of a fighter plane from World War II hung from the high ceiling. Its wingspan was about ten feet.

A long workbench stood against the glass wall facing the forest. In the middle was a T-Rex 700 Nitro helicopter in the final stages of assembly. Almost five feet long, it was made of carbon fiber and had a yellow canopy.

Outside, the black trees of Grunewald tossed wildly, and the snowflakes spun in a mad dance under the bright lights.

Alex called the Brussels station, one of the major Mossad outposts in Europe. It provided firepower, security, logistics, and technological services to Mossad stations in neighboring countries.

"Can't help you, Bartal. No one's going anywhere," the station chief, Sammy Zengot, said. "They're all being kept busy on security details. The PM isn't approving any active operations in Europe."

The chief of the Brussels station held the same rank as Alex. Alex couldn't impose his authority on him.

"Do I have to get Reuven involved?" Alex asked.

"Don't threaten me. You'll get the same answer from him."

Alex didn't waste any time.

Reuven texted back: You'll have a search team in two hours. Only for the night.

Alex sank into the soft gray sofa and stared out at the forest. The view was monochrome, lifeless, and exciting.

Jane rested her head on his chest. Ever since they'd first met twenty-five years ago, they'd had their own private language, without any words.

He would never forget the endless wait, the time that had stretched out like an infinite thread between their first meeting and the moment they could no longer restrain themselves, back when they were younger.

In the center of the room, near the glass wall opposite the gap in the bookshelves, was a delicate bronze sculpture reminiscent of Alberto Giacometti's *Walking Man*. The thin figure was human height. The arms were close to the body, and the stride was long and confident.

The image of Justus's dolphin brow flashed through Alex's

mind. He pictured the mane of white hair and the intelligent blue eyes. If he were still alive, they would undoubtedly have discovered that they had a lot in common. A love of books and art, for instance, and, of course, they'd both recently lost their wives. Alex wondered how it felt after a year or so.

His thoughts turned to Naomi. He felt a strange sense of nostalgia for the good years they'd had. Then again, maybe time had smoothed the rough edges of his memories. His heart ached.

Jane's body relaxed. She cuddled up next to him. He knew that if he suggested it, or just took her by the hand and led her upstairs, she'd come willingly. But his legs were welded in place, like the legs of the bronze *Walking Man*.

"Alex," she said, and his heart jumped. He'd thought she'd fallen asleep.

She raised her eyes to him. "Were you together?"

He felt her breath on his chin.

"Who?"

"You and Galia."

"Almost," he answered.

Jane nodded, but there was a troubled look on her face. "What does *almost* mean?"

"Almost means no."

"Are you hungry?" Jane asked.

"Starving."

"There's a good grill house not far away," she said.

Alex nodded. "Go out the front gate, get the car, and meet me at the corner."

Jane responded with a reluctant nod.

Alex crossed the backyard, climbed over the fence with its lethal finials, and stood perfectly still. Everything was quiet. He peered into the neighboring yards and scanned the edge of the forest before hunching over and taking off at a rapid pace, making footprints in the snow.

By the time she picked him up, the heater in the car was roaring. They drove in silence.

The branches of the black trees were swaying violently, scattering the snow that had collected on them like motes of dust in the air. Wind whipped at the wooden sign with curling neon letters reading SCHLAFF BIERKELLER UND GRILL.

They entered a small lobby and took the stairs down to a spacious cellar. The benches beside the long tables were filled with locals devouring mounds of meat and washing them down with large steins of beer. Opposite, whole pigs were turning slowly on a row of spits. Hearty laughter and roars issued from the throats of drunken men whose eyes gleamed with greed and lust.

They found seats at the crowded bar. The shrill German music was deafening. The bartender was filling jugs of beer to the brim, the foam spilling over. A young waitress in a checked dress and white apron gathered them up and hurried off, five jugs in each hand.

"This was Justus's favorite place. He came here often," Jane said.

"He knew how to live," Alex said.

"You envy him, don't you?" she asked with a smile.

A mansion in the most prestigious section of Berlin, fine works of art, a hefty bank account, a dream library, and freedom. Oh, yes, he certainly did.

"A little," he said. "Don't you?"

She didn't. The only daughter of wealthy elderly parents, she stood to inherit tens of millions. Pounds sterling, that is. She smiled. "Don't. He was terribly lonely."

"And we're not?" he asked, the words issuing straight from his heart before he could hold them back.

She caressed his face, wrapped her slender arm around his shoulder, and leaned her head against his neck. Her hair smelled wonderful and her skin gave off the pleasant aroma of soap. They were surrounded by Germans. He gazed at them with animosity.

Alex admired the masterful precision of the Berlin Philharmonic; was impressed by the excellent German cars, and, living in a country as chaotic as Israel, often yearned for a bit of German order and discipline. He was in awe of the might of German industry and inspired by the great writers, poets, philosophers, and engineers that the German nation had given birth to. But there was one thing he was still incapable of.

Forgiving.

Two seats away was a man around fifty with shoulder-length blond hair. He looked like he'd fallen asleep in a tanning bed. He was wearing a black turtleneck sweater and was totally focused on the dark red wine spinning in circles in the balloon glass he was twisting in his hand. He scrutinized the liquid, shoved his nose deep into the glass, and shut his blue eyes. Then he smiled.

"I think he's the owner," Jane whispered.

They ordered pork chops and salad and waited in silence, cringing from the noise. Without warning, Jane grinned, brought her face closer, and kissed him on the lips.

"Are you trying to kill me?" he whispered.

"Should we order wine?"

"What's he drinking?" Alex asked.

The man rose, smiled at Jane, and walked away. He came back carrying a bottle of wine, which he deftly uncorked. He smelled the dark stain at the bottom of the cork before pouring a taste into a balloon glass he placed in front of her.

"Brunello di Montalcino, Poggio di Sotto 2001. It's a treasure. You enjoyed it the last time you were here," he said in English with a heavy German accent. "I'm Oskar," he introduced himself as he poured out two glasses with a broad smile. His skin was too taut. "You were here a few weeks ago with a regular patron of my establishment who is also a good friend. Justus bought several cases at the Brunello winery in Montalcino. In lieu of a corking fee, I got one bottle from each case. The rest belongs to him," he explained, touching his glass to each of theirs.

The roasted pork chops were served sizzling in black cast-iron skillets together with wooden bowls of green salad that gleamed with a vinaigrette dressing.

"Enjoy your meal," Oskar said. He moved aside to answer the phone.

They emptied their glasses and turned their heads to look out over the crowded restaurant. By the time they turned back to the bar, their glasses were full again.

"Do you think we'll be drunk soon?" Alex said. A delighted grin spread across Jane's face.

The last time was in Madrid. They were young then. In order to kill the taste of the cheap wine they were drinking, they finished off four cans of sardines. She'd said he smelled like a well-behaved dolphin after a training session.

He kissed her, and he saw the surprise in her eyes. Immediately, she shut them and let herself savor the sensation. Recalling the sardines, he burst out laughing, breaking off the kiss.

"What's so funny?" she asked good-naturedly.

Someone touched his shoulder.

A slim waitress in a white apron said, "This is for you," and handed him a folded paper napkin.

"Who's it from?" he asked.

"I don't know."

"Who gave it to you?"

"He left."

Alex glanced at the phone. 23:18.

He unfolded the napkin, which had the ornate letters of Schlaff's logo in the corner. The message read:

"I saw you at the train station in Frankfurt in 2006. You went back to the freight car and set the bomb when the girl could not do it. I was standing watch. Somebody tried to kill me tonight. Justus is not answering his phone. He is not at home and he is not here. Something may be wrong. Meet me in the forest by the abandoned NSA station on Teufelsberg at a quarter to twelve. Upper level of the building with the three radomes. Come alone. Berlin."

In German, Teufelsberg means "devil's mountain."

DIARY

27 June 1943

The Germans wish to suck the marrow of pleasure out of Paris, but our city is already gaunt and feeble. There is a worrisome shortage of goods. The black market is thriving, and prices are sky-high. We have stopped serving lunch in the café. Income is plummeting.

28 June 1943

I close the café after midnight. The leavened dough rises until four in the morning. Then I return and bake a smaller version of the baguette de tradition for widows and the needy. Fortunately, our apartment is above the boulangerie, so the curfew does not prevent me from working. Jasmine pleads with me to charge money for these smaller baguettes.

I refuse. We will continue to cut down on our expenses.

We are all still together, still alive, and there is food on the table.

11 July 1943

I miss the rich yellow butter from Normandy. I could smell the sun in it, and the blue sky, and a lust for life. I dream about raisins from the Loire, about their robust, concentrated taste and their deceptive, salty sweetness. Where have the pheasants of Périgord disappeared to?

"I'm coming with you," Jane said, reaching for her purse.

"He said to come alone."

"It's too dangerous, Alex. It could be a trap."

"He must be Berlin. And he knows that Justus is missing. He could be the lead we've been looking for. If I'm not back in an hour, take a cab to Justus's house."

"Alex . . ." she began, her eyes clouded with apprehension. He made a lame attempt at a smile, kissed her, and left.

Outside, the heavy bass notes from the cellar pounded on the dark, cold air. The parking lot reached to the edge of the frozen lake. He got into the Mercedes, checked his Glock, and studied the map.

The road was dark and empty, with dirty snow piled up on either side.

Berlin wrote *Somebody had tried to kill him tonight.*

Alex took out his phone, turned on the scrambler app, and punched in a number. At Glilot, HQ answered immediately.

"I need the plans for the NSA listening station on Teufelsberg. Blueprints and satellite images. It's urgent."

The traffic on snowy Route 115 was light. Alex sped northward, quickly leaving behind the luxury homes of Grunewald. The Mercedes's tires gripped the compacted snow well. He passed Charlottenburg and turned west and then south, into the dark forest. In the car's strong headlights he could see solid oaks and lindens and slender pine trees, their branches white with snow.

Racing along Teufelsseechaussee, he suddenly saw a terrified animal in the middle of the road. His headlights made its big ears seem almost transparent. A young red fox. He slammed on the brakes and switched off the headlights. Glancing at his watch, he realized that he was cutting it close.

He turned the lights back on. The road was empty. His phone vibrated. The blueprints and sat photos had arrived. He studied them hurriedly.

The moon was hidden. The narrow road twisted and turned as it rose up the mountain. The Military Technology Faculty of the Third Reich was buried under the man-made mound above Berlin.

The station had been abandoned when the Berlin Wall fell and the two Germanys were reunited.

In the dim moonlight, Alex saw the outlines of the three giant geodesic domes covered in tarps. They used to house thirty-six-foot satellite dishes, but the radomes were empty now. The snow was coming down harder, turning the black night white.

As Alex circled the tower bearing a smaller radome, the car lost traction on the slick ice. The trees pushed up to the verges of the narrow road.

In front of him was the main building with the three radomes on the roof, the middle one positioned high on a tall tower. He parked at the foot of an exterior flight of concrete steps, pulled out his gun, and zipped up his jacket. His body was buffeted by the strong wind and his face stung from the freezing snow. The forest was filled with night sounds: distant growls, chilling shrieks, hoarse croaking.

Nearby, under a layer of ice, flowed the Havel River. It felt as if the wind was about to uproot the whole mountain. A mysterious whistling pierced the air.

The wall along the steps was tattooed with overlapping bursts of graffiti, and the acrid stench of urine hung in the air. As he climbed to the second floor, his high hiking boots crushed shards of glass and ice underfoot.

Somebody tried to kill me tonight.

His foot hit a heavy metal disk, causing it to spin away noisily. He heard the creaking of a steel door. He froze, straining to listen. The mysterious whistling grew louder. He tightened his grip on the Glock. The gale swirled around him, and he was almost blind in the spectral darkness. Dull footsteps sounded somewhere above him. The wind lashed at the tarps over the radomes as if they were giant tom-toms. He continued upward, sticking close to the wall and trying not to slip on the ice under his feet, until he saw an interior set of steps leading up to the roof.

Slowly he climbed the stairs, all his senses primed. He glanced at his watch: he was two minutes early. The whistling was louder, almost deafening. He heard a groan and took the last few steps at a run.

Footsteps were gradually fading into the distance. He hid behind a flap of canvas. Then he moved forward, holding the gun out in front of him. The snow was coming down hard, turning the air white. Toward the east he caught a view of the needlelike TV tower.

"Berlin?" he whispered into the darkness.

A nocturnal bird of prey shrieked overhead.

Alex entered the first radome, five stories high.

"Berlin?"

Crouching, he exited quickly and scanned the roof before

entering the second radome. Graffiti-covered torn Teflon sheets flapped in the driving wind. His phone told him that the time set for the meeting had passed.

Alex turned on his flashlight and passed the beam over the concrete floor. A rusty metal frame in the shape of a hexagon was anchored to the floor by fat screws as big as soda bottles. Near the edge of the radome, the beam landed on a dark mass.

The hair on his neck stood up.

Someone was there.

The man was lying on the floor surrounded by a dark stain. Blood spurted upward like water in a fountain. His throat had been ripped open, the damaged windpipe visible. His eyes gaped in terror.

"Who did this to you?" Alex demanded.

A weak gurgle.

"Who?" he repeated, louder.

"Kahl." The single syllable issued directly from the torn throat, together with bubbles of blood.

"Who?"

The blood slowed. "Kei . . . keine Augenbrauen."

The man shuddered, his hips rising and then dropping heavily to the floor. He emitted a long sigh, followed by silence.

Keeping hold of his pistol, Alex felt with his free hand for the artery in the man's sticky red neck. No pulse.

Was this Berlin?

He used his phone to check the meaning of the man's last words. "Bald. No eyebrows."

Leaving the radome, he jogged around the edge of the roof, peering into the darkness below. There was no one there. In the distance, he heard an off-road motorcycle start up, the wind distorting the sound of the rough roar. The beam of a headlight flitted among the dark trees and disappeared.

Shit. The motorcycle was already out of range of his gun.

Whoever had attacked Berlin could easily have come after him as well. The killer had followed Berlin here for the sole purpose of taking his life. As soon as he'd done what he came for, he left. He had no interest in Alex. But what about Jane? She was a Nibelung. If the killer knew Berlin's identity, he might also know hers. Alarmed, Alex realized he'd left her alone in the restaurant.

Nevertheless, he went back to the dead body and looked through the pockets of his clothes. Nothing there. Moving back, he passed the flashlight over the filthy floor. He saw a cable resembling a bicycle brake cable. The silvery fibers were stained red with blood. The reek of feces hung in the air.

Alex heard a noise behind him. He spun around, holding the flashlight parallel to the Glock. A human shape!

His finger tightened on the trigger.

"Alex!"

A woman.

Jane.

Fuck! He raised the flashlight to her face.

"Don't shoot!"

He could see her breath.

What was she doing here? He moved the beam to the slaughtered body.

"Dead?" she asked with no sign of panic.

"Very."

"Berlin?"

"Maybe."

"Maybe?"

"He said something about a bald man with no eyebrows."

"There should be a chip."

"Where?"

"Right side of the groin. Close to the artery."

"I told you to wait in the restaurant."

"I was worried. Pull down his pants."

"How did you get here?"

"I stole a car. Pull down his pants."

She wasn't supposed to be here.

Alex slid the glove off the right hand of the corpse.

"What are you doing?" she asked.

"I don't know. Checking."

The hand was wrapped in a bloodstained cloth. Alex unwound it and saw a long cut across the palm. He glanced at the shiny steel cable on the floor. The picture was clear.

The stench coming from the body was getting stronger. Death by strangulation causes the sphincter to relax. Alex pulled down the pants, breathing through his mouth. "Where is it?" he asked. Jane crouched down and felt along the edge of the fouled underwear.

Alex tasted bile rising in his throat.

"I found it!" she said, coughing.

He aimed the flashlight at the man's groin. "I don't see anything."

"You can't see it. I can feel it under his skin," she said, pressing her fingers into the dead flesh. "I can feel the chip. Oh God," she blurted in fear. "It's Berlin, no question!"

"I almost shot you," Alex said.

"Look how deep the garrote went. Whoever strangled him wanted to make certain he couldn't talk."

"Jane?"

"What?"

"His throat is cut. What makes you think he was strangled?"

The silence between them was heavy. The wind outside was raging and whistling. The seconds ticked by slowly.

Why wasn't she answering him?

"Can't you smell it?" she said finally.

"What?"

"Semen, Alex. He discharged semen. That's what happens when a man is strangled."

"You're questioning me as if I were a suspect," Jane said, not without resentment.

"The search team should be arriving at Justus's house soon," he said.

She gripped the steering wheel of the Mercedes, taking a curve without slowing down. The tires screeched and the rear wheels skidded.

"Answer me. Am I a suspect?"

Yes. Alex kept silent.

She braked violently opposite the gate to the Erlichmann house and got out, not waiting for him and not looking back. He followed her into the warm house.

Jane threw herself onto the sofa, sticking her legs out in front of her and crossing her arms over her chest. Alex watched her from the kitchen. She'd had time to steal a vehicle and she'd known exactly where to go.

"Just stop it, okay?" she called out to him.

"Stop what?"

"You're wrong."

"Someone in the restaurant was watching Berlin and followed him into the forest, probably on a motorcycle. They got to Teufelsberg before me."

"It wasn't me!" she said angrily.

The doorbell rang. They both froze.

Alex walked to the front door. The hall was brightly lit by an antique crystal chandelier. Just inside the entrance stood the ancient marble torso of a soldier, minus the arms.

Justus had lived on a different planet.

Outside was a scrawny man with gigantic elephant ears and huge black eyes in a small face. The lenses of his glasses were thick like the crystal prisms in the chandelier. His head was covered in silvery fuzz and his features were almost swallowed up by a broad smile. In a rich voice he said, "I brought you a dozen voles." Grabbing Alex around the waist, he burst out laughing.

It was Akiva Ancona, a little man with great talent. Brussels's chief operative, he was a tough, experienced investigator and an unparalleled master at organizing a search. "I saw a doghouse in the yard. Where's the dog?"

"Not here."

Twelve men filed in with black gym bags and aluminum cases on wheels. Not one of them smiled in greeting.

"What are we looking for?" Ancona asked.

"A list with a few dozen names or phone numbers or bank accounts. Maybe a code."

"Format?"

"Unknown."

"Show me around. I want to get started right away."

The searchers took off their jackets and got into their gear: white nylon coveralls, surgeons' caps, and overshoes. They pulled latex gloves from their wrappers, stretched them on, and let go with a snap.

Then they covered the front and side windows with black plastic.

"Start praying, Alex," Ancona said, rubbing his hand over the fuzz on the top of his head. "If it's for daily use, that means it's hidden someplace where you can get at it quickly and easily, and that means it'll be a piece of cake. But if it's just for backup, that means three whole days of mega digging and aggro."

Alex grinned. They went up the three wide steps into the living room.

"Wow," Ancona exclaimed when he saw the screen of glass facing the forest.

Ancona swiveled around and gawked like a cartoon character. Then he eyeballed the bookshelves, doing calculations in his head. His black eyes flashed. "Good God! Four thousand books . . . twenty-five seconds apiece—twenty-eight hours—six men—four hours and forty minutes." He chose the men and gave them whispered instructions, and they went to work.

Next he checked out the open cabinets in Justus's study.

"About eight feet of documents . . . a hundred and eighty pages an inch . . . two pages a second . . . ten hours." He gestured to two searchers, who immediately set a digital camera on a tripod and connected it to a satellite modem.

A pale, thin youngster was already typing furiously at Justus's computer, connecting it to the network that would enable Mossad specialists to suck it dry.

"How are you going to get into the safe?" Alex asked.

"Have you seen the tick?"

A short, chubby man was affixing a device to the safe door. It consisted of six thin carbon-fiber legs, an earpiece, and a silicone suction plate that fit over the combination lock. The computerized safecracking tool worked on a lithium battery.

"It's new," Ancona said. "The tick picks up the sounds of the locking gears when you turn the dial and computes the code."

"Wouldn't a drill be easier?"

"It's a Breitenbach, pal. The mechanism is booby-trapped."

Ancona gave the rest of the team their assignments and went through the house, making sure they were all doing their jobs.

"Now we can get some air," he said, pulling out a crushed pack of Gitanes. "Let's go outside. Twenty-six plus sixteen times two . . ."

"Fifty-eight," Alex said.

"Times forty-five seconds . . ."

"Forty-four minutes?"

"You're good! Together we can get it done in twenty-two minutes. You ever fondle a wall?"

"Not since high school."

It was cold outside. Ancona grinned, the cigarette nearly falling from his lips. Squinting through the smoke, he felt along the exterior wall of the house, starting at the ground and reaching as far as he could above his head. He held his ear to the wall as he tapped at it randomly with the knuckle of his index finger.

Nothing there.

"Who's the lady in the living room?" Ancona whispered to Alex.

"A friend."

"One of us?"

"Not exactly," Alex answered.

"Can she be trusted?"

Good question.

They hurried back inside and Ancona went down to the cellar. Alex stared out at the forest, uneasy. He couldn't get the events at Teufelsberg out of his head. What was Jane hiding?

The restaurant owner recognized her. She was close to Justus. Too close? And Justus had been killed.

Was she a threat?

Horrified by the idea, he shook his head.

Were Justus, Istanbul, and Lisbon all slaughtered with the same brute force?

It took massive arms to cut a man's throat open with a bicycle brake cable.

He was chasing a ghost. It was time to bring in the heavy artillery.

A spoon scraped the last of the Nutella from the bottom of the jar. In a dimly lit room opposite four huge screens lived a 365-pound creature. His fans said he was worth his weight in gold. The eight-core processor in his brain ran on sugar, chocolate, and junk food.

"What the fuck? The Coke is salty!" He moved the red can away from his round face and belched.

Tufts of bleached blond hair rose from his head like a cockscomb. He pushed himself out of his reinforced chair. His baggy rapper jeans hung off his enormous butt like a sack, revealing boxer shorts covered with images of Tweety Bird.

The name of the man who ran Mossad's IT division was Ethan Pinchas, but everyone called him Butthead.

The phone on the desk chirped. He reached out an arm that weighed as much as the average leg, nearly crushing the cupcakes waiting their turn like a line of condemned prisoners.

"Hello?"

"It's two in the morning, Butthead. Don't you have a home to go to?"

"Hey, man. I heard you're living the wild life in Berlin."

"Not quite. Are you writing this down?"

"Typing."

"Justus Erlichmann. Grunewald, Berlin."

"Who's Prince Charming?"

"That's what I want to find out. They tell me you can access his computer now. Do some digging. Fast."

"What do I get in return?"

"Your salary."

"We're on overtime."

"A pound of Leonidas?"

"You don't trust me," Jane said.

Alex remained standing at the foot of the steps.

He lowered his eyes.

"Say something."

"I almost shot you."

"Are you crazy? You think I killed Berlin?"

"You took me by surprise," he said. Maybe he was wrong.

Her stomach rumbled. She rubbed it.

"I'm confused, more than anything else," he said.

"Tactfully put."

"What would you think in my place?"

"I'd concentrate on what's important. Nibelungs are being killed, right now, in the middle of the night. We can put a stop to it. We may be the only people who can."

She had come as soon as he called, just like she had three months ago in London.

"Let's go down to the cellar, Alex. They're turning the rest of the house upside down. We can search Nelli's boxes."

"Nelli?"

"His wife."

He remembered the odor of his empty apartment.

"I can't."

Jane started down the stairs, stopping a moment to breathe him in. Then she descended to the cellar alone.

Naomi once said that the cellar is the house's subconscious. That's where you store the things you want to forget but can't abandon completely.

Ancona appeared out of nowhere. "The house is plastered with microphones. The system's connected to the Internet, but it's not on. The only security cameras we found are outside. They're top-of-the-line."

Alex nodded.

"There's a pile of books beside the bed," Ancona said. "They all have bookmarks stuck in the first few pages. Your man was troubled."

Alex gazed at Ancona. Straightforward and efficient; no crises, no drama.

Reuven called.

"I just got back from a meeting with the PM. He doesn't want us to dig into Erlichmann. It could do more harm than good."

Too late.

"Anything new on the crisis in Turkey?" Alex asked.

"With Galia dead and nobody to confess to being responsible for the Iranian's death, there's a good chance the whole incident will die down and be forgotten, unless the Istanbul Nibelung suddenly turns up and ruins everything. But that's not likely to happen. The foreign press is losing interest. Did you find anything in the house?"

"Not yet."

Reuven hung up.

It was after three in the morning in Israel. He brought the phone back to his ear.

"Reuven Hetz's office, shalom," came a chirpy female voice he knew well.

"It's me, Alex. Did the chief just meet with the prime minister?"

"The prime minister is in secret meetings in Paris. He's expected back soon."

"How long has he been in Paris?"

"Since yesterday."

She was born in Cambridge, England. When she was twenty-two she moved to Israel, and joined Mossad. After special field training, she was attached to the elite cadre of assassins known as Kidon. After she was seriously injured, her life as a field agent was over.

Exodus belonged to Mossad's Economics Division, where she'd served as director for the past seven months. Tough and fearless, she didn't pull any punches.

Her division was responsible for creating fictitious companies and other business entities to support Mossad operations. It was also capable of stripping targets of all their assets within minutes, as well as tracing covert financial activity anywhere in the world.

Justus Erlichmann would be easy prey for her.

Alex told her what he knew about him and asked for her help.

"I just got a memo from the head of Mossad telling me not to investigate a man by the name of Justus Erlichmann or to provide you with any information regarding said gentleman," Exodus informed him.

"He's connected to the fuckup in Bolu," Alex said.

"How?"

"And the murder of Galia."

Exodus had grown close to Galia during her time in the field.

"And you want me to ignore a direct order from the chief?"

There was a trace of irony in her voice. She wasn't one of Reuven Hetz's biggest fans.

"Affirmative."

"And why should I do that?"

"Justus ran foreign operatives for us. In the past twenty-four hours they've started dying off."

"He's not cooperating?" she asked.

"He's no longer among the living."

After a long pause, Exodus said, "What do we want to know about him?"

"Everything."

Nelli Erlichmann's study seemed frozen in time. There wasn't a speck of dust anywhere. On the wall were the diplomas of the noted professor of endocrinology at the Charité Campus Virchow-Klinikum, written in ornate Gothic script. An old laptop sat closed on the desk.

Alex felt as if he'd entered a shrine. The same deathly silence lay over Naomi's empty clinic. Time didn't move inside those four walls.

"You have to know how to grieve," Naomi once said when they were going to pay their respects to a family in mourning. He'd buried her quickly. At least, he thought he had.

Jane was in the cellar, keeping her distance, still under suspicion. His life seemed hopeless and meaningless, and his breath was tight as if all his organs were out of place.

Alex went back out into the hall and tried to regain his composure, but he was struck by a wave of repulsion at the abhorrent German character of everything around him, the icy tone of the harsh language ringing in his ears.

"Those-Germans-may-they-rot-in-hell," his mother called them, as if that were their full name, first and last. Would it help to splash some German water on his face?

The floor of Justus's luxurious bathroom was tiled in black and white marble. The room spun around him, the contrasting squares on the floor making him dizzy. He leaned on the gleaming double sink to steady himself. He had to get a grip. He was covered in cold sweat.

The cold water on his face felt bracing. He stood there, leaning on the sink, and waited.

Then he went into the master bedroom. Two large dark wardrobes stood opposite each other at the far end of the room. The one on the right was empty. In the wardrobe on the left he found Justus's clothes arranged precisely. He felt in the pockets and cuffs, shook the shoes out, undid the neatly rolled-up socks, and rooted around in the drawers.

On the top shelf he found a pair of skinny jeans, two red thongs, and a box of sanitary napkins. Holding the jeans up in front of him, he looked in the mirror. The owner was about five inches shorter than he was. The box of napkins was eleven units short. The start of a routine.

He found Jane in the living room. She'd just returned from the cellar.

"It's so sad," she said. "The boxes downstairs were once a living, breathing woman."

Alex walked to the thin bronze figure of the *Walking Man*. The sculpture was deceptive. The man was leaning forward as if he was about to start moving, but his feet were welded in place.

"He had a girlfriend," he said.

"How do you know?"

"Slim, about six feet. Short visits."

"There's nothing wrong with that."

"Do you have any idea who she was?"

"No," she lied.

After hours of fruitless work, the search team took a break, spreading a black tarp on the floor of the pantry in front of a large cupboard.

Ancona handed out sandwiches. The pungent odor of plastic mixed with the smell of roast beef and mustard. They were all crammed into the small room, which filled with sounds of chewing. In their white nylon coveralls they looked like a hungry octopus.

Alex went back to the living room, to the view of the forest. At the far edge of the lawn, under the bare trees, he spotted a rabbit with long ears staring at a linden. Something startled it and it took off, hopping agilely between the bars of the fence and disappearing into the dark forest.

"Alex," Ancona called from the study.

Alex was beside him in an instant.

The sight of an open safe always gets the blood flowing. Alex knelt down and examined the contents. Four thick bundles of five-hundred-euro notes.

"How much?" he asked.

"A hundred thousand," Ancona declared.

There was also a Sig Sauer pistol gleaming with oil, and a BMW fob from which a key with circular indentations was hanging.

"What's it for?" Ancona asked a short man with a double chin beside him, handing him the key.

The man scrutinized its shape and size. "A large bank vault," he stated finally in an unexpectedly high-pitched voice.

At the bottom of the safe was an olive-wood box. Alex opened it to find a medal resting in a depression in the red velvet lining. On the medal, beside a small image of a tree, was an inscription

in Hebrew and German: "In gratitude from the people of Israel."
It was accompanied by a document laminated in yellowing plastic: "On this day, 10 October 1963, a tree was planted at your request in the Garden of the Righteous Among the Nations on the Mount of Remembrance in Jerusalem, in honor of Herr Gunter Erlichmann, who risked his life to save thousands of Jews during the Nazi persecutions. Israel will never forget his noble spirit and courage." At the bottom was the verse: "I will give them an everlasting name that shall not be cut off."

"Did you know about this?" Ancona asked.

Too shaken to speak, Alex merely shook his head.

Ancona put a hand on his shoulder and patted it gently before moving away.

Black-and-white photographs were arranged on the low cabinet in the study. The attractive smiling face of a woman, presumably Nelli, her hair pulled back in a bun, was enclosed in a thick black frame. A smaller photo showed Justus with his arms around an elderly man with a dolphinlike forehead and a mane of white hair. His eyes seemed unfocused.

A tiny picture with frayed edges was encased in Perspex. A young man was standing proudly in front of an art-deco café. Paris? Alex turned it over. Written on the back in sinuous script was the year 1942. The man was grinning broadly.

If Alex had examined the face through a magnifying glass, he would have seen a wide gap between the front teeth.

Alex took refuge under a linden and filled his lungs with bracing air so cold it made his chest shudder. As he gazed at the dark forest, away from the foreign legion that had invaded the house, the memories came.

A five-year-old girl, all alone and shivering in fear, hiding in the forest in the middle of the night. It was his late mother, whom he couldn't save. Shrapnel from the stories of her early life tore at his heart.

In his mind's eye, they were always there, those Germans.

His chest rose and fell with an inner churning. He was consumed by sorrow for her lost childhood and his own sterile youth, strangled by the heavy onus of guilt.

The wind blew over his moist eyes. The bare branches of the linden tree above him creaked. Beyond was only black sky.

Alex tightened his arms around his chest, refusing to allow himself any consolation. He stood that way for a long time.

A gentle touch.

Slender arms embraced him from behind, and Jane leaned her head against his back. The cold had sent the bugs and crickets into hiding, and the silence was unbroken. His conscience gnawed at him.

She held him until his breathing slowed and they were enfolded in a calm stillness. Then they walked back in through the kitchen.

"Where've you been, Alex?" Ancona called from the sofa in the living room. The safecracker was standing beside him, holding a magnifying glass.

"Tell him what you told me," Ancona ordered the chubby man.

The safecracker pointed to the monumental picture on the wall and announced in his soprano voice, "It's a top-quality replica of a real Rothko. He must have the original someplace, but he wouldn't keep it in his house. We're talking seventy million dollars! And the little Jackson Pollock in the study—and it's very rare to find one that size—that painting alone is worth at least eighty million dollars. You with me?"

Stunned, Alex merely nodded.

"Giacometti's *Walking Man* is another one hundred and twenty million dollars! That's a small fortune already. And there are dozens of other drawings and lithographs, and the bronze sculpture outside is an original Henry Moore. Henry Moore!" he sputtered excitedly.

Stolid, modest Justus Erlichmann had an art collection worth hundreds of millions of dollars. The originals were tucked away somewhere. Maybe they were in the vault that the key they'd found in the safe opened.

"Ancona!" somebody called from upstairs.

Ancona jumped up and took the stairs two at a time on his little feet, with Alex right behind him. In the workroom at the end of the hall they saw a man standing on a ladder and pointing at the large-scale model plane hanging from the ceiling. "A Messer-schmitt, the Luftwaffe's main fighter craft. Do you recognize the pilot?" he asked Ancona.

The balsa-wood figure had high cheekbones and flowing blond hair that stuck out under the helmet.

Ancona nodded. "Erich Hartmann, a hero of the Luftwaffe and the greatest ace of all time. He shot down three hundred and fifty-two enemy planes. Whoever carved his face was a fan. You can see it in every detail. Just look."

The pure Aryan face was radiant and arrogant.

An eerie chill went through Alex's body. He crossed his arms over his chest.

"Look at the tail," the man on the ladder instructed. "This wasn't a kit. Every single part is handmade."

There was ice in his veins. Here in Berlin, it was a thousand times more horrifying.

A swastika.

DIARY

24 JULY 1943

There is no longer even a single glass of milk to be found in Paris. The bounteous udders of our homeland have dried up.

I am having trouble finding coffee beans. Across the street, at Hector's brasserie, they serve a hot drink made of acorns. Hector is a gentile and gives me looks.

26 JULY 1943

The sky is black now, and no hope is visible.

All that is left for us is the Resistance.

28 JULY 1943

Before dawn, when the sourish smell of fermenting yeast fills the air and the bread and pastries are slowly turning golden in the oven, I slip away down the hidden metal ladder that leads to the secret cellar and choose an expensive bottle of liquor for the commandant.

Rare bottles, bottles of freedom and life, guarantee our existence.

Your numbers are diminished.

6 AUGUST 1943

I worked up the courage and asked the deputy commandant to help me obtain the ingredients that are essential to my baking.

He said he will see what he can do.

That SS officer has good eyes, but I must not be misled.

He is SS.

Although the giant model was meant to be a precise replica of the Messerschmitt, Alex wondered whether the hand of Justus Erlichmann—the man whose father had been named a Righteous Among the Nations—had shaken when he painted the swastika.

Justus was a creature of contradictions.

The first row of trees in the forest beyond the intimidating fence showed clearly in the harsh lights on the lawn. It was already morning, but it was still dark outside. Berlin lay deep in winter.

The group of searchers gathered in the living room. Their faces said it all. A whole night of searching was drawing to an end, and there was a bitter taste in their mouths. They hadn't found what they were looking for.

"Did you look in the garage?" Alex asked.

"We pulled it apart, broke down any piece of the Mercedes that could be used as a hiding place. We even took apart the bikes, both the road bike and the mountain bike. Nothing," Ancona said. "If we had a few more days . . ."

"It's here," Alex said. "It has to be here. When we finally uncover it, we won't understand how we didn't find it sooner."

Ancona headed back up the stairs.

Jane's eyes were drooping. "They looked everywhere, Alex,"

she said. "They dismantled everything that comes apart. Maybe he didn't keep it here?"

Alex wanted nothing more than to close his scratchy eyes and get some sleep, but he shook his head. "We have to think."

"Alex!" Ancona shouted from the floor above.

He dragged his exhausted body up the stairs as quickly as he could. In the master bedroom, one of the two lamps with linen shades was spread out in pieces on the wide bed.

"It was in the metal base," Ancona announced, handing him a BlackBerry identical to the one Justus had been carrying. "This must be what we've been searching for!"

Ancona pressed the power key. Nothing happened. He passed the phone to the chubby safecracker, "Check it out."

The man took the back off, pulled out the battery, and licked it. He made a face. "The battery's charged. The phone isn't working."

"We'll give it to the lab techs in Brussels," Ancona said.

"Can't you solve the problem here?" Alex asked.

"It could be secured, programmed to lock or wipe the memory if anyone fiddles with it," the man said. "We've seen it before."

"It's easy to steal a phone," Jane said. "Justus wouldn't use it to keep his most closely guarded secrets."

The group fell silent.

Alex said, "They weren't his most closely guarded secrets."

The first light fell on the lawn. The forest was wrapped in mist. The spindly trunks of pine trees stood out in the glare of the strong garden lights. Ancona and his team were gathering up their equipment. Jane was asleep on the sofa, curled up in the fetal position. The contour of her curvaceous hip aroused a pleasant memory. Alex sat down on the sofa opposite and watched her sleep. Then he passed his eyes over the massive library.

He nodded off several times before he stopped fighting his exhaustion and sank into a dreamless sleep.

When he awoke, it was twenty past ten. The house was empty. Ancona and his voles were gone. Jane was still sleeping, her limbs now stretched out loosely. Alex went to sit beside her. Her feet touched his thigh. She was shifting in her sleep. He placed his hand gently on her shin and felt the warmth of her body. Her eyelids twitched.

"Come on, it's time to get up. We'll have some coffee and then fly to Davos," he whispered in her ear.

She cracked her eyes open, smiling at the feel of his hand on her face. "Davos?"

"Gunter."

"Let me talk to him first."

"To who?"

"He might remember me. He recruited me."

"Gunter?"

"In '86. He's a very imposing man, an almost-extinct species. Have you ever met him?"

His phone vibrated.

Reuven.

"I've got the lab results from the blood you found at the cemetery," he said, exhaling loudly. "It's Justus's. He's dead."

He hung up.

Alex filled Jane in immediately.

With glistening eyes, she said quietly, "I prayed all night that you were wrong, that he was still alive."

Alex leaned over and hugged her to him. She brushed away a stray tear. "He was always there when I needed him."

Alex thought about enigmatic Justus, dead Justus.

They locked up the house and hurried to Tegel Airport.

They were going to try to draw water from a dry well.

A pair of F-16s flying in formation over Masada.

The PM at the head of the March of the Living in Auschwitz, carrying a wreath.

Signed photographs in silver frames graced the walls of the holy of holies of Israeli politics.

The prime minister kept his distance, essentially barricading himself behind his massive desk. He looked tired, perhaps the result of his visit to Paris.

"We're getting very disturbing reports about our relations with Turkey from the Ministry of Foreign Affairs situation room. And it's still in the early stages. I understand that you lost your most critical asset, Justus Erlichmann," the PM said, raising an eyebrow.

"*Our* most critical asset, sir. Yes."

The PM looked around the room, checking theatrically in the corners and behind him, and then looked piercingly at Reuven. "Ours?" With a fake smile he asked, "Do you see anyone here besides you?"

It was as if a ninja star was flying around the room, and the two men were doing their best to duck. It's called an election year.

Reuven hadn't been born yesterday. Or the day before. He'd been speaking spin from birth, and he knew very well that a successful Mossad op meant press photos of the two of them smiling, shaking hands, and patting each other on the back. But if something went wrong, heaven forbid, the head of Mossad wouldn't get any farther than the PM's secretary.

"There is a serious leak in the Nibelung Ring. We have to consider the possibility that the whole Ring has been blown and we'll have to shut it down. The Justus Erlichmann I knew couldn't have been the source of the leak," the prime minister said, taking a breath before going on. "Find the rotten apple, Reuven, before it spoils the whole barrel."

Reuven remained silent.

A short, thin man, the prime minister raised his shoulders in an effort to appear more daunting. He played with a gilt letter opener, testing the sharpness of the blade.

"What's the connection between your man in Istanbul and the spice warehouse in Bolu?" he asked.

"There's no connection," Reuven fired back, feeling an irritating itch in his nose.

The PM nodded deliberately.

"As far as Justus Erlichmann and the Nibelung Ring are concerned, nothing gets leaked to the press. It never happened. No leaks, no spins," the PM ordered.

"Alex is handling the crisis, sir."

"Coward," the PM muttered, as if talking to himself. "You should be handling it yourself."

The last time Reuven had seen Justus was three weeks ago. They met in the Grunewald forest at night in a heavy rain, sitting in an armored car that belonged to the Israeli embassy in Berlin. Their conversation was somber. Justus looked pale, and one of his eyelids twitched.

"You still with me?" the PM snapped, interrupting Reuven's reverie. He glanced at the digital Breitling watch on his hairy wrist. "Okay, it's decision time."

Reuven held his water glass up to his lips. It was empty.

"In view of the attacks on the Nibelung Ring and the painful fact that Mossad's protective shield has been breached, we may be forced to shut the Ring down. Do whatever it takes to keep the situation from snowballing out of control."

"But Mr. Prime Minister, sir—"

The PM raised a hand to cut him off, then used it to straighten his blue tie. "It's all yours, the authority and the accountability."

"That's not entirely accurate, sir," Reuven said. The leather couch creaked beneath him.

"My dear Mr. Hetz. Perhaps I haven't made myself clear. You chose to fill me in on the crisis in Turkey only after it had grown to monstrous proportions. You screwed up badly there. You lost a highly regarded senior agent and the Istanbul Nibelung. After that, you lost another Nibelung in Lisbon, and Justus Erlichmann himself. You gave yourself the authority. Accountability goes along with it. And don't wave the Nibelung charter in my face. That document is sealed, and it has been locked in the safe of the prime minister's office since the sixties. It's never been opened. Nor has the third copy, held by the government's legal adviser. The guidelines for the Ring are nevertheless clear."

"But, sir—"

"I'm not done!" the PM silenced him, raising his voice.

Reuven stared down at the tips of his black shoes and the carpet beyond. He felt like a snake trying to swallow a goat.

"As of this moment, if another Nibelung disappears you are to disband the Ring immediately."

"Sir, there's something I have to say."

The PM walked to the door of the office and opened it wide. He was clearly determined to deny any responsibility, at all costs.

But Reuven wasn't here to crawl or kiss ass. "The Nibelung charter specifies explicitly that the prime minister alone has authority over the group's activities, sir," he said. "My job is merely to coordinate with the Ring when necessary and use its services as I see fit."

By the time he finished, he was nearly shouting. A small spray of spittle flew from his lips onto the PM's immaculately pressed white shirt.

A heavy silence fell over the room.

"Reuven," the PM said, bringing his bald head closer and speaking barely above a whisper. "A little bird told me that you said—off the record, of course—that Israel needed a prime minister who had experience as head of Mossad. You mentioned, if I remember correctly, Vladimir Putin, who used to head the FSB, and George H. W. Bush, a former CIA chief. And you hinted at this coming November."

In a country where the carcass of an ideology lay rotting for all to see and opportunism and cynicism ruled, Reuven felt he had something to offer in the political arena. A lot to offer, in fact. An eager expression spread across his face. Just a few nights ago he had dreamed he heard the chanting of a crowd, gaining in strength until it became a roar: *Reuven Hetz, the next prime minister!*

"Reuven," the PM barked. "I can see that you're lusting after my seat." With a sinister smile he added, "Maybe you haven't noticed, but it's already taken."

Reuven left without saying good-bye.

Later, sitting in the dimness in the backseat of the Volvo taking him home, he felt as if the car was falling into a sinkhole.

Jane hadn't said a word since they left Berlin.

The road wound its way up the snow-covered Alps. The frozen conifers bent under the weight of the snow. Even behind dark glasses, the light was blinding. Alex drove in uncomfortable silence.

The Magic Mountain Sanatorium had been built in the nineteenth century to treat tuberculosis patients. In 1971 it was converted into a home for wealthy retirees with pulmonary diseases. From an altitude of more than five thousand feet, the four-story building looked out over the Landwasser Valley, with Davos below like a giant mint candy.

Reuven called.

"I thought you were at Justus's house."

"We're in Davos."

"It's a wasted trip. Five months ago Gunter had a massive stroke, and he's also at an advanced stage of Alzheimer's."

Alex disconnected.

The lobby of the sanatorium was studded with arches and broad staircases with oak banisters. A modern elevator took them to the third floor. The steel walls smelled of disinfectant.

"Justus always read to Gunter from *The Magic Mountain*. When they finished the book, Gunter would ask him to start again from the beginning," Jane said. "A few months ago, he stopped asking."

The elevator halted and they got out. The sobering odor of old age and medications hung in the air.

"Herr Erlichmann is over here," said a nurse in her sixties. Her hair was pulled back with a disturbing severity. The shadow of a mustache could be seen under her broad nose. Her gilt name tag was engraved with the name CHRISTA. She opened the door on a blinding light. Alex put his sunglasses back on.

"Ten minutes. No more. Those are the regulations." The nurse left.

A scrawny young man with a sharp nose and round glasses was holding a spoonful of porridge to Gunter's mouth. There was no mistaking the dolphin brow and blue eyes. His skeletal body was engulfed in an orthopedic chair. A thin tube hanging from his ears pumped oxygen into his nostrils.

The young man returned the spoon to the bowl and reached out his hand. His name was Gustav. "I understand that you came all this way to talk to Gunter," he said. "You should know that since the stroke, he hasn't been able to speak or write."

Alex nodded.

The comfortable studio apartment was furnished with a high hospital bed, a television, a small refrigerator, a Biedermeier wardrobe, chairs, and an antique desk with a writing surface lined with faded green felt. A gilt-framed photo showed Justus and Nelli on their front lawn in Grunewald, with the grand house and the tall linden in full bloom in the background.

Gunter's skin was wrinkled and spotted with the signs of age. Beneath his dry eyelids there was an expression of confusion that did not match the carefully combed waves of his white mane.

The room they were standing in was like a solarium, with wood-framed glass walls on three sides. It was as bright as a greenhouse, and the heat was turned up to the maximum. The room was stifling and dazzling.

Alex took his coat off.

The view was breathtaking. The horizon was filled with a row of snow-covered peaks of different heights, like an EKG graph.

"I'll be right outside," Gustav said, leaving.

Gunter was sitting at the far end of the room, staring out at the valley. His withered body was wrapped in a rough gray sweater and thick woolen blanket. His eyes were cloudy.

Jane went to him and wiped the remnants of porridge from his mouth with a paper napkin. Her forehead was glistening. The faint whirr of a helicopter could be heard in the distance.

"Gunter, der Ring des Nibelungen," she said, stressing each syllable.

His blue eyes showed confusion.

"I'm London," she said, speaking louder and pointing to herself. "I'm London, Gunter. London. Do you remember me?"

The old man stared unseeingly at the white peaks.

"Der Ring des Nibelungs, remember?" Jane repeated, as if she were climbing a slippery wall.

Gunter's dry lips parted slightly.

"Paris. Barcelona. Moscow. Athens . . ." she said loudly, and then pointed to herself again. "London. I'm London."

No response.

Alex opened one of the glass panels, and the bracing air stung his face.

Gunter smiled. The left side of his face sagged.

"Where is the list of the Nibelung Ring?" Jane asked.

The old German turned and looked at Alex.

"Help me, Gunter, please. It's important."

An emaciated hand peeked out from the brown blanket. The back of the hand was wrinkled and covered in liver spots. Jane took it in her own. Gunter pulled his hand away and pointed falteringly at the photo.

Jane got the picture and handed it to him. He brought it up to his eyes. His lower lip was trembling.

With a shaking hand, he pointed to Justus.

"Yes, Justus has the list. Where does he keep it?"

Gunter pushed the photo into Jane's hands.

"What is he trying to tell us?"

The old man pointed to the picture with a limp finger.

"The list is in Justus's house," Jane said. "Where in the house, Gunter?"

Gunter's eyes again looked unfocused.

Jane got a sheet of paper from the desk and drew a house. She showed it to Gunter. The wheels in the old man's head seemed to have stopped turning.

"Where in the house?"

The door opened and Nurse Christa announced firmly, "Your ten minutes are up. You have to leave."

"In a minute," Jane said as she handed the sheet of paper to Gunter and placed a pen in his hand.

He stared at her, not understanding what she wanted from him.

"No minute. Right now!" Christa barked.

The noise of the helicopter was getting louder.

Alex positioned himself in front of the nurse. "We're here on a very important matter, madam. I'll thank you to give us a few more minutes of privacy."

Gustav fidgeted uncomfortably.

Jane again showed Gunter the drawing of the house. "Where?" she insisted.

"Now!" Christa roared. "Herr Erlichmann has had a stroke. You interrogate him without any consideration for his condition."

Alex quickly scanned the room. Opposite the bed was a tiny security camera. Had she been listening in on their conversation?

Gunter struggled to draw something.

An arch?

The helicopter was nearby. Alex searched for it in the sky, but the snow was blinding.

"It's very important, madam. Please go away and let us finish," he said.

Gunter was absorbed in his effort to move the pen over the paper. But it wasn't an arch he was trying to draw. What was it?

Gustav approached Alex and Christa, obviously seeking to negotiate a peace between the two warring parties. "Look," he began, but Christa dismissed him with a wave of her hand. "I call security!" she declared. Taking a small beeperlike device from her pocket, she pressed the button, smirking at them triumphantly.

That's when Alex saw it.

A miniature RC helicopter, about five feet in length, rose above the wooden support wall beneath the glass windows. Its black carbon-fiber body was topped by a yellow canopy. Smoke issued from an exhaust pipe as the rotors shrieked in the air. They all gazed at it in wonder. The helicopter drew closer to the open window.

Gunter was intent on his drawing.

A lens in the nose of the chopper glinted in the sunlight. The wind carried in the odor of burning nitro engine fuel.

"What's that?" Jane blurted.

Alex suddenly caught sight of what was hanging from the chopper's underbelly and leaped at Jane, pulling her toward the door, slamming her to the floor, and lying down on top of her. She hit her head as she fell, but her cry of pain was lost in a blinding flash that ended in a deafening explosion. Objects rose into the air and crashed onto the floor. The glass walls shattered, sending shards flying around the room.

Afterward, there was only an eerie silence and a blast of air from a dislodged tube.

Alex opened his eyes. The solarium was filled with thick smoke. Nurse Christa was lying on the floor, blood spurting from her neck. She was gasping for air.

With the glass walls gone, a freezing wind struck Alex in the face. Gunter was still in his chair by the window, but something was missing. Alex stood up and peered out over the remains of the wooden wall. An odd movement below caught his eye. Rolling down the slope of the Magic Mountain was Gunter Erlichmann's head, leaving behind a trail of red blood on the white snow.

Jane's face was covered in grime. Her moist eyes were wide open. As she picked herself up off the floor, she saw Gunter's headless body. Hunching over, she opened her mouth and puked.

Smoke and dust filled the room. A wailing siren could be heard somewhere. The sound of a motorbike riding into the distance carried on the wind, but the slope beyond the ruined wall was empty. There was no one there. Alex's ears were ringing, and there was a sharp pain in his eardrum.

The nurse was lying in a large pool of blood studded with shards of glass that glittered like diamonds. Her eyes were open, and her body was twitching.

Gustav had cuts on his limbs and face. His blood was squirting onto the floor, and fear showed in his eyes.

Jane's face was tight. "The police will be here any minute," she said.

"Bring the car around to the front. I'll be right there."

Jane was frozen in place.

"Go now. We don't have time," Alex ordered.

She hesitated, taking in the floor, the bed, and the shards of glass. "Aren't you coming?"

"In a minute. Go!"

She bent down and picked up a sheet of paper. It was covered in blood. Gently, she shook off the dust and wood splinters and took it with her.

Alex ran toward the hall, slipping on the glass and skidding across the floor until he banged into the sink near the door. He grabbed bandages and antiseptic off a medical cart outside and raced back into the room. Nurse Christa had fallen silent. Her eyes were glazed over.

As he wrapped tourniquets around Gustav's arms and legs, he saw that blood was also spurting from his neck. He held a large bandage to the wound and pressed down hard. Blood flowed out between his fingers.

"I'm cold," Gustav said, shivering.

"You'll be fine."

A young doctor in a white coat hurried in, followed by a nurse. They both froze in the doorway. The nurse covered her mouth with her hand, a look of horror on her face.

"Over here," Alex called to the doctor. "Keep the pressure on," he shouted, his voice too loud. The awful ringing in his ears was coming from inside his head.

Sweat marks showed under the doctor's arms. He pressed down on the red bandage. Alex pulled a gray blanket from the bed, shook off the glass, and threw it over what was left of Gunter Erlichmann. A dark stain appeared at the top.

"Code Blue!" the doctor shouted into the hallway. Instantly, medical personnel came rushing in. Under cover of the commotion, Alex slipped out of the room.

The asphalt in the parking lot was dotted with snow.

He searched for Jane between the parked cars. The sirens were getting closer. They had to get out of there. He found her kneeling beside their rental car, hurling. She didn't see him. The car door was open. He found a bottle of water and handed it to her. Without a word, she rinsed her face, took a sip, and spit it out. She was pale and sweaty. He helped her up and settled her in the car. As soon as she seemed calm enough, he turned the key in the ignition.

A red fire truck and two ambulances appeared around a bend, their red lights flashing as they sped up the snowy mountain. Alex made the descent at a measured speed. The ringing in his ears was becoming intolerable.

After a while, they left the Landwasser Valley and Davos behind.

The bomber that killed Gunter was identical to the RC helicopter that Justus had built.

A tear escaped from Jane's eye. She wiped it away with her sleeve. "Did you see his head?"

He touched her shoulder gently. She leaned her head on the window. "If we hadn't come, he'd still be alive."

He couldn't find the words to comfort her.

A few minutes later he whispered into his cell phone, "Someone blew up Gunter Erlichmann."

Reuven took a deep breath. "Are you serious?"

"Plastic explosives attached to a small remote-controlled helicopter. Justus built one just like it. We're on our way back to Berlin."

"What are you planning?" Reuven asked.

"To pull Justus's house apart until we find the list of Nibelungs, and then warn the ones we still can."

"Okay. Do whatever you want, but you're on your own. No calling Buthed or Exodus."

"I want Butthead and his staff to find out all they can about Erlichmann, and I want Exodus and her people involved, too. I need to know everything," Alex demanded.

"The PM is adamant. No secret ops, and that goes for Butt-head and Exodus, too."

Alex didn't give up. "The list of Nibelungs isn't hanging from a magnet on Justus's refrigerator. We have to find it. I need to know the man better. We don't have time."

Reuven hung up.

Jane didn't utter a word. She'd been crying quietly.

Alex reached out and caressed her wet face. She pressed her cheek against his large hand and closed her eyes.

Alex glanced at the stained sheet of paper Jane had picked up.

"What's that?" Alex asked.

"Gunter's drawing," she said, showing it to him.

Alex stuck the drawing on the steering wheel and examined it while he drove. A large section of the naive depiction was covered in blood, but the image was clearly identifiable.

A croissant.

DIARY

8 AUGUST 1943

The trains returning empty from the East will bring fresh supplies from the Vaterland, the deputy commandant said. Sacks of flour, yellow butter, eggs, real coffee, sugar, salt, milk powder—even raisins.

Now that he serves his customers a drink made of acorns instead of coffee, how will Hector, the gentile from the brasserie, take the news?

13 AUGUST 1943

Where have you gone, you nights filled with the joy of life, when cognac, calvados, and pastis were sipped from glasses; Château Margaux was poured slowly; Dom Pérignon foamed and overflowed? People drank and dreamed and fell in love. Back then, the Café Trezeguet was suffused with the intoxicating aroma of a full, rich life.

17 AUGUST 1943

I use the supplies that arrived from Germany to surreptitiously bake sixty small baguettes de tradition. Before dawn, at the back door to the boulangerie, I give them to widows and the needy.

I am digging my own grave.

Winter had its claws in Berlin. The sun was sinking listlessly in the cloudy graphite sky. In Grunewald, the lawns were buried under snow. The tall trees in the forest behind the houses were as bare as fish bones.

Croissant crumbs were still scattered on Justus's kitchen counter. As he wiped them away, Alex recalled the sketch Gunter had drawn seconds before he died. What did it mean?

He opened the freezer of the Sub-Zero refrigerator and rooted around among the neatly arranged plastic containers. He found frozen croissants, chicken stock, and beef stew, but no list of Nibelungs.

Alex switched on the TV. On one of the German channels, the Israeli prime minister was standing in front of a wall of microphones bearing foreign media logos. Speaking in Hebrew, he said, "Israel will never apologize for exercising its legitimate right to defend itself in all places and ensure the security of its citizens at all times."

Cut to the dead body of Karabashi.

Alex went over to the glass wall and gazed out mournfully at the forest. He remained standing there for a long time. Finally, he turned around and was struck once more by the monumental size of the library.

The Bebelplatz rose up from the depths of his memory. The empty bookshelves buried in the subconscious of the frozen square, in the subconscious of Berlin. Justus was a man of books; a man of many faces; an enigma.

Alex scanned the shelves, struggling to grasp the logic of their organization. He mapped the subjects and their locations on a piece of paper. German literature; Austrian, French, Russian, Italian, American, British, and Spanish literature; even Israeli literature in German translation.

The upper shelves held reference books and volumes of history, philosophy, and poetry. The bottom shelves were reserved for anthologies of art and architecture, and books on science and mechanics. All the German greats were represented, a sea of icons. Symbols of the cultural distinction of the German nation. An august array.

Six guides to identifying and growing orchids ignited a glimmer of hope. There was no greenhouse on the grounds and not a single orchid anywhere. Alex paged through them carefully but found nothing.

Were more Nibelungs being murdered in the meantime? He had to warn them, save them. Each Nibelung was a whole world. Each killing seriously jeopardized Mossad and forced them to halt operations in that territory.

Alex remembered the underground memorial at the Bebelplatz again. The empty bookshelves crying out to the world. What was Justus trying to tell him by meeting him there? Was he giving him a clue in case anything happened to him?

All the shelves were full, except one: the lowest one on the far left, closest to Justus's study.

A biography of Jane Austen caught his eye. For some reason, it wasn't with the other biographies on the right-hand side of the library but on the half-empty shelf on the left. Next to it was a book in Italian describing how to butcher a cow.

What is a celebrated author like yourself, dear Miss Austen, doing here beside a guide for beginning butchers?

Alex took the thick British volume into the kitchen and laid it on the counter. He paged through it impatiently.

Nothing.

He felt the dust cover and shook the book. Nothing fell out.

Alex shoved the book aside. Outside, the light had grown dimmer. Jane was snoring gently. He returned to the book and carefully scrutinized each page.

On page 286 he found a tiny crumb under the page number and tried to wipe it away.

It didn't move.

It wasn't a crumb.

He brought the book closer to his eyes. It wasn't a stain, either.

The mark had been made deliberately.

He felt a tiny flutter of hope in his belly. He examined every page closely and found another mark on page 351.

He wrote down the two page numbers: 286–351.

The difference between them was 65. Did that mean something?

What if he put them together: 286351.

It was too short to be a telephone number, unless the prefix was missing. What else could it be?

He sat down on the sofa beside Jane and touched her shoulder. Her eyelids twitched. She opened her eyes with a smile, but there was a look of confusion on her face.

"We're in Justus's house in Berlin," he whispered.

Jane sat up, folding her long legs under her.

"Did Justus transfer your money into a special account?" he asked.

"What time is it?"

"Do you have a special bank account?"

"Yes. It's late, isn't it?"

"Do you remember the number?"

"286351."

Golden rays of light seemed to dance through the room. For the first time in a long while, Alex's mood lightened. He ran to the library and examined the other books on the bottom-left shelf.

He found the same marks in a book of conversations with Isaiah Berlin, as well as in a French baking guide. Berlin and Paris. London was here with him, and Rome must be the butcher. He had found the answer.

Forty-eight books were bunched together on the shelf, and each had tiny marks under three-figure page numbers.

"Justus was a genius," he announced.

Working together, they made a list of all the Nibelungs and their six-figure account numbers, revealing the structure and extent of the ring. The most urgent thing now was to decipher the spare BlackBerry Ancona's team had found.

Alex called the Brussels station. "I'm sending you a list of codes to decipher. They are bank accounts, but also partial phone numbers. Try to figure it out," Alex said.

Zengot let out a sigh. "Alex, I've got my best people working for you, but for God's sake, you're not an only child."

"Sammy, while we're wasting time talking, our people are being killed."

It was freezing outside. The wind had died down, and the trees in the forest were still. A bird shrieked in the distance. A grunt issued from deep in the woods. The piercing cold hurt the man's skin. He couldn't feel his toes. His body was numb from long hours without moving.

He had gathered branches and woven them into the netting of his camouflage suit. His wait was nearing its end.

The clear glass wall along the width of the house gave him an advantage. He knew the house well.

When he'd arrived in the middle of the night, the two of them were already there. Then the white coveralls came and tore the place apart.

Moving as silently as a cat, he climbed down out of the linden tree in the yard.

It was time.

Jane had gone to wash up in the guest bathroom upstairs. Alex lay on the sofa in the living room, conjuring up images of her young naked body. He would gladly have joined her in the shower right now, but something still stood between them, keeping them apart.

His eyes closed and he nodded off.

Naomi appeared in his dream. Pale linoleum. A dark pool of blood spreading out around her. He opened his eyes, shaken and horrified. God, how long would it go on?

He got up and went into the kitchen. The last vestiges of daylight cast a blue tinge over the wooden floorboards. A soft, comforting snow was falling.

He ground fresh coffee beans. Then he packed down the grounds with the tamper and slowly lowered the lever of the La Pavoni machine. Thick, speckled espresso dripped into the cup, suffusing the air with a heady aroma. In the stainless-steel jug, milk gurgled and frothed.

Jane joined him, fresh and sweet smelling, her wet hair combed back. She sliced an onion, beat eggs in a bowl, and started frying a thick omelet. Alex got cheese and sausage from the refrigerator.

The landline rang.

The fork fell from Jane's hand, striking aplate. Alex turned to stare at Justus's desk at the other end of the house. Who was calling the late Justus Erlichmann?

"Should we answer it?" she asked.

"Not yet."

After six rings the phone fell silent. They went back to cooking. The ringing started up again.

Alex crossed the living room at a run and picked up the phone. An unfamiliar voice with a foreign accent said, "There's a silver Audi A6 parked outside, near the gate. Open the trunk."

"Who is this?"

"Go now. Alone."

The man hung up.

Alex got his Glock and pulled back the slide. There was a bullet in the chamber.

"What's going on?" Jane asked.

"There's a man outside who wants something from us."

"Let's go," she said, getting up. She pulled her own Glock from her bag and cocked it with a practiced motion. "He can see us," Alex said. "He told me to come alone."

"He's in the forest?"

Alex nodded and looked out the window. The snow was coming down harder, turning everything white. The eggs were sizzling.

Jane covered the pan with a plate and turned the omelet out onto it. "We're totally exposed. It's too dangerous here."

Alex went into the pantry and raised the edge of the curtain. She was right behind him.

"Where outside?"

"Over there. The silver Audi," he said, pointing with the Glock.

"I hope it isn't Justus."

"Where?"

"In the trunk."

The red Calder mobile at the far end of the hall hung motionlessly in the air. When Alex opened the front door, it began to swing erratically.

Visibility was limited in the snow-filled dusk. He walked through the gate and looked back at the house one last time. She was standing at the window.

Alex moved toward the Audi, checking the street. A motocross bike roared by, leaving a black stripe in the fresh snow.

Alex circled the car parked along the fence. He couldn't see anyone. He tugged on the passenger-seat door handle. The door glided open.

He leaped back, slipping on the ice and nearly losing his balance. At the last minute, he managed to grab hold of the freezing fence and stop his fall.

She was watching him from the pantry window.

Kneeling, he looked under the car. Then he stood up and reached out for the trunk-release button. If it was booby-trapped, he'd have nowhere to run.

Alex took out the Glock and pressed the button with his left hand. The lid of the trunk began to rise slowly. As he leaped back, he almost discharged the gun.

The trunk was empty.

He glanced over at the window.

Jane wasn't there.

Jane didn't answer her phone.

There was a cold throbbing in his neck. He closed the trunk lid with the hand holding the gun.

The unfamiliar voice answered Jane's phone. "Come to the living room. Try anything and the woman dies."

The call was disconnected.

Who was he? How did he get into the house?

Alex made his way quickly back, his boots crunching on the snow. The service door was ajar. He pushed it open with the barrel of his Glock and quietly entered the kitchen.

"Don't turn around!" ordered a man behind him. "One false move and the woman dies."

He'd fallen into another trap. He was desperate to turn around, pull the trigger, and empty the magazine into the intruder.

"Put the gun on the floor and go sit on the sofa. Hands on your head." The stranger's voice was steady.

Alex swiveled around sharply, his gun pointed.

Jane's pale face was in his sights. A gun barrel fitted with a silencer was pressed to her head. Her eyes burned with fury. The stranger had her in a headlock from behind. He was shorter than she was. His eyes peered over her shoulder as he used her body as a shield.

Suddenly she dropped to the floor, exposing the man behind her, but he immediately swung his arm around her neck and pulled her back up in front of him.

Alex didn't have enough time to get off a shot.

But the man's head was still visible. Alex aimed his gun at his forehead. The stranger lowered his weapon and pulled the trigger.

Pkow. A silenced shot. The bullet entered the wooden floorboards no more than an inch from Alex's toes. The bastard was a pro.

"Put the gun on the carpet!" he hissed. "The next time, I'll aim for your dick."

Alex placed his gun on the living room carpet and retreated to the sofa.

"Sit next to him," he ordered Jane, shoving her in his direction. "Hands on your head!"

Jane swung around and kneed him hard in the balls. He grunted and folded over. His face went red. Then he struck her in the head with his gun.

She let out a scream, her face scrunching up in pain. She wobbled a little but didn't fall.

Fuck. Alex's gun was too far away.

The stranger thrust the silencer between her eyes. His body was as massive as a Hummer. He had a broad face and oily skin. The veins stood out on his neck, as thick as a tree trunk.

Blood trickled from Jane's temple. "Do that again and I'll kill you," she breathed.

Through the stranger's quilted jacket, Alex could see the contours of his burly arms. Compared to the size of his body, his hands were huge.

"Who are you?" Alex asked.

"Shut up!" The man's small brown eyes flared. He was sharp and experienced.

Jane pulled a crumpled tissue from the pocket of her jeans and held it to the cut on her forehead.

"How do you know Justus?" Alex said.

Pkow. A silenced bullet whistled past his ear. A chunk of plaster fell to the floor behind him.

"I'm the one with the gun," the man said.

"So shoot, chatterbox," Alex goaded.

"Who are you?" the stranger asked.

Jane examined the bloodstained tissue. "Friends of Justus," she said.

"Liar!" Again he pointed the gun at her head. His expression grew more serious, and a deep furrow appeared between his eyes. "What were you looking for?"

"Who are *you*?" Alex demanded.

"Where is Justus?" the stranger thundered.

"What's he to you?" Alex said.

"We have a connection."

"What kind?"

"Friends."

"Are you in the habit of sitting in trees and spying on your friends?"

"I could tell something was wrong, so I came."

"From where?" Jane asked.

"Paris." He checked for their reaction. "You're Mossad?"

"Maybe," Alex said.

"One of your guys was tailing me in Paris."

"How do you know it was one of our guys?"

"He's dead."

The stranger placed his gun on the glass table and sat down opposite them.

"What happens if I grab the gun?" Alex asked.

"Take it," the stranger handed it to him.

Alex exchanged a quick glance with Jane, took the icy gun, and pulled back the slide. A bullet fell from the chamber and rolled noisily onto the wooden floorboards. Alex didn't bend down to retrieve it. The stranger's face was expressionless, but his body was tense.

A soft hissing issued from the heating system. Alex scrutinized the man. Something about his face seemed familiar. What was it?

"Come," the stranger said suddenly, standing up and crossing the living room.

Exchanging another glance, Alex and Jane followed. The cold outside penetrated their clothing. They went out to the street and stopped by the silver Audi, but the stranger kept going.

"This one's mine," he said, pointing to a beat-up blue Renault Mégane parked in front of the Audi. "Over here."

They flanked him. From this position, they could easily grab him by the throat and break his neck. Spots of sap glittered on his jacket. Snowflakes were piled up on his head and broad shoulders. His little eyes scanned the street. Empty.

A delivery truck filled with tall gas canisters drove slowly by, its cargo rattling in the back.

The stranger opened the trunk of the car. The bottom was covered with a thick sheet of plastic.

Jane flinched.

A white plastic body bag. He pulled down the zipper. The body inside was putrid, curled up in the fetal position. The man's gray face showed dark bruising around the closed eyes. The jaw was dislocated and the right eye socket was damaged.

"You know him?"

Jane shook her head, holding her stomach.

"Why did you kill him?" Alex asked.

"I didn't."

"So what happened, he died in his sleep?"

"Do you know him?" the stranger repeated.

"Not one of ours."

"I was sure he was."

"Ours don't look like that."

"What do you mean, *like that*?"

"Dead."

"So where did he come from?"

"Clean him up and then maybe I can tell you," Alex said.

The stranger zipped up the body bag and slammed the trunk shut. A sheet of ice slid off the car and splintered on the road.

"Back inside," the stranger said. His intensity was more intimidating than the barrel of the loaded gun.

"Do you often ride around with a body in the trunk of your car?" Jane asked.

"He followed me home. Tailed me up the stairs to the fifth floor. Fucking amateur. I took him by surprise and he lost his balance and sailed through the window into the courtyard. I left a message for Justus."

"Where?"

"Where I'm supposed to. He never got back to me. I called. He didn't answer. So I came."

"From Paris?"

The stranger nodded.

"Six hundred miles with a body in the trunk?"

"Six hundred and sixty-three." He smiled. There was a space between his front teeth.

The house was warm, and the living room smelled of books.

There was a bullet wound in the oak flooring.

The stranger removed his quilted jacket, revealing his muscular arms.

"I'm Paris."

The Frenchman had massive arms and prominent veins that came from hard work.

Alex remembered Teufelsberg and the steel cable on the ground at the feet of Berlin, his throat torn open.

"I'm London," Jane said.

"And you're . . . ?" Paris asked Alex.

"Alex. Justus is dead."

A shadow crossed Paris's face. His heavy shoulders sagged. Catching his breath, he muttered only, "What?"

He fell silent, sunk in thought, an unreadable expression on his face.

"Were you close?" Jane asked.

"What about the others?"

"What others?" Alex asked.

"The other Nibelungs."

He examined Paris's face. It was a mask.

Paris drew himself erect. "I was being followed. The guy who was tailing me is dead. You say that Justus was killed. You're here. She's London. You're Mossad."

Alex said, "Istanbul, Lisbon, and Berlin were murdered. Maybe others, too. I need the key to the Renault."

With a grim look, Paris threw him the keys with their diamond-shaped symbols. Alex was surprised.

"I've seen a lot of faces," Paris said. "Yours isn't dangerous."

Outside, the bitter cold made it hard for Alex to breathe.

The face of the man in the trunk was gray and battered. Alex snapped five photos from different angles and then scouted the street. It was quiet. He lifted a stiff arm out of the body bag and pressed a finger to the corner of his phone screen, where an app performed a high-resolution scan of the print. He sent the images to Butthead with the message: "Urgent. I need an ID."

There were dark footprints everywhere, but the street was white and silent. Rough sand and pebbles drew a stripe down the middle of the sidewalk. Alex went back inside.

He scrubbed his hands in the kitchen sink.

"Arab?" Paris asked.

"Too pale. It's hard to say. Did you search him?"

"Nothing in the pockets. Labels cut off. No wallet. No phone. Cheap watch. Fifty euros and change."

"You took it?"

"Let's say he paid his share of the gas," Paris said with a sneer.

"Did he say anything?"

"Would you say anything after falling five flights?"

"Get rid of him. Your car looks out of place here. It'll attract attention."

Paris nodded.

"How did you get in?" Jane asked.

Paris smiled, half closing his small eyes.

"I need proof you're Paris," Jane said.

"I need proof you're London."

"You first," she insisted.

His thick fingers struggled with the button on his jeans. He gave her a sheepish grin.

"Okay, okay, that's enough," Jane said.

"Where did you spend the night?" Alex asked.

Paris gestured toward the shadowy forest. "Out there."

"We can't ID the body," Butthead said over the phone.

"Did you check international databases?"

"Yup. We also tried face recognition, did a little artwork on the jaw. Nothing."

"Anything on Justus's computer?"

"Still digging. When there's something to report, you'll hear it."

He hung up.

The bronze silhouette of the *Walking Man* stood out against the blue-tinged scene beyond the windows. The day was dying. The lights on the lawn came on, casting a bright yellow glow over the cherry trees.

The forest had sent them this strange man, Paris. He'd spent the night up a tree after crossing Europe with a dead body in the trunk.

"You said you left Justus a message. Where?"

"Don't you know?"

"Where?" Alex repeated.

"At crazyheli.com. He always answers within twenty seconds. Ask London."

"Is that true?"

Jane nodded.

Alex's phone vibrated. The name of the caller appeared on the screen. Daniella!

"Hello," Alex answered.

Silence.

"Daniella?"

Breathing.

"Can you hear me?"

Silence.

"Hello?"

Nothing.

"I'll call you back."

He dialed.

Someone picked up. Muted sounds.

"Can you hear me now?"

Silence.

"Is something wrong?"

A hand covered the speaker, cutting off the sound of weeping.

His daughter was crying!

"Daniella, are you all right?"

The call was disconnected.

Shit!

"What did she say?" Jane asked.

He redialed.

No answer.

"She was crying."

"Was she alone?"

Alex threw Paris a steely look and checked him out from head to toe. His weirdness was disturbing. Should he stay or go? Daniella was in trouble. Could he leave Jane with this strange man? Fuck.

"Maybe they can send someone from the Rome station," Jane suggested.

"She's my only child."

"I meant in the meantime, until you get there."

Alex gazed at her. "I'm going."

She didn't volunteer her company, but the offer was in her eyes.

"We'll find a better time for the two of you to meet," Alex said. "I want that to happen."

Paris stroked his chin, examining Alex with his little eyes.

"Are you okay to be alone with him?" Alex whispered in her ear.

"It'll give me a chance to get to know him better."

"You're not scared?"

"Go to Daniella. I'll be fine." She pressed her body to his.

"Keep your gun with you at all times," he whispered.

When she nodded, her chin rubbed up against his chest.

The streets were empty and the roads were covered in compacted snow. The heater purred contentedly. An elderly man wearing a cap was walking a thick-tailed beagle in a red sweater.

Alex called Reuven and informed him that he was on his way to Tuscany.

"Daniella isn't in kindergarten and we're not nursemaids. You're the head of Operations. You can't just get up and leave in the middle of a critical op because you think you heard her crying. Did she say anything?"

"She couldn't talk. I know her, Reuven. She's in danger."

"She's in danger . . ." Reuven said dismissively. "The whole Nibelung Ring is in danger! Mossad is in danger!"

"So why aren't you handling it yourself? Admit it, Reuven.

You don't give a damn about the Nibelungs. You're already fanta-
sizing about your next job."

"I'm your boss! I don't have to explain anything to you. You
don't like it—you can quit."

"Someone's trying to get to me where I'm most vulnerable. I
can't stay in Berlin and forget about her."

"You're not going!"

Alex's long career in Mossad flashed before his eyes. It didn't
mean shit to him.

He called Butthead.

"I need a flight from Berlin to Tuscany right away."

"Give me a minute," Butthead wheezed. Alex heard his fingers
race across the keyboard.

"Air Berlin from Tegel to Fiumicino in Rome. It's a little longer than the flight to Milan, but it's a shorter drive."

"When?"

"Fifty-five minutes. Are you okay?"

"Find something on Erlichmann for me."

"Exodus has something. I was there a little while ago. They're
all hysterical up there."

"Why didn't she tell me?"

"You know her. If it isn't a hundred percent, it doesn't exist."

The mounds of dirty snow at the sides of the busy road were
streaked with the red glare of brake lights.

"Where did you get this fucking BlackBerry," Sammy Zengot
grumbled from Brussels.

"Have you hacked it yet?"

"Hacked it? The fucking thing doesn't have an operating

system. There's no way to turn it on, no way to dial a number."

"Figure it out, Sammy."

"I've got seven people working on it."

"Could it be a cloud—the operating system only works when you key in the code?"

"We can't key in a code without getting into the system. Get it?"

He got it, and he disconnected.

A semitrailer loaded with Volkswagen Passats was blocking the left lane. In the right lane, traffic was crawling. The Air Berlin flight to Rome was looking less and less likely. He felt like screaming.

He called Butthead. "Check the location of Daniella's phone and get me the farm in Bucine."

"Right away, man."

He hung up.

"Move already!" he yelled at the traffic inching ahead. He gazed out into the darkness, his knuckles white with frustration.

The congestion eased a little.

He was washed by a wave of panic. Too late, he saw the red lights rushing toward him. He slammed on the brakes and the Mercedes skidded on the ice. The back of the massive semi grew rapidly larger, as if it had been shot from a cannon in his direction. He pumped the brake pedal. The car slowed and slid sideways before stopping. The muscles in his back seized up. *Shit, that was close.*

Butthead called. "Daniella's phone is on. It's somewhere on the farm, outside Pogi. There's no answer in the office. Sorry."

He should have tried to stop her. He'd suggested that she talk to someone, but she'd said, "I'll do better on my own."

He finally made it to Tegel.

"You're late," the woman at the check-in desk scolded him. She wouldn't promise that the plane would wait. A man flying alone without any luggage demanded a thorough body search. German hands felt him up, invading his privacy, as the minutes ticked by.

He prayed that she hadn't been attacked again. He prayed that he wasn't too late.

He was about to waste two precious hours in the black sky.

"Coffee?"

"What?"

"Coffee, sir?"

A flight attendant with a pale, moon-shaped face smiled down at him. He shook his head. The smile vanished. She turned her attention to the passengers in the next row. Lights flickered between the clouds.

Three rows back, a bald man bit his fingernails as he kept an eye on Alex.

The agent at the car-rental desk in Fiumicino had pointed side-burns and calf eyes. He moved like a toy monkey drummer whose battery was running down. His thick fingers lumbered across the keyboard while he chewed on a disposable pen. Finally, he scowled, took the pen from his mouth, and handed it, gleaming with saliva, to Alex.

"Sign here."

Traffic on the highway was light. Alex circled Rome from the north in the rental Alfa Romeo Giulietta, going more than a hundred miles an hour until a flashing blue light up ahead forced him to slow down.

Leaving the lights of Umbria behind, he sped into the Tuscan night.

What if he was too late?

Sinkholes of fear opened beneath him. His knuckles on the steering wheel were white. Periodically he glanced in the rear-view mirror, checking out the dazzling lights behind him, but he found nothing suspicious.

Glowing orange traffic cones blocked the right lane. Red lights flashed in the distance. Scraps of slashed black rubber were strewn along the road. At the side of the highway, a wounded truck lay on its damaged tires like a collapsed beast in a slaughterhouse. The line of cars snaked forward at an exasperating crawl. Everyone had to get a look.

Alex called her when he got off the highway in Monte San Savino. Her phone was off.

A white fog hung in the dark air at the entrance to Pogi, blurring the shoulders of the road. He raced onward between the trees into the dark forest. The Giulietta shuddered violently, its engine groaning and its shock absorbers struggling to keep up. Tree trunks flashed by in the night as he sped down the winding road; his headlights were reflected back blindingly by the fog. All of a sudden a large deer leaped out of the forest in front of him. Alex braked wildly. The fog gushed toward him like smoke. The deer disappeared into the vineyard. As he took the final rise to the farm, he felt in his pocket for his gun.

The Glock was back in Berlin.

He parked the car, switched off the engine. Outside, everything lay in heavy silence.

The front lawn was dimly lit, but the houses were dark. A single light flickered in a second-story window of a nearby building. Steep terra-cotta steps led to a covered veranda. He tiptoed up the stairs. Her red mountain bike was beside the door. The cypresses on the lawn sighed in the wind. Alex's heart was pumping with adrenaline and fear. He saw a thin strip of light under a heavy gray curtain behind a double-glazed door.

A petrifying growl issued from the forest.

He knocked on the glass, the blood pulsating in his temples.

Nothing.

He pressed down on the handle.

Locked.

Alex picked up a small wrought-iron table and stepped back to give himself enough momentum to break the glass.

Then he froze.

The curtain had moved.

Daniella gaped at him. Her green eyes were swollen; her face was damp. She'd lost a lot of weight.

There was no gun at her back, no knife at her throat. Alex lowered the table and put it back where it belonged.

Thank God. She was alive.

She opened the door and he spread his arms wide. His daughter flinched, resisting his embrace.

"What's wrong?"

Daniella shrugged and gave him a piercing look.

"Why didn't you answer my call, Daniella?"

"I couldn't," she wailed in fury.

"My girl, what's wrong?"

"Your girl . . . " she spat back at him contemptuously.

"I tried to see you . . . I was here—"

"Liar!"

"You wheeled your red bike past my car and rode into the forest."

"Why didn't you tell me?"

"Tell you what?"

"You're pathetic!"

"What's wrong, Daniella?"

"Reuven . . . he called . . . this afternoon."

Alex felt a wave of heat in his face and painful pressure in his chest.

"I didn't understand what he was talking about," she said.

"What did he say?"

Her shoulders shuddered. "That you're not my father . . . he is. He said Mom told him." She burst into tears, wiping her face on the sleeve of her stained sweatshirt. "Is it true?"

Reuven had set a trap for him. He'd brought out his deadliest weapon and delivered the terrible blow to Daniella. And the motherfucker had done it over the phone. She'd cried out for Alex, and Reuven had forbidden him to go to her, cornering him and forcing him to make a decision that would cost him his chance to become the next head of Mossad.

If Reuven were here now, Alex would wring his neck.

"Can I hold you?"

She was hunched up in the corner of the sofa, childlike and helpless, a tiny figure in a large square room.

Since Naomi died, he'd done everything he could to avoid this moment. He sat down beside her. "I'm your father, Daniella."

The marble counter in the kitchenette was cluttered with dirty dishes and leftover scraps of food. An empty wine bottle lay on its side.

He reached out a tentative hand and stroked her hair in a familiar gesture. There was a wary look in her swollen eyes, but at least she didn't pull away.

In a broken voice he said, "I love you."

Her weeping grew more intense, her shoulders shaking.

His despair grew deeper.

Eventually she calmed down and leaned her head on his shoulder. He kissed it. Her hair smelled rancid and her body odor was rank. He put his arms around her and held her tight.

A black moth flew in through the open glass door and was sucked into the floor lamp in the corner. Its heavy body thumped against the taut linen shade.

"My whole world is crashing down," she said quietly.

Still shaking, she twisted around and rested her head in his lap.

"Mom . . ." she mumbled, her chin trembling.

He pulled her closer, struggling not to break down.

"I'd almost come to terms with her death. I was feeling stronger. And then my world fell apart. Why didn't you tell me?"

The moth landed on the floor near his feet, bare and motionless.

He sighed. "I was afraid I would lose you."

"I don't have anyone," Daniella said, light-years away.

"You have me," he said softly, stroking her hair.

"Did you always know?" Her face tensed, ready to take the blow.

"Of course not."

"When did you find out?"

"They were your mother's last words."

"And you didn't sense anything before that?"

"There was nothing to sense. You're mine."

The gap was widening.

"Tell me what happened."

"When?"

"Before I was born. How I was born. Everything. I have to know."

"Come home, dear." Unconsciously, he bit down on his lip. "I'll tell you at home, when things have quieted down. I promise."

She shook her head.

He closed his eyes. Wings fluttered on his cheek. He waved the insect away. A moment later, the irksome thumping against the lampshade started up again.

"I was younger than you are now. I was sent out on a prolonged operation. I was supposed to be off the grid for about a year. In the end, it turned out to be much longer. There were four of us. Mom was at home, alone. They didn't let us see each other until a year into the op, when we met in a hotel in Zurich. I always believed that you were conceived there."

"What really happened?"

"Reuven was looking after the families. He took advantage of—"

"Of what?"

"The bottom line is, they had an affair. That's it."

She made an effort to hide her astonishment.

He nodded sadly.

"And you were with that British woman . . ."

"Jane."

"Did you sleep with her, Dad? Did you cheat on Mom?"

"I was lonely, under pressure. We lived in constant fear."

"So you fucked the British woman," she stated.

Her innocence was gone. She was hardened, aggressive, and demanding. He knew her well enough to know that she wouldn't cut him any slack. "You know what? Yes. I fucked her, okay? Happy now?"

"Did Mom know?"

"No."

"Are you positive?"

"No."

"Why didn't you leave her for the British woman?"

Alex inhaled deeply. Her questions weighed on him. But there was something liberating about finally revealing the secrets in his history.

"When I got home, your mother was pregnant with you. About six months along."

"And all the years you lived together, you were having an affair on the side with the British woman?"

"I didn't have any contact with her."

She brushed the hair off her face. "Did you stay with Mom because of me?"

"I loved your mother."

"And the British woman?"

"Jane. Call her by her name. You owe her that, at least."

"I don't owe her shit."

He'd never heard her talk like this. "She saved your life in London. She saved both our lives."

Daniella sat in silence, turning the information over in her mind.

"Okay, Jane," she conceded. "We'll call her Jane. Were you in love with Jane all those years?"

"Maybe."

"And you didn't do anything about it?"

"You and your mother were more important."

She pulled her head back and searched his eyes for the truth.

"So you don't have anyone, either," she said softly.

"I have you."

The sorrowful look remained on her face.

A breeze entered through the open door and wafted around the room, caressing their faces.

"Why didn't you answer the phone when I called?"

She shook her head and clenched her teeth. "I was angry."

"Because it wasn't me who told you?"

She nodded timidly. "Scared, too."

"Of what?"

Daniella smiled, and the tears welled up in her eyes again. "Scared that now that I know, you won't want me anymore."

He kissed her brow and held her tighter.

"I miss Mom so much. I have no one to talk to."

"You have me."

"You're a man. It's not the same."

She got ice cubes from the freezer, wrapped them in a dirty towel, and pressed them to her swollen eyes.

Alex looked around him. The walls were painted in Tuscan yellow stucco. Angled oak beams supported a terra-cotta ceiling. Under different circumstances, this place could be heaven.

She came back to the sofa and leaned her head against his shoulder, and they sat there in silence. Only the stubborn moth kept thumping.

"It didn't take you long to get here," she said.

"I was in Berlin."

"Do you have to get back?"

"Quiet!" he whispered, placing his hand over hers. He rose silently and moved to the open door. He stood still and listened to the night. Glancing back at Daniella, he saw that her face had gone white. He went out onto the covered veranda, which cast a long shadow on the railing and its sleeping flower boxes.

There was no one there. He came back inside. "We have to get out of here."

"When?"

"Now. It isn't safe here."

"I can't. I have to pay my bill, I have to say good-bye—"

"Leave a note. Do you have enough money?" he asked, taking out his wallet.

"I have to pack."

"Go take a shower. You'll feel better. Put on some clean clothes, and then I'll help you pack. Meanwhile, I'll find us a flight."

"Can I come to Berlin with you?"

"It's too dangerous."

"Is Jane there?" she asked.

"Why?"

"I want to meet her."

"You'll meet her soon, but not now. You've been through enough. I'll make us something to eat. Go."

"Do I smell?"

He threw her a smile.

Alex closed his eyes, feeling drained and exhausted. The sound of running water came from down the hall.

On the kitchen counter he found a bag of dry Tuscan bread hidden among the dirty dishes. The small refrigerator yielded butter, aging mozzarella, and prosciutto whose edges had gone stiff. He washed a plate and a knife, made sandwiches, and wrapped them in aluminum foil.

Bone-weary, he sank heavily onto a rustic wooden chair. He would have liked nothing better than to shut his eyes and get some sleep. He gazed out at the veranda through the open door. The red bike was standing there.

The brake cable was missing.

The blade of the pickax landed with a clang in the dark, hitting stone and sending shards flying. The surface of the ground was cracked and crumbly. Nocturnal predators shrieked in the depths of the Grunewald forest, and a mysterious groan issued from among the dense trees.

The flashlight warmed Jane's hand. The strong, haloed light shone on the rectangular contour of a pit in the snow, just about big enough for a human body folded up in the fetal position.

Paris put down the ax and picked up a heavy shovel. His hands were encased in black work gloves. The night air was filled with the smell of moss and exposed roots. White vapor issued from his mouth. His breathing was labored. The shovel whistled while it dug into the ground. The heap of soil beside the pit grew higher.

Paris took off his dirty jacket and hung it on a branch. Jane turned the beam of light on him. His face was sweaty. His body, as solid as a tree trunk, was waist-deep in the pit. The silence was eerie.

"What do you do for a living?" she asked.

"All sorts of things—odd jobs," he answered in the darkness. "I don't have a steady job."

"So what do you do all day?"

Paris stopped digging and gave her an unreadable look. Turning back to the task at hand, he said, "Wait. I wait."

A hundred flashlights wouldn't shed any more light on this man.

The wind wailed through the trees. It was cold in the forest. She was about to ask what he waited for when he got in ahead of her. "Are you married?"

"Single."

"And the man, Alex. What's he to you?"

Good question.

"What about you?" she asked.

"On my own."

Something buzzed too close to her ear. She shuddered and waved it away.

"Was Justus a friend?" she asked.

"You could say that."

The shovel hit a stone.

"How so?"

Paris stopped shoveling, took a deep breath. "It's a long story."

A bird of prey flew over their heads, breaking through the darkness.

"I'll go get him," he said. "Bring the flashlight."

Jane followed him. The beam of light dancing in front of them revealed their footprints in the snow and the tangled roots of the birch trees. Paris opened the trunk of his car, and they were assaulted by a sickening odor. He pulled the white plastic bag toward him, encircled the corpse's waist with his mighty arms, and threw it over his shoulder. Fluid collected in the bottom of the bag.

Jane's stomach heaved. Bile rose in her throat.

"Shine the light on the pit," he instructed, dropping the body, which landed with a dull thud.

"Why didn't you drag him over here?" she asked.

"Have you ever tried to get the air out of a hundred pounds of rising dough? You have to grab it in the middle, hoist it in the air, and fold it over."

He wiped the sweat from his brow, crouched down, and opened the zipper of the body bag. "Give me some light."

Paris cradled the man's chin in his hand and scrutinized the pale face. The beam of light trembled.

"What are you looking at?" Jane asked.

A sudden blast of cold wind numbed her face.

The corpse's eyes were open.

"Look!" Jane shrieked.

"What happened?"

"He closed his eyes!"

"Don't be—"

And then the corpse coughed, and pink fluid spilled from his mouth.

"He's alive!" Jane stammered, fighting off a wave of nausea. She couldn't allow herself to hurl, to leave incriminating DNA at the scene.

"That's impossible!" Paris sputtered. "There was no pulse."

The white plastic banged against the snow dotted with footprints.

"Maybe he can talk," Jane said.

Paris picked up the shovel. "Don't look!"

"Don't you dare!"

"Shut your eyes."

"No!"

"I'm not waiting."

"Maybe he can talk," she repeated, but Paris had already raised the shovel in the air. He brought it down on the skull. The gruesome sound of bones being crushed. He continued to beat at the skull until the head hung on the neck at an unnatural angle.

"You're a psychopath!"

"He was already gone."

I can't puke, she thought, forcing herself to breathe through her nose. Why wasn't Alex here when she needed him the most?

Was Paris afraid of what the man might say? What was the Frenchman hiding?

He went on digging in the dark. Only his head extended past

the edge of the hole. She shone the light on the grave. A shudder ran down her spine. It seemed deeper and wider than necessary. Pulling out her gun, she held it parallel to the flashlight.

"Get out!"

"What's wrong?"

"Out!"

"Madame London, I have to finish the work."

Pointing the Glock at his head, she warned, "Get out, or I shoot."

"Okay, okay," he chuckled warily, climbing out of the pit and standing beside it.

She moved back, beyond reach of his arm.

"Lie down on the ground!"

"What's going on, London?"

"Do it!"

He lay down on his back, his eyes fixed on her and on the silencer attached to the barrel of the gun.

She aimed the gun and the light at his head.

"Pull down your pants!"

"You're to blame for the fuckup in Turkey. It's your fault Galia is dead. Justus told me about you and the warehouse, and I kept my mouth shut. Then you landed me with the Nibelung shit—and what do I get in return? You go for Daniella like a rabid dog!" Alex fumed into the phone.

"What are you going on about? It's three in the morning," Reuven said, his voice blurred by sleep.

A chef's knife was lying on the counter. Alex grabbed it by the handle.

"You should have talked to me. We could have done it right, shown some sensitivity."

"Control told me you'd made a stop in Florence. I assumed you'd seen her and told her yourself. It's not my fault you couldn't find the time—"

"Reuven, the girl was raped! Her mother was killed. She was molested by the Iranians. She's hurting. She's trying to recover. Have you seen what she looks like? Do you have the slightest inkling of what she's going through?"

"Come off it, Alex. Don't play the perfect dad."

Alex disconnected and thrust the knife tip into the cutting board.

Daniella was still in the shower, under the cleansing water.

He called HQ in Glilot. There was no plane available at the moment.

He leaned against the cool marble. A refreshing breeze blew in through the open door, circled the room, and soothed his neck. He shut his eyes.

The shower was still running.

"Is everything all right?" he called out. No answer. Maybe she couldn't hear him.

"Daniella?"

He reacted too slowly. Something metallic glimmered in the corner of his eye and was instantly wrapped tightly around his neck. He barely had time to stick his hands between his throat and the steel cable. The cable was pulled tighter from behind with enormous force. He tried to flip the attacker on his back, but the man was too strong and too determined. He managed to get close enough to the counter to knock over a glass, which shattered on the floor. Panting, the assailant strengthened his stranglehold. Alex struggled to free his right hand, but the cable tore into it, cutting a deep wound. Blood flowed from his hand. He got a glimpse of the man's reflection in the window. He tried to push him backward into the table. The floor lamp wobbled and fell over.

Alex tried to elbow his attacker in the face, but he couldn't move his hands, couldn't even shift position. He grunted, and with a huge effort he hurled himself and the stranger at the flat-screen TV. The man pulled him back savagely. Alex's hands were on fire, throbbing in pain. He kicked at the screen, which fell to the floor with a crash, smashing into pieces.

The shower was still running.

Black spots swam before his eyes, and his head was threatening to explode. Blood flowed down his arms and onto the floor. The steel cable went deeper, and then there was a harsh grunt.

It hadn't come from him. The hold around his neck loosened. Something had happened. His attacker was now pressing his whole weight against Alex's back, presumably attempting to drop him or break his neck. With the last of his strength, Alex pulled the cable away and slipped out of the noose. He fought to take in air through his injured windpipe. The assailant slumped to the floor.

The man was lying on his stomach. The chef's knife was stuck deep in his back, just behind the heart, only the black handle visible.

Daniella was standing there in panties and a red T-shirt. Her hair was wet. Her eyes burned with horror and fury.

"Are you okay?" Alex asked.

"I heard a groan and something breaking," Daniella said.

Fat drops of blood were falling from his hands. The pain was becoming more intense, radiating to his shoulders. He raised his hands above his head, but the bleeding didn't stop.

"You're bleeding from the neck, too," she said.

He remembered the swaddled infant he had held moments after her birth. "You saved my life," he said. "He would've killed me." He looked with repulsion at the dead man on the floor. He was about six feet tall, with a tight, muscular body. His hands were protected by black Gore-Tex gloves reinforced with what appeared to be Kevlar strips. The shiny steel brake cable was still wrapped around his hands.

Alex hurried into the bathroom. The water was still running in the shower, and the room was steamy. Daniella followed right behind him. He stuck his hands under the water. It burned like white-hot iron. The floor of the shower turned red, and the glass walls became spattered with pink dots. He breathed deeply, bit his lips.

"I killed him."

"You saved my life. Both our lives. Get some towels."

She stared, mesmerized, at the floor of the shower stall. "It's so red."

"Daniella, give me a towel!" he ordered. Pain was shooting

from his hands to the top of his head. He kept forcing himself to breathe deeply, fighting not to scream.

Daniella didn't respond. Gingerly removing his hands from the water, he shuffled toward the towel rack on the opposite wall. Bloody water dripped down his arms, staining the floor. He wrapped his throbbing hands in the white towels and let out a groan. His blurred image was reflected in the steamy mirror over the sink. Blood was still issuing from the cut in his neck. He soaked it up with the white towel around his hand. A smell of iron wafted around the room, carried by the steam.

They had to get out of there. He moved toward Daniella. She flinched, staring in terror at the towels, which were quickly turning red.

"Is there anyone else on the farm?" he asked.

She shook her head.

"Can you get yourself ready to leave?"

She gave him a puzzled look.

"Go pack your things. I'll take care of the rest."

He found some kitchen towels, poured some grappa on them, and replaced the bloody dressings on his hands. It hurt like hell. He covered the towels with cling wrap, using his teeth to tear holes for his fingers.

Outside, he noticed an old wooden door beside the steps. Inside were towels, linen, and cleaning products. The storeroom produced another treasure: a huge roll of plastic wrap, the kind used by movers.

Back in the living room, he pulled the knife from the man's back. His gleaming bald head shone like a persimmon. The eyes were open and looked strange. They looked crazed and frightening.

"He doesn't have any eyebrows," Daniella said behind him. No eyelashes, either. The eyes seemed to have been pinned into his forehead.

As Alex removed the dead man's jacket and sweater, he remembered the words Berlin had mumbled on Teufelsberg— "bald, no eyebrows." The stranger's body was smooth and completely hairless. It looked as if he'd just been through a course of chemotherapy.

He was undoubtedly the same man who'd attacked Berlin on Teufelsberg. The MO was identical. And it was very likely that he was responsible for the deaths of Justus and the other Nibelungs.

It was over.

The man's pockets were empty. Alex stripped him bare and searched for identifying marks. There were no tattoos, no scars, no birthmarks. He spread two white sheets on the dark wooden floorboards, moving awkwardly because of the dressings on his hands. For the moment, the pain was bearable. He attempted to hold his phone steady to snap a picture, but the device slipped from his fingers.

"Daniella?"

She reacted immediately.

"Take a picture of his face."

Nodding, she did as he asked.

"What else?"

"Do you know how to scan his fingerprint with the phone?"

She nodded reluctantly, compressing her lips as she picked up the man's right hand. She grasped the thumb, grimacing in disgust. Then she examined his index and ring fingers and finally released the hand with a somber expression. "Take a look," she said.

"At what?"

"No fingerprints."

Alex came closer and scrutinized the man's fingers. The prints had been burned off with acid. He could see the scars. "Take a picture of the fingertips."

Daniella took the photos.

"That's it, I'll be done with him soon," he announced. "Finish packing."

He forwarded the pictures to Glilot. A second later, Butthead called. "Are you all right?"

Alex filled him in on the attack.

"No one would burn off his own prints," Alex said.

The next call was from HQ. There was no available plane in the vicinity. It would take a while. He was told to make his way to Milan as quickly as possible. If they located a plane, they'd direct it there.

Alex struggled to silence the racket in his head. He'd been in Tuscany *before* his meeting with Justus in Berlin. His phone was secure; it couldn't be hacked. So whoever was gunning for the Nibelungs had no way of knowing about Daniella.

Had he picked up a tail on Bebelplatz? If that were the case, the man who killed Berlin on Teufelsberg would have killed him, too, and brought the whole Ring down then and there.

The only logical conclusion was that the attacker had been watching Justus's house and had followed him to the airport, gotten on the plane with him, and tailed him here.

The back of his neck went cold. Someone had been tracking him for a long time, and he hadn't had a clue.

Alex turned his attention back to the body. He rolled the corpse in the sheets and wound layers of plastic wrap around the still-warm human bundle. It was hard work. He scrubbed the blood off the dark wood and then went into the bathroom, where he used some bleach to get rid of as much of the spattered blood as he could. The cleanup took a long time.

Daniella put her suitcase in the backseat of the Giulietta. On the table in the living room she left six hundred euros and a note apologizing for her hasty departure and the broken TV and providing her credit-card number to pay for the damage.

They crammed the corpse into the trunk of the car. They drove through the forest in a thick fog that curled itself around the trunks of the bare trees. They followed the signs south, toward Siena. A few minutes later, Alex left the roadway and drove up to the top of a hill, where he dumped the naked body near a ruined building. He burned the plastic wrap and bloody sheets in a garbage pit. Then he returned to the roadway and headed in the opposite direction. His hands gripping the steering wheel throbbed.

They turned onto the highway to Florence. After a while, Alex pulled into an Autogrill rest area, stopping at the far end of the large parking lot. Daniella went in alone while he waited in the car.

She returned with coffee, pastries, medical supplies, and extra large black gloves. She undid his improvised bandages and bathed the gaping wounds in Betadine. Alex breathed deeply. Then she wrapped his hands in clean white bandages and pulled the gloves over them. They pressed painfully on the open wounds.

"Where are we going, Dad?"

She'd called him *dad*. Maybe she did it without thinking.

"Milan. We'll take a plane from there."

"Are you coming home with me?"

"I wish I could."

Her face fell.

Daniella closed her eyes and leaned her head on the window. It was quiet in the car. Jane would still be asleep in the house in Grunewald. It was too early to call.

"I knew you'd come," she said softly, her eyes still shut. He stroked her head with his gloved hand. A little before five in the morning, they passed Florence on the way north to Bologna. It was still dark out.

She was strong. The harsh blows she'd suffered hadn't broken her. Look how she'd run out of the shower without a moment's hesitation and plunged the knife into his attacker's back, saving both their lives. She might be young, but she was stronger than him, and ten times tougher.

Trucks were racing past in the opposite lane, their headlights blinding.

He had to force himself not to cry.

Daniella's eyelids twitched. They were nearing Parma. He called Jane and hung up after eight rings. She must be in the shower.

He rang her again at six thirty.

No answer.

A cord of concern wrapped itself around his heart.

Paris. Unreadable Paris. The man of the dead body and the stakeout in the forest.

He tried Jane's number a third time, with no luck.

Paris. Shit!

Was it possible that Paris wasn't really Paris?

Apprehensive, he tried Jane again.

Still no answer.

He called Butthead.

"Check the logs of the emergency services in Berlin starting from last night. Check the hospitals." He kept his voice low. His stomach was churning.

"What are we looking for?"

"Jane Thompson, British citizen, forty-six, slender build, five ten."

He glanced at Daniella, praying that she couldn't hear him.

Hammers were pounding in his head. First Daniella, now Jane.

The sky was slowly turning a cloudless blue.

Butthead called.

"Sorry, Alex—"

"Spit it out," he barked, panicking.

"A Jane Doe answering that description was brought to the Charité Mitte in Wedding."

"What's her condition?"

"She's not in the system yet. She was brought to the emergency room by ambulance and was taken straight into surgery."

"No!"

"Dad?" Daniella asked quietly. "What's the matter?"

"What?"

"You're crying."

"Charité Mitte, guten Morgen," a thick female voice recited.

"You admitted a surgical emergency this morning around six o'clock. A Jane Doe. Can you tell me her condition?"

The Gulfstream started its descent into Tegel.

"I'm sorry, sir. We don't give out medical information over the telephone."

"I'm on a plane on my way to Berlin, and I'm very concerned. Please, I just want to know her condition."

"I'm sorry. It is forbidden. Are you a relative?"

"I'm her husband."

"You should be here, sir."

Alex hugged Daniella tight, burying his face in her sweet-smelling hair. He shouldn't be abandoning her now. He prayed that he'd chosen the best of the bad options he had.

"Go, Dad," she said, giving him a kiss. "Be strong."

Tense and agitated, he disembarked from the plane in the dry chill of Berlin. He gazed at her from the rear window. She waved at him from the door of the plane.

Alex took the elevator to the Surgical Trauma and Intensive Care Unit on the seventh floor. The nurse at the desk had heavy thighs and no lips. Her mouth was no more than a thin line. Stonily, she made it clear that he would not be able to see the patient in the recovery room.

The hospital smells, the intense dry heat, and the presence of police detectives all urged Alex want to get out into the fresh air to cool off. He had to think carefully before he made a move.

He waited for the elevator, his eyes fixed on the ceiling. When it finally arrived, he got in last and took a position close to the door, facing front.

His phone beeped.

"Do you need me?" It was a text from Paris.

If he could get his hands on Paris, he'd squeeze the life out of him.

The elevator stopped on the second floor with a ding. All the passengers except one spilled out and headed off in different directions with worried faces. Alex stayed where he was. The doors closed.

He texted back: "Where are you?"

Within a second, his phone beeped again.

"Behind you."

Paris was dressed in scrubs, his face hidden behind a surgical mask.

Alex grabbed Paris by the throat and started squeezing as hard as he could. Making no attempt to defend himself, Paris croaked, "It wasn't me."

The Frenchman's face was turning red. He finally rammed his fingers between his throat and Alex's hands, his small eyes bulging. Alex squeezed harder, but the man had the neck of a bull. He managed to break away, crashing into the corner of the elevator, where he gasped for breath. "I swear on my children's lives, I didn't do it!"

They settled themselves on a freezing wooden bench on snow-covered Robert-Koch-Platz. An ambulance drove by with flashing orange lights, its siren silent.

Alex gave Paris a piercing look. "What happened to her?"

"I was digging a deep grave. She got nervous. Maybe she thought I was making it big enough to hold her, too. I just wanted it deep. There are wild boars out there. She drew her gun on me. I let her feel my chip and she calmed down. I went back to the house and she stayed outside, alone. I heard a scream. I ran out. Someone was strangling her from behind with a thin steel cable. He was stocky and strong. I saw him. A bald guy.

"He was cutting into her neck. When he saw me he ran away. She was losing blood. I bandaged the wound and called an ambulance."

"You said he was bald?"

"He's scary. Sick."

"Someone tried to kill me with a steel cable, too," Alex said.

"This stinks," Paris said. "Two attacks the same way at the same time."

Alex took out his phone and flipped to the picture of the dead body of his attacker. He enlarged it and showed it to Paris. "This is the man who attacked me."

Paris looked at the photo and laughed. "You're kidding me, right?"

"Why?"

"That's the man who attacked Jane."

"She has been sedated since the operation," the nurse whispered.

The harsh neon lights were reflected on the linoleum floor, which was bare save for a few widely spaced beds.

Jane twisted fitfully under the sheet. Alex reached out and touched her hand. "I'm here, honey."

She tried to clear her throat and grimaced in pain, her eyelids drooping. She mouthed, "Water."

"Later," the doctor said firmly. "Not yet." She headed for the door. Alex hurried to catch up with her.

"How is she?" he asked.

"She has deep cuts on her neck. She was lucky. Another quarter inch at most and the artery would have been severed, but as it is she should recover quickly. If there are no complications, we should be able to release her in two days."

The doctor went away.

Alex called Butthead. "Look for identical twins, assassins for hire. And look for strangulation with a steel cable."

"Have you heard from Exodus or the econ division?" Butthead asked.

"No."

"I hope you're lying down when she calls. I wouldn't want you to fall over."

In the early afternoon they slipped out of the hospital, leaving behind fake identities. Jane gripped the armrests of the wheelchair as tightly as she could.

When they reached Justus's house, she collapsed onto the bed and fell asleep. Alex sprawled beside her and slept.

He awoke to the aroma of root vegetables stewing in the kitchen. A view of the forest filled the glass wall opposite the bed. Jane was sleeping on her side, breathing heavily.

The day was waning, growing colder and tinting the snow blue. At the edge of the forest, the bleak conifers were swaying in the wind. The last remnants of daylight gradually disappeared as darkness fell on the snow-covered lawn. The outside lights glowed, blazing orange.

Alex sat in the gloom, listening to Jane's troubled breathing. Her face was bathed in a dim glow. It's always odd to watch someone you love when they're sleeping, stripped of all expression. He suddenly felt apprehensive, concerned about the effort it would take to make their relationship work.

His phone vibrated.

"We're in," Sammy Zengot informed him. "Like you thought, the system was in a cloud. We got it to work by keying in one of the codes you gave us with two plus signs in front. The guys say the owner of the phone has to have a chip with all the codes on it implanted somewhere in his body. The chip communicates with the BlackBerry by Bluetooth. Happy now?"

"Very. What came up on the screen?"

"On the screen? A list of major European cities. Why?"

"How many?"

"Give me a few seconds to count them."

The seconds felt like minutes.

"Thirteen."

Alex's temples were pounding. "How many?"

"Thirteen. Why?"

"You sure, Sammy?"

"Sorry, make that fourteen."

"How come?"

"Grunewald's on the list, too."

Mossad's immune system was compromised. For the next few months at least, it would be impossible to operate in any city where a Nibelung had been killed. Someone had declared war on the Ring and had planned the attack meticulously.

Jane listened openmouthed as he told her what he'd learned.

"How many signal types does the chip have?" he asked.

"Five," she whispered.

"Is there an emergency alert, one for imminent danger?"

"The fifth signal."

He called Sammy.

"Find the menu for the signals in the phone and send out the fifth to all the numbers I gave you."

"That'll take a while."

"What's the last city on the list?"

"The last one?"

"Yes, Sammy, the last one."

"Vienna."

"When?"

"10:51 this morning."

"I need the BlackBerry," Alex said.

"On its way."

He hung up.

Alex reported to Reuven the loss of fourteen Nibelungs, including Justus.

Reuven heaved a sigh. "It's an operational disaster."

This wasn't a good time to be the chief. Very soon, Reuven would have to report to the prime minister. It could cost him his head. Alex was surprised to find that he felt sorry for the man.

"Alex," Jane said.

"Did you get an alert?"

She nodded gingerly.

Finally, the dormant Nibelungs were being awakened. The vulnerable targets could become lethal weapons.

Alex went down to the kitchen. The stainless-steel counter was hidden under bulging shopping bags from Kaiser's supermarket. Paris was using a wooden spoon to stir the contents of a blue cast-iron pot. He tasted what looked like orange soup and threw in a pinch of salt.

Baby carrots were cooking in an integrated steamer in the counter. The Frenchman ground cumin and cardamom with a mortar and pestle and added the aromatic mixture to the carrots. Three brushed-stainless-steel Iittala saucepans with their crisp Scandinavian design were arranged on the counter beside two copper pots.

Paris displayed a two-pound cut of marbled entrecôte to Alex. "Hungry?" he asked.

Alex nodded and looked through the red grocery bags. He found a round country loaf, salami, cheese, mustard, mayonnaise, onions, garlic and fresh thyme.

The Frenchman was unaware of the crisis.

"Even in bad times, you have to eat," he said.

"I'm sorry," Alex said.

"You're not hungry?"

"Sorry I didn't trust you. I apologize."

"Sometimes I act strange," Paris smiled. He cut the meat into two substantial steaks and studded them with sprigs of thyme.

"How did Justus communicate with the Nibelungs?" Alex asked.

The Frenchman arranged boiled potatoes in a deep pan, adding a generous splash of olive oil, coarse salt, ground black pepper and thyme leaves. He put the pan in the hot oven and then sat down.

At least he didn't decide to organize the cupboards first, Alex thought.

"Never by phone," Paris said. "Not cellular or landline. There can't be a direct link between the Nibelungs. Not under any circumstances."

"So how did you communicate?"

"Justus built nitro RC helicopters. He started a fictitious forum on the web, crazyheli.com, and installed a special search engine that got questions and answers off other forums. It would seem perfectly innocent to anyone who happened onto it. If I needed something from him, I left a coded message there. It sent an alert to Justus's phone. He'd respond with a signal to the chip in my crotch. It vibrates."

Things were beginning to make sense.

"Each Nibelung has their own username and password," Paris went on. "If Justus wanted to set up a meeting, he'd send a signal to my chip. I'd go into the forum and find a coded message with the details.

"I just got an alert," Paris said, getting up. He chopped a few cloves of garlic and rubbed them into the steaks. Then he opened the oven door, and the kitchen was filled with the aroma of roasting potatoes and thyme.

Why did Paris wait until now to tell him about the vibrations in his crotch? He might have heard Alex give the order to send out an alert. The man could be setting a trap. Alex had to be sure of his identity. But there was no way to check him out, no one to ask.

Dinner was ready. The two men took their places at the bar. The roasted sprigs of thyme gave the steak an earthy aroma. The golden potatoes were roasted perfectly. They sat there chewing and eyeing each other. Alex filled their glasses with fine Tignanello he'd found in the wine cellar.

"No dessert," the Frenchman apologized. They were silent, giving Alex time to think. Whoever was killing the Nibelungs was going from country to country, stalking his victim, taking them out, and then immediately moving on to the next target. Someone else had to be getting rid of the bodies. The legwork must also have been done before the assassin arrived. It demanded painstaking information-gathering over an extended period of time. An operation of that size could only be organized by the secret agency of a sovereign country with embassies and consulates throughout Europe. It would require dozens of field agents, sophisticated covert infrastructure, and secure communications.

Alex's phone vibrated against the thin stem of the wineglass. Exodus was calling.

"We dug deep, Alex. According to our preliminary estimate, Justus Erlichmann was worth roughly three hundred million euros. He might also have had additional income from property in Berlin that we haven't found yet. We're looking under every rock. His name is never mentioned in the media. But that's not why I'm calling."

All that remained from the wine was a dry, salty taste.

"Alex, Justus Erlichmann has been contributing large sums of money to a neo-Nazi organization."

Alex fled to the snowy lawn behind the house, the piercing cold striking at his burning face. Out of earshot of the Frenchman, he whispered into the phone, "Justus? Neo-Nazis? Are you positive?"

"We checked and rechecked," Exodus said. "We broke down his annual outlays and crossed off the regular expenses. In the end we were left with a monthly bank transfer of thirty thousand euros. We couldn't explain it, so we kept digging."

A chill ran down his back.

"Where exactly was the money going?"

"Into the account of what was supposedly a Swiss NGO for Alzheimer's research."

"His father had Alzheimer's. Couldn't they have been legit donations?"

"I sent someone to the address in Lucerne."

"And?"

"It's an empty lot."

"Maybe they moved."

"It's been empty for nineteen years. The heirs are fighting over the property. We checked out the bank account. Justus Erlichmann was the only depositor. It was opened specifically for him."

Thoughts were racing through Alex's head. "Does Reuven know about this?" he asked finally.

"I thought I'd give you the pleasure."

"When was the first money transfer?"

"October 1994."

"More than twenty years ago," he said. It was freezing outside.

"Last month it was ten times as much as usual, three hundred thousand euros," Exodus said. "The total figure is almost six million!"

Even a fire hose wouldn't have relieved the dryness in his mouth.

Justus Erlichmann—the champion of Zionism and faithful servant of the State of Israel—had a dark side.

"The NGO funnels funds to neo-Nazis?" he asked.

"We milked a reliable source in the German Federal Office for the Protection of the Constitution. They know the organization. It's a front for a neo-Nazi group, but they don't know anything else about it. All they know is that it exists."

"What's the name of the group?"

"The Fourth Reich."

Alex looked back at the home of Justus Erlichmann. The exquisite house suddenly seemed hostile, its rooms contaminated. The imposing, tastefully lit library was infested with vermin. The artwork glittered like gold-plated shackles, and the thought of the swastika on the tail of the Messerschmitt made him sick to his stomach.

Repressed monsters threatened to soar up out of the depths of his memory. The Holocaust had lived in his parents' home like an unmovable tenant. Silent and bleeding, it had lain among the clothes in the closet and beside the empty bottles on the balcony,

puncturing his sleep with nightmares, slashing into his childhood with terror.

His mother's stories about Treblinka and Auschwitz. Her
father hanged before her eyes. Aunts and uncles sent to the gas
chamber or shot in the back and falling into open pits. The heavy
barrel of a gun slamming into her little neck. A bullet penetrating
her body. Unendurable pain.

He felt a pressing need to get as far away from this house as
possible, but some dark, unnameable force urged him to stay, to
resist and fight back. He'd let himself believe that his intimate
conversation with Justus in Café Einstein had forged a genuine
link between them. Now he knew that the despicable German
had deceived him.

"That's utterly ridiculous!" Reuven declared. "Justus never gave
money to neo-Nazis!"

"Exodus can fill you in on the details," Alex told him.

"I already told you, the PM doesn't want us to investigate
Justus Erlichmann. I gave you a direct order not to ask econ or
intel to look into him. You chose to ignore my order, and now you
want to embarrass me in front of the PM? How am I supposed to
tell him your idiotic suspicions after he explicitly told me to leave
Justus alone?"

That's your problem, Alex thought. "When did Gunter find out
he had Alzheimer's?"

"You're ignoring me," Reuven said hotly.

"Do you really want to discuss what orders you gave or didn't
give, or are you ready to deal with the fact that Justus had close
ties to a neo-Nazi group?"

Reuven remained silent.

"Can we move on, Reuven? When was Gunter diagnosed with Alzheimer's?"

Reuven let out a sigh.

"Nineteen-ninety-four," he said quietly. "The director needed to find a successor. Gunter suggested his son, Justus. The PM said it looked too much like nepotism. He didn't approve Justus's appointment until after the elections."

"Isn't it strange," Alex said, "that Justus transferred hundreds of thousands of euros to neo-Nazis just before he was killed?"

Reuven didn't respond.

"Maybe Gunter was the one who started giving them money," Alex went on, thinking out loud. "No one ever looked into the Erlichmann family?"

A bottle uncorked. Liquid poured. A swallow.

"What difference does it make now?" Reuven said. "I have to bring all this shit to the PM."

He hung up.

A light snow rustled through the trees. Snowflakes landed on Alex's face and melted away.

The photo of the dead machine gunner from the Time–Life album floated up before him. His lifeless body lay with his legs on the balcony and his head on the wooden floorboards of the room inside. The dark pool of blood grew bigger from picture to picture.

Alex went back inside under a cloud of grief mixed with rage. His body shook from adrenaline and cold. He climbed the stairs to the bedroom and sat down beside Jane, telling her in a soft voice about Justus's secret donations to neo-Nazis.

"That's not possible," she whispered back.

He nodded, his head as heavy as a church bell.

"He was more loyal to Israel than to his own homeland," she said. "At most he might have made a small donation. Justus was no traitor!"

If only she was right. "He gave them close to six million euros."

Jane's face fell. She lay there in silence.

It was almost midnight. The doorbell rang. Alex hurried downstairs, his Glock in his hand. He met Paris in the entrance hall and handed him the gun. Then he opened the door while the Frenchman covered him.

It was a courier with a thick envelope containing Justus's BlackBerry.

Alex went back upstairs, undressed, and got into bed. A night-light cast a soft glow over Jane's face.

"We're in for some tough days ahead," he said, moving closer. She reached out and put her arm around his neck. Alex switched off the light.

The silent BlackBerry on the bedside table blinked blue.

Within seconds, he had sunk into a deep sleep, dreaming of the bronze sculpture of the *Walking Man*. The figure was hunched over in despair.

On its chest was a yellow Star of David.

DIARY

4 September 1943

I looked into the new commandant's eyes and saw dark, icy tundra. Since his arrival, the waves of arrests have multiplied alarmingly. The transports to the East are more frequent, and those who have been transported vanish without a trace.

5 October 1943

Jewish families are disappearing. Apartments are emptying out. An ill wind whistles through abandoned living rooms.

Today I baked croissants with Nazi butter.

6 October 1943

The commandant came into the café this evening, drunk with power.

Champagne! he cried. Champagne and six glasses!

A sign that he had sent a packed transport to the East.

7 October 1943

Yesterday, 967 of our children were transported. Tonight, I had to pour a rare bottle of Châteauneuf-du-Pape for the beasts from the SS.

I am the whore of merchandise.

There is no forgiveness.

The aroma of fresh espresso and buttery croissants rose from the kitchen. Paris had risen early. He was lying on the sofa in the living room, reading a book. Outside, the sky was clear.

Alex went into the kitchen, shading his eyes against the gleam of the white snow in the morning sun. Jane made her way downstairs and sat down at the breakfast bar. Alex dipped a silver knife into a pot of prune jam, spread the dark fruit on a piece of warm croissant, and placed it on the plate in front of Jane.

"More coffee?" Alex called out to Paris.

The Frenchman nodded, got up from the sofa, and padded into the kitchen on bare feet. He pulled off the end of a croissant and stuffed it into his mouth. Beyond the window, crows were pecking at the snow.

The BlackBerry in Alex's pocket beeped. Anxiously, he looked at the screen: Barcelona $.

"What's going on?" Jane whispered.

Alex turned the BlackBerry so Paris could see it. "What does it mean?"

"There's a message on the forum," the Frenchman said. "May I?" He reached out and took the phone from Alex.

Paris went to crazyheli.com. "It's from Barcelona," he announced. "It says, 'I've got a live one.'"

"How do we know someone didn't seize Barcelona and force him to reveal how he communicates with Justus?" Alex asked.

Paris and Jane exchanged a nod. "If Barcelona had sent the message against his will," Paris explained, "there'd be an exclamation point at the end."

"And what if it wasn't Barcelona who sent the message?"

"The sender has to enter his code a second time at the beginning of the message. You can't see it, but if it's not entered, the system automatically adds the exclamation point," Jane said.

"Ask him when and where we can meet."

"I already did," Paris said, pulling on socks and shoving his feet into his shoes.

Alex nodded. "Do you want to stay here?" he whispered to Jane.

A delightful lemony perfume wafted from her neck. "This time I'm coming with you," she said, standing up and grabbing her coat off the back of a chair.

"And you'll wait here till we get back?" Alex asked Paris.

A hint of envy flitted across the Frenchman's face. He swallowed. Finally, he nodded.

The warm Mediterranean sun thawed the Berlin frost out of him and charged him with renewed energy. On the northern edge of El Papiol, a mature chestnut tree cast its shade over an old stone house. Rusty iron scaffolding clung to the front of the building.

"Barcelona is expecting Justus, not us," Jane said.

"It'll be okay," Alex said, pulling up next to the scaffolding.

The ground was strewn with black buckets stained with dry plaster. A hoe and a pile of dusty bags of cement were leaning against the wall. A light breeze blew through the trees. The unfenced yard was covered in wild grass dotted with daisies. Alex knocked on the rustic wooden door while Jane shaded her eyes from the sharp arrows of light thrown by the sun.

They heard footsteps approaching. An ancient peephole opened and a pair of black eyes stared out at them. The peephole closed, and the door opened to reveal the barrel of a Sig Sauer pointed at Alex's face.

"Can I help you?" a woman asked.

Her skin was deeply tanned, her hair was pulled back in a loose bun, and her eyes bored into Alex and Jane. Dark armpit stains showed on her denim shirt and sweat dripped from her face, but she didn't bother to wipe it away.

"Justus isn't coming," Alex said.

"Who are you?" She had a deep voice, almost a baritone.

"We'll tell you inside."

"No."

"Justus is dead. Thirteen Nibelungs have been killed. Someone knows about the Ring. You're in danger. We're the ones who sent the alert last night and got your message on the helicopter forum. We're here to help, but only if you let us in. Please."

The barrel of the gun didn't budge. After giving Alex a quick once-over, the woman passed her eyes slowly over Jane, checking her out from head to toe.

"I'm London. They're after me, too. That's Alex. He's Mossad," Jane explained.

A shutter creaked in the wind, and somewhere a dog barked. Barcelona opened the door and lowered her gun. The tough expression on her face was replaced by a look of wariness. "Come in," she said, leading them into the dim interior of the house. Pencil drawings on parchment paper lined the stone walls. The mosaic floor was almost entirely occupied by models made from cardboard and wood. Barcelona brought them a carafe of water and two freshly rinsed glasses and placed them on a wrought-iron table. A ray of light seeping in through a high window painted prisms in the water.

"Where is he?" Alex took a sip of water.

"What do you know about me?" Barcelona asked guardedly.

"Nothing. Just that you're in danger." He saw her looking suspiciously at the inflamed scars on his hands.

"Where is he?" he repeated.

"All I found on him was some cash and this," she said, pulling a Third World cellphone from her pocket. She handed it to Alex.

There were pictures. One showed Barcelona beside a blue truck in front of the Basílica de la Sagrada Família. Another was a distorted face shot from too close up. Above the pictures was a long series of digits: the number to which the photos had been sent.

They finally had a lead.

Alex called Butthead and told him to trace the number.

"Where did you take him down?" he asked.

"At La Sagrada Família, where I work. He was shadowing me. I knocked him out and brought him here."

"Show us," Alex said, appraising her with male eyes. She was fleshy and rugged.

They walked through a small bedroom to the rocky yard behind the house, grass sprouting between the stones. "He's over there," Barcelona said, pointing to a small, windowless stone building.

A current ran through Alex's body, as tingly and stimulating as speed. He opened the rusty iron door, its hinges creaking. The dark interior was lit by a single bare bulb hanging from the ceiling. In the puddle of dim light, a man in a gray suit was tied to a chair, a black plastic bag over his head. A hole had been torn for his mouth. The bag rose and fell in time with his breathing.

The prisoner sat up straight.

The walls were covered in gray egg-crate acoustic foam. In the corner was a worn black leather case and a music stand.

"I play my trumpet here," Barcelona said quietly.

Jane closed the heavy door.

"Was he carrying a weapon?" Alex asked.

The bronze-skinned Catalan shook her head.

"Give me your gun."

Barcelona reluctantly handed Alex her gun. The butt was warm.

Alex moved closer to the prisoner. His hands were bound

tightly to the arms of the chair with silver duct tape. Alex pulled the bag off his head. The man's face was pasty, his chin was slumped on his chest, his eyes were half-closed, and his black mustache was stiff.

He looked Turkish.

"What's your name?" Alex asked.

No response.

"Mute?"

No response.

"Deaf mute?"

No response.

A sharp slap landed on the prisoner's cheek. His head was thrown sideways.

There was a deathly silence. Jane lowered her eyes.

"Are you going to answer me?"

No response.

"I need a chair, a bucket of water, and some kind of club," he said over his shoulder to Barcelona, sticking the barrel of the gun against the man's thigh. The prisoner's eyes bulged in fright. Alex was pretty sure the acoustic foam would absorb the noise.

He fired.

A howl of pain burst from the man's throat. The smell of gun-powder spread through the room. Fat globules of thick blood fell from the wound onto the floor: plip-plip-plip. The man fought for breath.

"You don't have much time," Alex said.

"Where are you from?" Alex asked.

The bare bulb above their heads was reflected in the pool of blood collecting on the floor. The veins in the man's neck bulged. He clenched his teeth and breathed through his nose.

"Syria," he croaked.

"Where in Syria?"

The man shut his eyes and coughed.

"I asked you where in Syria."

"Idarat al-Mukhabarat al-Jawiyya," he declared in pride and pain, spitting on the floor.

Syria's Air Force Intelligence Directorate has little to do with aerial intelligence. It is under the direct command of the Syrian president, Bashar al-Assad. Bashar's father, Hafez al-Assad, formerly the commander of the air force, brought its intelligence agency under his wing and used it to bolster his totalitarian rule. Ever since, it has been charged with the country's most sensitive covert operations overseas and plays an important role in safeguarding the regime.

"Are you killing our agents?"

The prisoner shook his head. Sweat dripped from his chin.

"We just gather information."

"You're lying!" Alex thundered, sticking the gun against the man's other thigh.

Jane looked away. Barcelona watched, mesmerized.

"Information about who?"

"Everybody." The man's face twisted, and his breathing became raspy.

"Who killed the agents?"

The Syrian gazed at him with tortured eyes.

Alex moved the gun to the man's temple. His finger on the trigger was taut. He leaned over the prisoner. He could see the blue veins in his eyelids. The Syrian had halitosis.

"I asked you who killed the agents."

"I don't know," the Syrian said pleadingly.

"Where did you send the pictures?"

"I don't know."

Alex took the gun away from the prisoner's temple and used it to strike him savagely across the chin. Something broke. The man groaned. Blood flowed from his mouth, and he spit out splinters of broken teeth. Blood was still dripping from his thigh.

Jane turned her back and covered her ears with her hands. She was standing next to Barcelona, who was exhibiting increasing fascination with the scene.

"Where did you send the pictures?" Alex repeated in a whisper, his lips almost touching the Syrian's face.

Blood was spilling from his mouth onto his chin. "To the number they—"

"The Mukhabarat assassins?"

"No."

Barcelona came closer and whispered something in Alex's ear. The prisoner stared at them in alarm.

"The lady says you're not very good at surveillance," Alex said.

The Syrian lowered his eyes. His shirt was stained with sweat and blood.

Without warning, Alex grabbed him by the hair. His eyes gaped wide in pain and his breathing quickened. He was as white as a sheet.

"Who sent an amateur like you on a covert op?"

"I work at headquarters . . . behind a desk . . ." the man said, sighing deeply.

"So why did they send you?"

"The agents were all in the field. . . . They didn't have anyone else . . ." he whined.

Alex retreated.

Watching the man crack and crumble was making him uneasy. He felt sorry for him. The Syrian was sitting in a pool of his own blood, his teeth were broken, and he was crying.

There was a cold lump in Alex's chest.

Alex went outside into the blinding sunlight. He was still holding the blood-spattered Sig Sauer.

He had to stop for a minute pull himself together and start thinking straight.

If the Syrian and his fellow Mukhabarat agents were just doing the legwork, gathering intel on the Nibelungs, who was attacking them?

He had no time and no other options. He had to ramp up the pressure. He went back inside the dark, soundproofed building, slammed the door, held the gun to the man's other thigh.

Bam.

A shriek of pain shook the small room and was swallowed up without an echo. The Syrian was seized by a fit of tears, gasping for breath as blood flowed out of him. "What do you want to know?" he mumbled from within the knot of pain.

"Who killed the agents?"

The prisoner shook his head slowly. His eyes were starting to glaze over.

"What did they do with the bodies?"

Plip-plip-plip. The man was sobbing quietly.

"Give me something that will persuade me to save your life."

The man shook his head. His chin slumped to his chest.

"You don't have much longer to live."

"I don't know . . ." the man muttered.

"As soon as you lose another quart of blood—which won't be long now—you'll start to feel confused. To stay alive, you'll need twelve pints of saline—twelve bags! That can only happen in a hospital. Are you ready to talk to me yet?"

The prisoner's face was ashen. Alex touched his brow. The clamminess was gone; the skin was dry and cold.

"In a minute or two you won't be able to talk, and I won't be able to help you."

The odor of iron rose from the blood on the floor. The door opened and the room was flooded with dazzling light. Jane's silhouette vanished into the glare. The door slammed shut.

"Who are you working for?" Time was running out.

The Syrian's breathing was shallow. "Hattab . . ."

"Omar Hattab, the head of the Mukhabarat?"

The Syrian nodded weakly.

"On Friday . . . Hattab . . . is meeting . . ."

"Who?"

"In Zenobia . . ." he mumbled.

"Who?"

"Ten o'clock . . ."

"Who is Hattab meeting in Zenobia?"

"The Israelite . . ."

"What Israelite?"

Alex aimed the Sig Sauer at the Syrian's shoulder and turned his head away.

Bam.

Something struck the gun. Blood sprayed onto Alex. He swiveled his head around and looked at the Syrian. He was stunned. Half the man's head was gone. Alex's stomach churned. The bullet had missed the shoulder. "What happened?" he mumbled to himself.

"He shoved his head in front of the gun," said Barcelona.

"Why?"

She rolled her eyes and then gave him a sour smile.

"Death seemed the better option."

Alex looked down at his hand holding the gun. It was spattered with blood and fragments of broken teeth.

Outside, Jane was crouched down beside the tree, vomiting. He moved closer, putting his clean hand on her shoulder. She straightened up and retreated from him, then hurled again.

She shouldn't have come.

The silvery olive-tree leaves glittered in the blazing sun. No wind was blowing.

Rage was building inside him.

Jane was still crouching, spitting on the ground. Her eyes were red and there was a sour expression on her face. Once more he tried to touch her, but the look she gave him was stony.

"Why did you have to torture him?"

"What would you have done, asked him nicely?"

She remained silent.

"It's easy to watch from the sidelines and pass judgment," he said. "You left the dirty work to me. We're out of time."

Jane didn't respond. All of a sudden, the years showed clearly on her face.

Alex walked away. His finger was still frozen on the trigger. He relaxed his hand and returned the Sig Sauer to Barcelona without wiping it off. It had been repulsive and unforgivable, but eventually she might understand that he'd had no choice.

"You have so much anger," Jane called after him.

His figure cast a harsh shadow on the rocky soil. He felt his heart clench. He was sick and tired of his thankless job. Without turning to look at her, he shot back, "Why are you taking pity on him? His friends killed the Nibelungs. They killed Justus."

Alex called Butthead.

"Find Zenobia. It's a place. Start in Syria. I also need a profile of Omar Hattab, the head of the Syrian Mukhabarat. Just the highlights."

"Will do. You asked me to trace a number. It's a prepaid SIM, no way to identify the owner. We tracked its location. For the past seventeen minutes it's been in the Syrian Air office."

"Where?"

"Berlin."

Very good. Berlin. Justus Erlichmann. Omar Hattab. Mukhabarat . . . As soon as he had a moment of peace and quiet, he'd try to connect the dots.

Who was the Israelite?

One of theirs? Someone in Mossad?

Maybe he wasn't Jewish. Alex knew a person who fit the description. A German who secretly donated money to a neo-Nazi organization and had recently been killed.

He called Butthead again. "We're looking for somebody called the Israelite."

"There are millions of them."

"We can't be sure he's Israeli. It might be a code name. Cast your net as wide as you can. Try associative searches."

"Anything else?"

"A log of the incoming and outgoing calls from the cellphone in the Syrian Air office in Berlin."

"How far back?"

"Start with the past week."

Alex's next call was to Reuven. "The Syrians are involved. But they're not working alone. They're surveilling the Nibelungs. Somebody else is orchestrating the attacks."

"How do you know?" Reuven asked.

Alex told him about Barcelona and the Syrian prisoner.

"Two days from now, Omar Hattab, head of the Mukhabarat, is meeting with someone called the Israelite. Butthead's checking into it. I need people in Damascus and a team in Berlin. There's a link to the Berlin Syrian Air office."

"The Syrians wouldn't dare do something like this on their own," Reuven said. "They'd be too afraid of the consequences. Assad's regime is hanging by a thread. But they wouldn't mind helping out, as long as somebody else paid the bill and took the flak in the end. Get as much as you can out of the Syrian."

"I already did."

"Get him to spill what's going on in Berlin."

"He's in no condition to talk."

Reuven hung up.

Alex caught himself before he threw the phone against the wall.

A second later, the phone vibrated in his sticky hand. It slid out of his grip onto the grass. Butthead would have to wait. Alex was beginning to disgust himself. He had to wash his hands.

Barcelona strode across the yard without a glance in his direction.

"Where can I wash myself off?" he called after her.

After a deliberate pause, she stopped and pulled a pale rubber hose from the long grass. She handed him the cracked end and went to turn on the faucet. A spray of warm, murky water burst from the hose. Alex waited until it flowed clear and cool, darkening the soil. Then he rinsed his hands. Bloodred strands floated in the silvery flowing water.

Once his hands were clean, he splashed some water on his face. The gentle breeze that had started up cooled his wet skin. Finally, he drank from the hose. Butthead called back.

"Zenobia is apparently the name of a park in the Abu Rumaneh section of Damascus. It's a high-class district, lots of embassies, fancy homes, government offices."

"Sounds right," Alex said.

Alex had seen Jane stumble in the direction of the front yard. He circled the old house and found her leaning on the rusty scaffolding, drinking from a tall glass of water. She was pale. Barcelona was standing next to her, an arm around her shoulders, stroking her head.

"What are you doing?" he heard himself say.

Barcelona gave him a contemptuous look.

"I'm comforting her."

Jane was as neutral as Switzerland. She handed the empty glass to her new ally.

The unbound breasts under Barcelona's shirt swung lazily. Alex could see her bare flesh between the buttons, but it didn't arouse his interest in the slightest. The Catalan had elbowed her way into the gap that had opened between him and Jane.

Jane gazed at his wet hands. He came closer, but she shied away from him. The glass fell from Barcelona's hand, shattering on a rock. Frightened pigeons flew out of the eaves of the house, flapping their wings noisily.

"Give us a few minutes alone," he said quietly to Barcelona.

The Catalan didn't move.

Jane rested her head on the strong shoulder of her new friend. The women held each other. Barcelona stroked Jane's face, and Jane closed her eyes.

"Leave her alone," Barcelona said. "Leave *us* alone."

Alex felt a flash of jealousy. Salty sweat dripped into his open mouth. He bent over and spat it out.

Ashamed of what he was feeling, Alex turned and walked away. He called the Brussels station. Sammy Zengot was unusually cooperative. A team of six men would soon be in the Wilmersdorf district of Berlin, maintaining round-the-clock surveillance of the Syrian Air office at 20 Bundesallee. They'd be listening in on conversations, snapping photos, and intercepting messages. Most important, they'd find out whether the seemingly innocent airline office was a front for a Mukhabarat station.

Butthead called next. "In the past week there've been two hundred and ninety-six calls from fifty-one different numbers to the Syrian Air office. All incoming, no outgoing. All the numbers are European. We're tracing them, but it'll take time."

"See whether any of the calls came from Israel or Berlin."

He couldn't wait to get away from here. Just climb in the car, get on a plane, and vanish. Leaning against the olive tree, he closed his eyes.

"What are we going to do with the body?" Barcelona demanded, breaking into the rare moment of silence. Alex looked at her. Her eyes were averted. Jane was hiding behind her. How long had it been since he'd shut his eyes?

He wasn't going to make it easy for her. "Dump it somewhere far away and get rid of the gun," he said.

At least she wasn't questioning his authority. Time was slipping away. The sun disappeared behind a cloud, and the scene grew somber. The wild grass in the yard became darker, and the edges of the sharp shadows softened. A cool breeze sent a shiver along his skin.

After a while he hardened his heart, pulled Jane roughly from Barcelona's side, and shoved her into the car. In the rearview mirror he saw the Catalan watching them with her penetrating eyes as they drove away. Her figure gradually grew smaller. He breathed a sigh of relief and turned on the radio, exposing them to an assault of blaring ads.

In the dim light of dusk, he examined his hands on the wheel. He didn't see any blood. In a conciliatory tone he said, "Don't be mad at me."

Jane didn't respond.

"The Syrian wanted Barcelona dead, just like Berlin and the others," he went on.

He recalled the terror in the prisoner's eyes.

"I'm having trouble coping right now," Jane said in a weak voice. "All the violence . . . the brutality."

"I get it. But if I hadn't applied pressure, he wouldn't have talked."

"Did you have to shoot him again and again?"

"What would you have done?"

"I don't know. I guess I'm not as tough as I thought I was."

The countryside was growing darker, the blue sky gradually turning black. The day was drawing to an end. They crossed Barcelona on Avinguda Diagonal, the street that cuts through the city from northwest to southeast. Alex placed his hand over hers. She cringed and hunched up against the door.

"What's wrong?"

A heavy, desertlike silence hung between them. Alex suddenly realized that he was in love with the woman she used to be. Time had polished his memories, rounded off the sharp edges. He'd allowed himself to be drawn into an illusory cocktail of fantasy and nostalgia. She had changed over the years. Now he couldn't predict her reactions. In the dark car driving through the center of Barcelona, she whispered, "That part of you, Alex . . . It scares me."

"Your assassin was taken out in Tuscany by his target, Alex Bartal, who flew to Barcelona this morning with Jane Thompson,
the London Nibelung. It appears that your team didn't manage
to finish her off, either," says the tall man in the gray raincoat and
black woolen cap. His face is badly disfigured. When he talks, he
gestures with his left hand alone.

The wind angles the rain into his eyes. The asphalt on the
broad street is slick. There were clear skies in the morning, but
that feels like a long time ago. Now the weather is wet and stormy
and he should be inside, at home. But home is far away.

"Where are we going?" asks Disfigured Face.

"Trust me," says the man in the black cycling suit. The tight
pants accentuate the thick mass of quads in his thighs.

"Where?"

"To one of my favorite spots," the cyclist says.

"Did you bring proof?"

"Stop fretting."

"Did you?"

On the seam between the two halves of the city, traffic is
heavy. Dark umbrellas sail past. People are in a hurry.

The cyclist takes a brown envelope from his black nylon
jacket. "In only one week, they lost more agents than ever before.
Can you believe it?" His eyes shine with self-approval. "In a day

or two, the Ring will be history. We are making history. Are you trying to make history?"

"I'm just doing my job," says Disfigured Face, moving aside. He opens the envelope and studies the document. His face goes white, and the pale lips under his mustache open. The teeth aren't his. They're implants.

The cyclist scratches his ear. "Did you know that you have to boil a noose for an hour and then stretch it out to dry to make it lose its flexibility?"

The Disfigured Face hardens. "If you wish to see your partner again, you had better stop trying my patience."

The cyclist bursts out laughing. "You're threatening me? You are, aren't you? You just threatened me!"

"I have come to thank you for your part in Stage One." He looks like he is being forced to chew on a dead cat. "The boss has given the order to move on to Stage Two."

"That's all?" the cyclist says derisively.

"We have to agree on the terms for Stage Two."

"Payment?"

"Terms. We only pay for goods on delivery," says Disfigured Face as if he is speaking to someone mentally challenged.

"Forget it," says the cyclist, coughing up phlegm and spitting a green wad onto the dark pavement. "Did you know that if the rope is too short, you don't lose consciousness? You die of strangulation, very slowly."

Disfigured Face stops short. "Then there is no deal." He knows he cannot go home without concluding the transaction. He thrusts his hands into his coat pockets. Even his nearby hotel room is too far away. He needs to scrub himself down in a steaming hot shower to get rid of the filthy residue of this meeting.

"Did you know that if the gallows floor is too high, you get decapitated?" the cyclist says.

"You are a sick man," says Distorted Face. "You need help."

The rain starts coming down harder.

"Payment up front—or you lose your head," says the cyclist with a chilling smirk.

"You will get your money in cash when we have proof of completion and it is reported in the press."

"It's been nice knowing you," the cyclist says dismissively. "We both know that you can't go home without closing the deal," he adds, chuckling with self-satisfaction. "By the way, did you know that there are no eyeholes in the hood they put over your head? It's pitch-black and stifling underneath. You can't see a thing."

"No payment until delivery. It is not open to negotiation."

"I expected you to be more appreciative," the cyclist spits. "We saved you and your fucking prosthesis from the noose."

Disfigured Face bites down on his pale lip, pulls at what is left of his nose, and gazes into the distance. Then he turns his eyes back to the cyclist. "You did your job and you got paid for it. Take your medication and shut up."

They reach a crosswalk. A black Volkswagen Touareg passes them, driving slowly.

In its tinted windows are reflected the concrete slabs of the Holocaust Memorial.

The hair dryer roared behind the closed door of the bathroom in the Claris Hotel.

When it was his turn, Alex got into the shower and scrubbed his fingers raw. The hot water washed the putrid refuse of the day off his body. Within minutes, the bathroom looked like a steam room.

There was nowhere to rush off to, nowhere to fly to. They could take this night to rest and shore up their strength. Alex still cherished the hope that the precious hours of quiet ahead would bring them close again.

The water was soothing and purifying.

Buzzing.

He turned off the water and pulled the shower curtain aside. His phone was vibrating on the marble countertop, inching its way to the edge of the sink. Butthead had the profile of Omar Hattab.

"I'll call you back," Alex said, preparing to step back into the shower. Then he stopped in his tracks. In the silence, he could hear her hoarse voice on the other side of the door.

She was talking on the phone.

Flight.

London.

As soon as possible.

Despite the friction in El Papiol, the fragments of conversation he overheard were cutting and painful. He fled back under the stream of hot water, desperate to escape his thoughts.

A knock on the bathroom door.

"Alex?"

He turned off the water.

"What?"

"I'll be in the lobby."

He heard the hall door open and close.

Alex shaved. Wrapped in a towel, he sat down on the lid of the toilet. He'd taken on the odious part of the operation, and now she was mad at him. Or maybe he was mad at her. He wouldn't get another chance.

He left the bathroom, dressed, and splashed cologne on his smooth cheeks.

The decor of the lobby was a bizarre cocktail of New York and the Middle East: a mix of ancient Egyptian artifacts and Andy Warhol lithographs. She was sunk deep in the cushions of a brown couch, staring out at the street. He walked over to her and leaned down. "You smell wonderful," he whispered.

She recoiled. He sat down beside her.

A young mocha-complexioned woman with generous curves stepped out of the elevator. The lights of the lobby were reflected in her dark eyes. She smiled, revealing perfect teeth.

"What did I do?" he asked.

Jane shook her head. "I'm sorry."

"Did I hurt you?"

"You've changed."

"How?"

"You're harder."

"Because of my interrogation techniques?"

"Crueler."

Alex folded his arms over his chest.

"You didn't have to kill him," she said.

"He committed suicide."

"If you'd been in his shoes, you would have, too."

"I aimed for his shoulder. He stuck his head in front of the gun."

"And you didn't see him do it?"

"He wanted to die."

"You didn't see him do it?"

"I turned my head away."

"Why?"

"I'd seen enough."

Jane shifted her eyes back to the street. He wasn't going to get her companionship tonight.

"You know very well that the Nibelung Ring isn't devoted to saving the whales or rescuing pandas. We were covered in shit, and somebody had to clean it up. You ran, and your friend Barcelona rolled her eyes."

"Barcelona has nothing to do with it. Leave her out of this."

"Do you want to go back to London?"

Her face froze.

"I'm sorry," Alex said. "I was wrong to get you mixed up in this."

"You didn't get me mixed up in it. I'm part of it."

"I'll finish it on my own."

"That's it?" she asked in a hoarse whisper.

"What do you mean?"

"We go our separate ways?"

He could easily fall asleep right here on the brown couch. But when Jane put a gentle hand on his arm in the middle of the bright, bustling lobby, he was caught in her web once again. He shook his head.

"This is who I am now. It's what I've become," he said. "It's not easy for me."

She wrapped her arms around his neck and rested her head on his shoulder. He moved closer, feeling exhausted and drained. "You need time to recover," he said.

She nodded. It was the first time they seemed to be in sync since that morning.

"Maybe it's best if we try again some other time," he heard himself say. "When there's a chance we can make it work."

"We have to stick together," she replied. "Together we can get through this. It's the only way."

Hesitantly, his lips reached for hers. They kissed, but with a trace of desperation.

"Let's go outside, where there's more life," she said. "Barcelona is waiting for us."

Alex froze.

"The city," she said with a smile. "Barcelona the city."

They went out onto the street, their arms intertwined, and were instantly absorbed into the high spirits and vivaciousness of the Latin city.

He'd never held her in public before.

As she walked beside him with her arm around his waist, he finally felt her softness, and she smelled wonderful. He made an effort to erase the memory of the events in El Papiol.

"Are you ready for a good meal?"

She nodded.

"There's a great place for tapas and seafood on the beach," he said.

"It's only a quarter to seven. The restaurants are still closed. Let's take a walk first."

"Are you up to it?"

"Yes," she said.

His phone vibrated.

"Is now a good time?" Butthead asked.

"General Omar Hattab has been head of the Mukhabarat for seven years. He was a young air-force pilot during the Yom Kippur War," Butthead read out to Alex from the profile. "His plane was hit and caught fire, but he didn't bail out. He insisted on landing it and suffered burns over most of his body. Since then, he has risen steadily through the ranks. He's sixty-three, married, yadda yadda... Here it is! Since he's been in charge, there've been some serious fuckups. There are details here from our operations portfolio: the bombing of the nuclear facility in Deir ez-Zor; the assassination of Imad Mughniyeh; the explosion at the chemical weapons factory; the car bomb in Damascus that took out a senior Iranian official, and there are more—"

"What do the analysts say?" Alex asked. "Why doesn't Assad get rid of him?"

"He's some kind of cousin. And he's a loyalist."

The call was disconnected.

Under ordinary circumstances, Assad would boot him out, maybe even order his hanging. The Mukhabarat chief had a very strong motive to prove himself if he wanted to stay alive.

They walked into the wind blowing from the sea. A yellow roadster, its roof down, drove by, growling roughly. Even after it passed, Alex's diaphragm continued to vibrate.

"Did you hear me?" Jane asked.

"What?"

"I said I'm sorry."

"For what?"

"For getting so upset. I'm not as tough as you anymore. My shell has gotten thinner. I lead a quiet life. I get action and stress no more than one week out of the year, and even that's just training exercises, or, as Justus used to call it, operating system updates. I'm already on my way out. You're still in the thick of it all."

Traffic was clogged along Via Laietana. Brake lights painted the facades of the imposing Catalan Modernista buildings in red. Built at the beginning of the previous century, they mimicked the style of the buildings on the great thoroughfares of Madrid.

"Stay with me," Alex said.

The streetlamps shone on a bare plaza with an abstract pop art sculpture in the center. Alex breathed in the bracing sea air. A flock of gulls flew over their heads, their shrieks carried off by the wind. Alex and Jane strolled on, their two bodies casting a single shadow.

Reuven called.

"Who do you think the Syrians are working with?"

"I have to go to Syria. The answers are there," Alex said.

"The PM has you on the list of new appointments this summer. He won't let you risk your neck."

"The Israelite will be there," Alex said. "That's who they're working with."

"Where are you?"

"The Israelite could be one of us," Alex said.

"No way."

Reuven hung up.

The waves lapped up against the concrete piers and retreated back into the sea. A field of masts and steel cables clattered in the wind. The air tasted salty and smelled of rotting seaweed. A dark-skinned man with a shaved head bumped Alex's shoulder as he passed. He didn't bother to apologize. When Alex turned his head, he was already gone, swallowed up by the other strolling people.

"We'll head back to Berlin in the morning," he said into the wind.

Every time he uttered the word *Berlin*, the disturbing Time–Life album rose up before him.

They joined the long line outside Restaurante El Pulpo. Within a few minutes the doors opened and the crowd snaked into a cloud of garlic and melted butter, and the sounds of dizzying flamenco music played on an acoustic guitar. Yellow cloths covered the tightly spaced tables filled with eager diners.

Alex ordered a bottle of cava. The cork flew up to the ceiling, and the bubbling wine climbed to the tops of their narrow glasses.

A green salad with tuna was followed by thin slices of *jamón ibérico*. The lightly salted cured ham was delicious. The bubbly cava tickled Alex's tongue. Laughter came from the tables around them. The waiter placed a plate of *boquerones* between them. The white flesh of the anchovies was pleasantly sour and salty.

"You look sad," Jane said.

"Worried."

"You always are, a little."

"A little what?"

"Sad."

He refilled their glasses.

"All the people around us are happy," she said.

Alex put down his fork. "Do you have a happy life?"

Jane chewed on an anchovy before answering. "You've never been happy."

"Just drop it."

"I read an article about the children of Holocaust survivors."

Alex nodded with manifest distaste.

"You suffer from feelings of guilt and existential angst, and you have abandonment issues."

"Guilt for what?"

"Maybe you feel guilty that you weren't able to save her."

"Who?"

"Your mother."

"How could I?" he said quietly.

"You couldn't."

The conspiracy of silence. The anxieties over food. The fear of what tomorrow would bring. The fragility of life. Survivor's guilt. Life in his childhood home had been grim. He couldn't afford to open that box right now. Not here. Not in his condition.

Distracted, he reached out for his cava glass and knocked it over. A dark stain spread across the yellow cloth. It reminded him of the pool of blood beneath the Syrian's feet.

"Let's try to enjoy ourselves," he said sadly.

The waiter brought a large plate of black mussels and left.

The guitar quartet, decked out in frilly white shirts and heavy gold chains, was making its way toward them. The entertainers attached themselves to their table like leeches. Giving the couple a veiled look, the broad-nostrilled leader opened his mouth and began singing a treacly serenade. Alex glared at them. He pulled a two-euro coin from his pocket. The guitarists bowed and smiled before moving on, taking their irritating strings with them.

After a long pause, Alex asked, "Were you having an affair with Justus?"

"What makes you ask that?"

"When we found the skinny jeans in his closet, you tried to look surprised, but I had the sense that you were hurt."

Jane examined her fingernails and then scanned the other diners. Her expression darkened. She remained silent for a long time. Finally she said, "I wonder how things would have turned out if this crisis with the Nibelungs had never happened. I wonder if we could have lived a quiet life together." She looked him in the eye. "Do you think we could have pulled it off?"

Alex groped for the passion Jane had once aroused, but his attraction to her now felt like a foot that had fallen asleep.

It was obvious that it was hard for her to be with him. She couldn't cope with who he was.

For a fleeting moment, he got a glimpse into his own soul and recognized the part he had played in his failed relationship with Naomi. Maybe he wasn't cut out for the sustained intimacy of being a couple. Maybe he could only find release in wide-open spaces, far from anyone else, alone on his barren inner tundra.

He covered his face with his hands. Between his fingers, he saw her doleful smile.

"Sometimes I think your job keeps you from having to deal with life," she said.

On the way to the restroom, Alex bumped into a chubby wait-ress encased in a tight dress, nearly causing her to drop the heavy tray she was carrying. She flashed him a smile, revealing a dark tongue. In her deep cleavage, there was a gold cross.

A cross . . .

Christian . . .

Alex made sure he was alone in the restroom before calling Butthead.

"Find out about a racist group that calls itself Christian Iden-tity."

Alex had come across the name in a survey of far-right fringe groups and messianic cults in Western countries.

"What do you want to know?" Butthead asked.

"Who they refer to as Israelites."

He returned to the table.

The waiter brought them a plate piled high with langoustines. Jane peeled the shell off one and placed the white flesh on his plate. Butter dripped from her fingers.

His phone vibrated.

"Sorry," Alex mouthed.

"Christian Identity is a white supremacist religious move-ment," Butthead reported. "They believe that white Europeans are the true Israelites and that the Jews are the offspring of Satan. All the rest are 'mud people,' soulless human trash. They're affili-

226 | RONI DUNEVICH

ated with racist organizations like the Aryan Nations, the Aryan Brotherhood prison gangs, the Redeemer ministries, the Phineas Priesthood, and the loony redneck militias in the American Midwest. According to these other groups, only Caucasians have souls and only whites go to heaven. The Jews are the descendants of Satan, so naturally we go to hell, and when Jesus is resurrected we'll all be exterminated."

"What's their connection to neo-Nazis?"

"There's almost no connection. Most neo-Nazis don't want anything to do with them. They claim that Christian Identity is a Jewish invention."

"So according to Christian Identity, the Israelite can't be an Israeli or a Jew," Alex said.

"And he would hate Jews because they're the lowest of the low."

"But we don't know if he's a neo-Nazi or not," Alex added.

"Not yet."

"Find out what links do exist between Christian Identity and neo-Nazis."

A plate of squid arrived at the table, but Alex had lost interest in the food. The cava was making him feel sluggish. His mind was fighting a headwind.

"Sorry about all the phone calls."

She nodded, but she seemed upset.

"The Israelite is probably a Jew-hating Christian," he said.

"What about us?" she asked bluntly.

"We'll get through this," he said, too quickly. "What do *you* want?"

"Where will we live?"

"We'll figure it out."

"You're dreaming, Alex. I love you, but you're dreaming."

"Would you come to Tel Aviv?"

"My life is in London. I'm in the middle of a research project that's going to keep me busy for years."

The creases in her face grew deeper. The image of what she would look like as an old woman flashed through his mind. She would still be beautiful.

His phone vibrated. He dropped his shoulders in a show of despair.

She didn't reward him with so much as a nod. Alex glanced at her as he got up. Jane was deep in thought, staring at the screen of her phone.

He went outside.

It was Reuven.

"Christian Identity is an interesting idea, but it's not very likely," his boss said. "Butthead just sent me a memo. It's a fringe group. The neo-Nazis among them are outside the mainstream. Mostly, they just make noise and pick on easy targets."

"The Syrian said the man they were working with was called the Israelite," Alex insisted.

"He could have been lying."

"He said it at the stage when you don't lie."

"Sorry, but I don't think you're on the right track. Try a different direction."

"Okay. Don't hang up."

"Who's hanging up?"

Alex surveyed the street and the alley alongside the restaurant. A row of different-colored recycling bins; a dog with its tail between its legs and fear in its eyes. He heard voices speaking English with American accents. A tourist walked by, a camera with a huge lens hanging from his thick neck. Guitar music. The quartet of musical leeches was standing in the entrance to the alley. A white truck started backing into the narrow space. The guitarists went on strumming as they moved aside.

"Don't we have a source high up in the Federal Office for the Protection of the Constitution in Germany?" Alex asked.

"Parsifal? Not anymore."

"He's dead?"

"No, Parsifal's not dead. He caused a major diplomatic incident between us and Germany. After that, he slammed the door in our faces."

"He was an agent?"

"No, an asset. A Jewish psychiatrist who made his way up the ranks in the office. He passed on information that happened to cross his desk, and he didn't want any money for it. The Germans caught on to him in 2004. We offered to pay for an attorney and anything else he needed, but he couldn't take the pressure. He gave up his handler, our agricultural attaché at the embassy in Berlin, and they let him keep his job. The attaché was deported the same night, and Parsifal cut off all contact with us. We've tried, but he doesn't want anything more to do with us. He's retiring soon. Forget about him."

"What put them on to him?"

"He wasn't computer savvy. He didn't understand that as soon as he switched from paper to computers, every keystroke was recorded. They had their eye on him for a long time. They suspected him of leaking information."

"What's he doing these days?"

"He's a senior profiler in the unit that tracks extreme right-wing movements."

"Neo-Nazis?"

"Them, too. But I don't believe neo-Nazis are behind this. They're nothing but simple-minded, marginal rejects. It's not them. The people we're fighting are powerful, organized, and professional."

"We don't have any other leads," Alex said.

"So keep looking. The answers aren't under our noses."

"Give me Parsifal's phone number."

"You're wasting your time."

Alex waited. Finally he heard the familiar sound of Reuven's office safe swinging open. The chief read out the number and then hung up.

Should he go back inside, or call now? There was no point in going in and coming right back out again. Jane's patience had a limit.

Alex dialed the number. It went to voice mail.

Jane was going to be upset.

He dialed again.

"Ja?" said a polite German voice.

"Are you alone?" Alex said.

"Who is this?"

"Can you talk?"

"Yes, and I can sing, too. It depends on who you are."

"Somebody from your past."

The call was disconnected.

Alex redialed.

"A psychiatrist isn't supposed to be afraid of the past," he said.

"What do you want?"

"Parsifal?"

The German hung up.

But Alex wasn't ready to give up. He called the number again.

"It won't be hard for me to find you," Parsifal said. His tone had become aggressive.

"Don't bother. I'd be happy to come see you."

"What do you want?"

"I'm looking for a man called the Israelite."

He heard the German light a cigarette and inhale. He was stalling.

"Do not dare call this number again," Parsifal said and hung up.

Alex walked unsteadily back inside. The odors in the restaurant were overwhelming. He passed a waiter carrying a tray loaded with steaming plates. El Pulpo was jumping, the atmosphere lively and buoyant. Five drunken men were roaring with laughter at a table near the door.

As far as he was concerned, they could pay the bill and leave. They'd take a taxi back to the hotel. He'd turn his phone off for an hour or two. The world could wait. It took him a minute to locate their table.

Jane was gone.

A shudder of fear ran through Alex like a low-frequency wave. Waiters carrying heavy trays emerged from the kitchen one after another. A bottle was uncorked, and raucous cheering filled the crowded restaurant. The noise was brutal.

Jane's cellphone was on the table.

A fish sat on her plate, its pale flesh partially eaten.

She must be in the restroom.

The abominable phone in his hand vibrated.

"Alex?" said a deep voice.

"Who is this?"

"I told you it wouldn't be hard for me to find you," Parsifal gloated.

"Can you help?"

"It is risky. I would be jeopardizing my pension. Do you have a pension, or are you one of those Israelis who is expecting an exit that will make him a millionaire overnight?"

"Who's the Israelite?"

"I have no idea."

Alex took the phone away from his ear and glared at it. "So what did you call for?"

"Reuven asked me to. I am a Jew, but my roots are here in Berlin. My family was one of the few that were not deported during the war."

"I'm looking for the Israelite."

"Have you ever heard of a movement called Christian Identity?" Parsifal asked.

The conversation was beginning to sound like yesterday's news.

"Yes. Who's the Israelite?"

"I told you, I do not know. But if he is not an Israeli, he could be an Aryan who believes in the purity of the race."

"Are you going to help me?"

Parsifal pulled on his cigarette and exhaled noisily.

"Look for the Mud Man."

Parsifal hung up.

Alex called him back. The asshole had turned off his phone.

He left two hundred euros on the table, grabbed Jane's phone, and checked the floor. There was nothing there. She was probably throwing up again. He'd wait for her outside the restroom. Time slipped by frustratingly. Why didn't she come out?

Butthead had mentioned "mud people" when he told him about Christian Identity. Alex glanced at his watch. He'd been standing there for eight minutes.

He went into the ladies' restroom. Two stalls, one locked. The sound of flushing came from it. He heard muffled coughing from behind the door. Poor thing—he was right, she was puking again.

The lock turned, and the door opened. Two round eyes gaped at him, and a deafening scream rocked the small space.

"Sorry . . . I'm looking for my wife. She felt sick . . . I thought she was in here."

Another scream.

Alex retreated. As he exited the ladies' room, he bumped into a waiter and an older gentleman in a blue suit with a trim white beard. Both men had amused expressions on their faces. The waiter burst out laughing and patted his shoulder as if he were drunk.

Jane wasn't there.

He knew she hadn't left the restaurant. He would have seen

her when he was talking on the phone right outside the door. He went into the kitchen, ignoring the disapproving looks from the chef, line cooks, and dishwashers. The kitchen was hot. The air was steamy and humid and filled with cooking noises. Something moist was thrown into a pot of sizzling oil.

Alex scanned the workstations. Cooks were concentrating on their tasks: stainless-steel counters; pots and pans.

He found the back door and pushed against it. It was locked.

He felt a vague pressure in his chest. The man in the blue suit came up behind him. He must be the manager.

"Is there another exit?" he asked.

"Is something wrong, sir?" the man asked politely, an amiable look in his eyes.

"I can't find my wife. Where's the emergency exit?"

Nodding, the man steered him to a black door between the restrooms and the kitchen. "We keep it locked," he said, leaning on the handle to demonstrate. He fell forward as the door opened, revealing a paved enclosure behind the restaurant that was occupied solely by garbage bins in need of a good scrubbing and tall gas canisters.

Alex had a sinking feeling. The enclosure led out to the alley.

The flagstones were too filthy to tell whether there were any drops of blood.

He'd wasted precious time standing around waiting.

White Beard mumbled something, but Alex was already checking out the alley. He went into every yard and stairwell, searching for signs of a struggle or blood smears, his pulse pounding painfully in his temples. His desperation grew with each empty yard.

No more than an hour had passed since he'd asked her to stay.

He kicked wildly at a trash can, knocking it over. The contents spilled out over the street. The stench filled the air.

He returned to the restaurant and surveyed each table and every high-spirited diner. Not one of them so much as glanced in his direction. He went back outside, his temples throbbing with the knowledge that it was a lost cause. Justus's BlackBerry beeped in his pocket. He mouthed a silent prayer, but the pain in his chest was already unbearable. Looking at the screen, he howled until his throat burned and tears of fury welled up in his eyes.

His prayer had been in vain.

London's heart had stopped.

Alex went back to the alley. She couldn't have disappeared into thin air. Shit. He had to figure out what had changed.

The guitar players were gone. What else?

He'd seen them move aside to make room for a truck backing in. Where was the truck?

He found the restaurant manager near the door. "There was a truck in the alley before. Who does it belong to?"

"We only take deliveries before noon," the manager answered with a worried look. "Why?"

Alex returned to the alley and scrutinized each of the buildings from the ground up. No security cameras.

"Can I be of help, sir?" the manager asked behind him. Alex ran down the alley to the other end, where it was blocked by a low post. He pulled on it, and the post came out in his hands.

The picture was becoming clearer. The motherfuckers were using trucks.

He needed backup, urgently. He couldn't do it on his own. He considered calling Barcelona in El Papiol. She was a tough, well-trained operative. But it would take her too long to get here.

He called HQ in Glilot and instructed them to contact the Madrid station. "Give me your precise location," the female voice at the Operations Center said. He gave her the address.

"Just a second."

After a short pause, she was back. "A mile and a quarter to

your southwest, at the old port, there's a point jutting into the sea. On the beach at the far end is a bare tract of land about two hundred feet square. A medevac chopper from El Prat will pick you up there in twenty minutes. It's red and white. The pilot's name is Pepe. He's one of ours. He's not allowed to land there, so he can't be on the ground for more than two minutes."

Alex steeled himself and took off at a run. His chest was tight, and his head throbbed. The lights spun around him. A cold sweat ran down his back, and his face was icy. He glanced at his watch: no time. Finally he reached the port, where the colored lights of the city rippled on the black water. The air was warm and thick with oily fumes.

A light drizzle began falling. He couldn't afford to be late.

He found the empty tract of beach. Nothing there. He called Parsifal, but his phone was still off. His tiny window of opportunity had been sealed shut.

The wind was carrying the faint beat of a rotor. The noise got louder. Lights suddenly appeared in the sky, coming closer. The pilot turned on a bright spotlight that lit up the beach below, and he began maneuvering the aircraft into the middle of the square landing site. The rotor shrieked in the salty air.

Pepe's chin was flanked by long black sideburns. A diamond winked in his earlobe. Within seconds the helicopter was off the ground again, the rain spattering the windshield as it rose.

"We're looking for a light-colored refrigerated delivery truck that left Barcelona and is probably heading for central Europe. What's the quickest route?"

"How much of a lead do they have on us?"

Alex looked at his watch. "About forty minutes."

"The fastest route is the Autopista del Mediterráneo. They

could get on it anywhere. Considering their head start, I say we go straight to Girona and fly low toward the oncoming traffic. That way, we won't miss them on a side street."

Pepe handed Alex night-vision goggles. "We'll be in Girona in twenty-six minutes."

They made the flight in silence, Alex trying to remember every detail of the truck in the alley. He'd noticed it immediately because its light color had made it stand out in the dark. It could be white. What else? Lettering? Stickers? Dents?

"Keep your eyes on the exits," Pepe said as he descended. Through the goggles, the cold highway looked white and the speeding cars black.

Semis and large trucks rolled down the left-hand lane.

"Let's hover here," Alex said.

The chopper held its position in the air, making the traffic appear to slow down. Alex swung the goggles back and forth across the road like a radar dish, checking out every commercial vehicle.

A delivery truck!

It had rounded corners in the back. The one in the alley had sharp corners. He was positive.

The highway followed the winding path of the Tordera River. The pale moon was reflected on the water.

The cars thinned out. The first pangs of hopelessness began to gnaw at him. Maybe his whole truck theory was flawed.

The image of Jane pushed all other thoughts out of his mind. It pulsated in his temples, danced before his eyes. The loss was overwhelming.

A police car passed one of the semitrailers, its lights flashing black. The night in negative. The semi slowed and pulled onto the shoulder. Alex nearly missed the light-colored truck that sped past it.

"That's it, Pepe!" he shouted, pointing.

The Catalan turned the chopper around and started following the truck.

"Go down. Let's try to block it," Alex instructed.

The road rapidly loomed closer.

"Faster!"

Pepe hovered fifteen feet above the highway.

Flashing his headlights and leaning on the horn, the truck driver screeched to a halt in alarm. He stopped about sixty feet from the nose of the chopper. Pepe brought it down onto the road.

"Do you have a gun?" Alex asked.

Pepe shook his head.

"Flares?"

Blinding lights piled up behind the truck. The police would be there any minute. Pepe pulled out the emergency kit and handed Alex a flare gun. Alex climbed out and walked over to the truck. He hadn't the slightest idea what he'd find when he got there. Sticking the flare gun up against the driver's window, he ordered, "Pull over and show me your license and registration."

"Who are you?" asked the young driver, an albino with red eyes. Another man was sitting in the passenger seat.

Alex aimed the gun at the albino's head. "Pull onto the shoulder."

The passenger's black eyes opened wide. The two men nodded compliantly.

The truck inched onto the shoulder of the road. The chopper rose and hovered above the highway, raising a cloud of dust.

Alex signaled to the other vehicles to move along, but the curious drivers only crept forward at a snail's pace, their eyes fixed on the unusual scene. Cars honked; the chopper's engine growled and its rotor shrieked. The albino stepped out of the truck and handed Alex his documents.

"Open the back."

The driver nodded, fear showing in his red eyes.

"Give me the keys and get in," Alex ordered.

The albino climbed in, with Alex on his tail. The refrigerated van appeared to be empty. Alex walked down its length, knocking on the scratched metal floor as he went, and then jumped out and examined the undercarriage. His nostrils filled with the stench of hot rubber and diesel fuel, but he didn't see anything suspicious.

"Is there something wrong, señor?" the albino asked.

Alex didn't bother to answer. He went over to the passenger door and ordered the black-eyed man out. Quickly, he patted down the two men. A look of protest was beginning to form on the albino's face. A search of the cabin was equally fruitless. Alex glanced at the license and registration. They were fairly new. He returned them to the driver.

"Sorry," he said, gesturing for Pepe to land.

The medevac chopper came down on the bare shoulder, spraying dirt and pebbles in Alex's face. The truck roared to life. It pulled back onto the road and disappeared. The helicopter rose.

Alex called the Claris Hotel. There was no one in his room, and the lady had not returned. For a long time the chopper continued to hover over the highway, but it was a wasted effort.

If Alex had been listening in on cellphone communications in the area, he would have heard the truck driver reporting, "He's gone. We're on our way."

The sea was stormy, the waves breaking on the shore and retreating in dismay. Climbing down from the helicopter felt like surrender. Alex watched its lights grow smaller until it disappeared, leaving behind an empty black sky. His feet sank into the sand.

On the cab ride back to the hotel, he prayed that he would find Jane waiting for him in the room, as furious as she liked, just there.

The room was empty.

Alex lay down on the bed in his clothes. Muted, unintelligible voices seeped through the wall. After a while he undressed and got into the shower, but he quickly lost patience, turned off the water, and dried himself off.

He stretched out on the bed again and shut his eyes for a second. The room spun around him as if he'd drunk too much. The dead machine gunner in Leipzig floated up from the depths of his memory, bringing with him the unbearable fragility of life.

Reuven called. Alex told him about Jane. There was a long silence before the chief finally said, "I'm sorry to hear that."

"I'm going back to Berlin. I want to get eyes on the people working out of the Syrian Air office. Parsifal told me to look for the Mud Man. Does that mean anything to you?"

"No. You have to fly to Lyon in the morning."

"Lyon can wait."

"No, it can't. A woman will be waiting for you in Crémieu. You don't know her."

"Berlin is more urgent," Alex insisted.

"The Nibelungs were just the beginning."

"The beginning of what, Reuven? What's in Lyon? It's all tied to Berlin. As soon as the Nibelungs started disappearing—"

"Disappearing?" Reuven cut in. "Don't be a child, Alex. They didn't disappear. Neither did Jane. She's dead. They're all dead."

Reuven was a prick, but he was right. Alex had to let go of his fantasies. She was dead.

He was filled with a debilitating mixture of despair and rage. Craving revenge, he paced back and forth in the empty hotel room.

Everything led back to Berlin, to the Germans. Those Germans-may-they-rot-in-hell.

Text from Zengot: Contact Ancona. Urgent.

Thank God Sammy had sent the right man. But what could be so urgent in the middle of the night?

"We're in Berlin," Ancona informed him. There was the sound of a match being lit. Ancona blew out smoke. "I need you here."

"I'm in Barcelona."

"You have to get here fast," Ancona said, drawing on his cigarette.

"What happened?"

"We grabbed someone from the Syrian Air office. We had a short conversation with her. She has information, and she'll give it up."

"Where will I find you?"

"Spandau. I'll text you the details."

If he left right away, he'd have an hour or two in Berlin before the flight to Lyon in the morning.

He called Paris from the plane, waking him out of a deep sleep, and filled him in on the events of the evening.

"Do you want me to come to Barcelona?" Paris asked.

"It's a lost cause."

"I can help."

"I know. But at the moment there's nothing we can do. We'll talk in the morning."

"Where will you be?"

"I have no idea."

"Be careful, Alex. They did not give up on Jane, and they will come looking for you again, too."

The lights of Barcelona faded from the window, and with them any hope he still harbored of finding Jane alive.

The plane approached Spandau. A glimmer of hope flickered in the darkness. Ancona had sounded confident, and Ancona was as scarred as a street dog.

Three weary men were sprawled on the wooden floor of a cellar that reeked of mildew and diesel fuel. Not far away, a rusty iron anvil sat on a heavy worktable. One of the men was chewing gum, another was listening to music on his iPhone, and the third was chugging beer from a bottle and scratching his balls. They acknowledged Alex's arrival with unsmiling nods.

Akiva Ancona was standing next to a slender woman in a cheap blue suit seated on a straight-backed chair. Her hands were tied behind her back, and her feet were bound to the chair legs. The edge of a pale neck and dark purple scarf peeked out from under the burlap bag over her head.

Ancona strode over to Alex silently, thanks to the soundproofing in the soles of his shoes. An unlit cigarette was stuck between his teeth. The men on the floor waited.

"Let me introduce you," he said quietly. "An intel officer in an airline uniform. She was posted to the Berlin station by Mukhabarat HQ in Damascus. We picked her up outside the Syrian Air office.

"They've been working around the clock in shifts of six for the past ten days."

Ancona lit the cigarette with a bent match and inhaled. He crushed the filter between his teeth. Spirals of smoke issued from his nostrils as he gave Alex a nod.

Alex swiveled around and stood with his back to the prisoner.

The sounds of slapping and punching bounced off the walls of the cellar, followed by howling and groaning, crying and gasping. Ancona never uttered a single word. Saying nothing, asking nothing, he went on beating, punching, inflicting pain.

Ancona pulled off the filthy burlap bag. Her eyes were closed. He poured a bucket of water over her head.

She groaned. Her long, dark hair was pulled back in a ponytail held by a simple blue rubber band. She had an olive complexion, high cheekbones, and well-defined features. Or at least, they had been before. Now blood was dripping from her nose, her mouth, and a cut above her right eyebrow. Her frightened eyes were half-closed to shield them from the light.

Ancona leaned down and whispered something in her ear.

She turned her head away.

He grabbed her chin roughly and pulled her head back, repeating his whispered threat.

The woman began mumbling a long monologue. Ancona held a small digital recorder to her lips, catching every word. Finally, she fell silent.

With a loud snap of his fingers, Ancona summoned one of the men. The burly agent rose, set down his beer bottle, and came over. His massive muscles seemed slack, like those of an out-of-shape former bodybuilder. His limbs were chunky, his fingers short and square. He undid his zipper, pulled down his pants and boxers, and took hold of his limp cock with an awkward grin. He rubbed it until it was erect, tore open a packet of condoms with his teeth, and sheathed his dick hurriedly, as if he was afraid that the erection wouldn't last. His pants were down around his ankles.

The cellar shook from the woman's bloodcurdling scream.

Ancona walked over to Alex. "They've got more than fifty operatives on surveillance detail all over Europe. She knows about the
Zionist agents who were crossed off the list. The operatives have
been sending the intel they gathered to the Syrian Air office. She
says the basement belongs to the Mukhabarat's Berlin station."

"Where does the Berlin station send the intel?"

"The operation was halted yesterday. She says that seven Syrian trackers reported being blown."

"I asked where they send the intel."

"She doesn't know, Alex."

"Are you positive?"

"I will be in a minute."

Ancona's man was rubbing his cock against her face. Her eyes
were bulging in terror. Tears flowed down her cheeks. Her thighs
were as narrow as a young girl's. A dark wet stain spread over her
legs. Urine dripped to the floor.

Ancona went up to the eager agent and touched his shoulder.
The man moved off with glazed eyes. The woman's face was damp
with tears and blood.

"Where did you send the intel?" Ancona demanded.

She shook her head.

"Do you want to suck his cock?"

She swung her head wildly, terrified.

"I'm not going to ask you again."

"I don't know . . . I swear."

Ancona gestured to the agent, who came closer and used
his thick fingers to pry the prisoner's mouth open. He shoved
his cock in. The woman gagged and he pulled out and retreated.
Coughing, she vomited on herself. Ancona again whispered in
her ear.

She was no longer crying, just shaking her head with a chilling detachment.

Ancona went back to Alex and gazed at him with his huge, sad eyes. He stank of cigarettes, sweat, and alcohol. "She has nothing more to give us."

"Sorry. One last nudge," Alex said.

With a nod, Ancona walked over to the man whose pants were still around his ankles and spoke to him softly. Alex saw the flash of the switchblade in his hand. With quick thrusts, he cut the ropes binding the prisoner's hands and feet.

Once again the cellar shook from the screams of the slender Syrian woman as the man tore off her clothes, threw her down on her stomach on the grimy wooden floor, and climbed on top of her.

"Stop!" Alex shouted.

The agent froze. The expression on his face reminded Alex of a sex doll's.

Ancona looked at him quizzically.

"That's far enough!" Alex ordered.

But the woman was already at the depths of the abyss, muttering, choking, pleading, her legs beating at the floor. She was trembling, her breathing shallow. Ancona put on a callous expression and held the recorder up to her mouth. "Talk."

She shook her head. Ancona landed a slap. She uttered two unintelligible words before white foam spilled from her mouth, along with a wail of despair. She shuddered violently, and then her arms and legs convulsed and her body curled up into a ball, twitching as if an electric current was running through her.

The agent recoiled. He pulled his pants back up and tossed

the condom onto the floor. The red rubber he had shed leaked shame.

"What's wrong with her?" Ancona asked nervously.

"She's having an epileptic seizure. What was the last thing she said," Alex asked stiffly.

"Two words: Mud Man."

The two men went outside. Dawn was about to break. A cold morning wind was blowing, biting at their faces. It was growing lighter. Ancona was silent. His mouth was curled down and there were deep lines around his eyes. He crouched down and spat, then lit a cigarette and inhaled, squinting to avoid the smoke. He spat again, stuck the cigarette between his teeth, and folded his arms over his chest.

They stood there side by side, staring unseeingly into the dark courtyard.

"Too bad about her," Ancona said, drawing deeply on the cigarette. The end glowed orange. He didn't exhale. "Too bad, that's all," he said sadly.

In the distance, a bird called out to the empty sky.

"What are you going to do with her?" Alex asked.

Alex pushed away his untouched breakfast tray. The plane climbed into the gray sky until it was above a floor of pillowy clouds. The light outside grew brighter. They were heading southwest, toward Lyon in France.

The satphone chirped. Alex took a deep breath, gathering up the last crumbs of his patience.

Reuven said, "Orchidea is waiting for you in Crémieu, outside Lyon. She runs the Orchid Farm."

"I shouldn't have left Berlin," Alex said. "The Syrian woman confirmed that they're working with someone called the Mud Man. He must be the one responsible for the deaths of the Nibelungs—Parsifal also told me to look for the Mud Man. Berlin is where it's going down, Reuven. Not on some orchid farm."

"The farm is just a front," Reuven said.

"For what?"

"Orchidea will fill you in."

Alex didn't reply. Everything he said was falling on deaf ears.

"What are you doing about the meeting in Damascus tomorrow?" Reuven asked.

"We'll send our people in."

"Too risky. You need the PM to sign off on it."

The head of Mossad was hiding behind the PM's skirt. "Sign off on it yourself," Alex snapped. "What's so special about the Orchid Farm?"

"The Hothouse."

"Go yourself, Reuven."

There was a pause before Reuven answered with forced civility, "If you gave me a second, I'd have a chance to explain. The Hothouse is the Ring's training facility. It's a very sensitive site."

"What's so urgent about it now?"

"Orchidea will fill you in."

"What does she know?"

"That Justus is dead. That's all."

"Berlin is the key."

"Berlin can wait."

He hung up.

The patch of sky outside the small window was gray.

Butthead called.

"The man who attacked you in Tuscany was Bruno Mauser. He had a twin brother named Sepp. They were assassins for the Stasi until the wall came down. They were known as *die Mauser Zwillinge*, the Mauser twins. It's believed that they were responsible for the deaths of thirty-seven people. Dangerous men."

"The Stasi?" Alex said.

"That's right." Candy wrappers rustled, followed by the sound of biting and vigorous chewing.

"It fits," Alex said. "The Stasi used acid to burn the prints off their assassins."

"There's just one tiny problem," Butthead said.

"What?"

"Their apartment in Berlin burned down in April 1990." Butthead paused before adding, "The Stasi twins were burned alive."

DIARY

3 December 1943

Even if I pierced the commandant's heart with a white-hot knife, the Nazi monster would whelp another devil to take his place.

I am a defeatist. There is no forgiveness.

12 December 1943

My shoes make noise. The Wehrmacht has stolen our entire supply of leather to make occupiers' jackboots. The soles of my shoes are pieces of wood held together by rubber strips. They are clumsy but they provide good insulation against the terrible cold that escapes from the winter earth.

20 December 1943

The SS officers clink glasses lustily. Drunk, they boast of their crimes, releasing bits of precious information. I write everything down in pencil on pieces of the dried parchment paper that Président butter comes wrapped in and give it to my comrades in the Resistance.

21 December 1943

My diary is hidden in the yard. Dear diary, my refuge from a wretched reality.

Jane is close to him, her skin touching his. Her body gives off heat. She is upset, crying and apologizing. He strokes her face. Blood spurts out of her neck, spilling on them both.

Alex awakened from the short nap in a daze. His shirt was stuck to his back. He was alone. He got up, hunched over, and made his way to the cockpit.

"Where are we?" he asked.

The epaulets on the pilot's blue sweater were dotted with dandruff. "Between Karlsruhe and Strasbourg. Twenty-seven minutes out of Lyon."

Alex sank back down in his seat, feeling totally drained.

When the Berlin Wall fell, the Stasi twins set their apartment on fire and disappeared, expunging their murderous past. In the bureaucratic chaos surrounding the reunification of Germany, the unreliability of the new population registry would have made it relatively easy for them to pop up somewhere else under new, untarnished identities.

But the Stasi twins were only the executive branch of the operation. They weren't the brains behind it. Were they taking their orders from the Mud Man?

The satphone chirped, interrupting Alex's train of thought.

It was Exodus.

"We're starting to fill in the blanks about Justus Erlichmann,

Alex. Immediately after the wall fell, he purchased two massive apartment complexes on the eastern side, one on Karl-Marx-Allee and the other on Leipziger Strasse. More than a thousand units altogether. He renovated the buildings and resold them at a huge profit a year and a half ago. We've found cash and assets totaling more than a billion euros, and we're not done yet. He had dozens of bank accounts. We've already located accounts at Deutsche Bank, Crédit Agricole, HSBC Trinkaus, Credit Suisse, and the Royal Bank of Scotland.

"Back in the 1950s, his father, Gunter, purchased works by artists who had not yet made names for themselves. He didn't pay more than a few thousand dollars for any of them. Similar artworks have recently sold at auction for tens of millions. We're talking artists like Jackson Pollock, Mark Rothko, Robert Motherwell, Henry Moore, and Alexander Calder. He also acquired three sculptures by Giacometti. Not long ago, one of the pieces in the *Walking Man* series sold for more than one hundred million dollars. Justus had sold two of the three in his collection. He was liquidating his assets. He had a lot of ready money."

Alex was stunned by the extent of Justus's fortune. "Find out what you can about the neo-Nazi organization he was funding."

Beyond the windows on the left, the majestic peaks of the Swiss Alps soared into the sky. Alex felt pressure in his ears. The plane was making a left turn, swinging around as it began its descent into Lyon's Saint Exupéry Airport.

The sky was like a midwinter black. A heavy rain battered down on the roof of the rental car.

The GPS directed him eastward to the town of Crémieu, thirteen miles from the airport. Alex stopped the car in a puddle at the side of the road and called Orchidea.

Her voice was soft and pleasant, like a cat rubbing up against its owner's leg. She'd meet him at the Café des Touristes in the center of town at nine thirty.

The rain was coming down in buckets. The streets of Crémieu were flooded. A stooped old lady in black tried to escape from the deluge by taking cover against the wall of a building, shielding the baskets she was carrying.

Reuven called.

"The PM refuses to let us send anyone to Damascus. Too dangerous, he says. It's an election year. He doesn't want Israeli hostages in Syria. It would spell the end for him."

"Our people will be there," Alex said.

"Forget it!"

"Why don't you want me in Berlin?"

Reuven hung up.

On the corner of Rue Lieutenant-Colonel Bel, Alex saw a building as orange as a cheap hotdog. The facade was decorated with white line drawings of artisans from the Middle Ages.

Three tipsy old men were sitting near the door, their empty beer mugs pushed to the center of the table. The game of dominoes in front of them had reached a standstill. Each of the men was gazing off in a different direction. Aside from them, the café was empty.

Alex passed his fingers through his wet hair. Where was she?

The middle-aged woman behind the bar smiled and pointed to the coatrack behind him. He sat down at a corner table in the back facing the door and waited.

The espresso tasted of sand. He asked for a glass of water and set his phone and Justus's spare BlackBerry on the table.

The head of one of the elderly men drooped. His chest rose and fell in time with his snores.

Where was she?

Alex leafed through a copy of *L'Équipe* that had already seen a lot of hands that morning. Then the door opened and an unusually tall woman with a stunning figure walked in. She was dressed in skinny jeans and a red Jack Wolfskin coat spotted with rain. Her lips matched the color of the coat, and her hair was as golden as ripe wheat.

When she caught sight of him, her red lips turned up in a charmingly crooked smile. Alex stood up, and she reached out a cold hand and surprised him with the firmness of her handshake. She sat down without a word. Her eyes sparkled like an untamed animal's. They examined each other in silence, the smile never leaving her face.

A television was chattering in the distance. The waitress brought over a mug of café au lait the size of a soup bowl and a small basket of croissants. Orchidea picked up the huge mug with both hands and took a sip of the pale liquid without taking her eyes off Alex.

The image of a fig opening, dripping with juice, floated up before him.

He ordered another double espresso. Orchidea still hadn't spoken. She scrutinized him unashamedly, studying him with her brown eyes. The silence stretched out until talking seemed almost impossible.

She put down her coffee. There was a drop of foam on the tip of her nose.

She wiped it with a finger. "I'm Orchidea."

"So I assumed."

"Croissant?" she offered, pushing the small basket toward him.

He shook his head.

"It's awful about Justus," she said.

Did she know that Justus was a traitor? That he had been funding neo-Nazis? Alex decided to keep his thoughts to himself.

"Did you know him?" she asked.

"I met him."

"He was an extraordinary man," she said sadly.

She was either cunning and dangerous or naive and harmless. He forced himself to nod.

She looked out at the narrow street. A bolt of lightning turned the interior of the café blue, and the picture on the TV screen flickered. Thunder split heaven and earth.

"Were you close to him?" he asked.

"We all were."

She had a strong presence, one of those women who demanded all your attention until you forgot someone was waiting for you at home.

She got up and removed her coat. Her breasts swelled under her black sweater. Making an effort to appear indifferent, he raised his eyes and asked, "Why am I here?"

She sat down again and bit slowly on a croissant. She looked troubled.

"Do you know what's at the Orchid Farm?" she asked.

Alex sat up, and his chair creaked as he leaned toward her. "The Nibelung training facility," he whispered, shoving a piece of croissant into his mouth. She smiled. Then she said, "The Field

Training Unit. We don't do basic training. Nibelungs come here after they've already gotten their pulse down to fifty; after they can empty a whole magazine into a box of cigarettes from fifty feet. This is where they're tortured and deprived of sleep; where rubber bullets are fired at them at close range; where they're shot up with alcohol and have to perform delicate motor tasks when their heart is beating at close to one-ninety a minute; where they learn to make tough decisions under extreme pressure. Every Nibelung comes here once a year for a weeklong refresher course. They lose ten pounds in those seven days. They're taught to withstand prolonged interrogation, humiliation, torture. It all happens in our training facility—the Hothouse."

"But that's not why I'm here," Alex said, taking a sip of his espresso. It was cold.

"Have you heard of the Cube?"

He put his cup down. "No."

"It's a concrete cube, about a third of which is aboveground. The cellar is secured. It holds refrigeration units with orchid seeds. Justus bought the farm eleven years ago. He planned to fund the Hothouse by raising rare orchids."

She allowed herself a small smile.

"Do you really grow orchids?" he asked.

"Only the expensive kind."

"What's expensive?"

"One to five thousand euros."

"For how many?"

She burst out laughing. Her face was radiant. "For one."

"What else is in the refrigerators?"

"Have you ever heard of Hochstadt-Lancet?"

"What's that?" he asked.

"HL2436. It's a lethal virus that was developed at the Israel Institute for Biological Research in Ness Ziona by Professor Severin Hochstadt and Dr. Elimelech Lancet. It destroys the respiratory center in the brain. You breathe it in and then it lies dormant for thirty-six hours before it comes to life and attacks. You're dead within twenty-four hours. The thirty-six-hour delay is meant to give operatives time to make it out of the country after they release it."

"What's the delivery mechanism?"

"A Ventolin inhaler. Do you know anyone with asthma?"

"I get the picture."

"The virus is kept alive in a culture made from chicken kidneys. To arm the inhaler, you have to turn the canister clockwise three times and counterclockwise once. Then you can release the virus."

"Why is it kept here?"

"We're close to the international airport in Lyon and several major highways, the area is quiet and isolated, and the farm is the perfect cover. The locals know that the orchids we grow are worth a lot of money, so they don't think twice about the tight security."

"Is there a vaccine for Hochstadt-Lancet?"

"It's in very short supply. Just three inhalers. They're in the

Cube. You have to take it twenty-four hours before you're exposed to the virus."

She smoothed her hair.

"Are you Jewish?" Alex asked.

Orchidea smiled. "My mother is Jewish. My father ran the original Orchid Farm from the 1950s until Justus bought it. Then he retired. Justus offered me the job. I'm very proficient at propagating orchids from seed and breeding special varieties. Justus helped me hone my skills. He sent me to some of the most prominent orchid growers in the world and to countries where orchids grow wild. It was a long time before he told me about the Ring and the training facility he planned to build here. Before the Hothouse, they conducted the training wherever they could find someplace out of the way. They didn't have a dedicated facility with the proper conditions."

The head of the sleeping old man fell to the table, striking the black domino tiles and knocking them over.

"Where did you do your training?" Alex asked.

"Most of it was at HQ in Glilot. After that, I worked out of the stations in London, Paris, and Brussels for a year. I think I saw you in Paris once."

He didn't think so. He wouldn't forget a woman like her.

"Justus dreamed up things that didn't exist in any other secret agency, not even the American ones, with all their bells and whistles. Thanks to him, we're ahead of our time." Her eyes lit up whenever she mentioned Justus's name.

"Aside from Justus, you're the only one who knows all the Nibelungs personally. You know their real identities," Alex said.

"I don't."

"But they come to the Hothouse every year, right?"

"I've never seen their faces."

Alex leaned back and smile.

"Before they come through the gate, they put on ski masks, and they don't take them off until they leave. The only time they're allowed to remove them is when they're alone in their rooms at night. The masks are Dri-FIT."

"So how do you tell them apart? And how can you be sure that none of them is an impostor?" Alex asked.

"The Nibelungs all have chips implanted in their crotches. All we know is the identity code. Six figures, like a bar code. And the numbers aren't consecutive. When they're on the firing range or doing exercises, they wear a bib on their chest, like athletes."

"You mentioned tight security. What does that mean exactly?"

"They make an excellent flourless chocolate cake here. Would you like something sweet?"

"I never say no to cake."

She gestured to the woman behind the bar.

"Most of the systems are robotic. The only human security is at the gate. If you're less than a hundred yards from the wall, we'll know it. Less than thirty yards without a chip, and the system opens fire. The sights acquire the target and lock on to it."

"Unless you have a chip in . . ."

"Your crotch."

"Exactly. Do you have one?" Alex asked.

She examined his face before nodding.

"What else?" he asked.

The chocolate cake arrived. Alex cut into it with his fork. Butter, cream, rich Belgian chocolate, and a hint of Cointreau. "That's the owner," she whispered. "She does the baking. It's incredible, isn't it?"

"Were you sleeping with Justus?"

"Excuse me?" She blushed right up to the roots of her hair. He kept his eyes fixed on her.

"You have a lot of nerve," she said.

"I found your clothes in his bedroom closet."

She turned her head away. "How do you know they're mine?"

"Skinny jeans, just like the ones you're wearing. You're six feet tall, and you're a beautiful woman."

"It's none of your business."

"Actually, it is. That's why I'm here. Justus is dead. You were having an affair with him. You were close to him."

"It was over. It happened, and then it was over."

"You left your clothes there."

"I left my heart there, too. So what?"

"So now you tell me everything."

"Why? Who are you?"

"The last one who can still save the Nibelungs. Maybe you, too."

She stared out at the storm lashing the abandoned street and took a deep breath. "There's nothing to tell. There was chemistry between us almost from the beginning. I was attracted to him because he was an amazing man. We had some sex, but we both knew it couldn't last."

"Why?"

"It ended four months ago."

"Why?"

"That's enough."

She looked sad. Alex realized that her eyes were puffy. She'd been crying.

"He was old enough to be your father," he said.

"Alex, some people only eat veal. But sometimes there's nothing better than an aged entrecôte from a cow that's already tasted all the herbs in the pasture. You've never fantasized about a twenty-five-year-old?"

Her brown eyes waited expectantly for his answer.

"You mean a girl my daughter's age?"

"I mean sometimes it's the ultimate connection."

"Was Nelli still alive?"

She winced at the insinuation. "I can see that you didn't know him. It started one year and two days after she died. I thought eventually we'd go back to being good friends, but we didn't get the chance. Justus's clock stopped. For me, he'll always be what he was until the day before yesterday: an unsolved riddle. Are you married?"

"My wife died."

It was the first time he'd ever uttered the phrase. His lips felt numb.

She stopped chewing. "You're not kidding?"

"No. And yesterday my best friend disappeared."

"A Nibelung?"

"London."

"I knew her."

"I thought you weren't supposed to know who they were."

"I met her through Justus."

"How did that happen?"

"It happened. What's your connection to her?"

"She was a good friend."

Unabashedly, she appraised his face, hands, and body.

"How old are you?"

Alex smiled.

Her face took on a distant expression. "You don't trust me?"

"Not at all."

She gave him a bitter smile. "As soon as Justus was killed, Reuven took over the Nibelung Ring. He called and told me you were coming to check on the cellar, the inhalers, and the security system."

"Fourteen Nibelungs have been killed, not counting Justus."

Her face clouded over. "What?"

He nodded slowly.

She shook her head. "How? They're the best-trained operatives."

"We took a bad hit. Do you have any idea what went wrong?"

"No."

"You were close to Justus, and you were very familiar with the Ring," he pressed.

Leaning in, she whispered, "An orchid seed can lie in the dark on the ground in a rainforest in Borneo for years, and nothing happens. And then one day, for some reason that has nothing to do with the seed, a tree falls nearby and lets a single ray of light through the canopy, and it lands on the seed. The seed opens up, and an incredibly beautiful orchid emerges. It's called the butterfly effect. Chaos."

Bullshit.

"Justus couldn't have children," she went on. "He wanted me to have a family. He said that not having kids was terrible. That's why he dumped me, even though he still loved me." Her eyes were moist. "Let it go, Alex. It hurts to talk about it. But believe me, it was over."

The BlackBerry pinged. Alex glanced at the screen.

"What's wrong?" she asked.

"Florence. He was on the list of the dead Nibelungs."

The color drained from her face.

"What happened to him?"

"He was just removed from the list."

"What does this mean? Where is he?" Alex sputtered.

She grabbed the BlackBerry from his hand and stared at the screen. Her eyes opened wide.

"He's at the gate of the Orchid Farm!"

She jumped up and he followed reluctantly, tired of the constant surprises. He ran after her into the angry storm. His dainty café companion had suddenly turned into a wild animal. Water sprayed from the wheels of her Land Cruiser. She was holding her cellphone to her ear. After a few seconds she muttered, "The guards at the gate aren't answering!"

His body tensed.

Emerging from the narrow streets of the town, she veered onto the Route de Siccieu. The road ran between two heavily forested hills. She sped up, and his body sank deeper into the passenger seat. The windshield wipers couldn't keep up with the pouring rain.

"Press on the bottom of your door," she said.

A lid opened, revealing a secret compartment that contained a Sig Sauer and three full magazines. Alex slid in a magazine and cocked the gun, sending a bullet into the chamber.

Château de Saint-Julien cast its shadow over Étang de Ry. Orchidea turned sharply to the south with screeching tires, almost overturning the SUV, and sped along the shore of the small lake, whose surface was riddled with the barrage of rain. They raced through a deep puddle, raising high walls of water on each side. Alex's knuckles were white as he held on to the door handle. The carcasses of dead frogs floated in the puddles at the sides of the road.

At the edge of the lake she turned left and drove for a quarter of a mile through the trees, then made a sharp right onto an unmarked dirt road that rose steeply up a hill through thick forest. The Land Cruiser shook and heaved as if it wanted to spit them out, but she took the turns with precision despite her speed.

The BlackBerry pinged.

"What's up?" she asked.

Alex looked at the screen. "Florence is back on the list of the dead Nibelungs!"

Biting her lip, she sped up even more. Her breasts rose and fell against her shirt as the SUV jolted wildly. He nearly bit his tongue. She made it past a rough tree trunk by mere inches. Light began to appear through the pine trees, reflecting off the surface of the puddles.

At the end of the road was a clearing and a ten-foot-high concrete perimeter wall. Through the open gate he could see low structures that looked like greenhouses.

Orchidea braked at the entrance and jumped out, holding a gun at her side. Alex ran toward the concrete guard post. Its upper section was made of thick bulletproof glass. He moved up close in a crouch, the air crackling with tension and filled with the smell of iron.

There was a look of terror in Orchidea's eyes.

The guard was on the floor, leaning against a wall. There was a hole in the middle of his forehead. Fresh blood flowed down his face. The wall behind him was smeared with blood and gray brain matter. An H&K submachine gun was beside him. She felt his neck.

"Joseph . . ." she whispered, shaking her head.

The second guard was seated in an office chair in front of two dark flat-screens. He was bleeding from a wound in his right cheek. His lifeless eyes stared.

She checked the computer under the desk.

"They took the hard drive!"

"Take me to the Cube!" Alex ordered.

She grabbed the submachine gun next to the dead guard.

"Hurry up!" Alex barked.

"What's this?" She froze, taking care not to step on something on the floor.

The chocolate cake he'd eaten earlier threatened to rise up again.

Two shiny white spheres, smaller than Ping-Pong balls, lay in front of the door.

"Florence's eyes," Alex said. "That's why it looked like he'd come back to life."

"They used them to get in," she said, her face white. "They cut the chip out of him and gouged out his eyes. Fucking animals!"

A portable iris scanner lay beside the eyeballs. The lens was smashed.

Pulling herself together, Orchidea took off at a run. "This way!"

Alex matched her long, rapid stride. Large, brilliantly lit greenhouses filled with orchids lined the path.

A figure was lying on the ground.

A man.

Two bleeding holes gaped in the center of his forehead. He

lay in a small pool of blood turned pink from the rain. She felt his neck.

"Who is it?" Alex asked, panting.

"Bernard. The fitness trainer. He's dead," she said with a grim expression.

"Let's go!"

She stopped in front of a glass greenhouse about twenty-five feet square. Inside was an artificial rainforest. At the door was an iris scanner, a small control panel, and a screen that glowed pale blue. The rain pummeling the roof was deafening.

She struggled to catch her breath as she tried the door. "This is the Cube. It looks like we're in luck. They didn't manage to break in."

She held her eye up to the scanner. It beeped. With a tight stomach, Alex surveyed the ground in front of the door.

Nothing there.

She tapped in a long code. A muted buzzer sounded. As she leaned her weight on the door, Alex passed his eye along the path, then followed her in.

It wasn't a greenhouse, and there weren't any orchids. It was a concrete cube a few feet smaller than the outer glass walls. Dozens of tiny projectors screened images of a rainforest onto the glass.

Set into the rough concrete wall was a stainless-steel double door. Orchidea tapped in a code. An elevator rose.

Tensing, Alex aimed his gun at the center of the elevator doors, whose shiny surface reflected their distorted images. The bulbs overhead threw broken light on Orchidea's face.

"Thank God the Cube hasn't been breached," she muttered to herself.

The doors opened. The elevator was empty. They descended to the cellar; the Fort Knox of the orchid world.

Standing close to her, he got a whiff of an unusual mysterious perfume on her neck.

The elevator came to a stop. First out was the Sig Sauer, followed by Alex and Orchidea.

Harsh neon lighting illuminated a space that hummed with the chilly sound of compressors. Six long white refrigeration units, measuring about six feet by four feet, occupied the smooth concrete floor. The heavy lids were made of reinforced glass.

Orchidea went to one of the units. Inside were tall piles of petri dishes. Lined up beside them, as if on parade, were hundreds of glass jars with green seedlings.

She lifted the lid and let out a shriek.

"The inhalers are gone!"

Alex hurried over. The refrigerator was filled to the top, save for one empty rectangular space the size of a laptop. How was that possible? They'd seen no sign of a break-in.

"Where's the vaccine?" he asked.

"They took everything!"

"Can you tell whether the thief released the virus here?"

Her face grew somber. "No."

"Who has access?"

"The inhalers were in a reinforced case."

"Orchidea, who has access?"

"Besides me?"

"Yes!"

"Justus and Reuven."

"Does the scanner keep a record of everyone who enters?"

"Just the last three people to enter."

"Let's go upstairs."

He grabbed her hand. The elevator was confining. Alex suddenly imagined a carnivorous plant that attracted its prey with an intoxicating perfume.

They went outside into the relentless rain. Orchidea worked the control panel. A line of text appeared on the screen.

Ice ran through his veins. He read it over and over. On the blue background, the black letters read:

11:31 Justus Erlichmann. Duration: 02:13 minutes.

"You said it recorded the last three entries. Who was here before him?"

She pressed a button.

There was no end to the surprises.

She cringed.

"What were you doing in the cellar sixteen minutes before you met me at the café?" Alex asked.

"What?"

"You were late, Orchidea. I checked my watch. What were you doing in the cellar?"

"I just wanted to make sure everything was okay."

"You mean you didn't *know* that everything was okay?"

"The case was where it was supposed to be. I opened it. It was all there: six inhalers with the virus, and three with the vaccine."

"All three of you use the same code?"

"No. Each iris has to be matched with its own code. Keying in the wrong number twice locks the Cube for fifty minutes."

"So if someone was using Justus's eyeball, he also needed Justus's code?"

There was a look of repulsion on her face. She nodded.

"If it was Justus himself, why would he pretend to be Florence to get into the farm?" she asked.

"If Justus were alive, he'd have used his own code at the gate and then come for the inhalers," Alex said.

Her eyes darted wildly.

"Do the guards know that Justus is dead?" he asked.

"Of course. They all know."

"So he couldn't use his own identity to get in without alerting security. He put on a ski mask, came in as Florence, and then used his real identity to enter the Cube. And he didn't leave any witnesses. He took out everyone who saw his face, grabbed the case, and ran."

"Do you really believe that?"

"Do any other roads lead to the farm?"

"No."

"Any other ways to get out?"

"No."

"We didn't pass any cars on the way in. Whoever broke in could only have gotten away on an off-road motorcycle or a quad."

"Or a helicopter," she said.

"We would have heard it."

Leaving her there, he ran through the drenching rain to the open grass in the center of the farm. Behind a large greenhouse he found a man sprawled on the ground, a gunshot wound in his neck. His ski mask was torn apart and his face was slashed.

Alex entered the greenhouse. At the far end was a black projection screen, about twenty feet wide, that was dotted with a random array of tiny holes. A ball machine stood in front of it, surrounded by dozens of lime-colored tennis balls.

A petite woman was lying on the floor in a pool of blood, a gun just out of reach of her hand. Her face was hidden by a black ski mask, revealing only a pair of lifeless eyes staring up at him.

"The Estonian Nibelung, Tallinn," he heard behind him.

He spun around, ready to fire.

Orchidea froze.

"There's nothing here," he said, heading for the door. He ran back across the farm and past the guard post, and exited through the gate. The fresh tire tracks made by the Land Cruiser were clearly visible. But he was looking for something else. She caught up to him, her hair dripping and her eyes blazing with fury.

Beyond the gate he found a single track, about six inches wide. "We have to catch him!" he shouted.

They ran to the SUV. "I'll drive," Orchidea said.

Raising a screen of mud, they sped through the gate onto the perimeter road and followed the deep track. At the corner of the front wall, Orchidea slammed on the brakes, throwing Alex forward. She continued in the wake of the fresh tire track as it wound its way down the hill. Branches struck the side mirrors of the Land Cruiser on the narrow path. She stopped short inches in front of a tree trunk, reversed, and edged the SUV around it. The forest grew increasingly dense the farther in they went. When she opened her window to get a better view, a sharp branch hit her shoulder. Orchidea rode the Land Cruiser like a wild horse.

"Stop!"

"What's wrong?"

"Stop!"

She put the car in neutral. The diesel engine growled. Through the rain beating down on the trees, they heard the rumbling of a motorcycle.

"I know where it's coming from!" she said.

Skidding through the mud, the SUV rubbed up against one tree after another, periodically rising in the air and landing heavily. Alex grunted as Orchidea navigated the sea of trees. Suddenly, something streaked through the thick forest like a flash of lightning. Alex aimed and fired off three quick rounds. The third hit a nearby trunk, sending chips of bark flying in their direction.

"I saw him," she cried, turning sharply in an effort to avoid a large, crooked tree. The bumper crushed against it, but she didn't slow down until the road became totally impassable. She hit the brake and punched the steering wheel over and over, swearing ferociously. Finally, she stared out at the dark forest, panting heavily.

She shook her head in frustration. "We were so close . . ."

"Where can he go from here?"

"Anywhere."

The tree trunks closed in on them like iron bars. Inside the SUV, the smell of gunpowder hung in the air. Everything was crystal clear, cold, and unforgiving. They returned to the Orchid Farm. It reminded Alex of an empty operating room after an unsuccessful surgery: the dead patient hastily covered by a sheet and the remains of the procedure left behind on the floor—used syringes, bloody gauze, discarded gloves.

He reported the break-in and the theft of the inhalers to Reuven.

"It looks like the work of Justus," he concluded. He didn't need to be present in the chief's office to know that the next sounds he heard were a bottle being opened, whiskey being poured, and a long swallow.

"Are you still there?" Alex asked.

A glass hit something hard and shattered. Reuven Hetz didn't utter a word before hanging up.

Sammy Zengot, on the other hand, was eager to help. He promised to send a team from Brussels right away to keep watch over the compromised Orchid Farm.

"What's there?" Zengot asked.

"Nothing anymore," Alex answered before hanging up.

Orchidea stopped the SUV just inside the gate. She turned off the windshield wipers, and the window was immediately covered by a sheet of water.

"Am I a suspect?" she asked.

"What does that matter now?"

A streak of lightning lit up the interior of the car, revealing the hopeless expression on her face. She examined her fingernails and glanced at the dashboard before saying with a trembling chin, "I'll do anything to get the inhalers back. Anything."

Alex nodded. In his mind, the pieces were already falling into place.

Reuven called.

"What do we know?" Evidently he was buzzed.

Alex opened the door and went out into the rain, moving away from the SUV. "A few minutes before Orchidea left the farm to meet me, she went down to the cellar of the Cube. She claims she just wanted to make sure everything was all right."

"Are you positive it was Justus?"

"Someone got into the Cube by holding Justus's eye up to the scanner and keying in a code that only he knew."

A long swallow.

"Don't hang up, Reuven."

Reuven grumbled and then exhaled loudly. "I have an urgent meeting with the PM. He's going to want to hear that we're looking under every rock in Europe to get the inhalers back. What should I tell him?"

Alex didn't have a chance to answer before Reuven continued his rant. "The Hochstadt-Lancet virus cannot fall into enemy hands!" he shouted. "We don't have vaccines for the whole population. It'd take months, maybe even years, to make enough. Hundreds of thousands of Israelis could die. Maybe a million, or more."

"It's no good running around like a chicken without a head just to impress the PM," Alex said.

He heard the loud thud of Reuven's palm striking his desk. Ignoring it, he went on. "Europe has a million train stations, airports, and roads. We don't have the manpower to cover them all. Or the time."

"So what do you suggest?" Reuven said.

"I don't think the virus is going to be sold on the open market. In my opinion, whoever took it is planning to save it for a rainy day. We have to employ the same tactic Zvi Malkin used to catch Adolf Eichmann. Instead of trying to track him down, we set traps for him in the places he's likely to go. It'll save manpower and reduce the risk of exposure. We have to find out who the Syrians are working with. Then we'll know where to apply pressure to prevent the release of the virus."

"So what do I tell the PM?" Reuven made no effort to conceal his desperation.

"The truth. The inhalers were stolen by the Syrians and their German partner. We're vulnerable. We have to make the Syrians understand that if they use the virus against us, we'll destroy them."

"Through diplomatic channels?" Reuven interjected.

"We don't have time for that."

"So how?"

"We show the Syrians we mean business. Action, not talk."

Reuven let out a sigh. "Are you okay, Alex?"

Alex didn't fall into the trap. The chief's question didn't come from a sudden attack of good manners or concern. He was simply embarrassed.

"Put the tactical squad on alert," Alex said. "We have to leave our options open."

"What else?"

"We need someone in Damascus tomorrow."

"I already told you, the PM won't allow it."

"To hell with the PM. He doesn't have to know. He's replaceable, just like you and me. The country isn't."

"He'll have my balls."

Alex hung up.

Dripping wet, he returned to the Land Cruiser. The rain drummed its fingers on the roof.

"Whoever broke into the farm needed Nibelung eyes," Orchidea said. "He wanted us to think he was targeting the Nibelungs, but he was really after the virus. Killing the Nibelungs was just the first stage, the foreplay."

"Makes sense. But if that's what Justus wanted, he'd have had no trouble getting into the farm, going down to the cellar, and taking whatever he liked. He owns the place. Who would have known?" he said.

"Sooner or later I'd have found out, but it wasn't Justus," Orchidea said. "He wasn't like that."

She went to the café every morning. Somebody could have been watching, waiting for her to leave the farm. He'd know exactly how much time he had.

"There's something you ought to know," Alex said quietly.

It seemed that her thoughts were already racing ahead. She blinked and caught her bottom lip between her teeth. "What?"

"Justus donated large sums of money to a neo-Nazi organization in Germany."

"That's ridiculous!"

"Almost six million euros. He did it for years."

"I don't want to hear it."

"You're blinded."

"Really?"

"By love."

Her face turned bright red. "You know nothing."

"I'm sorry if I offended you," Alex said, breaking the silence in the car.

Orchidea stopped the Land Cruiser on the gravel path that ran down the middle of the farm and looked him straight in the eye. "You did," she said.

"I need answers. I leaned on you too hard. It's been a hard couple of days."

"I understand, but Justus is gone. I don't know what Justus you met, but the man I knew wasn't capable of such horrible things," she said, fighting back tears.

"Maybe."

"Not maybe. Absolutely."

"Isn't it possible you put your trust in the wrong man, that Justus is behind everything that's been going on?"

"Why? What would he gain from it?"

Alex didn't answer. She took her foot off the brake, and the SUV edged forward along the path.

"I've given the best years of my life to the Ring and the Hothouse and the Orchid Farm. Then catastrophe strikes and you show up out of nowhere and you're suspicious of me and you make accusations against Justus. And you won't even let me in on what you're thinking. You're a brute."

Her face twisted in a grimace as she swerved to avoid a body sprawled on the path.

"You went into the Cube just before you came to meet me. You were late. Then you ordered chocolate cake to draw our meeting out. It's the perfect alibi. At that very moment, someone was breaking into the farm and knew exactly what to do and where to go. So, yes, Orchidea, it definitely looks suspicious."

Her face grew grim.

Alex's phone vibrated and the screen lit up.

Outside the SUV, the fucking rain wasn't letting up. His clothes were drenched. A sudden gust of wind sent a chill through him. He felt like he was in a car wash. What he wanted most of all was to snuggle under a thick blanket in a warm bed.

Behind him, the door of the SUV opened and closed. Alex felt a hand on his shoulder and swiveled around. Orchidea motioned for him to follow her.

"What's up?" he asked.

She led him to a windowless concrete building with a re-inforced door and keyed in a code on a tiny panel. A buzzer sounded softly.

She pushed the door open and smiled. "It's dry inside. I'll wait out here."

The door closed behind him. He was standing in a small ante-chamber in front of a second door. He pushed it open. The space was dark and humid, and the air was thick with intoxicating fruity fragrances, reminding him of the perfume floor in a classy depart-ment store. Life buzzed around him. Something flitted across his cheek, humming faintly like a power line. Insects swarmed around him, and glowworms twinkled in the dark.

"I'm in the prime minister's office, Alex," Reuven announced. "You're on speaker."

This was his moment. He had nothing more to lose. "Tomorrow morning in Damascus. The head of the Mukhabarat is meeting the man the Syrians are collaborating with. They call him the Israelite. He's responsible for the assault on the Ring and the theft of the virus. We have to be there."

"Alex, I expected you to be more responsible," Reuven scolded. "Forget your personal interest in Damascus. That's not what matters now."

"The answers are there."

"Bullshit!" Reuven cut in.

"If we have people in place, we'll be able to find out where the virus is and what happened to the Nibelungs."

"No, we won't!" Reuven barked. "You only want to go because of Jane."

"Who's Jane?" the prime minister asked.

"Jane Thompson," Reuven said quickly, "the London Nibelung. She disappeared in Barcelona last night."

Alex paced impatiently back and forth on the dark walkway. A light mist sprayed down on him from above. A buzzing insect passed too close to his ear, making him shiver. He was standing in water.

"What's your connection to Jane Thompson?" the prime minister asked Alex.

"She's his lover," Reuven said before Alex could answer. "That's not a good enough reason to risk the lives of our people on a fool's errand in Damascus."

"Is he right?" the prime minister asked.

"She isn't my lover, she's a good friend. And, yes, among other things, I'd like to find out what happened to her, but it's more important to find the guilty parties, make them pay, and recover the virus. The Syrians are involved, but they're not the ones getting their hands dirty. The Nibelungs have covered for us on hundreds of operations; they're our own flesh and blood. At the very least, Israel owes it to them to make an effort."

Standing in dripping clothes, Alex felt the full weight of the fatigue that had been building for months.

"Okay, Reuven," the prime minister said firmly. "I think we've found the man with the proper motivation."

"Pardon me?" Reuven said.

"Alex, as of this moment and until you hear otherwise, I'm putting you in charge of the Nibelung Ring. But on one condition—you don't go to Damascus."

"Mr. Prime Minister," Reuven objected, "that goes against the Nibelung charter!"

"Sending Alex Bartal to deal with the crisis instead of going yourself also goes against the charter. And as you said, Reuven—I alone have authority over the Ring."

Alex heard Reuven step back and state for protocol, "Mr. Prime Minister, I consider this a dangerous and unjustified decision."

The dog could go on barking, but Alex now had the authority to issue orders to the Nibelungs without needing anyone else's approval.

With a sense of foreboding, Alex stepped out of the darkness of the rainforest and covered his eyes. He climbed into the SUV. It was cold in the car, cold and wet, and Orchidea looked despairing. Morosely, she said, "The farm was broken into, the virus is gone, Justus is dead, the Ring has been crushed—it's all over."

With a hopeless shrug of her shoulders, she added, "What am I supposed to do tomorrow morning?"

It was time to take a gamble. "You're going to Damascus."

"Tomorrow morning?"

"Tonight."

"What—"

"You said you'd do anything."

"Damascus?"

If she was part of the conspiracy, he wasn't telling her anything new.

"There's a meeting in Damascus tomorrow between the head of the Syrian Mukhabarat and whoever they're collaborating with, the man behind the attacks on the Nibelungs and probably the theft of the virus as well. When we find out who he is, we'll have our answers."

"Will it be dangerous?"

"You'll be risking your life."

Orchidea lowered her eyes. Her eyelids were translucent. "How much of a life do I have anymore?"

Her words hung in the damp air. The rain drummed on the roof.

"We have to do something with the bodies," Alex said.

"Lance can put them in an empty refrigerator in the Cube. When I get back from Damascus, we'll take care of them."

How could she be so sure she'd make it back safely?

"You're coming with me, aren't you?"

"Where?"

"To Damascus."

He shook his head.

"It's my birthday tomorrow," she said.

"Would you rather not go?"

"It's just kind of weird celebrating my birthday in Damascus."

"What's that place I was in before?" Alex asked.

"The paphs greenhouse."

"Sorry?"

"Paphiopedilum. It's a genus of orchid that produces some of the most amazing varieties in the world." The light was back in her eyes. "Like the ghost orchid. It can sell for more than fifteen hundred euros."

"Who pays that kind of money for a flower?" Alex asked, thumbing through the list of contacts on his phone.

Orchidea smiled.

He wondered how she would function under threat on enemy soil.

"What are you doing right now?" Alex asked into the phone.

"Waiting for you to call," Paris answered with a chuckle.

Alex told him about the break-in at the Orchid Farm.

"Can you go to Damascus?"

"When?"

"Tonight."

"Alone?"

"With Orchidea."

"From the Hothouse?"

"That's right."

"You're out of your mind. She doesn't have any field experience."

"You do. Are you in?"

"What do I have to do?"

"Tomorrow morning, ten o'clock local time, the head of the Mukhabarat, Omar Hattab, is meeting with the man behind the assault on the Ring. We want to know the man's identity. Take pictures, try to get ears on the conversation. Then stay on his tail until you find out who he is. He might be armed, and he's dangerous. They call him the Israelite."

"He's Israeli?"

"God knows. Take a flight to Brussels and go see the head of our station there, Sammy Zengot. He'll tell you what to do and fit you out with the gear you'll need. I'll call him right away."

"I told you we'd screw the motherfuckers in the end. I'm happy to do the honors," Paris said.

The call was disconnected.

"You mentioned somebody named Lance," Alex said. "Can he stay here until the security guards from Brussels arrive?"

"He went to the supermarket in Genas. He should be back by now. He's the only one left."

"Except for you."

"What are you trying to say?"

"That if you want, I'll drive you to the airport."

She gave him a long, piercing look. She was a worthy woman.

"I need a few minutes to get organized and pack. Come on—in the meantime you can see where I live," she said, opening the door of the Land Cruiser.

Alex heard his internal brakes squealing.

"I'll wait here."

"How did we wind up in this ugly mess?" the prime minister asked, getting up and pacing the floor.

"Sir, if you so wish, I will tender my resignation immediately," Reuven said, pausing before he added, "but, of course, then the media will start rooting around in *your* backyard."

"I'll try to keep that in mind, Reuven. But let's focus on the real problem. What can we do right now to get the virus back?"

Reuven scratched his head and brushed his shoulder. Then he kept silent.

"Are you saying there's nothing we can do?" the prime minister protested, straightening his tie.

Reuven felt as if the ceiling were descending on him. "We don't have the thousands of operatives it would take to search all over Europe for the stolen inhalers. And they could already be on another continent."

"Pretend for a moment that you are prime minister, Reuven," the PM said with a cynical smile. "Just pretend." He paused to let the words sink in. "And you're responsible for the Nibelung Ring and the Hochstadt-Lancet virus. What would you do?"

Reuven was a cunning rat and a master of devious tricks. He wasn't tempted by the smell of the cheese in the trap.

"I understand," the PM said.

Muffled voices came from beyond the thick door. A telephone rang.

"With all due respect, Mr. Prime Minister, if I understand correctly, you're telling me that you are authorizing the insertion of our agents into Damascus?"

The prime minister licked his pale lips. "Yes." Then he added, "Why? Do you have some objection?"

"No, sir. I trust your judgment implicitly. It's your decision to make."

"Exactly."

"And at your behest, Alex Bartal is now in charge of what's left of the Nibelung Ring?"

"Yes, Reuven," the prime minister said, dismissing him coldly.

Later, in the backseat of the Volvo taking him back to his office, Reuven turned off the tiny recorder he had concealed in the pocket of his suit jacket.

"Had Justus seemed unusually tense lately?" Alex asked her on the way to Saint Exupéry Airport.

"Maybe a little. But once it was over between us, he kept his distance."

"How long has it been since he ended it?"

"Two months and six days."

The rain was finally letting up. The truck in front of them sprayed mud onto their windshield.

Alex switched on the radio and searched for a station that was playing soothing music. All he found was cacophony and the shrill voices of announcers on speed. He turned the radio off.

In the ensuing silence, she said, "I told you. He wanted me to have a family." She bit her lip. "Aphids destroyed more than half of the greenhouse. I didn't catch it in time. We had to burn orchids worth almost four hundred thousand euros. Justus was furious. The farm isn't insured. He didn't say anything, but he couldn't forgive me. Five days later, he broke it off."

In the rental car parking at the airport she said, "Maybe we'll meet again, at a better time." Reaching out a cold hand, she stroked his face, then leaned in and hugged him, her eyes gazing into his. Taken by surprise, he froze, confused by the quiver of lust that ran through his body. Her breath smelled fresh. She was so young. He wanted to bury his head between her breasts.

"Thank you for giving me the chance to make things right. I won't forget it," she said, giving him a quick kiss on the lips.

Alex's heart pounded. Orchidea released her embrace, got out, and walked away, disappearing into the sea of cars.

He sat there for a long time without moving.

Standing in front of the flight departures board, he couldn't remember where he was supposed to be going.

There was no reason to rush off anywhere, no place he had to be, no one waiting for him.

The Grunewald house was empty. There were no direct flights to Berlin, and the next flight to Zurich left in four hours. He bought a one-way ticket and at a bookstand found a detective novel with a lurid cover. Leaving the crowds behind, he took a seat in a quiet corner of the terminal. He looked around him. He was alone. He called Sammy Zengot in Brussels. They discussed the details of Paris and Orchidea's mission in Damascus.

"What's their cover?" Alex asked.

"False identities similar to their real ones. The trip is a surprise for her birthday. They leave tonight. Where will you be?"

"Damascus is dangerous, Sammy. It could be her last birthday. Buy her something."

Sammy chuckled. "We'll look after her."

Alex hung up.

He searched his mind for Jane, but the cells that stored her memory had clouded over. Orchidea intensified the sense of loss. He opened the book he'd bought, but after no more than half a page he realized that the words weren't sinking in.

His phone vibrated.

Parsifal!

The German said in his deep voice, "I've decided to tell you about the Mud Man."

"Does he have a name?"

"No."

"Is he connected to the Israelite?"

"Both terms come from Christian Identity doctrine. I don't know who he is, but I can tell you that the Mud Man is a sociopath."

"Have you penetrated his organization?"

"We sent in two undercover agents," Parsifal said.

"What did they find out?"

"They disappeared. We never found the bodies."

"How did you learn about him?"

"I interviewed him. They wanted my opinion as a psychiatrist. There was a black screen between us. I never saw him, and they never showed me his file or picture. Nothing."

"What did they want to know about him?"

"Whether he was reliable. Whether he could be trusted."

"And what was your conclusion?"

"That even the opposite of what he said was a lie."

"Give me something I can use to find him."

"Be careful with the Mud Man, Alex. At the age of eight he was sent to a reform school in Nuremberg. One night they found him wandering around the dormitory, totally naked. All he had on was an armband he'd made from toilet paper. It had a swastika on it."

As the plane made its way from Zurich to Berlin through a dark sky, Alex's body tingled. At last, Mossad was silently reaching out its long tentacles to squeeze the life out of the demon.

Below, lights flickered in the distance.

Germany, the black box; the eye of the storm; the axis of torsion. Its dark past pulled at him, undermined his foundations. At times he felt that if he could only look the evil in the eye, he would be healed.

Germany had cleaned itself off and moved on. But he was still caught in the web of his fixations, held back by his insistence on delving into its crimes, like a creditor who refused to forgive a debt.

The plane touched down.

Grunewald was covered in ice. Behind the bars, the windows of the house were dark. He got the Glock from the doghouse, where he had stored it, and slid a round into the chamber. It was snowing lightly.

The drawn gun made its way into the silent space, where the smell of thyme and grilled meat hung in the air.

A chilly welcome: the heating wasn't on. He tried everything he could think of, but it didn't do any good. Then he checked the fuse box. Everything was in working order. Dammit, there must be a fault in the heating system.

He checked the ghostly house room by room, stunned again by the works of art.

The living room was dimly lit by the outside lights. The thin legs of the *Walking Man* cast a long shadow.

An empty house is a dangerous house.

Zengot called from Brussels.

"They're taking a Turkish Airlines flight at 23:30. It lands in Damascus at 1:30."

"What are their chances of making it out of there alive, Sammy?"

"We did what we could in no time. Their cover is too thin."

Alex banged his open hand on the glass wall. His fingers burned.

Paris was a street cat. Even if you threw him off the roof of a nine-story building, he'd land on his feet. Orchidea wouldn't. The thought of her made Alex regret his decision. He'd taken advantage of her weakness.

Even a good night's sleep wouldn't cure his fatigue. But his body was on fire, his muscles ached, and the madness would start in the morning. The bedrooms weren't safe. He'd be too exposed.

The deep cupboard in the pantry smelled of onion and garlic, but it was a good place to hide from the nasty cold. The bottom shelf was empty. It was about five feet long and two and a half feet wide. He folded his body into it, covering himself with his jacket and a woolen blanket he found in a closet. Exhausted, he sank into a troubled sleep.

About half the women were wearing hijabs. Some had their faces veiled. The men were all dressed in cheap suits. The cabin of the 737 reeked of pungent body odor. Paris seemed to be the only man without a mustache.

The lights of the hostile city twinkled like bait on a hook.

Zengot's deep voice still echoed in her ears, raising the horror of underground torture chambers and dungeons in infamous Adra Prison to the north of Damascus.

The line at passport control didn't move. The air stank of cigarette smoke. The portrait of President Bashar al-Assad looked down from every wall, as was only proper for a dictator under threat.

At the last minute she found an empty stall in the ladies' room. A hole in the floor. She vomited up her meager dinner.

The Nissan Primera they rented had seen better days, about sixty thousand miles ago. Paris was driving. Antiquated yellow cabs raced along the brightly lit road, and dozens of minarets pierced the night sky.

They cut around Damascus from the east, passing the poor tin shacks of the Jaramana refugee camp, where a stray dog was rummaging through an overturned trash pail. The wind carried the smell of burning garbage.

Damascus receded behind them until its lights vanished, and they entered the moonscape of the M1. The countryside was silent and desolate. On their left were the Anti-Lebanon Mountains. Yellow lights flickered in distant towns.

Paris was shorter than she was and not very attractive, but he was solid and well-built, with narrow hips and a broad chest. He wasn't arrogant or patronizing or full of himself.

But he was hiding something.

He smiled at her.

Orchidea tried to smile back, but her face was frozen. And she was dying of thirst.

The road rose slowly to a barren, rocky plain. The Anti-Lebanon Mountains still towered over them imposingly on the left.

Paris glanced at the dashboard. "Seven and a half miles to Al-Qutayfah. The turnoff is just past it."

The asphalt illuminated by their headlights was swallowed beneath them.

Finally the lights of Maaloula, situated on a steep hillside in the Qalamoun Mountains, flickered above them. The houses clinging to the scarred land looked as if they had been built one atop the other. They entered the town, its empty streets dimly lit by weak streetlamps. Pistachio trees grew everywhere. A tired mule raised its head and gazed at them indifferently as they passed.

The crosses and domes of ancient churches appeared around every corner. Religious murals adorned the front walls of the houses. Zengot had told them that some of the locals spoke modern Aramaic, the language of Christ.

"The house is on the outskirts of Maaloula, about half a mile after the last building on this street," Paris whispered. "Look for a stone house that has arched windows with bars on them."

An icon on a tiny church showed the Virgin cradling Jesus, a baby with a golden halo. Paris sped up, turned into a narrow alley, and switched off the engine. He checked the mirrors. After a few minutes he reversed, turned around, and drove into the black night with the lights off, going so slowly that Orchidea barely felt the car moving. He kept a close watch on the numbers on the odometer.

Orchidea opened the window, letting in the sounds of insects buzzing and whistling and crickets chirping. The calm was seductive—and deceptive.

The Nissan wheezed, its springs creaking on the dirt road. A row of pistachio trees on the right was heavy with green clusters of unripe fruit.

A red cross with the word *Doctor* below was painted on a white tin sign on a low stone fence. The word was written in English, French, Arabic, and some unfamiliar language, maybe Aramaic.

Paris stopped the car and turned off the engine. The radiator fan continued to roar for a few seconds before switching off. Somewhere, a dog barked. After that, there was silence. They got out of the car. It was cold on the mountain.

Orchidea knocked on the door. The metal was icy.

Lights came on in the house. The silhouette of a man with a huge potbelly moved past the big windows, a bolt slid aside, and the heavy double door opened. Light flowed out onto the path. The potbellied man filled the doorway, throwing a large shadow on the front yard.

Breathing heavily, Dr. Petrus Abu Luka held out a small, clammy hand and moved aside to allow them entry. He smelled of cigarettes. In his fifties, with one leg shorter than the other, he walked with a pronounced limp. He was dressed in a white *jellabiya* sheer enough to afford a clear view of his underwear.

They crossed the modest living room and entered the doctor's office, with its distinct medicinal odor. The walls were painted a pale blue, and the meager furniture consisted solely of a desk, three chairs, a gray tin cabinet, and a narrow, battered examination table. On the wall was a clock with a tapestry face, an embroidered inscription in Aramaic, and a diploma from Damascus University.

Begging their pardon, Dr. Abu Luka left the room. They looked around themselves and then at each other. The sound of the doctor's limping walk echoed through the high-ceilinged living room. Their host returned carrying a hammered copper tray with three small cups of coffee.

He then locked the door and closed the shutters. He gave them a meaningful look and rolled his eyes toward the ceiling before taking out of the cabinet a cardboard box with the Bayer logo.

They heard a noise above them. The doctor froze.

Orchidea stared at the locked door.

"Passports," the doctor whispered abruptly.

They handed him their passports. He paged through them, looking for the secret mark. Finally, the worry lines vanished from his brow. Dr. Abu Luka's face glowed with perspiration. He removed the contents of the cardboard box and arranged them on the desk like a display of spoils of war.

After transferring the items into a gray nylon carryall, the doctor got to his feet. They followed him to the door. As they were leaving, he patted Paris on the shoulder, his round face dripping with sweat, and handed Orchidea a small white box.

"What's this?" she asked.

"Freshly baked *kanafeh*. My wife made it this evening."

He sent them on their way.

DIARY

23 March 1944

The deputy commandant has good eyes. Resolve shines from them. Tonight, it cracked.

2 April 1944

The deputy commandant said that Germany would regain its honor through occupation and force, but not by extermination of the Jews. Not for that did I join the army of the Reich, he said.

Are his eyes truly good, or is he laying a trap for me?

3 May 1944

My children are still small, and Jasmin and I are young. We have our whole lives.

I hope the German is not luring me into a trap.

17 May 1944

He knew that I was Resistance. He knew that I'd know how to take him to the Catacombs. He knew that we are Jews and that our papers were forged.

So why didn't you turn me in, I asked.

Because you suit me.

18 May 1944

He signaled me with his eyes to follow him to the toilet. My body grew terribly cold and my heart was pounding. He stood at a urinal and urinated.

I remained at a distance.

He gestured for me to approach.

I was embarrassed.

I have decided to desert, he whispered.

20 MAY 1944

The monster could pursue you for the rest of your life. Are you prepared? the deputy commandant asked me tonight.

I nodded unhesitatingly. He is likely to do that, he added. The commandant will never forgive you, and he will hunt you down until one of you dies.

I nodded again.

Finally, I saw a spark of hope in his eyes.

21 MAY 1944

The deputy commandant said that the commandant had worked with a man named Adolf Eichmann. He is in charge of the extermination of millions.

Millions of what? I asked.

Jews, millions of Jews.

He must have been exaggerating. Perhaps he'd been drinking.

Every sound sent a chill down Orchidea's spine. Every approaching vehicle made her seize up.

Jabal Qasioun overlooks Damascus from the north. Muslims believe that it is the place where Cain killed Abel. Red lights flickered on the peak. The face of Assad was plastered everywhere, screaming: *Don't forget who controls you; don't forget who controls Syria.*

They entered Damascus through Al-Sades min Tishreen. Since 1973, everything has been called Tishreen: Tishreen Park, the *Tishreen* newspaper, Tishreen Street. *Tishreen* means October, and October 1973 marked the first victory over the Zionists after a long line of humiliations.

Paris turned onto Al-Tawara Road. They passed through three tunnels that crossed the northern sectors of the city and turned west onto Al-Ittihad Road. It was the middle of the night, but the Sunni capital with its thousands of mosques was buzzing with life.

The fronds of the short palm trees on Shukri Al Quatli Street flapped in the wind. The street runs alongside the Barada River, which flows through Damascus, held in check by concrete embankments.

Le Méridien Hotel has always been a favorite of the Syrian government. Some say that the government actually owns the hotel. Not long ago, the name was changed to Dedeman.

They took their trolley bags with them, leaving the black duffel bag they got in Brussels and the gray carryall they got from Dr. Abu Luka in the trunk of the car.

They were greeted by a doughy reception clerk who was barely awake. Paris handed him their French EU passports. The man's ears were as hairy as a squirrel's. The portrait of Hafez al-Assad peered out from between the pages of one of the passports, gracing a thousand-Syrian-pound note.

The ceiling of the lobby was supported by marble-faced columns in alternating vertical stripes the colors of maple syrup and tahini. Their room on the seventh floor, designated the Royal Club, had a pale parquet floor and peach walls. The balcony afforded a view of Jabal Qasioun.

"Do you want to wash up?" Orchidea asked.

"You go first."

Both of them noted the single king-size bed.

The hot water was soothing. She hadn't thought to get her pajamas out of her suitcase, and now she would have to come out in her underwear. She looked at herself in the mirror. Her breasts moved under the thin white T-shirt. Treacherous nipples.

She opened the bathroom door. Paris was sitting on the bed in his underpants. He rose, grabbed his toiletry kit, and walked past her, taking care not to brush against her. His body was even more solid and muscular than she had imagined.

Paris whistled in the shower. Orchidea smiled as she looked through the glass door of the balcony at the prestigious Abu Rumaneh district. The dark triangle of Zenobia Park stood out clearly. Beyond it were the houses of the Al-Muhajireen sector, clinging to the slopes of Jabal Qasioun.

Paris came out of the bathroom, lay down on the bed on his

side, and turned off the light. It was dark in the room. He'd used the tiny bottle of soap provided by the hotel, and he smelled like an apple orchard in full bloom.

Hostile Damascus was right outside. It had all happened too fast. Justus was killed, the Orchid Farm was broken into, the inhalers were stolen, her staff was murdered. Orchidea wrapped herself in her solitude, sinking into a bout of birthday blues.

Paris was still awake, his breathing steady. She was too restless to sleep, and anyway, morning was only a couple of hours away. Everything seemed so hopeless.

"Hold me," she said.

DIARY

22 MAY 1944

He handed me the red card with the golden eagle insignia on it—his Nazi Party membership card—his laissez-passer, his entry permit to the Drancy camp, and his Obergruppenführer certificate. He gave me his officer's bars and put his life in my hands. And all he said was, Take me to them.

23 MAY 1944

The pharmacist on the Rue de Buci took us to the back room, where the salves were prepared. There, he opened a concealed door in the floor, and the deputy commandant and I went down a steep flight of stairs. The air in the sewage tunnels was dank. We entered the labyrinth of the Catacombs.

The comrades undressed him and checked his blood type, which was tattooed on his underarm. I handed over his papers. Gaston took a revolver and removed all but one bullet. Only then did he give the gun to the deputy commandant and say, Follow me. He took him by the arm and led him to the young SS officer our comrades had captured the night before near the Madeleine. Shoot him, he said, and then he touched my arm and we went to an adjoining room.

The prisoner had been gagged with a sock, but his gaping eyes were uncovered. The deputy commandant sobbed. There was a stench of sewage, and the air was soaked with sorrow.

The deputy commandant wept out loud.

Then there was silence.

A shot thundered.

An irritating hum was coming from Alex's hand, waking him from a sound sleep. When he tried to turn over, he banged his elbow on the wall, sending a shooting pain through his arm. Attempting to sit up, he hit his head on the ceiling. The cold air smelled of onions.

It took him a moment to remember where he was: in the pantry cupboard. His phone was vibrating, lighting up the cramped space.

It was Exodus. Unconsciously he clenched his stomach, as if he were expecting a kick.

"Justus Erlichmann made a single deposit in the account of a company called Dopo Domani Holdings," she said. "It's registered in the British Virgin Islands. We can't find any reason for it, or any records."

"How much?"

"One million, two hundred thousand euros."

"When?"

"Seventeen days ago."

"Maybe it's one of his donations to the neo-Nazi organization?"

"No way. Those were made regularly, through fixed channels. Are you all right?"

"Why?"

"You sound weird."

"I'm in a closet."

Muttering to herself, Exodus hung up.

It was almost seven, and he was wide awake. He pushed the sliding door aside. His body was stiff from fatigue and cold. He rolled off the shelf and stood up. He stretched, vowing never to sleep in a cupboard again.

Dopo Domani Holdings, €1,200,000. What was Justus up to this time?

Alex heard a soft thud somewhere nearby. He tensed and raised his Glock, swiveling around to survey the darkness.

Something was moving inside the house!

Holding his breath, he began scanning the rooms, adrenaline racing through his veins, tingling and spurring him on.

The sun wasn't up yet, and the house was lit only by the nighttime lights that filtered in from outside. He inched along the library wall in the living room but didn't see anything. As he climbed the stairs to the second floor, he heard a click and turned around sharply.

No one was there.

Alex reached the upstairs landing. Nelli's study lay in silence, and the guest room opposite was equally quiet. In Justus's work-room at the end of the hall, the disgusting swastika still adorned the tail of the Messerschmitt, but the room was empty. He entered the large master bedroom, his finger tightening on the trigger of the silenced gun. The wide bed was empty.

All that remained was the cellar.

Alex went down two flights and stopped in front of the wine cellar. A dim, warm light shone on shelves upon shelves of expensive bottles.

Maybe an animal, some forest creature, had penetrated into the house? The kitchen and the living room were silent.

He sat down on the soft gray sofa in the living room to wait for sunrise, but he soon nodded off again. He awoke from a nightmare and could still hear himself groaning. The sky was as heavy as graphite. Exodus was calling again, and he was grateful to her for pulling him up out of the depths of his nightmares.

"There's something strange, Alex. Are you awake?"

"Absolutely."

"Erlichmann was a billionaire and a lawyer, and he was involved in dangerous activities."

"What's strange about that?"

"We haven't found his will."

Justus's will might shed light on his dark side.

But you don't hide a will in a secret drawer. Ancona and his voles had already searched the house and hadn't found it.

The house was empty. The damned heating didn't work, and the cold was painful. Alex needed time to think. He left the house and was surprised to hear birds chirping outside. It was pleasant and comforting.

In a café near the Grunewald S-Bahn station he ordered espresso and a vanilla cream croissant. It was still early, not quite light out, and few people were up and about. He wondered if he wasn't taking too much of a risk showing his face like this, but he needed a break from the oppressive mood in Justus's house. He had to find a clue that would lead him to the German's will.

In the corner was an Aryan lady in her seventies who, by the look of things, had this morning put her makeup on twice. She was leafing through a newspaper. On the floor beside her was a young Doberman. The lights in the café were reflected in its black fur.

A stocky German with silvery stubble was wolfing down a pink sausage. A young blond girl with thin black eyebrows came in and looked Alex over. It was too early for smiles. Alex bit into his croissant. The girl carried her cup over to the counter. His hand slipped automatically to the gun under his jacket. She sat down on a barstool next to him, tilting her head back slightly so that her nose was in the air. The imprint of a wrinkled blanket was etched on her cheek.

She was holding a huge set of keys, like a prison guard's.

Keys.

A key.

The key!

Alex sped back to the house and rushed into Justus's study. The safe was locked. He called Ancona, waking him up. "Give me the code to the safe in the Erlichmann house," he said.

"I must have the code written down somewhere. Give me a few minutes."

"Ancona."

"What?"

"Now."

Alex heard distant grumbling, followed by slipper-clad feet shuffling along the floor, papers being ruffled, and tuneless whistling.

Ancona gave him the code. "Don't hang up," Alex said.

The dial turned, clicking quietly, and the safe door swung open. The key was still hanging from the BMW fob. He examined it under the desk lamp. At the top was the mark B-776.

"I'm sending you a photo of a key. Your expert said it belongs to a bank vault. Tell him to find out what bank it's from."

He hung up.

Alex went outside and studied Henry Moore's reclining woman. The lights on the lawn flattered her ponderous bronze curves. Snow had collected on her large breasts and small head. It was quiet on the Erlichmann lawn. The sun was coming up, and the cold was becoming bearable.

Orchidea was celebrating her birthday in Damascus with unreadable Paris. And Alex was on his own. But he was still alive. Jane wasn't. He touched the bronze woman. She was as cold as the moon.

The trees of the forest were reflected on the glass wall. A pair of wild geese with long necks crossed the sky above him.

Ancona called.

"Berghoff Bank. B-776 is a secure basement vault for sculptures and large paintings like the ones in the living room. The bank has only one branch, on the Ku'damm near the Kaiser Wilhelm Memorial Church. It's open from ten in the morning to one in the afternoon, and again from four to seven in the evening. You need two keys to open a vault—the customer's and the bank's master key—and they're familiar with every one of their customers. If you're thinking about getting into Justus's vault, forget it. The bank hasn't had a break-in since it was founded in 1882."

A large icy drop of water fell on Alex's neck from the linden tree he was standing under. He shivered.

He went back into the living room to try to devise a strategy to get through Berghoff Bank's security.

He had a long day ahead of him.

DIARY

25 May 1944

The commandant was here this evening. He ate and drank, and his eyes blazed. The Gestapo is investigating the disappearance of the deputy commandant and conducting surprise searches. My heart shudders now. For in the end, the truck will stop in front of the café. The Wehrmacht soldiers will climb down, and their hobnailed jackboots will desecrate the old black-and-white-checkered marble floor. They will smash the furniture and rip out the brass railings that were the work of an artist. The only things they won't be able to shatter are the windows, because they have already been shattered by bullets and the shockwaves from the bombings. Hateful wooden boards hide the light of day, impose darkness.

When will the sun return and warm the floor of the café?

27 May 1944

A dozen Wehrmacht flamethrowers washed the innards of the Catacombs with hellfire. Someone betrayed us. Some comrades suffocated; others burned.

7 June 1944

Despite the fierce resistance of the Wehrmacht, Allied forces have succeeded in establishing an iron grip on the Normandy coast. It is a long way to our capital, but Paris will be liberated. Paris must be liberated.

His dark face looked as if it had been drawn in pencil and then brutally erased. His neck and left hand were disfigured, as well. In place of his right arm was a rigid, old-fashioned prosthesis that didn't move. The man had been burned from head to toe.

Omar Hattab, the head of the Syrian Mukhabarat, was just under six foot two. He was wearing a dark gray suit and a blue tie that was wound around his long neck like a noose.

He was flanked by two armed bodyguards who seemed more wired than necessary. A third bodyguard was waiting in a black Mercedes S600 parked illegally.

"That's him," Paris whispered under his fake mustache. He had a kaffiyeh on his head, held in place with a black *agal*.

Orchidea's heart was fluttering. She was dressed in the loose slacks and blouse worn by Syrian Sunni women, her head covered by a hijab. Less than thirty yards separated them from Hattab and his bodyguards.

Last evening in Brussels, they had studied up-to-date pictures of the triangular park and memorized possible escape routes. Zengot had crammed an enormous amount of information into their heads in a short time.

The sun shone through the palms and pine trees that cast long shadows on the neglected public park. The locals called it Subchi Park, after the street that ran along its western leg. The paths were paved in white stone, and the lawns were bordered by a row of small yellow wrought-iron arches that had been painted over innumerable times.

It was cold out. They'd left the hotel looking like a pair of tourists and changed on the way. A tiny camera in the frames of Orchidea's plain sunglasses enlarged the picture it captured and projected it like a translucent overlay onto the inner surface of the dark lenses.

The lenses were now covered by the figure of Omar Hattab, with trees swaying in the background.

Orchidea's hand was on a small remote in her pocket. She pressed the button again and again.

Strapped to Paris's chest under his cheap gray jacket was a thin dish antenna with a narrow range that would enable him to listen in on Hattab's conversation. The sounds it picked up were transmitted to the white earbuds hidden beneath his kaffiyeh.

Everyone was waiting. Orchidea felt a nervous twitch in her stomach.

Five young men were sitting on the sandy grass, dressed in cheap knockoffs of Western designer jeans. They were laughing at something.

Subchi Park bustled with activity.

Omar Hattab glanced at his watch. His bodyguards looked like a pair of hand grenades with their pins removed.

Five after ten. Orchidea felt as if she could actually hear the buzz of time passing.

Between Paris and Orchidea and Hattab was a sinuous pond with a lifeless fountain in the middle. The water was a stagnant green. Casually dressed Damascenes were relaxing on the park benches.

They were the only foreigners.

Nearby, a woman in a hijab pushed her daughter on a swing planted in the sand. The young girl's fingernails were painted red.

Hattab looked at his watch again.

Orchidea and Paris strolled casually around the pond.

The dog showed up first.

It was scrawny, and there were bald patches in its mangy fur. It touched its pale nose to the edge of General Omar Hattab's highly polished shoes and sniffed at his pant leg.

A figure approached Hattab, moving slowly.

Orchidea muttered, "That can't be him . . ."

Small, quick steps. A gaunt, stooped body. His eyes were hidden by large sunglasses and a cap. His pale skin hung from his face like a drape, but the square jaw under his thinning gray mustache was firm. His hands were encased in leather gloves, and he was carrying an empty plastic bag. He stopped directly in front of Omar Hattab and, as if he were performing a military ritual, straightened his back, bent with age, to the best of his ability.

The much taller Hattab looked down on him with a forced smile.

The old man held out his right hand.

Hattab's distorted face scowled. He clenched his lips. After a long pause, the old man nodded to himself as if recalling a joke, and then theatrically offered Hattab his left hand.

Hattab recoiled. The old man seemed amused.

"At least it's not Justus." She released a sigh of relief.

"Justus is dead," Paris said.

"He must be from around here," she said. "He couldn't walk far."

Paris nodded.

"He was over by the swings before," she said.

Paris nodded again.

The mangy dog stuck close to his master's feet. They began pacing slowly along the path around the pond. Paris kept his chest pointed in their direction.

Veiled women were pushing strollers. An infant howled, buses drove by, and car horns blared. Traffic was heavy on Abdul Aziz Street.

"It won't work," Paris muttered. "Too much noise. I can't hear anything."

"What are we going to do?" she asked. "We made it this far, and now . . ."

"We've already lost three critical minutes," he grumbled. A large fly was buzzing around him. He chased it away with his hand, but the stubborn insect returned and settled on his nose. The Frenchman rolled his eyes.

"Give me a second," she said. Hiding behind him, she thrust her hand under her blouse and pulled from her bra a small plastic pouch that Zengot had given her. It held three black dots, each the size of a pinhead. She peeled one off and stuck it to the tip of her finger, and then started toward Hattab and his companions.

The old dog had grown tired and was lagging behind his master.

Orchidea went over to the dog, crouched down with a smile, and stretched her hand out to pet it. Growling, the animal bared its teeth and retreated. A bodyguard rushed to plant himself between her and Hattab, his hand reaching for the gun under his polyester suit jacket. He mumbled something.

The old man turned around, clenching his jaw.

Orchidea slowly held out an open palm, making her intentions clear. The old man's face grew softer. Nodding, he smiled, momentarily revealing a nearly gumless jaw.

Swallowing, she tried to stroke the dog. It growled and barked in the wrong direction, reluctant to come any closer. Finally, it gave in to temptation and moved toward her hesitantly, lowering its head, sniffing her hand, and licking at the air. She petted its head and then rose with a smile.

Hattab threw her a suspicious look. The old man smiled back at her, and the entourage resumed its walk along the path.

On the grass nearby, a group of boys was kicking around a tattered ball, shouting at one another. Orchidea looked behind her. Paris was petting a wide-jawed mastiff with its tongue hanging out. He gestured for her to come back and threw a stick in the direction of the men. The mastiff took off at a run.

The old man's dog yelped in fright. Its master turned around and picked it up quickly. With a growl, the mastiff leaped into the air. A bodyguard grabbed the collar of the attacking animal, who clamped its teeth down on his hand. Swearing, the man struggled to free it. Suddenly there was a loud whistle and the bloodthirsty dog froze, lay down on the ground, and lowered its head submissively.

The bodyguard's hand was bleeding. Hattab offered him a tissue. The group moved on, the old man still clutching his dog in his arms.

Paris was grinning. Orchidea could smell his sweat, and she found the odor oddly appealing.

"Is it working?" she asked.

"Perfectly!" he whispered.

There was no longer any need for the ungainly antenna strapped to his chest. The tiny microphone was transmitting the conversation between Hattab and the old man directly into Paris's ears.

"I don't know a word of Arabic," he said.

It was all being recorded. Later it would be translated into Hebrew at Mossad HQ in Glilot.

"The old man has a foreign accent," he said.

"Israeli?" Orchidea asked.

"Don't know."

"Hattab despises him."

"How do you know?"

"Look at Hattab's feet. They're pointing outward. He keeps trying to put distance between them, but the old man just moves closer."

Orchidea pressed up against Paris, took an earbud from his ear, and stuck it in her own.

The old man had started speaking English. His accent was pronounced. Maybe he was trying to emphasize his foreignness.

"Stop to lick me with compliments. Stage One is over. It is history. It achieve its purpose," he said sharply to Hattab. English obviously wasn't his mother tongue.

"And you have been paid in full," Hattab cut in.

"You were supposed to transfer ninety-six million euros for Stage Two yesterday. I check just before I come. The account is still empty. I thought you are serious."

"I do not have the authority to approve such a large sum," Hattab apologized.

"So talk to someone who has."

"It will take time. He has a country to run."

"We do not have time. You don't understand?! We do not have time!" the old man sputtered, his jaw trembling.

"Give me one more day."

The man snorted contemptuously. "One more day? I take Max for walk so he can do his business. I be back in five minutes." He grinned, exposing his bare jaw. It was a chilling sight. "When we be back, I want to hear the transfer go through."

Spittle gleamed in the corners of the old man's mouth.

"That is not possible," Hattab said angrily, looking like a raging guard dog that had leaped into the air only to discover that the chain around its neck was shorter than it had thought.

The old man gave him a patronizing look. He took a step back, held up five gloved fingers, and said firmly, "Five minutes, Omar!"

The spittle spraying from his lips glittered in the harsh sunlight.

The old man turned his back on the head of the Mukhabarat and walked away. The dog straggled along beside him, bumping into its master's feet and sniffing its way.

Hattab was already on the phone. Repressing his resentment, he clenched his teeth, barked orders excitedly, nodded, and disconnected. Then he loosened his blue tie.

A few minutes later, the old man returned and stuck his smile into Hattab's disfigured face. Hattab nodded, not hiding his disgust.

The old man pulled out a telephone.

Hattab marveled.

"I am old, not stupid," the man said, his lips turning up in a cold smirk under his graying mustache. He brought the phone up to his eyes until it was touching his sunglasses, punched in a number, and turned his back to Hattab. He spoke into the phone and then turned around again, nodding vigorously. Returning the phone to his pocket, he reached out his right hand.

Hattab used his left hand to raise the prosthetic right one. Without flinching, the old man shook it and then twisted it sharply.

Hattab grimaced in pain and said indignantly, "Look at the ground you are standing on. It is Syrian soil. You are a guest here, a guest who has overstayed his welcome. Very soon, you are liable to discover that even our famed hospitality has its limits."

The old man's jaw trembled. Muttering something to himself, he looked piercingly at Hattab's long neck. Then he let out another snort of contempt and hissed, "Omar, you should show respect for person who save you from the gallows."

Hattab turned around and walked off, his bodyguards close behind. They were swallowed up by the black Mercedes and disappeared down Abdul Aziz Street with squealing tires.

"If the old man isn't Syrian, where is he from?" Orchidea asked.

"No clue," Paris lied.

The old man exited Subchi Park onto Hafez Ibrahim Street, carrying his blind dog in his arms. Paris and Orchidea followed him to the Sha'alan Street bazaar, in the heart of the prestigious Abu Rumaneh district.

A young beggar in rags rattled a tin can. His corneas were cloudy.

The old man entered a shop with canaries in cages out front. The delicate chirping of the birds mingled with the melancholy trills of the Arabic music issuing at full volume from a nearby shop. Violins wailed, and a singer keened and moaned.

A dark, modern bus pulled up. Light-skinned tourists poured out into the bazaar, chattering in Dutch.

Paris took advantage of the wait to send the recording and photos they'd collected to the Brussels station via the satphone.

"How is the old man connected to the murder of the Nibelungs?" Orchidea asked in a low voice.

"It's weird, right?"

The old man left the pet shop and walked in their direction. Paris threw his arm around Orchidea's shoulder and pulled her into a shop selling pirated CDs.

The man walked past them, returned to Subchi Park, and settled himself on a cracked bench with rusty screws, sending a flight of pigeons into the air. The dog lay listlessly at his feet. He drew from his jacket pocket a fist-sized bundle wrapped in newspaper. The headlines were in Latin letters. Unwrapping the bundle, he took a pinch of birdseed and threw it on the ground in front of him. The pigeons alit one by one, grousing and jockeying for space. The feeble dog didn't even bother to bark.

The park was crowded with local residents. A young boy came up and stamped his foot. The pigeons flew off in alarm, flapping their wings noisily.

Orchidea watched them fly away and perch on a nearby power line.

When she looked back down at the bench, it was empty. Her heart skipped a beat.

A few tense seconds later, she caught sight of the old man's shuffling stride in the crowd. They hurried after him. He crossed the park and turned right onto Hadad Street.

The old man walked with surprising agility. At the corner of busy Abdul Aziz Street, he stopped at a red light. The traffic was crawling and jittery. Horns honked in deafening frustration, and curses were spat through open windows. A man on a bicycle wound his way among the cars, a square wooden tray filled with pita bread balanced on his head.

Paris didn't speak. From time to time he touched her arm protectively.

The light changed. The old man continued down Hadad Street and stopped at a solid black iron gate in front of a yellow apartment building. From the top of the fence, a security camera peered down.

A buzzer sounded and the gate opened. The old man disappeared inside.

"He lives here," she whispered. "The guard recognized him."

Paris nodded. There was a troubled look on his face.

"What's the matter?"

"Nothing."

"Liar," she said, adding a smile.

He looked at her in silence and led her into a cool stairwell across the street. Without warning, he came closer and kissed her on the lips.

"Wait here. I'll get the car," he said, his lips still glistening.

Before leaving, he fixed his eyes on the yellow building and then looked back at her.

Suffused with a delightful warmth, she smiled at the retreating figure. From within the darkness of the stairwell, she kept her eyes on the iron gate across the street.

Time passed slowly.

DIARY

12 June 1944

A truck pulled up in front of the café. The barbarian invaders bayoneted the precious sacks of flour, emptied the wooden cases of dough, and toppled the proofing cabinet. The starter dough, the apple of my late father's eye, lay contaminated on the floor.

Evil paid a visit here today. Evil will return. When the avenues of investigation of the circumstances surrounding the deputy commandant's disappearance become blocked, it will return bayoneted and savaged.

10 July 1944

The ground is burning. I tried to persuade Jasmine. Once again, I pleaded with her to listen to me. In the end, the commandant will come. It will all come to an end, and my prayers will be of no use. I am crying now, and I did not cry when my father died or when my mother was taken.

12 July 1944

Jasmine is begging for help. Tonight the commandant drank until he was intoxicated, called her over, put his arms around her waist, and demanded that she caress him. She looked at me with gaping eyes. I averted my gaze and stared down at the floor. He touched the intimate parts of her body, and I was weak and contemptible and helpless. She fled to the kitchen in tears, and the commandant's eyes *flickered with the aroused look of a street dog smelling a bitch in heat.*

I embraced her as tightly as I could. We both cried.

14 JULY 1944

I avoid my elongated image reflected in the side of the espresso machine.

15 JULY 1944

Tonight, at long last, I participated in a Resistance operation. We stopped a train heading east and saved 803 Jews. An entire transport!

16 JULY 1944

Jasmine has agreed to escape with the children, but only if I come with them. I cannot desert the battle. Not now. Not when the deputy commandant is on our side and we are rescuing full trains from death. I pleaded with her to escape with the children.

She wept and wept.

In the end, she refused.

"Where were you?" she asked his shadow in the entrance to the stairwell.

"Were you worried about me?"

She nodded.

"It's a long time since anyone was worried about me.

"I'm coming out," she said.

Paris nodded.

She stepped out of the cool stairwell into the hot blinding sun and crossed the street to the iron gate in front of 7 Hadad Street. The worn head of a metal bell button gleamed in the bright light. There was no name beneath it. Orchidea continued down the street and crossed back to the cool stairwell. With Paris there, she felt safe.

"There's too much light and too much traffic. We'll have to wait," he said.

"It could be hours."

We can't stay here. Everyone knows everyone around here."

"What do you suggest?"

Paris smiled. "Wait here."

He left and came back a short while later carrying two yellow bags with Arab lettering she couldn't read. "This one's yours," he said.

Paris put a bra on over his shirt and filled the large cups with rolled-up socks. Then they both pulled on over their clothes musty black abayas that smelled of onions. They hid their faces behind black burkas. Paris looked like a Muslim woman, his face covered and only his eyes and thin eyebrows showing. She smiled, thrust her hand into her backpack, and felt around for the flat shoes she had packed. Her fingers encountered the gun and silencer. The feel of the cold steel gave her confidence. Paris hid his square hands inside black gloves.

"Check your phone and see how you say 'for sale' in Arabic," he said.

"Why?"

"I'll be right back," he said, his burka fluttering as he spoke.

Google Translate gave her what she was looking for. The Arabic letters looked like a family of earthworms pulled from rotting soil.

Paris returned. "Find it?"

Orchidea showed him the screen. He nodded. "Let's go."

"Where?"

"I found us an apartment," announced the French street cat.

They left the stairwell together, walking side by side. Two houses down, a tin sign was hanging from a balcony railing. Orchidea recognized the word.

"Here," he whispered under his veil. "Third floor."

They entered the building and climbed the stairs. She prayed that no neighbor would come out and speak to them in Arabic.

Paris raised the skirt of his abaya and took a red Swiss Army knife from the pocket of his jeans. He stuck the midsize blade into the lock and followed it with a thin pair of tweezers, and moved them around gently.

The light came on in the stairwell. Footsteps on the stairs.

Paris twisted the blade, and the lock finally admitted defeat.

They hurried inside, closing the door behind them. Paris stuck his eye up to the peephole.

The apartment was empty. Dust and the sweetish smell of a dead animal hung in the air. Orchidea fought back a sneeze.

On the painted floor in the entrance hall sat an old telephone. The line was disconnected. The kitchen cabinets were bare. Dust bunnies rolled around on the floor where the refrigerator should be. They found the source of the stink: the half-gnawed carcass of a dead rat. Flies buzzed around it. They closed the kitchen door, blocking off the odor.

When they turned the faucet in the bathroom they heard distant rumblings, but no water came out.

The old wooden shutters were painted green. The slats were pointed downward, affording a view of the street. Perfect.

Somebody was blanching chicken necks in boiling water. The smell was nauseating.

"What happens if someone shows up?" she asked softly.

"We kill him," Paris replied.

The hours passed, and their time in the hideout, their safe time, slowly ran down. Sooner or later someone would come. In the end, the illusion of safety would be shattered.

Orchidea stood quietly by the window, listening to the sound of her breathing against the green shutters. Her eyes were glued to the street.

All of a sudden she was startled by the sound of a frog croaking. Turning around, she was blinded by a red glare. She averted her eyes.

Paris was holding a bright green plastic frog. He pressed a button and the frog opened its mouth, a red light came on, and the toy croaked. There was a huge grin on his face.

"You can't fit candles into *kanafeh* or baklava," he said. "Happy birthday."

Orchidea touched his cheek, and his face glowed. She passed her fingers through his hair. "He's lovely, your frog." A surge of passion inside her threatened to erupt.

They fell silent, absorbed in their thoughts.

"Get some sleep," Paris said. He was holding his burka in his hand. His eyes were pinned on the spaces between the slats. Stripes of light ran across his face.

In the kitchen she found an old newspaper, brought it into the living room, and spread it out on the dusty floor. She sat down on it, her back against the wall, and gazed at the broad back of the dark figure who filled her with a sense of peace. A peace she'd never known.

She fell asleep instantly.

In the basement, Alex found a stiff aluminum case designed to carry small works of art. A steel handcuff was welded to the handle.

Just before four, he cuffed the case to his wrist, put the Glock back in its hiding place in the doghouse, and left. The bracing walk to the Grunewald S-Bahn station warmed his body.

The sign over the decaying platform read GLEIS 17, giving no hint of its use in Berlin's dark past. It was from here that fifty thousand of Berlin's Jews had been transported to extermination camps.

Alex took S-Bahn 7 in the direction of Wartenberg. During the ride, the German passengers remained silent, stern-faced, and distant. A few stole a glance at the aluminum case cuffed to his wrist.

Their fathers and grandfathers had built the dens of evil on Prinz-Albrecht-Strasse: the headquarters of the Gestapo, the SD, and the SS. Members of their families had shot Jews in the head at close range.

He had no intention of forgiving or forgetting. As far as he was concerned, they would wear their ancestors' shame on their foreheads for the rest of time.

An elderly accordion player boarded the train at Savignyplatz, sporting a bowler hat and a weary smile. He started playing a begrudgingly cheerful melody. An old couple moved away to the end of the car.

Alex tightened his grip on the case. Nobody held out a single coin, and the air went out of the accordion and it fell silent. The voice of the conductor came over the loudspeaker: "Nächste Station, Zoologischer Garten." He added in his guttural German, "Ausstieg: links."

Outside the busy station, it was a rare sunny afternoon; the weather had drawn crowds to the stores on the Kurfürstendamm. Mounds of dirty snow lined the curbs.

But Alex wasn't here to shop. He found the building easily. On the green marble facade was a polished copper sign with black letters reading:

BERGHOFF BANK
SEIT 1882

The guards at the entrance were dressed in black uniforms and armed with H&K submachine guns. They had a cold, distant look in their eyes. Inside, facing the door, were three well-preserved antique oak counters.

A scrawny, somber clerk escorted Alex to the manager's office, his sharp nose leading the way. Wood paneling ran halfway up the walls, and thick carpet absorbed the sound of their footsteps.

The manager had a shrewd smile on his face, although he seemed to be mistakenly wearing a silver-coated pet terrier on his head. He immediately began sniffing and licking, complimenting the new prospective client and playing with a large square gold ring on his finger. He asked to be called Herr Berghoff and requested Alex's passport.

Herr Berghoff examined the fake Italian passport, paging through it and wrinkling his brow before looking back up at Alex. "May I inquire as to the gentleman's occupation?"

"I'm a winemaker in the Chianti Classico region."

Nodding, Berghoff said, "If you wish to open an account with us, you must deposit fifty thousand euros, yes?"

Alex drew from a brown paper bag five packets of bills neatly held together with rubber bands.

The cash on the desk seemed to cause the German discomfort.

"Do you understand where you are, sir?" Berghoff huffed condescendingly.

"I've brought a valuable artwork I wish to leave with you. Is your basement vault room secure?"

Berghoff seemed amused. He studied his manicured nails and said, "Herr Visconti, Berghoff Bank has been through the worst possible times, and it is still standing. No one has ever succeeded in breaking into our vaults, not even in November 1943, when countless tons of bombs fell on this street. The Allies—as you are Italian, I can speak freely—the Allied bastards showed no mercy to the area of the zoo and the Ku'damm. The same horrific bombs that destroyed the Kaiser Wilhelm Memorial Church landed on the zoo, sending wild animals out onto the Ku'damm. They also turned this building into rubble. And what happened to the vaults?"

He looked expectantly at Alex like a pedagogue waiting for a slow pupil to answer his question. Alex nodded, impatient for the entertainment part of the program to be over.

But Berghoff wasn't finished. "A concrete beam fell on the door of the vault room. First the Americans and then the Soviets tried to blow the door open, but they could not get inside. They used hundreds of pounds of explosives, but it did not work."

Herr Berghoff brought the tip of a finger to his pink tongue and then reached out and trapped an errant speck of dust on the gleaming cherry wood desk separating the two men.

Nodding gravely, Alex said, "In this country, a distinguished history is a rare commodity."

"Tell me about Florence and the wine business," the German said, leaning back in his black leather chair.

"Florence is paradise. I would be happy to invite you to dinner and offer you a taste of some fine wines. Are you planning a trip to Italy in the near future?"

The German smiled, picked up the phone, and spoke into it quietly. Alex wondered whether he had even heard his invitation. The door opened and a clerk in a conservative gray suit entered, then reached out to shake Alex's hand.

"My name is Adolf," the man said with a smile, revealing horse teeth.

They made a fine pair, these two: Berghoff with a terrier on his head and Adolf with a horse's mouth.

Adolf glanced at the pile of cash as if the money had come from trafficking in children. "Would you like to follow me to the vault?"

Alex stood up and shook Berghoff's hand. "Do you happen to have a free vault with the number seven in it? It's my lucky number," he said.

Berghoff typed something into his computer with circumspection.

"Seven seven seven?"

"Perfect!"

"That is most interesting," Berghoff said. "The number is of significance in the Jewish kabbalah, yes?"

"Is it?" Alex asked quizzically. "What's the kabbalah?"

"The vaults that begin with the number seven are the largest ones," Berghoff said, resuming his pedagogical tone. "They measure thirteen feet by two and a half feet. You appear to have brought a miniature."

"I plan on bringing more pieces, including a life-size bronze sculpture."

"In that case, Adolf will show you the way, yes?"

"Your belt, too," Adolf instructed with a smile. He had a dandified gait.

Alex unlocked the handcuff and handed the aluminum case to the guard, emptied his pockets, and passed through the metal detector. The machine remained silent. The stern-faced guard opened the case, glanced at the picture covered with protective felt, jabbed his fingers into the case, and nodded.

Adolf smiled in relief. Red capillaries drew a grid on his bulbous nose.

The elevator stopped, the gleaming wooden doors opened, and Alex could finally breathe again. Two armed guards stood stock-still like mannequins in front of the round, nickel-plated steel door to the vault room. Alex counted twenty-four bolts. The door was open, but the entrance was blocked by a screen of closely spaced metal bars. A set of keys attached to a coiled metal chain hung from Adolf's belt. He fit a key into the lock and turned it. The bars rose silently, and they went through.

"The basement vault room provides optimal conditions for the storage of artworks. Six years ago we installed a sophisticated climate-control system that keeps the vaults at a constant temperature of twenty-two degrees Celsius. It is accurate to a tenth of a degree. The humidity is a constant fifty percent. When we entered, the sensors picked up the change caused by our body heat and made the necessary adjustments."

"No security cameras?" Alex asked with a tone of concern.

"We are not in the habit of violating our clients' privacy," Adolf scolded, raising his nose haughtily.

"But isn't that a risk?"

"For whom?" Adolf asked as he handed Alex a key. He led the way to vault 777 and inserted another key into the left-hand lock. Alex inserted his in the lock on the right.

"Counterclockwise," Adolf instructed. The two men turned their keys simultaneously, and the bars swung open.

In the adjacent vault Alex noticed a huge canvas covered with a tarp, most likely the Rothko original. He walked into 777 and placed the aluminum case on a high wooden shelf.

"You are leaving the case here?" Adolf asked in surprise.

"I'll be bringing three more pieces next week. I'll get it then."

The guards outside were hidden behind the wall. Alex dropped his key, and Adolf hastened to bend down solicitously to pick it up. As he straightened up, he was elbowed harshly in the back of the neck. He let out a groan and collapsed, his head striking the marble floor and drool trickling from his mouth.

Alex leaned down for the keys hanging from the German's belt. The one he'd found in Justus's house was already in his hand. The chain was too short. He dragged the unconscious body closer to the door of Justus's vault. The chain still didn't reach. Grasping Adolf's limp body, he held it up to the bars, inserted the two keys in the locks, opened the vault, and dropped the German over his shoulder.

He looked toward the entrance of the vault room. The guards were still out of sight. He went into Justus's vault and did a quick search among the artworks. The original of Giacometti's *Walking Man* was in the back. There were dozens of paintings and drawings. He didn't have much time. Adolf could regain consciousness at any moment. The guards weren't far away, and he knew they would do whatever it took to prevent Berghoff Bank's first robbery.

He heard a voice behind him and spun around.

Adolf was struggling to raise himself on his elbows. The glazed look in his eyes was starting to clear. Alex hurried over. The German grabbed his leg in an effort to pull him down.

Alex swung his arms around Adolf's neck and applied just the right amount of pressure to his Adam's apple and the arteries in his neck. The banker kicked and grunted. Alex tightened his stranglehold, but Adolf stuck his effeminate fingers into his wrist. Then suddenly Adolf went limp, and an unnerving shudder ran through his body.

Footsteps were approaching. He lay Adolf on the green marble floor and returned to Justus's vault. He had the troubling thought that he might be risking himself for nothing. On the floor behind the last painting, his foot banged into a wooden box. He lifted the lid.

A sealed envelope.

Adolf groaned.

Alex stuck the envelope in his pocket and exited the vault. Throwing Adolf over his shoulder again, he used the woozy German's key to lock the door.

The banker shook his head and moaned. Alex dragged him away from Justus's vault and banged his head on the floor. He lifted his eyelids to make sure he was out and then shouted to the guards, "I need help! Quick!"

The two armed guards came running, their rubber soles squeaking on the marble. One aimed his gun at Alex, who knelt down and started undoing the buttons on the shirt of the unconscious Adolf. "Call an ambulance!" he yelled to the stunned security guard.

"What happened to him?" the other guard asked, his eyes taking in the open door of the vault.

"Stop pointing that thing at me!" Alex barked. "He mumbled something about not feeling well, and then his eyes rolled back and he collapsed. Call an ambulance. What are you waiting for?"

The guard brought his radio to his lips and called for help.

Alex slapped Adolf's face.

"What's taking so long?" he said reproachfully to the bewildered guards.

Security officers in black suits arrived in the vault room, followed by the agitated Herr Berghoff, who gave Alex a hostile look.

"Does he have a medical condition?" Alex asked.

"A mild case of diabetes," Berghoff replied. "What happened?"

"He just collapsed," Alex said, slapping him again. Adolf was as still as a corpse. Alex felt his neck. "There's a pulse."

Berghoff issued orders to the security guards, who split up and started checking each vault thoroughly. Still on his knees. All the vaults were locked except for his.

"You are finished with the vault?" Berghoff demanded.

He nodded.

"Then we must lock it immediately."

Berghoff had his own master key. Together they relocked the vault.

"Come with me," Berghoff instructed. Alex looked back, as if he were reluctant to leave Adolf lying on the floor unconscious.

"Come. You must leave," Berghoff insisted.

"Why?"

The bank director gestured for a security guard to accompany them. The hefty man picked up his gun and kept it pointed at Alex's back.

"In an emergency, clients are forbidden to be in the vault room," Berghoff explained.

"Someone has to stay with him," Alex said.

"It is very odd," Berghoff said, scratching his terrier-like head. "Adolf takes medication for his diabetes. It is under control. He has never fainted before."

Alex halted. "Tell him not to point that gun at me."

Berghoff gave him an appraising look. His pandering manner was gone. He signaled to the guard to lower his weapon.

They took the small elevator up to ground level. The German placed a firm hand on Alex's arm. "Please wait in my office until the ambulance arrives. We must complete our security check before I can allow you to leave."

"Gladly," Alex said, following Berghoff into his office and settling into an armchair. Berghoff whispered something in the guard's ear. Nodding, the man took up a position behind Alex.

Alex picked up a copy of the *Financial Times* and leafed through its pale salmon pages. A siren approached. Through the open door, he could see EMTs in white uniforms running down the hall, pushing an orange gurney that rattled.

He rose, moved toward the door, and felt the security guard's body heat. A rough hand landed on his shoulder. Alex grabbed it with both hands, twisted the guard's arm, and hurled him at the wall as hard as he could. The man's nose struck the wall, and Alex heard the sickening sound of shattering bones.

Undeterred by his bloody face, the guard spun around quickly and sent his knee into Alex's gut. The blow to his liver was debilitating. The room became blurry, his head felt heavy, and his legs threatened to collapse. Taking a deep breath, he grasped the guard by the collar, swung him around, and slammed a fist into his thick red neck. The German moaned but continued to fight. The second punch to his neck knocked him out, and he fell to the floor.

Alex hugged his stomach, gasping for breath. Then he wiped the cold sweat from his forehead with the sleeve of his coat and walked out of the room. Striding calmly, he passed the guards at the front door, the *Financial Times* under his arm. He exited onto the Ku'damm, the chilly wind whipping at his face.

DIARY

17 July 1944

The commandant came to the café this evening and neither ate nor drank. He simply stared at me with that chilling glance of his. I buried my trembling hands in my pockets.

He knows, and he is waiting.

When he left with his evil entourage, I slipped away to the flour pantry and let the deputy commandant out of his hiding place.

18 July 1944

How much longer must Jasmine endure the commandant's brutish urges? He defiles her body and sullies her honor. And I hide behind the counter and, ashamed, bury myself in the order slips.

If I stab him in the heart with a kitchen knife—we will all die.

I cry out to the heavens, but they are empty.

21 July 1944

I have removed my diary from its hiding place in the yard and I carry it with me.

So far, we have not managed to do anything.

At six o'clock sharp, the iron gate finally opened. The blind dog emerged, sniffing at the air, and the old man followed it out onto Hadad Street. They headed south, toward Subchi Park.

Paris was dozing, his face weary. Orchidea touched his shoulder. He opened his eyes and straightened up.

"What's going on?"

"We have to get going."

Paris stood up, stretched, and yawned. He was momentarily taken aback by his own attire.

She cracked the door open and peered out into the stairwell. Male voices were coming from below. She went out wrapped in her burka and looked down at the bottom of the stairs. Two brawny moving men were struggling with an ancient refrigerator that was blocking the hallway. In their apartment there was no refrigerator!

Paris came up behind her, only his eyes exposed. He pulled at her arm. She followed him back into the empty apartment.

"They're coming here," she said.

"Let's leave the clothes here. They might talk to us in Arabic," Paris said, removing his burka and bra. Orchidea followed suit. She looked through the blinds at Hadad Street. It was getting dark. The old man was getting farther away, his figure growing smaller. The men's voices became louder and rougher, their breathing heavier. A curse word was sent into the air.

"We can't lose him," Paris said. As they descended the stairs to the second floor, they came face-to-face with the older of the two men with the wide, dingy refrigerator. They were wasting time. The face of the stocky older man was shiny, and his mustache was stiff. The younger man peeked out from behind the refrigerator. He was just a boy. He looked at them apologetically. The older man said something.

"We're late for dinner. Can we get by?" Paris said in French.

No response.

He said it again in English.

The stout Arab took a deep breath and repeated himself in Arabic, louder this time.

Just get out of there.

Paris climbed up on the handrail and came down on the outer edge of the steps, sticking his feet between the wrought-iron posts. The older man gaped. Orchidea followed, climbing onto the handrail and taking care not to look down. She passed the Syrian moving men and the refrigerator. The youngster burst out laughing in astonishment.

They ran down the last flight and a half, the older man calling out to them from behind. Ignoring him, she left the building first and walked quickly toward the park. There was no sign of the old man. Bile rose in her throat. When she reached the corner, she turned around. Paris was right behind her.

"How are we going to find him?" she asked.

The Frenchman scanned the streets. Traffic was heavy.

"There he is!" he said.

They passed the park. The old man picked up the dog and turned into Hafez Ibrahim Street, entering a smoke-filled local café. They followed him in.

The large space was crowded with elderly men, lifeless drones, and young men in cheap leather jackets. Dice bounced off a wooden frame, coffee and tea were sipped noisily, and men with glassy eyes puffed on narghiles. A female singer keened, and violins wailed. The rancid air was filled with green flies buzzing around semolina cakes topped with pistachio nuts and dripping with honey.

The old man wiped off a rickety wooden chair with his hand, grumbling to himself, and sat down at a turquoise table, cradling the mangy dog in his arms.

An obese waiter with a pockmarked face approached the table with an air of deference, a stained kitchen towel over his shoulder. They spoke briefly.

Pockmarked Face moved off. After a while he returned and placed a glass of hot water on the table.

The old man did not remove his dark sunglasses, cap, or leather gloves. He took a bundle wrapped in newspaper from his pocket and opened it on the table. It held an herb Orchidea couldn't identify. Pulling off a few leaves, he tossed them into the glass. Then he drank the green infusion silently.

Pockmarked Face returned again and smiled, revealing discolored teeth. They spoke in Arabic, the old man gesturing with his hands.

Pockmarked Face ran from table to table, carrying a beat-up copper tray. He brought Paris and Orchidea the black coffee they'd ordered, and Paris paid the bill on the spot.

A cell phone rang deafeningly. The locals froze, staring. The old man stuck his hand in his pocket and pulled out a phone. The ringing got even louder. He nearly lost hold of the dog.

He raised his dark glasses for a moment to examine the screen.

Her stomach constricted. His left eye socket was empty.

The camera in Paris's cap was snapping one close-up after another. The old man had a brief conversation, disconnected, and brought the glasses back down over his eyes.

They decided to split up: she would follow their target while Paris hurried back to the man's house on Hadad Street. It was nearly dark out, and getting chilly. Hafez Ibrahim Street was cast in blue, the shadows black.

The old man packed up his things and left the café, Orchidea on his tail. The streetlamps had just been lit. He entered Subchi Park, which was filled with children at play, and paused in front of a fenced-in bed of gladioli. Then he walked home and disappeared through the iron gate.

Behind a wooden blind on the fourth floor, a light came on.

Paris joined her. "It's getting dangerous. We've been here too long. We have to talk to him."

"There's at least one guard," she said. "Maybe two."

Paris was silent. Going back to the apartment they had commandeered was too risky. They climbed up to the roof of the house across the street.

"Let's go," Orchidea said.

"Where?"

She spelled out her plan. Paris smiled, and then his face grew serious. "Are you sure?"

Orchidea nodded. She reached behind her back and undid her bra, pulling it out through the sleeve of her blouse. The cold made her flesh tingle.

They went back down to the street. Orchidea rang the bell on the iron gate. Paris waited across the street.

No response.

She pressed the button again.

No response.

She smiled up at the camera above.

Still no response.

Her heart pounding, she pressed down on the button and held it there.

A buzzer sounded. Orchidea pushed the gate open. A young, dark-complexioned man in a blue sweater was already coming toward her from the far end of the walkway. His eyes homed in on her blouse and the abundant jiggling flesh beneath it. Entering the courtyard, she met him halfway down the path. "I'm looking for the Polish embassy," she said with a flirty smile. "They told me it was here."

The guard's eyes were glued to her blouse. He shook his head. "Follow me," he said. As he circled around her, he rubbed up against her right breast, seemingly by accident. He led her back to the gate.

"What did you say your name was?" he asked.

She shot him in the back of the neck.

"I didn't say."

Her hand trembled as she lowered the silenced gun.

Paris appeared and dragged the body into the stairwell while she covered the bloodstain on the walkway with dirt. At the security desk inside, she found an old-fashioned black-and-white monitor divided into six squares. There was no recording device and no computer, merely real-time camera images that weren't saved.

There was no name on the last mailbox.

Nor on the dark wooden door on the fourth floor. Paris kicked the door, causing the frame to shake and a lump of plaster to fall at their feet. Something gave way, but the lock remained intact. The second kick did the trick. Guns pointed, they rushed in. The apartment was lit dimly by a few bare bulbs. The blinds were all closed. They checked it out room by room. The floor was painted.

"This isn't possible," Paris muttered.

The old man wasn't there.

The envelope was throbbing in Alex's pocket. Taking the S-Bahn was too dangerous. There were security cameras everywhere.

The obese cabdriver's body spilled over the seat. His chubby fingers were strangled by gaudy rings. The radio chattered quietly, and pale lines of text flickered on the display unit. Traffic was inching westward along 17th of June Street. It was dark in the back of the cab. The answers were waiting for him in the envelope. He would have to be patient.

The cabbie's round eyes glanced at him in the mirror. Alex ordered him to stop in Charlottenburg, just before the on-ramp to the A100 autobahn. He paid the fare and climbed out, and then rode southward in the company of an elderly Turkish driver who hummed to himself the whole way.

Alex got out in Grunewald center and made it the rest of the way by foot, the envelope and its secrets blazing in his pocket. He entered the yard of the late Justus Erlichmann, and rain mixed with snow began falling. The Glock was still in the doghouse. He opened the door, kept still, and listened.

A quick check of the large house revealed nothing. He sat down at the breakfast bar in the kitchen, opened the sealed envelope, and spread out the folded sheets of paper.

The clock on the wall ticked solemnly.

The dozens of items in Justus's estate were listed in meticulous detail over two pages. This was followed by a clause relating to Gunter: a large sum was to be set aside to provide for the care and burial of his elderly father should he outlive his son.

The shocker was contained in the next clause: Justus Erlichmann willed his entire estate to two individuals.

Alex instructed Butthead to find out who they were and to pass the information on to Exodus. It would take time.

He went over in his mind what he'd discovered, but he could find no logical explanation. A man and woman were about to learn that they had each come into more than half a billion euros in real estate, artwork, and German government bonds. Alex stared at the two names on the sheet of paper in front of him.

They meant nothing to him.

"Turn the place upside down," Paris said, his eyes flashing. "I'm going to find him."

"Maybe he has another apartment in the building?" Orchidea suggested.

"I don't think so," he said as he left. She heard his footsteps running up the stairs.

Inside the apartment, time had stopped in the seventies. The sparse furnishings conveyed a sense of emptiness.

The spartan bedroom contained nothing more than a bed, a chair, and a wardrobe. On the floor by the bed was a pile of three books, with a rectangular magnifying glass on top. She moved them apart with her foot. One was Nietzsche's *Beyond Good and Evil* in the original German, another a German guide to medicinal herbs. The last book was missing its cover, the tattered pages held together with a thick orange rubber band. Scraps of newspaper marked several pages. She bent down and picked it up. In small letters at the top of the page: *Adolf Hitler*. On the opposite page: *Mein Kampf*.

She dropped the book in repulsion and wiped her fingers on her coat. Gripping her gun, she aimed it ahead of her at a low angle as she opened the wardrobe. Cheap, old clothes and the smell of plain laundry powder and mothballs.

In the kitchen she found a small table and a single straight-backed chair. The corner of the refrigerator door was held together with a wide strip of masking tape. It was empty except for a few fruits and vegetables and some odd-looking seeds in a glass jar.

A transistor radio stood on the yellowing marble countertop, its brown leather casing scratched and cracked. Two bowls were on the floor, one holding water and the other a few scraps of dog food.

The bathtub was stained with rust. The cabinet revealed medicine bottles and suppositories, a red first-aid kit, and a tub of Vaseline.

The living room was bare save for an ancient television perched on a wooden crate in front of a worn upholstered armchair. A door led out to the balcony, but it was covered by a dusty blind; the pull tape was torn.

The study was furnished solely with a desk and a wooden chair. On the corner of the desk sat a pile of papers and documents arranged in perfect order, all the edges lined up. Beside it was a magnifying glass the size of an appetizer plate and an older-generation computer with a boxy monitor. The computer wasn't on. The only up-to-date item in the whole apartment lay next to the keyboard: a flash drive.

Orchidea downloaded the contents onto her phone. The drive held a single PowerPoint file.

She opened it.

Paris reached the top of the stairs, turned on his flashlight, and held it alongside his silenced gun. He pushed on the creaking door and stepped out onto the dark roof. As he spun to the right, the flashlight picked up a jumble of small satellite dishes. He shifted to the left. The old man was sitting on a stool, trapped in the sudden beam of light. He was gazing at a wooden cage with rusty metal netting.

He turned toward Paris slowly, and his jaw dropped.

Paris rushed at him. The sunglasses were gone. The man's left eye socket was empty.

Paris swallowed.

The old man raised his hands in the air, mumbling in Arabic.

Paris remained silent.

"No money," the man stuttered in English. The open door to the stairs shed murky light on the roof.

Paris gestured with his gun for the man to get up and stand by the wall of the stairwell.

The old man didn't move.

Paris came closer, pressing the silencer to his throat.

"No money!"

"Shut up and get going!"

The old man rose. From up close he looked shorter, older, and frailer. His clothing smelled of old age. Paris searched his skeletal body. Touching him made his flesh creep. Skin and bones and empty pockets, aside from the old cellphone. Two simple keys hung from a rusty ring attached to his belt.

"What do you want?" the old man asked, his chin trembling.

"Sit down."

The old man didn't move.

"*Sitz!*" Paris commanded.

He sat down. "Who are you?"

Paris took up position behind him and remained silent.

"What do you want?"

"Take off your gloves!"

"What?"

Paris pressed the silencer to his scrawny neck and bent over. "Take off your gloves and stop asking questions."

The beam of light quivered around the old man as he slowly removed his right glove. His hand was shrunken, dotted with dozens of liver spots.

"Your bodyguard is dead," Paris informed him. "There's no point trying to buy time."

A look of disgust spread over the old man's face. He removed his left glove.

Paris's heart started racing.

The only finger that remained on the left hand was the thumb.

The gun was shaking in Paris's hand. He looked into the distance and hugged himself. The red warning lights on top of Mount Qasioun were blurred by his tears.

DIARY

We were in the Catacombs. Charlotte burst in, agitated, and shouted, Get back to the café, fast!

What happened? I asked.

She handed me a gun.

I flew up the stairs and ran as fast as I could. A Gestapo truck was standing in front of the café behind the commandant's black car.

Didier the shopkeeper grabbed my arm. Don't go, he said. It would be a shame to remember Jasmine this way.

Did he hurt her? I asked.

Didier burst into tears and embraced me.

And the children?

I am so sorry, Didier wept. Run, Roger, run! At least save yourself, he called after me. I ran off and, mad with despair, climbed to the roof of the building that overlooked the café. I crawled to the edge of the roof and saw the commandant below, screaming, throwing objects around, and smashing tables and chairs.

Jasmine and Sophie and Albert were nowhere to be seen.

The Gestapo men climbed back into the truck. The commandant came out of the café carrying a tin container. He sprayed the remainder of its contents over the smashed tables and straw chairs lying on the sidewalk. He screamed something in German, and everyone moved back. Then he tossed the butt of his cigar over his shoulder into the dark puddle. Everything burst into flames. The fire climbed rapidly up to our apartment and began to consume everything.

Curious onlookers stared. Acquaintances wrung their hands. The firemen arrived too late. I lay on the edge of the roof and cried as the water flowed black from the burning café to the sidewalk, carrying with it the remains of my dear ones; of what I once was; of my life and my family—of all that I loved. A terrible pain cut through my heart. I have no country, no home, no family.

A stranger's hand stroked my head. Someone embraced me at the edge of the roof.

The deputy commandant.

Thick smoke darkened the street. Something exploded behind the café. Perhaps the small gas tanks.

I pray only that my dear ones were already dead when the flames engulfed them. I lay on the edge of the roof, the terrible smell of smoke and congealed tar filling my nose. I thought of hurling myself to the street. For I would never, never find consolation.

I remain alone in the world, uprooted, cut off from all that made me who I am.

We are like brothers, the deputy commandant said. We shall always be brothers.

He embraced me. We wept together.

"Justus ratted us out!" Orchidea called up to the dark roof. She saw the small moon of light cast by the flashlight, and then the silhouettes of Paris and the old man.

She waved the flash drive. "It's all here."

"What?!" Paris called in a choked voice, keeping the flashlight on the old man, who was snarling like a wild animal.

Her eyes gradually adjusted to the darkness. She came closer. Paris seemed agitated. "What's wrong?" she asked.

Taking advantage of the distraction, the old man rose with surprising agility and headed for the stairs. Paris leaped at him and grabbed him by the coat.

"Tell her who you are!" he snapped, his voice cracking.

"Don't shout," she said. "Someone might hear you."

"I . . . I am George Fischer. I am a Syrian citizen."

"Keep lying and I'll gouge out your other eye," Paris said, catching him in a headlock.

"That's the name on his papers," she confirmed.

"What do you want from me?" the old man pleaded.

Paris forced him back down on the stool.

"He's ninety-nine," he said.

"Unbelievable!" she exclaimed.

"Who are you people?" the old man said, raising his voice.

362 | **RONI DUNEVICH**

"I found a PowerPoint file on his flash drive," she told Paris. "He has a partner in Germany who's responsible for organizing the killing of the Nibelungs. The Mukhabarat surveilled them, and then the Germans took them out. There's a video that shows Justus telling them everything he knows about the Ring and how it operates, about the Orchid Farm and the inhalers. The filthy traitor. He sold us out."

"No way!" Paris sputtered. Bending over, he shrieked into the old man's face, "Do you know who I am?"

He aimed the flashlight at the German's face.

The man shook his head.

"You raped my father's first wife!"

"What?"

"You murdered her, and you murdered her children!"

"What do you want from me?"

"You burned them alive in a café in Paris!"

Fischer's face fell. His one eye gaped. "Who the hell are you?" he shouted in rage.

"My name is Trezeguet. *Trezeguet!* Gerard Trezeguet!"

The old man froze. The blood drained from his face.

"And you're going to die today!"

"Who is he?" Orchidea asked.

"I'm George Fischer," the old man said beseechingly.

"Liar!" Gerard screamed.

"So who is he?" she repeated.

"He's a Nazi war criminal."

"What?" The roof seemed to shake under her feet.

"He was the commandant of the Drancy concentration camp."

Paris's chin was trembling.

"He sent one hundred and twenty-five thousand Jews to their death!"

His breathing was labored, his chest rising and falling.

"He is SS-Hauptsturmführer Alois Brunner!"

"From France alone, he sent twenty-four thousand Jews to Auschwitz," Gerard went on.

"But, Gerard," she said. It felt strange to call him by his real name. "Alois Brunner is dead."

"Not yet!"

Without warning, he grabbed the old man's head and stuck his fingers into his mouth.

"What are you doing?" she cried out.

Gerard's strong fingers nearly dislocated Brunner's jaw. He felt around roughly between his false teeth.

"Stop it, Gerard!" she shouted.

"I have to be sure he's not hiding a cyanide capsule in his teeth," Gerard said, wiping his wet fingers on Brunner's coat. The old Nazi sat in silence, staring bitterly at the empty cage beside him.

"How do you know it's him?" she asked.

"He's been hiding out in Damascus since the fifties, alternating between this apartment and a suite in the Hotel Dedeman. I checked to see if he was upstairs in his suite last night when you were in the shower."

He nodded to himself. "Mossad managed to get two letter bombs into his hands. In the first explosion he lost his eye, and in the second—four fingers on his left hand. Show her your hand, Alois!"

"What if it's not him?"

"Show her your hand!" Gerard aimed the flashlight at Brunner's left hand.

The German raised it. His thumb was as wrinkled as lizard skin.

She felt sick to her stomach.

"It's him," Gerard said firmly. "I've seen his picture. I've been looking for him for years. Everyone thought he was dead, but nobody could point to a grave. Beate Klarsfeld tracked him to this address."

He raised his gun and aimed it at Brunner's forehead.

"Don't you dare shoot him!" she exclaimed. "Give me your gun."

Gerard lowered his weapon. "No way," he said with a snicker before raising it again.

Orchidea pointed her gun at Gerard's head. "Give it to me!"

"Have you lost your mind?" he growled.

"Hand it over!" she ordered.

"Okay, okay," he chuckled nervously, lowering the gun until it was pointing down at the whitewashed roof. "I won't hurt him."

"Give me the gun!" she demanded.

"Are you going to shoot me?"

"Just give it to me."

He handed her the gun.

"I'm sorry," she said.

It was getting cold.

"Why didn't you tell me about your family?" she asked.

"I didn't have a chance."

"I asked you in Subchi Park if you recognized him. You lied to me."

"I couldn't . . . I wasn't sure."

"Don't kill me," Alois Brunner said suddenly in a broken voice. They both looked at him.

All of a sudden there was a switchblade in Gerard's hand. He thrust the shining blade into the Nazi's heart.

"This is for my family!" he shouted, breathing heavily. He pulled the knife out and thrust it into the old man's abdomen. "This is for Roger Trezeguet!" Again he pulled it out and thrust it in. "This is for Jasmine!" Stabbing him for a fourth time, he shouted, "This is for Sophie and Albert!" Tears welled up in his eyes. Wailing, he wiped them away with his sleeve. He was crying out loud.

The knife was still stuck in Brunner's torn abdomen. Through clenched teeth, the German whispered hoarsely, "The Fourth Reich . . . is . . . already."

Thick black blood spilled from his mouth. His body was twitching. He fell to the floor, a pool of blood forming around his torso.

A shot rang out.

Gerard dropped the flashlight.

Gerard Trezeguet's body was thrown backward, hitting the cage. He clutched at the netting, tearing the top from the wooden frame. The cage cracked and collapsed, and he slid to the ground.

Orchidea spun in the direction of the open doorway to the stairs, where the shot had come from. Dropping and rolling across the roof, she fired two shots at the head of the broad figure she saw, followed by two to his midsection. The shooter slumped to the floor, and the gun fell from his hand. She went over to the cage, retrieved Gerard's flashlight, and examined him. "No!"

The Frenchman's breathing was shallow. His hands were pressed to his chest in an effort to stop the bleeding. She unzipped his fleece jacket and raised his shirt. Blood was bubbling from an entry wound near his heart.

She'd been relying on him to get her out of Damascus, and here he was, lying wounded and bleeding. She stroked his head and bit her lip. When the initial wave of panic subsided, her mind started racing. After the noise of the shots, the whole world would come running; they had to leave—now. She called Alex and told him that Brunner was dead and the Frenchman was injured.

"Why did he stab him?"

"He said something about his father . . . their family . . . murder. I didn't understand it all."

A gunshot wound to the chest meant that she had to get him to a hospital. But a hospital was out of the question. "What should I do?"

There was a pause.

"Take him to Dr. Abu Luka in Maaloula," Alex said finally.

DIARY

2 AUGUST 1944

He taught us the train routes and departure times, and the vulnerable spots along the tracks. He participates in every operation and saves Jews.

Such is the deputy commandant.

Yesterday we stopped a train that had departed from the Bourget-Drancy station. During a brief battle, we—a handful of Resistance fighters—succeeded in killing a dozen SS men and saving 278 children who were on their way to Auschwitz.

I couldn't save my own children.

3 AUGUST 1944

My embraces are empty. No trace is left of my family, no portrait, no smile or utterance. I am alone in the world, and my loneliness is beyond measure. Every thought of my loved ones floods my eyes with tears.

Justus Erlichmann was sitting in front of the camera in a white T-shirt, spilling everything about the makeup of the Ring and the identities of the Nibelungs: addresses, phone numbers, meeting places. He divulged details of his special relationship with the Israeli prime minister and the head of Mossad, the Hochstadt-Lancet virus, the design of the Cube, and how to arm the inhalers, with an appalling nonchalance and outrageous composure.

In one scene, speaking directly into the Syrians' camera, Erlichmann talked about the plans for the Bolu operation, including the abduction of the Iranian general, the location of the spice warehouse, and the identity of the Nibelung assigned with the task of getting rid of the body.

So the Syrians had known about the mission well in advance, but they had only passed the information on to the Turks after Istanbul was taken out, presumably hoping to spark a crisis between Israel and Turkey.

Justus had managed to fool the polygraph, Reuven, and everyone else. He had been collaborating with Alois Brunner, which explained the large sums he'd transferred to the neo-Nazi group. It seemed that the swastika had always been carved into his heart, but unfortunately Israel had never bothered to rummage through his activities.

The Nibelung Ring was history. The Syrian Mukhabarat had marked their targets and surveilled the Nibelungs. Then the

Mauser brothers—the Stasi twins—had gone from city to city, strangling their victims to death.

Her, too. Jane, too.

Despicable neo-Nazi house.

He struggled to put his thoughts in order. Alois Brunner was the Israelite. Was Justus Erlichmann the Mud Man?

Had Justus orchestrated the assassinations and hidden the bodies? Where? Why did he decide to kill his own people, the people he himself had recruited and trained?

And what about Brunner?

Alex had heard the story of the escaped Nazi war criminal early in his Mossad career. Alois Brunner had vanished after the war, turning up later in Egypt and then moving to Damascus in 1954. It was said that somewhere along the way, he had worked for the CIA. Six years after he arrived in Syria, he was arrested on suspicion of drug trafficking. As soon as he identified himself as a high-ranking SS officer, he was released.

Brunner taught the Mukhabarat the art of torture. His technique employed a modern version of the rack, born more than five hundred years ago in the dungeons of the Spanish Inquisition.

Israeli pilots who had been held captive in Syria spoke of ordeals similar to the ones described by survivors of the Drancy internment camp, over which Brunner had presided.

Brunner had also brokered a deal with the Stasi for the sale to the Mukhabarat of thousands of miniature listening devices. That was the start of the unholy trinity between the Nazi fugitive, the East German Stasi, and the Syrian Mukhabarat.

For decades Brunner had been in hiding, protected by armed guards, giving rise to the belief that he was dead.

The first letter bomb exploded in 1961 in a post office in Damascus, killing two Syrian postal workers and taking out one of Brunner's eyes. The second package was sent in 1980 by the German Society of Friends of Medicinal Herbs, and took off four fingers of his left hand.

But Alois Brunner refused to die.

The debt was still outstanding.

Along with the video, Orchidea had sent him two phone numbers she had found scrawled on a scrap of paper on Brunner's desk. Alex called Butthead and requested an immediate trace.

Then he called Reuven.

"Paris killed Alois Brunner, but Paris was shot by one of Brunner's guards. It's serious. Orchidea took out the guard. They're on their way to Dr. Abu Luka in Maaloula, but he can't do much more than bandage the wound. We have to get them out of there immediately."

A bottle was opened.

A drink was poured.

Sipping.

Pitiful.

Swallowing. A deep breath.

"Will you organize the extraction, Reuven?"

"It's too risky."

"They're our people."

"That's just it. They're not."

Alex disconnected.

His call to the prime minister's office was answered immediately.

Paris's gray jacket was stained black with blood, and his eyes were squeezed shut. Blood dripped onto the whitewashed roof. Air entered his chest through the hole, making a whistling sound. She knew that a punctured lung meant that his condition could deteriorate rapidly, and she knew what she had to do. She sat him up on the creaky wooden stool. His body swayed.

Clenching her jaw, she pulled the knife out of Alois Brunner's body and wiped the blade on his coat. She cut a five-inch square from the dead bodyguard's shirt and then ran down to Brunner's apartment and grabbed the first-aid kit and the tube of Vaseline from the bathroom cabinet.

Returning to the roof, she held the flashlight between her teeth as she lifted Gerard's shirt from behind. Damn! It was so dark. She felt around for an exit wound and finally convinced herself that there was none. Thank God.

His breathing was shallow. The light from the stairwell fell on his face. He was turning blue and shifting restlessly. The ominous trill of a muezzin's call rose into the night air.

She glanced at her watch and counted thirty-four breaths a minute. Way too fast. The injured lung could collapse. She disinfected the wound with a cotton ball soaked in alcohol, spread a thick layer of Vaseline around it, and placed the square of cotton over it, holding it in place with Band-Aids in three sides. The one-directional valve she had improvised should let out the air trapped in his chest without allowing new air in. The bandage rose and fell with each rasping breath.

After a few minutes, she noticed a slight improvement. Gerard was breathing noisily.

"Can you stand up?"

He nodded. She helped him up from the stool. He was heavy. She shoved her shoulder under his arm to support him and led him to the stairs, and he leaned on her, gritting his teeth in silence. They descended slowly, one step at a time.

He skipped a breath.

Her heart skipped a beat.

The stairs seemed endless. He sent a silent kiss into the air, managing to smile through his pain. His eyes sparkled bewitchingly. Hers, filled with tears.

The trek down the stairs went on and on. At last they reached the entrance, her blouse stuck to her back and her knees nearly buckling under her. She sat him down on the ground, leaning him against the wall just inside the iron gate.

"I'll be right back."

She raced to the Nissan. She could already hear the wail of sirens approaching, rapidly growing louder.

She drove the car onto the sidewalk in front of the gate. The veins in his neck looked a little less swollen, but his lips were purple. She counted eighteen breaths a minute. Better.

She sat him down in the backseat and buckled him in. His movements were lethargic. Sitting up meant that his internal organs wouldn't press on his diaphragm, making it easier for him to breathe. But Gerard was slipping away.

There was a blood smear on the door of the white Nissan. She wiped it away with her sleeve and jumped in.

She drove down Hadad Street and turned left into Al-Mahdi ben Barakeh, which cuts across Damascus diagonally toward the northeast.

The cursed Jabal Qasioun was up ahead. She was going in the right direction. She had to pass the mountain to the east, and then, if she was lucky, she'd make it onto the M1.

She looked for a sign pointing the way to the highway but didn't see one. She didn't look back. Nothing good could appear in the rearview mirror.

Police sirens shrieked nearby. The back of her neck went cold. She glanced at Gerard. He was quiet. She prayed for him to hold on.

Ben Barakeh Street was congested. Grasping the wheel with her left hand, she reached back and touched his face. It was cold and dry. Drivers honked incessantly. A shadow of despair fell over her heart.

"Why didn't you tell me who he was before we went up there?"

He coughed wetly and said hoarsely, "I wasn't positive . . ."

She didn't reply. After a long pause she said, "I'll get you out. You'll see."

"I'm sorry . . ."

In the north of the city, the traffic eased a bit, but time was against them.

"There's a morphine injector in the bag," he said.

"I have to ask the doctor."

Dr. Petrus Abu Luka picked up on the fourth ring. Sudden anxiety showed in his voice. He would make preparations for their arrival, and no, she shouldn't give morphine if there was a lung injury. It could suppress his breathing.

"It won't be long," she said to the dark interior of the car. Gerard's breathing was becoming more rapid. He slumped sideways on the backseat, twisting into an unnatural position. He could no longer restrain his groans.

Don't cry, she urged herself. *Keep it together.*

At Al-Sades min Tishreen, the road opened up, but not enough to allow the speedometer to climb past fifty-five. A flashing blue light would mean interrogation rooms, torture, and the gallows.

A large junction was coming up. She passed through it going straight, following the sign to Homs and Aleppo. Once again, traffic piled up, slowing her down. Maaloula was still far away.

Too far away.

DIARY

14 AUGUST 1944

I am diminished, my actions are limited, my time is allotted, and my room is cramped. Nothing remains of the objects that once filled my life.

I bake in someone else's boulangerie, and the mistress says that my croissants with berry jam are snatched up. Her face is always flushed. Perhaps she is trying to ease my suffering.

I want to father a child. So someone will remain after I am gone. So people will believe that I was here.

16 AUGUST 1944

The Resistance is growing. The buds of freedom are blossoming, and the air carries an intoxicating scent. The Allied forces are making their way to us, to Paris.

Yesterday, Parisians sunbathed on the sun-drenched banks of the Seine.

Paris will be liberated. Paris must be liberated.

24 AUGUST 1944

My comrades in the Catacombs beneath Le Meurice Hotel on the Rue de Rivoli can hear the Germans packing up. A lookout saw senior SS officers abandoning their headquarters and fleeing for their lives. The fountain pen shakes in my trembling hand. It is coming.

Paris will be liberated. Paris must be liberated.

25 AUGUST 1944

I was sitting alone in Arsène's café near the Champs-Élysées. On the saucer, next to the small cup, the spoon suddenly began to vibrate.

Later, I learned that tanks and armored vehicles from General Leclerc's Second Armored Division had swept through the Arc de Triomphe and the Champs-Élysées. Crowds cheered, and "La Marseillaise" echoed in the adjacent streets. There was an explosion of joy. Someone thrust a bottle of champagne to my mouth.

Dead people do not drink.

If only we had restrained ourselves. If the deputy commandant had waited a bit, Jasmine, Sophie, and Albert would be with me today, the café and the boulangerie would be bustling, and I would not be dead.

At Nazi headquarters in Le Meurice Hotel, General von Choltitz signed the surrender documents.

The foul-smelling jackboot has been removed from our faces. Here in Paris, the war has ended and the Germans are fleeing eastward.

I saw Parisians lynch a Wehrmacht soldier whose hands were raised above his head. He wept and pleaded for his life, and they ripped the flesh from his body. They did not heed his pleas, even as he was being torn to pieces.

Did the commandant hear the pleas of my loved ones?

"We're almost there," Orchidea said into the rearview mirror, searching for Gerard's face. His eyes were shut. He was barely conscious.

The narrow alleys of Maaloula were bewildering.

Suddenly she saw the gilded icon of the baby Jesus. Up ahead were the green pistachio trees. She sped past them.

The sight of the white tin sign with the red cross made her blood race. A light shone in the big living-room windows.

"We've arrived!" she cried.

Gerard responded with a shallow wheezing breath.

"Listen to me, you're going to make it!" she said, leaping out. She ran to the door and rang the bell. Her heart was pounding and her face was dripping with sweat, but there was a glimmer of hope in her heart. She held her ear to the door but didn't hear the doctor's footsteps approaching.

"Come on!" she muttered, pressing down on the bell.

Moving away from the door, she pressed her face to the window.

A scream escaped her lips.

Dr. Petrus Abu Luka was hanging in the living room.

"Get out of there!" Alex ordered her over the phone.

"Where to?" Orchidea asked.

"Don't touch anything. It might be a trap."

"Paris is dying!"

"Get in the car and drive away quietly. Keep your eyes open and make sure you're not being followed. The first chance you get, ditch the car and head back toward Damascus. Don't enter the city. Keep going south on the M1. We'll try to get you out."

"I have to save him!" she insisted, struggling to hold back tears.

She found a rusty iron bar in the yard and stuck its pointed end between the double doors. The heavy doors resisted. On the third try she heard something snap, and the lock gave way. She rushed in, her gun drawn. Ice flowed through her veins. The doctor's body was swaying gently. There was a dark stain on the front of his white *jellabiya*. His head was slumped on his chest, his neck broken and his face white.

She went into Abu Luka's clinic. In the tin cabinet she found bandages, disinfectant, ampoules, and syringes. She gathered it all up in a small cardboard box.

A blank white envelope had been placed on the living-room table. She opened it with shaking hands. On a scrap of paper were the words: "They are coming for me. Run."

Orchidea's heart was beating wildly. If they were on to Abu Luka, they were on to her and Gerard, too.

Gerard was utterly still in the backseat. She called his name, but he didn't respond. A wave of apprehension surged through her. His condition was bleak. So was hers. She switched on the overhead light and leaned over to him, planting a quick kiss on his cold forehead. She thought she saw his eyelids flutter.

She drove through the town and sped down the mountain until finally the lights of Maaloula disappeared behind her. Periodically Gerard sank into a fog, but each time he fought his way back up, groaning and muttering. He was still alive.

She turned onto the dark highway, where traffic was light. Gerard suddenly let out a loud sigh. Her heart seized. She leaned on the gas, passing cars, trucks, and a half-empty rickety bus. Very soon, the treacherous lights of Damascus appeared on the horizon.

At the entrance to the city, the highway became frustratingly clogged. She honked her horn at the crawling cars in front of her, helpless in the face of the congestion.

Meanwhile, in the backseat, Gerard's time was running out.

She weaved through traffic, forging a path until the houses in the southern sectors of Damascus had disappeared behind them and up ahead was the Yarmouk refugee camp and Kafar Souseh. Silent industrial buildings and dark warehouses flanked the road; beyond was the unbroken landscape of the night.

"Gerard?"

No response.

A pair of uneven headlights was approaching.

An old truck. It was hauling hundreds of filthy wooden cages. White feathers flew off into the night.

Hens to the slaughter.

DIARY

26 August 1944

A young woman with a shaved head was walking along Boulevard Saint-Germain. Some men attacked her, tore her dress and brassiere from her body, and spit in her face. As she sobbed and wailed, her bare breasts shook.

Word on the street was that she had consorted with Luftwaffe pilots.

She was Francine, the daughter of Hector from the brasserie.

General de Gaulle gave a speech at the Hôtel de Ville. How thirstily I drank in his words. Throughout the years of the occupation, he carried the flag of our honor.

De Gaulle said: Paris! Outraged Paris! Broken Paris! Martyred Paris! But liberated Paris! Liberated by itself, liberated by its people with help from the armies of France, with the help and support of the whole of France, of the France that is fighting, of the only France, of the real France, eternal France!

Hearing his voice, I burst into tears. Now, too, I weep.

26 September 1944

Yom Kippur eve. I shall go to the synagogue and stand before the holy ark and pray, and I hope I will be able to control myself and not burst into tears before the Almighty. For four years, I have been away from my Jewishness. Four years empty of faith.

I shall fast and suffer and plead, but God will never forgive me for my sins.

16 NOVEMBER 1949

In my apartment there is a table, a chair, and a bed. I wear most of the little clothing I have and keep the rest in a bag. I awaken at four o'clock in the morning and ride my bicycle to Pierre Poilâne's boulangerie on the Rue du Cherche-Midi. I save every franc. Sometimes I work shift after shift until my knees swell and ache. In the afternoon I return to my room, listen to the radio, and read old books that I find in the street.

One day I will have enough money to ask the bank for a loan.

Orchidea opened the window. The air brought with it the odor of fresh soil and horses. The night was dark and hopeless. Suddenly she froze. A light had appeared on the horizon. In the opposite lane, flashing red lights were coming toward them.

Thinking fast, she slowed the car and drove it onto the median strip between the two lanes. The undercarriage of the Nissan banged against the concrete. She switched on the hazard lights and signaled with her high beams as she drove toward the approaching vehicle.

An ambulance.

The driver slammed on the brakes and stopped in front of her. Hoarsely, she shouted, "My husband is seriously injured! Help us, please!" She gestured to the driver. He pulled the ambulance onto the shoulder and jumped out, together with two other men: a paramedic in a short white coat and an older gray-haired man.

"Quickly! He's in the backseat," she said, getting out.

The paramedic was the first to respond, disappearing behind the ambulance and opening the back doors. The older man took out a stethoscope, turned on a Maglite and held it between his teeth, pulled on latex gloves, and scrutinized Gerard.

"What happened, madam?" he asked in English with a heavy Arabic accent. His cheeks were covered in thick black stubble. His eyes showed compassion.

"He was shot."

The doctor froze. "We must notify the police."

Orchidea drew her gun. "No police. Take care of him!"

The doctor stood stock-still.

"Move!" she shouted, aiming the gun at his head.

The paramedic came over, stopped short, and dropped his first-aid kit. She pointed the gun at the driver's head. "Give me the keys!"

He obeyed and then raised his hands in the air.

"There's no need for that," she said, gesturing at his arms with the gun.

The doctor and the paramedic drew Gerard out of the car and sat him down on a rusty gurney. The doctor held the stethoscope to his chest and listened. Then he leaned Gerard forward and passed the flashlight over his back, nodding to himself. He examined the improvised bandage on his chest. "Did you do this?"

She nodded.

"You saved your husband's life."

A wave of joy surged through her.

The doctor knocked with his knuckle on Gerard's bare chest and then held two fingers to Gerard's wrist as he stared at his watch. He strapped a blood-pressure cuff around Gerard's arm and squeezed the bulb to inflate it.

Finally, he nodded. "Madam, your husband's condition is critical. His right lung has collapsed. There is fluid in his chest. Blood. His pulse is weak, and his blood pressure is low. It is very serious. It is urgent that we take him to a hospital. Come with us to Damascus."

"That's impossible."

The doctor nodded deliberately, and then took a syringe from his bag and filled it with the contents of a glass ampoule. He stuck the needle into Gerard's shoulder. Next he inserted an IV line into his arm and attached a plump infusion bag to the end. The driver held it in the air over Gerard's head.

"You are making a mistake, madam. He is losing blood," the doctor said. "He is strong, but he will not survive."

He issued orders in Arabic to the paramedic, and the driver pointed the flashlight at Gerard's chest. The doctor painted the skin between his ribs with brown Betadine. He was holding a scalpel, and he made an incision between the ribs and went deeper with a confident hand.

A weak groan.

The doctor tore the sterile wrapping off a chest drainage kit and thrust it into the bleeding incision. There was a sharp whistle as air was released through the tube, followed by dark blood. The paramedic ripped open a packet of large gauze squares to soak up the blood. Then the driver moved the flashlight up to the Frenchman's face.

She thought his eyelids fluttered.

Raising Gerard's eyelids, the doctor shone a small flashlight into Gerard's dark eyes. He said something to the paramedic, who hurried to the rear of the ambulance and returned with a rusty metal cylinder. The doctor placed an opaque mask over Gerard's nose and mouth.

"Oxygen," the paramedic explained.

"What I have done will keep your husband stable for a short time, but you must take him to a hospital soon. What do you wish us to do now?" the doctor asked.

"Put him in the ambulance."

"You are making the right decision, madam," he said with a strained smile.

The three men loaded Gerard into the back of the ambulance.

"And now?" the doctor asked, not without apprehension.

"Thank you, thank you very much . . ." she mumbled.

With her teeth clenched and tears in her eyes, she shot the doctor, the paramedic, and the driver.

DIARY

22 AUGUST 1953

I have not written a word in four years. I am lonely. Since Jasmine's death, I have not known a woman.

I am weeping now.

6 NOVEMBER 1954

I am alone. Utterly alone. I no longer weep.

9 JUNE 1957

The deputy commandant's wife gave birth to a son. A reason to rejoice has been born. I have no one to rejoice with.

3 FEBRUARY 1960

Finally, the manager of the bank in Saint-Germain has seen fit to give me a loan. The café stands in soot-blackened ruins. Its front is boarded up with rough wooden planks. The remains of my life are imprisoned there. When I enter for the first time and see my loved ones in my mind's eye, I will certainly collapse.

She kept seeing the doctor's face. She would never forget the spark of humanity in his eyes, the kind look on enemy territory. For the rest of her life she would despise herself for killing the ambulance crew. But she didn't have a choice; it was too dangerous to let them go. She'd dragged the bodies into the field and hidden them, and then covered the bloodstains on the road with dirt.

The wheel trembled in her hands. The battered ambulance creaked and bumped. The back of her blouse was soaked with perspiration. She found a map between the seats, but it was in Arabic.

"Gerard?"

No response.

Sammy Zengot called. "Where are you?"

"Syria. Have you ever been here?"

"Where in Syria?" he persisted in his deep voice.

"Twenty-three miles south of Damascus."

"You have enough gas?"

She glanced at the fuel gauge. "Almost empty."

"Too bad you didn't check before you left Damascus."

"It's not our car."

"You stole a car?"

"An ambulance."

"Where?"

"They took care of him, bandaged the wound."

"Are they with you?"

"It's late, Sammy."

"In about twenty-five miles you'll reach a large junction. Get on 109 East toward As-Suwayda."

"Can you see us?"

"Your phone location."

"What's in As-Suwayda?"

"It's a Druze town, but you're not going there. After ten miles on 109, turn right onto a dirt road going south. Leave your phone on."

He disconnected.

"Gerard?"

Silence.

"Gerard!"

Silence.

"GERARD!"

He coughed. That was a good sign.

Black basalt rocks, fractured like prisms, reached the shoulder of the road. A pear orchard, a vineyard. At an altitude of 2,500 feet, the black soil was fertile. She pressed the gas pedal to the floor. A blue sign announced: AS-SUWAYDA. The junction was approaching.

Just survive. Stay alive. Even as an invalid, but alive.

She turned on the dim interior light and checked the dark dashboard. The needle on the temperature gauge was pointing sharply to the right, close to the red zone.

Outside, the night was still and silent, a wind was blowing; but the darkness was endless, and her fear was bottomless.

It was a little past eleven, but it felt like the middle of the night. The weak engine squealed, and the silence inside the ambulance weighed heavily.

Suddenly the horizon was flickering blue. Her heart fell. About a quarter of a mile ahead, across the road, she noticed two blue flashers.

Four hundred yards.

Orchidea turned on the shrill siren and slowed down. The hair on her nape was standing up.

Three hundred yards.

She didn't speak a word of Arabic.

Two hundred yards.

Two dark jeeps.

One hundred yards.

A spike strip. A shadowy shape approached with a flashlight; its dazzling beam was running around. She held the silenced gun between her thighs. The safety was off. She glanced back and whispered, "I'll get us out of this."

He moaned and said something unintelligible. He was conscious. He might make it.

She rolled slowly up to the roadblock.

Fifty yards.

They'd never let her through. They must have found Alois Brunner's body by now, along with his dead bodyguards, and maybe the bodies of the ambulance crew as well . . . What a night!

Thirty yards.

Three figures armed with assault rifles with curved magazines—Kalashnikovs.

Ten yards.

She cracked the window, then replaced her left hand on the wheel, her right staying on the gun between her thighs. She stopped the ambulance. The air hummed and vibrated.

The barrel of a Kalashnikov was pointed at her face. A flashlight blinded her. The silhouette of a man was lit intermittently in blue by the flashing lights. There was another armed man behind him.

She forced a smile. The man came closer and roared, "Out!"

She nodded obediently, raised the gun, and fired two rounds into his face. His body was thrown backward.

A second Kalashnikov was aimed at her. She fired two more rapid shots. The man collapsed to the ground, squeezing off a long burst as he fell. The night shook.

A third man suddenly appeared a short distance away. He dropped to the asphalt and crawled behind a jeep. Orchidea fired into two of the tires. Then she sped around the roadblock and kept going. Terrifying bursts of gunfire thundered behind her. Through the rearview mirror, she saw the window in the back door of the ambulance go white and shatter.

Good God, Gerard was back there!

The ambulance zigzagged down the road, one wheel pulling hard to the right. She got on 109 in the direction of As-Suwayda. Several jeeps were on her heels. Her body went cold and rigid. The rubber from a torn tire hit the asphalt: *flack-flack-flack*. She fought the wheel with all her strength, but the flashing blue lights were getting closer, filling the rearview mirror.

DIARY

2 APRIL 1961

I have risen from the dead. I barely sleep. We work day and night. The restored café will open on 8 August.

Yesterday, an attractive brunette walked in and asked what was going to open here. Even now, I don't understand why I told her about the fire and my loved ones who were killed.

Her blue eyes glowed.

She returned today with a thermos of coffee she had made. She is at least fifteen years younger than I. Once my scarred soul is exposed, she will undoubtedly run for her life. I must make it clear to her that I am not interested.

Last night, I dreamed about Jasmine. Sophie and Albert were in her arms.

Flames engulfed their bodies.

Alois Brunner was the Israelite, the link between the Syrian Mukhabarat and the Mud Man.

Orchidea and Paris were still in Syria.

"We're not going to make it out of here," she yelled over the phone. In the background was the ominous sound of bullets hitting steel. The engine of the ambulance was shrieking and springs were creaking. Another thud.

"We'll get you out," Alex said with as much confidence as he could muster.

"Gerard won't make it," she said. "He's dying."

"Who?"

"Paris."

"What did you call him?"

"Gerard."

"Trezeguet?"

"Yes . . . Why?"

"Let me talk to him."

"He's in bad shape, Alex. He's lost a lot of blood."

"I understand. But it's important. Can he speak?"

"He's not responding."

"Let me try."

"Just a minute," she said. "I must keep my hands on the wheel. I lost a tire!"

Sirens screamed in the background. He heard her call out in a loud voice, "It's Alex!"

"Just a second," she said. "I'm trying to hand him the phone."

Alex heard a bang, followed by a yelp of pain. "The steering wheel!" she cried out in panic. "They're getting close!"

Alex picked up Justus's will and stared at the names of the heirs: Rachel Dresdener and Gerard Trezeguet.

The Frenchman's breathing was noisy and anguished.

"Gerard?" he tried.

A broken moan.

"Justus betrayed the Ring and handed it and the virus over to Brunner and the Syrians."

"No . . ." Gerard protested weakly.

Thank God, he was still responsive. "I saw it with my own eyes," Alex said.

"No . . . not Justus . . ."

"He donated a lot of money to a neo-Nazi group. He was doing it for years."

Gerard spat. "No."

"He was working with Brunner and the Syrians."

"No . . ."

"There's no one else."

"There is . . ."

"Who?"

"Blackmail . . ."

"Who was blackmailing whom?"

"Justus asked me . . . letter bomb . . ."

"What letter bomb?"

"Woman killed . . ."

"Who did he send a letter bomb to?"

"Blackmail . . ."

"Brunner?"

"Nazis . . . first Gunter . . ."

"Who was blackmailing them, Gerard?"

"The swine . . ."

"What swine?"

"The grill house . . ."

"What grill house?" Alex asked, a shiver going through his body.

"Schlaff . . . Oskar Schlaff."

Oskar Schlaff was the Mud Man.

Schlaff, the owner of the Schlaff Bierkeller und Grill; Justus's close friend; the man who kept a case of rare Brunello for him; the warmhearted host. Oh God.

The picture was becoming clearer. One of the Stasi twins had been tailing Berlin, had followed him that night from the grill house to Teufelsberg. The note the waitress passed to Alex linked him and Jane to Berlin. And Schlaff had also seen Jane in the restaurant with Justus.

"Are you positive?" Alex asked.

"It broke him . . ." Gerard said faintly.

"What's the connection between Schlaff and Brunner?"

"Nephew . . ."

"How?"

A cough. "Sister's son . . ."

"What did Schlaff have on Justus?"

Gerard coughed uncontrollably, gagging. "Don't know . . ."

"It's important, Gerard."

"They ate there for years . . . they paid . . . didn't know who . . . I found the bank . . ."

"What bank?"

"He withdrew the money . . . cash . . . I got pictures . . . Justus saw . . . the pictures . . ."

"Of who?"

"He cried . . . like a child . . ."

Gerard was wheezing. His lungs were choked.

"Where the hell is it . . ." Orchidea muttered in the background.

"And the body you brought from Paris?" Alex asked.

"Tailing me . . ."

"Why did you come to Berlin?"

"Justus didn't reply . . . I understood . . . something wrong . . ." He groaned in agony.

A bullet hit the ambulance. Glass shattered.

"Justus left you half a billion euros. Why did he do that?"

"In the war . . . my father and Gunter . . . like brothers . . ." He wheezed. "Papa owned a café . . . Brunner and the SS . . . always came . . . Gunter defected . . . Papa recruited him . . . Resistance . . . rescued Jews . . . thousands . . . children . . . Brunner raped, killed . . . wife and children . . . set fire . . ."

"Did you know that Brunner was still alive and hiding in Damascus?"

"I prayed . . . in Zenobia I suspected . . ."

"How?"

"Don't want to die . . ."

"How did you know it was him?"

"No eye . . . gloves . . . Justus died . . . died loyal . . . not traitor . . . dear Justus . . . dead . . ."

He wept softly. "Oh, Justus . . ."

Alex's heart ached for the Frenchman. His sobbing grew louder. He coughed and choked. "Dear Justus . . ."

Alex wiped his eyes.

"What's wrong, Gerard? Why are you crying?" Orchidea asked.

"My fault . . . didn't know . . ."

"Didn't know what, Gerard?"

"All connected . . . please . . . forgive me . . ."

"There's nothing to forgive."

"I did . . . what you wanted . . . Brunner was the Israelite . . ."

"I'll take care of Oskar Schlaff," Alex promised.

"So cold . . . Papa wrote . . ."

"What did Papa write?"

". . . Diary . . . please . . . kiss children for me . . . Gilbert . . . Gaston . . . kiss . . ."

"I will." Tears were streaming down Alex's face. "I promise."

Gerard fought for air.

"Who's Rachel Dresdener?"

Silence.

"Tell me, Gerard. Who's Rachel Dresdener?"

Silence.

"GERARD!"

The silence was unbroken.

Then Alex heard a whisper: "Shema Yisrael . . . Adonai Eloheinu . . . Adonai Echad."[1]

---

1   "Hear, O Israel . . . the Lord our God . . . the Lord is one."

DIARY

5 April 1961

The young woman returned to the café today. Her name is Arianne. I am not afraid of you, she said as she sat down beside me on the curb, where I devoured the egg-salad sandwich she had prepared. Her hair is coal black and her eyes clear blue. Her lips are as red as ripe fruit. Before she left, she gave me a quick kiss on the cheek.

6 August 1961

A while ago, I wrote a letter to the deputy commandant to tell him of the reopening that will take place in two days.

Today he appeared unexpectedly at the construction site, elegantly dressed and perfectly coiffed, and hugged me tightly. When he saw the restoration work we had done on the café, he burst into tears. He kissed both my hands. I told him that I had taken out a large loan. He left, explaining that he had a business meeting.

Later he returned and handed me a full cardboard box. What's in the box, I asked. The deputy commandant smiled. The box was packed with new five-hundred-franc notes.

Take it, he said. I have more than enough. And you sacrificed everything you had for me.

7 August 1961

Oh God, tomorrow is the opening.

"Look for a news item about a letter bomb in Berlin not long ago," Alex instructed Butthead.

"Why do you sound strange?"

"Strange how?"

"Sad."

He'd sent Gerard Trezeguet to his death without even knowing who he was, and had unwittingly allowed him to fulfill his destiny. The deep-rooted, courageous friendship between Gerard and Justus—born of an even stronger bond between their fathers—aroused a mixture of envy and sorrow. The words *Shema Yisrael*, traditionally recited by Jews on their deathbed, had never affected him so deeply.

Moments before he died, Gunter had drawn a croissant. He was trying to tell them to talk to Paris, but Alex had missed it.

Trezeguet . . . Trezeguet . . . He'd seen that name before . . . But where?

He hurried to Justus's study and looked at the photographs on the cabinet. He picked up the small faded picture encased in Perspex and examined it closely: a man in a white apron was standing in front of a Parisian café, his arms folded on his chest and a smile on his face. In the background, patrons occupied round tables. Above his head was a dark awning with the name CAFÉ TREZEGUET.

He found a magnifying glass in a desk drawer and held it up to the photo. There was a gap between the man's front teeth.

His phone vibrated.

"February 18 of this year," Butthead said. "A letter bomb exploded in the office of the Schlaff Bierkeller und Grill. It was addressed to Oskar Schlaff, supposedly from the Estonian Veterinary and Food Service, but it blew up in the hands of the restaurant manager, one Rosemarie Landwer. She was Schlaff's common-law wife. It contained three pounds of plastic explosives. It took five days to officially identify the body. No suspects have ever been detained."

Gerard had told the truth. Oskar Schlaff had been blackmailing the Erlichmanns. Justus tried to assassinate Schlaff, but he killed his common-law wife by mistake. From that point on, it became personal.

Schlaff wanted to hurt him badly and keep him paying. He took the gloves off, meted out punishment, and sentenced him to a heavy fine. That would explain Justus's last deposit, which was ten times the usual amount. So far, it all fit. But why did Justus hand over the Ring to Schlaff?

In the video, he seemed to be giving them the information of his own free will. But that didn't make sense. Something was missing. What was Schlaff holding over the Erlichmanns? What did he know that they would pay such a hefty price to keep secret?

And what about the swastika Justus had painted on the tail of the Messerschmitt? Maybe he simply wished to make it look authentic and hadn't painted it out of sympathy or worship.

Butthead called.

"We traced the two phone numbers they found in Brunner's

apartment. The first is Oskar Schlaff's cellphone. We're working on a preliminary profile of the guy.

"The second number belongs to Omar Hattab. We're analyzing the conversations between them over the past few months. After that, we'll see who else they were each in contact with."

"Well done, Butthead. I need Schlaff's home address and a satellite image of the area of the restaurant complex."

In his mind's eye, he saw the overly tight face of Oskar Schlaff. The long blond hair, bottle of Brunello, gracious hospitality, affection for Justus.

And, of course, skewered pigs.

The Syrian jeeps were closing in on them like a pack of hyenas that smelled blood. Her side mirrors were painted in intense blue light. Where was the fucking turnoff? Had she missed it?

She saw a black road sign with Arabic letters. Was it the turn-off? Impulsively, she decided to risk it and swerved sharply off the highway onto the dirt road, the ambulance jerking wildly. She banged her head on the roof. The rear punctured tire was wrenched from the rim. Black rubber scraps spun up and splashed on the road.

"Sammy?" she yelled into the phone, but she only heard hushed mumbling.

The phone emitted a flagging beep. The battery was dying.

"SAMMY!"

"You're almost there," came his deep voice.

"They're right behind me!"

"We know. Go straight for one-point-eight miles and stop."

"I lost a rear tire!"

"You are so close."

All of a sudden, a deafening blast rocked the night. The ambulance was thrown forward, bumping on the ground. In her rearview mirror, a huge bright orange fireball illuminated the night.

The first jeep behind them stopped at once, engulfed in flames. Then another explosion. The gas tank? She fought the unruly steering.

"What does the ambulance look like?" Sammy asked.

She glanced at the insignia on the steering wheel. "Mitsubishi. An old white van. The lettering is red or black."

The dirt road was treacherous, rutted and dotted with puddles of murky water. They passed a blighted olive grove followed by plowed fields, and she sped forward, not knowing where she was going. Behind her, a jeep was getting ominously close.

Shots were fired. The ambulance was hit. She bit down on her lip. A flash of light flew past her, and almost immediately she heard a petrifying whistle followed by a loud explosion. A second jeep flew into the air and crashed to the ground, breaking apart into dozens of burning fragments. The willful ambulance pulled to the right, nearly sinking into the soft shoulder.

They were here somewhere. She knew they were here. She just couldn't see them. She braked the ambulance and switched off the engine. There was another blast behind her, and a large flame rose into the sky. The odor of diesel fuel and burning rubber. She didn't look back.

"Can you hear anything?" Zengot asked.

The crackle of flames licking at another jeep. Glass breaking.

"What am I supposed to hear?"

"Hold on. Don't go any closer. Wait for instructions."

She searched the sky for lights. Nothing.

And then her ears caught the whiz of rotor blades—the most beautiful sound she'd ever heard.

The light cast by the flames rising from the jeeps revealed the outline of a giant steel bird descending awkwardly from the black sky. She turned her head, and a current ran through her: two more jeeps were rapidly approaching, the beams of their headlights bouncing on the road. They skirted the burning vehicle. It wouldn't end . . .

She turned the key, but the engine didn't catch. She tried again and again, the ambulance's battery weakening and her eyes welling with tears. Not now. Not like this.

In her last desperate attempt, the engine awoke, the ambulance shook, and she pressed down on the gas pedal as hard as she could, racing toward the Sikorsky CH-53. The titanic body was caught in her headlights. It landed in the dark, raising a cloud of sand. Its back ramp was facing her. Under its short wings hung external fuel tanks and missiles.

As the loading ramp opened, the blue lights of her pursuers licked at the rear of the ambulance. Her high beams exposed the empty belly of the chopper. She didn't slow down.

Four armed silhouettes jumped out. They spread out, lowered themselves to a kneeling position, and aimed a barrage of fire at the jeeps. Orchidea ignored their hand signals, steering the ambulance toward the center of the ramp as she screamed into the phone, "They're too close! I'm going in!"

"No!" Sammy shouted. "The chopper's roof is too low!"

Assessing the width of the opening and mouthing a prayer, she raced in. Something shattered. She braked. The ambulance skidded to a stop. Shards of red plastic fell from the roof. The headlights lit up the interior of the chopper, revealing several masked figures. Two of them quickly secured the ambulance to the floor as the four shooters ran back inside. The engine roared louder immediately and the chopper detached itself heavily from the ground, leaned forward, and rose into the night. The ramp whooshed closed.

The lights of As-Suwayda twinkled on the left.

A field hospital had been set up in the front of the chopper. A medical team rolled the gurney out of the ambulance, and she was right beside them. Gerard's face was white. They set to work at once.

As she climbed out of the ambulance, all eyes were on her. Someone held out a canteen of water, but she waved it aside, hurrying after the doctors. She touched Gerard's cold face. His eyes were shut. "Don't die . . ." she whispered. "Please don't die . . ."

Behind a clear plastic curtain, a surgeon held a stethoscope to Gerard's chest and listened intently before grabbing the paddles of a defibrillator.

The Frenchman's body jerked.

They tried again.

She burst into tears.

DIARY

9 August 1961

My hair is once again acrid with smoke. The deputy commandant has had a nervous breakdown. I sit at his bedside at the Hôpital Hôtel-Dieu in Île de la Cité.

You will not break, Roger, he whispered to me today when he awakened for a moment. I will give you money again.

I told him that I read in the newspaper that a Syrian tourist has been arrested on suspicion of having committed the crime.

His breath caught. Do you know who lives in Syria now? he asked.

I did not.

The commandant.

The room spun around me.

I remember a nurse and a glass syringe.

You are suffering, sir, the doctor whispered to me. We can help.

Not me, I replied. I am lost.

10 August 1961

Old wounds reopened. The fire department ruled that it was arson. The Syrian tourist confessed that he set fire to the café at 5:15 in the morning.

Less than three hours before the opening. There had been hope in my heart.

The smell of smoke and damp earth. My fresh grave.

Exodus called.

"Remember the deposit of one million, two hundred thousand euros we found?" The tension in her voice was tangible.

"Dopo Domani Holdings. I remember," Alex said.

"We traced the owner. Are you sitting down?"

What more did this night have in store for him? "Who is it?"

"Someone you know, Alex. Someone we all know."

"Spit it out."

"Reuven."

"What!? Reuven?! Are you sure?"

"A hundred percent."

Alex paced the kitchen, his mind in turmoil.

"Could it have something to do with the funding of the Ring?"

"Financially speaking, the Ring is totally autonomous. It has no links to Mossad whatsoever. It's funded directly by donations from Jewish communities in North America. If they needed more money, Erlichmann reached into his own pocket. We've found quite a lot of transactions like that."

"When was the deposit made?"

"Eighteen days ago."

"What could it be?"

"Only a bribe, Alex. That's what bribes look like."

Ever since the beginning of the crisis, there had been something fishy about Reuven's behavior. He'd put a spoke in every wheel; he'd lied and sabotaged their efforts—and failed them.

He'd even messed with Alex's personal life by making the call to Daniella.

Reuven was garbage. Reuven was a piece of shit. But Reuven wasn't a traitor. There was a difference.

He was about to be brought down—an earthquake—but strangely, Alex didn't have any feeling of schadenfreude, nor pity for the man. Mostly, he was disappointed. Reuven was dirty, and he wasn't a mere union rep in a factory in a forgotten town.

Alex felt sick to his stomach. The time had come to bring the ax down on Reuven, but he didn't intend to stoop to his level. Exodus had him pegged. If the tables were turned, Reuven would never give him the benefit of the doubt, but Alex felt that he had to hear his side of the story first.

Reuven picked up on the third ring. "I was just about to call you," he said.

"Were you?"

Reuven remained silent.

"We know that you took money from Justus Erlichmann, Reuven. One million, two hundred thousand euros deposited in the account of Dopo Domani Holdings. You're the sole owner."

"Alex?"

"Go to the prime minister and submit your resignation."

"Is this some kind of sick joke? Are you bored?"

"What was the money for?"

"That's enough, Alex. It's not funny anymore!"

"I don't have time to play games, Reuven. Resign now, or I'll contact the PM myself."

"What do you mean, *resign*?"

Glass striking glass. A bottle being opened. A gulp.

"Reuven, it's over."

"You don't decide what's over and what's not over!"

"You took a bribe."

"Why would Justus Erlichmann give me a million euros?"

"One million, two hundred thousand. This is your last chance, Reuven. I have to deal with Schlaff."

"Justus passed his last polygraph. If he gave me anything, Drucker would know, wouldn't he?"

"When did you start believing in polygraphs? All they're good for is putting the fear of God in junior agents. Squeeze your ass at the right time, and the fucking machine is blind."

"Is that what you did?"

"Resign now, and the press might never discover the real reason. You'll still have a future."

If Reuven went straight to the prime minister, things would take their course. The PM would call security, and the head of Mossad would not be allowed to return to his office. He'd be put under house arrest and stripped of his rights, he would be barred from leaving the country, and he would undergo interrogation. That seemed like enough for the time being.

"You can't stomach the thought that I'm Daniella's real father," Reuven said.

"Reuven, the only person who can't stomach that thought is Daniella."

DIARY

---

4 JULY 1967

I placed my hand on Arianne's hard, round belly. I felt the heart-beat of my child, his young heart lusting for life. I am fifty-six today, the age my father was when he died of heart disease.

Please, let me live long enough.

13 JULY 1967

The doctors say that my heart is functioning at 40 percent capacity. My breathing is labored, and simple tasks tire me out. Six years have passed since the café burned down for the second time, right before it was supposed to open. I am sated with disappointment and tragedy and pain. I do not have the strength to try again.

8 AUGUST 1967

I am the happiest man in the world. Our son was born this morning. A green bud in the black, smoking embers.

My Arianne is young and healthy. She will be his anchor in the world. Please, God, watch over her.

Arianne, my love, how were you able to pull me out of the grave?

16 AUGUST 1967

My comrades from the Resistance came to the circumcision ceremony in the synagogue. The deputy commandant and his wife ar-

rived from Berlin and brought their son. The boy is ten. During the ceremony he never laughed or played or made any noise; he simply watched as if hypnotized by Gerard, the baby.

I held my son in my arms, and tears wet my prayer shawl.

You were there with me, my scorched roots.

Once again the image of the machine gunner in Leipzig tried to rise from the dead.

His first order of business was to confront Oskar Schlaff face-to-face. Soon he would go to the cellar of the modern-day Nazi. Soon he would go there and rip out his heart.

Alex oiled the Glock and wiped it down with a kitchen towel. Then he checked the chamber. It was empty. He snapped a full magazine in place and cocked the gun.

His phone vibrated.

Reuven said falteringly, "Do I have your word?"

"About what?"

"The press."

A deep swallow.

"Are you going to the prime minister now?"

"I'm counting on you," Reuven said, his voice choked.

The call was disconnected.

Text message from HQ in Glilot: Gerard's condition critical but stable.

Oh God!

He slipped the Glock into his jacket pocket. Its heaviness was reassuring.

He went up to the workroom and selected several tools. Coming downstairs for the last time, he switched off the lights in Justus Erlichmann's home and left. As he trod through the snow on the street, he turned and took a final look at the house, knowing that he would never be back.

He drove south toward Wannsee, the dark forest emerging from between the fancy houses.

On Am Grossen Wannsee, the street leading to the grill house, he suddenly shuddered. Just down the road was the villa where Reinhard Heydrich, Adolf Eichmann, and their cohorts had plotted the Final Solution to the Jewish Question.

Here, on January 20, 1942, the Holocaust was born.

The curling neon letters of SCHLAFF were reflected on the ice that covered the parking lot. Alex parked the Mercedes behind a row of trees and watched the restaurant complex from a distance. The single-story structure aboveground was about a quarter of the area of the cellar. It was painted a mustard yellow. There were eleven cars in the lot. The elegant curves of a white Porsche Carrera stood out among the other vehicles.

An older couple came out, the wife supporting her husband's weight. His legs were like jelly. The woman burst into raucous laughter. The man slipped on the ice, losing his balance and nearly falling from her arms. They stumbled into a car and left.

One down.

Butthead called. "Do you have time for a quick profile?"

"Let's hear it," he whispered.

"Oskar Schlaff was born in 1957 under the name Fritz Jungbluth. His mother was Alois Brunner's sister. His father left when he was a year old. His mother died of cancer when Fritz was five. He was sent to an orphanage in Munich and thrown out before the age of ten. Reason unknown. He was transferred to a home for orphans and juvenile offenders in Nuremberg."

Alex cracked the window.

"At fourteen, he was gang-raped by six boys. Two weeks later, the body of the gang leader was found in the showers. He'd been strangled by a steel cable."

Alex took a deep breath.

"Listen to this, Alex: the other five all vanished and have never been found. Schlaff was questioned repeatedly by the police, but they were never able to tie him to their disappearances."

Chills ran up and down his spine.

"In 1975, on the day he turned eighteen, he officially changed his name to Oskar Schlaff. He had a number of short-lived jobs before he opened the restaurant in '79. He expanded it in '86 and then renovated it to look like it does now in 2005. It does very well.

"Schlaff also owns three pig farms. Their website says they mix special herbs into the feed to give the meat a flavor uniquely suited to the European palate. He operates a huge slaughterhouse about forty miles north of Berlin, and he's now negotiating a contract to market his pork outside Germany. He has a fleet of twenty-six trucks of different sizes."

Alex hit the steering wheel.

"He's about to go public on the Frankfurt Stock Exchange. A leading Berlin law firm is preparing the company prospectus for an IPO. He has a line of credit of around three million euros from a number of banks for business development. All his enterprises are profitable and financially stable."

"That's it?"

"I'm just getting started. In the early years, his restaurant was patronized by Americans working at the NSA listening station on Teufelsberg. They stopped coming when Schlaff was caught recording their conversations. Later he was suspected of sub-

versive activity for the far right and for neo-Nazis. He took part
in right-wing demonstrations in the late '70s and was picked up
three times, first by the police and then by the Federal Office for
the Protection of the Constitution. The last time he was arrested
was in 1981. His record is clean after that. It's possible he became
an informant. Mud Man could be his code name.

"Schlaff was also suspected of working for the Stasi right up
until the fall of the Berlin Wall. In 1993 they uncovered a tun-
nel leading from East Berlin—near Checkpoint Bravo on the
Glienicke Bridge—to the west. It came out in a pigsty Schlaff
owned. According to records in the Stasi archives, his restaurant
was the staging area for quite a few assassination attempts."

"Hold on a minute," Alex croaked. Afraid he was about to
puke, he breathed in and out deeply.

"Okay, go on."

"For the past thirteen years, he's been flying to Damascus
once a month. But in the last six weeks, he was there five times."

"Is there much more?"

"Seven pages."

"I'll get back to you later."

"Finish him off, Alex. He smells like an informant for the Federal Office for the Protection of the Constitution; that means he's
got immunity. The piece of garbage could walk away from this
without a scratch."

DIARY

17 August 1967

Yesterday, during the ceremony at the synagogue, the deputy commandant placed a hand on my shoulder. I am creating a secret Zionist organization, he said. Give me your son, your only son.

Gerard is a baby, only eight days old, I replied.

So we will wait, he said.

What will this secret organization do? I asked.

It will make sure that it doesn't happen again, he replied.

Gerard is yours, I said.

22 July 1970

My days are numbered. I lie in bed in the Hôpital Hôtel-Dieu. The deputy commandant does not leave my bedside. Arianne comes with our Gerard. He will be three soon. He kissed me on the lips.

Papa is crying, he said.

7 August 1970

Gerard is enchanting, small but strong. Tomorrow is his third birthday. He gets his beauty from my Arianne, and the space between his teeth from me. I hope that when he grows up, he will rebuild the Café Trezeguet, construct a proofing cabinet, and create a starter dough. I hope that he will once again fill the air with the scent of yeast.

A sudden gust of icy wind. Leafless branches swayed wildly. The air was charged with electricity. A bolt of lightning cut through the black sky, blinding him and lighting up the parking lot. A waitress in a white apron locked the front door of the restaurant from inside, turned off the neon sign and the lights on the first floor, and then disappeared down the stairs.

Moonlight shone on Wannsee's large lake. Cracking chunks of ice floated on the surface like sleeping animals. The narrow bank was crowded with boats wrapped in protective tarps. Mounds of dirty snow were piled up alongside the footpaths and roads.

Hunched down in the backseat of the Mercedes, Alex kept his eyes on the restaurant. The staff had finished their shifts and were exiting through a back door, puffing on cigarettes; the wind swallowed up the smoke. The last five cars pulled out together.

Only the white Porsche remained.

Alex called Butthead. "Block cell transmissions around the restaurant and cut off the landlines."

"For how long?"

"Just do it."

Alex got out of the car and listened to the night. The strong wind roared and a loose sheet of metal banged against a wall. There was a hum in the air as the storm gathered force. He pulled his jacket tighter, made his way to the restaurant, and began searching. On the other side of the door, everything seemed dark and lifeless.

He didn't see any sign of an alarm system or security cameras. The stairs going down to the back entrance and the kitchen were slippery with ice. The door was locked. He climbed back up and stopped next to a windowless structure about forty feet—the size of a shipping container. He checked the door. Locked.

The entrance to the restaurant consisted of two sets of doors with a small vestibule between them. The interior doors were locked. He took out the tools he had collected from Justus's workroom, chose two small screwdrivers, and started fiddling with the lock. The tools kept slipping from his fingers.

At last, he heard a click and the door opened. He froze and held his breath, listening for sounds from the sleeping restaurant. He pulled out a flashlight, held it with the Glock in a combined grip, and went in.

It was dark inside. The rough wooden floor was still damp from the mop. In the beam of his flashlight he saw wood benches upturned on the long tables.

Suddenly he heard a strange gurgling coming from the direction of the bar. He spun around, his finger tightening on the trigger, and walked quickly toward the sound.

No one there.

More gurgling. It was the movement of air in the beer taps.

He passed the beam of light over the bare brown brick walls and the large wine cooler with its heavy lock.

The stainless-steel counters in the kitchen gleamed. Blasts of cold, dry air washed over him as he opened the refrigerators. Slabs of pink meat were hanging silently from sharp hooks. The fire was out in the long, freshly cleaned grill. He rested his palm on it. Lukewarm.

The restrooms were painted mustard yellow and reeked of air freshener. He found a shiny black door he hadn't noticed before and aimed the Glock straight at it. The flashlight's reflection was blinding. He kicked the door open, burst in, and quickly scanned the room: desk, office chair, adding machine, files, documents, telephones, and a letter opener. Everything was in perfect order.

The remains of Rosemarie Landwer had been scraped from these walls.

Dozens of photos of grinning diners were pinned to a large corkboard, some of them obviously drunk, their nostrils flared. They had all been caught in the merciless glare of a camera flash. The pictures had been taken here, in the restaurant. Including one of Oskar Schlaff, Gunter Erlichmann, and his son, Justus. The old man seemed detached from his surroundings.

Where was Schlaff?

Alex climbed the stairs and exited the building. The white Porsche was still in the parking lot. He hid behind a row of cypress trees and examined the restaurant roof.

His heart stopped.

Smoke was billowing from the tall chimney.

The prime minister was buttoning his jacket, although the heat in his office was on high. He didn't offer Reuven a seat.

Reuven closed flaps and steeled himself.

"I have been informed by a member of your organization that you received one million, two hundred thousand euros from Justus Erlichmann. Unless you can provide a satisfactory explanation, you are officially under suspicion of accepting a bribe," the PM said, pausing meaningfully before continuing the attack. "Mr. Hetz, do you understand the gravity of your situation?"

Reuven didn't respond.

"The man from whom you took the money is a traitor whose actions have had catastrophic implications, on both the intelligence and operational levels."

Reuven didn't respond.

"Your silence is an admission of guilt?"

That was transparent. Reuven didn't respond.

A green vase with an enormous bouquet of red roses stood on a side table. The perks of power were so seductive.

"Since this crisis began, we have lost more agents than in the whole history of the country. We have lost the protective shield around Mossad, and Israel itself," the PM said, keeping up the assault.

Reuven didn't respond.

"I know you, Reuven. You're a cold fish. But you're not a traitor." Retreating behind his desk, he added, "Considering your fantasies of a career in politics, I tend to believe that the money was meant to fund your political campaign. I assume that you set up Dopo Domani Holdings to funnel questionable donations. Am I wrong?"

Reuven didn't respond.

"As head of Mossad, you are forbidden to accept gifts of any sort, anything that could be construed as a gift, or any sum of money from anyone who is not a member of your immediate family."

The motherfucker had spoken with his legal advisers.

"In view of the timing of the payment, it appears to be related to the Ring crisis. Perhaps you smelled a rat, and Erlichmann bought your silence? Perhaps he heard that you were hoping to occupy this office in the near future—and he pushed the button? Justus was a man who knew what buttons to push. He could always put his finger on the motive driving the person he was dealing with. He'd find it and use it to his advantage."

Reuven didn't respond.

He gazed at the photo of the F-16s flying over Masada and remembered the words of Eleazar ben Yair, the leader of the Sicarii rebels, during the first-century siege on the fortress: "Let us die unenslaved by our enemies and leave this world as free men."

Then, in a pragmatic frame of mind, he decided he would choose different pictures: high-tech, solar energy. Something green, up to date.

"If you wish to preserve what remains of your honor and ensure that your dirty laundry is not aired in the media, you must resign immediately; naturally, I will accept your resignation. You will be forbidden to enter politics, or to return to your office. Agreed?"

"Or else?"

The PM looked surprised. "Or else you will be held on suspicion of treason and will most likely face charges for compromising tens of Mossad operatives during a time of war, in exchange for money. If I am not mistaken, that alone is enough for several consecutive life sentences. I trust that you used the time it took you to get here to hire a good defense attorney?"

"I can see that you're scared to run against me in the next elections," Reuven said.

"Reuven, there is a neck under the guillotine and it isn't mine. For your own sake, you have to start thinking realistically."

Reuven remained silent.

The PM gave him the sort of look you give a rebellious teenager. "Okay, Reuven. Go wait outside. Think about it for two minutes and come back with your answer."

Reuven didn't nod. Instead, he moved closer to the PM and stood facing him, straight on.

The PM sniffed the air.

Maybe he smelled the whiskey on his breath. Who cared. It was his turn to talk.

"Mr. Prime Minister, you bear sole authority for the Nibelung Ring. It says so in the Nibelung charter. I presume you've never read it. I suggest that you use the two minutes you have left in this office to do it. I'll be outside."

The PM's face went red. His eyes narrowed with the wariness of a snake eyeing a mongoose.

Reuven smiled. "Either you deny the item about corruption

and stand behind me before the press, the attorney general, and the police, or I go to the media with the story of how you screwed over the Nibelungs. And that's without even mentioning how your incompetence enabled the Hochstadt-Lancet virus to fall into enemy hands, exposing Israel to the threat of another Holocaust. Do you think two minutes will be enough, Mr. Prime Minister?"

Leaving the safety of his hiding place, Alex made his way to the meat locker. He stuck the pair of screwdrivers into the lock. His heart was racing, his fingers were stiff, and the lock was stubborn. Time dripped by, burning his skin like hot wax.

Where was the smoke coming from?

A silent delivery vehicle was parked in the back—a white truck. He remembered his fruitless search of the white truck outside Girona. He should have stripped them all down—the truck, and the albino driver, and the idiot sitting next to him—and then fired a flare at the two motherfuckers and watched them burn. They had been hiding her somewhere in the truck. He might have been able to save her.

The wind whipped at his face. Lightning flashed from behind ominous clouds, and his fingers refused to do his bidding. He took a deep breath in an attempt to calm himself down, or, at the very least, to stop his hands from shaking.

There was a loud rumble of thunder, and a car alarm somewhere began blaring. Finally the lock gave way. He opened the heavy stainless-steel door. A neon light flickered on automatically. Inside, the sickening smell of dead flesh hung in the air. Dozens of headless half carcasses of pigs were hanging from steel hooks in the ceiling. He checked between the cold slabs of meat and scanned the floor the whole length of the meat locker. No one there.

Two sealed cartons were standing at the far end. He opened one, and the light sparkled over shiny, dark calf livers. The other contained pale pig toes.

On the floor beside them, barely visible, was a trapdoor the size of a suitcase, with a ring embedded in it. He pulled on it. The trapdoor opened.

He thrust his Glock into the opening, followed by the flashlight: a flight of stairs.

His body heavy from exhaustion, he lifted the trapdoor until it was leaning on the wall. Shining his flashlight into the hole, he saw a short corridor at the bottom of the steps. It led to a closed door.

There was a lump of ice in his chest. He could still leave and call Brussels for backup. And then wait for hours for the team to arrive? No. Every minute was precious.

Alex descended the stairs, hugging the wall, and aimed the Glock at the door in front of him. He pressed down on the handle. It resisted for a moment before opening. A light came on automatically, and he almost let off a round.

Another fucking corridor, about ten feet long. The walls were covered with white tile.

The door behind him suddenly swung closed, and bolts slid into place. Alex tugged at the handle. It was locked.

In front of him was another door with a protected peephole in the center. Something moved behind it.

He leaped at the door. Too late. He was locked in. A fucking trap!

He heard a hiss, and something slightly sweet sprayed on his face.

Then everything went black.

He hadn't been knocked out. It was a tight loss. But it was just the first round.

Even if he was ultimately forced to resign, he'd made it clear to the PM that he'd be going down with him.

"Get me a glass of ice water," Reuven ordered the secretary without a glance in her direction. He settled himself in the anteroom.

He had only one goal—to save his political career.

He used the couple of minutes he had to play a familiar game: actions and responses.

Then he went back into the PM's office.

"What's your decision, Reuven?" The PM's jacket was off now, relegated to a hanger together with his officialdom. He was looking for a political solution, and that was no actions and responses. It was haggling.

"I'm not resigning. You will not fire me but will ask me to stay on until the end of the year. You're going to promise Alex Bartal the directorship, but you and I are going to handpick his second-in-command, someone we can control. Nobody holds that post at the moment. Naturally, when the press asks for your comment, you deny everything.

"In return, I won't run against you in the next elections. That way, you'll have a fighting chance of keeping your job. Do you need time to consider it, or do you agree that this is the perfect solution?"

The PM's lips moved, but no sound came out. His face went red and he raised his shoulders threateningly. "How dare you!"

Reuven pulled the tiny recorder from his pocket. "Remember our last meeting, Mr. Prime Minister? You confirmed your responsibility for the Ring and ordered the insertion of two of our people into Damascus. Would you like to hear it again?"

The PM's face dripped with loathing. "You're filthy, Reuven."

"And you're the one who invented bleach."

"The public isn't sophisticated. They can only digest simple messages. If the media tells them there was a fuckup involving Mossad, they'll want the head of Mossad, not the prime minister. That's Mass Media 101."

"The judges who sit on the High Court of Justice are no fools," Reuven said.

"We both know that it will never reach the court," the PM cut in. He turned to look at the pictures on the wall. After a lengthy pause he said in a quieter voice, "What about the inhalers?"

Reuven's face broke into one of his rare, cold smiles.

"What inhalers?"

His cheek was pressed up against something cold. His stomach was cramping, and there was a sickeningly sweet taste in his mouth. He couldn't seem to open his eyes. Where was he?

Voices above him spoke in German. The words were spit out like sharp metal shards.

Stairs; a narrow corridor; trapped; gas—his memory was coming back.

They might be waiting for him to open his eyes. One of them was very close. His shoes smelled of damp earth. The other was farther away, barking orders.

He managed to crack his eyes open: muddy, rough work shoes and the bottom of dirty jeans; a black floor; the blurred reflection of something moving continuously; a black-and-white image; a huge screen; a large space. The barking one was wearing black moccasins polished to a high shine. A vague odor of sewage. His hand was lying on a cold metal lattice—a drain.

Where the hell was he?

A hand pulled at his hair, lifting his head until the vertebrae in his neck were stretched taut. A groan escaped his lips.

"Stand up, you piece of garbage!"

He opened his eyes and saw silvery walls covered with aluminum.

Oskar Schlaff had an evil smirk on his face. His long blond hair undulated like a swarm of worms.

From the other end of the room, he heard someone stifle a giggle. A third man. Short, almost dwarflike, he was leaning against the large screen. He couldn't be more than five feet tall, and he had piggy eyes. His ruddy bald pate was encircled by a brush of brown hair. The dwarf was rooting around in his ear with a finger. He brought what he found up to his nose and sniffed at it. He was holding an old-fashioned black leather medical bag between his feet, and he was clad in a shabby brown suit and pink shirt.

He must have gotten dressed in the dark.

He giggled again, an oink followed by a snort. His shoes were protected by stained white overshoes.

"Have you two met, Jew-boy?" Schlaff asked, like a convivial host at a cocktail party. "This is Dr. Rauch. Herr Dr. Rauch."

The dwarf snorted.

"Let me guess," Alex said. "His parents are siblings?"

"It would be worth your while to stay on his good side. The man is ruthless."

"It's always good to have a doctor around," Alex said.

"He is not a doctor," Schlaff chuckled. "He is a veterinarian."

Schlaff was wearing a custom-tailored gray blazer over a black turtleneck sweater. His face looked baked from excessive tanning, and the cold look in his eyes was as welcoming as liquid nitrogen. "Do you recognize this one?"

Alex turned his head.

Bald, no eyebrows. It was the other Stasi twin.

"Say hello to Sepp Mauser."

The twin's eyes were blazing with fury. He raised his upper lip, revealing the fangs of a predator.

"Sepp is mad at you," Schlaff said. "You killed his brother,

Bruno. I promised him he could spend some time with you before we started the ceremony."

A harsh kick hit the side of Alex's face, sending his head flying.

Something was crushed; bones were shattered—his eye socket. Blood flowed from his nose and forehead. Pressure throbbed behind his eye as if a spike had pierced his skull. He remained flat on the floor, buying time, but the pain intensified. Forced to protect his head with his hands, he felt a sharp kick to his exposed abdomen.

He moaned out loud. Snakes of pain twisted through his torso. He coughed and gagged, his head throbbing with pain. A bucket of cold water was thrown over him, making his teeth chatter.

He had to get away, get away and stand up.

He could hear a bucket being quickly filled with water in the far end of the room. A hand grabbed his hair and banged his head on the floor over and over again. The room was growing hazy, spinning around him.

Water landed heavily on his head. His clothes were drenched and he was shivering. Drawing in painful breaths, he turned on his side and held his stomach. A harsh kick to the back. He cried out in pain.

Schlaff rasped a short order in German, as if issuing a command to a trained dog.

Come on, you neo-Nazi Stasi twin, show your face . . .

He rolled away in an effort to evade another kick, and managed to catch a glimpse of Sepp Mauser's face. His eyes were protruding from their sockets and his lips were dripping with spittle.

A sharp kick to the kidneys. His whole upper body was a mass of searing pain. He coughed and spit out something salty.

"Mauser," Alex called out, struggling to produce a smile, "your brother begged me not to kill him." He grasped his stomach. "He pleaded like a little girl . . ."

A savage kick to the liver. Immediately, his body turned cold and everything went black.

Icy water landed on his face like a barbell. He groaned out loud. His injured cheek was burning. He remained on the floor, not moving. The room fell silent. The sound of his own breathing echoed in his head.

Schlaff issued an order. Sepp bent down and slapped him on his injured cheek. A wave of pain surged through his head, but he managed to stay still. Sepp held his short fingers to Alex's neck, feeling for a pulse.

Alex let out a deep sigh. Taken by surprise, Sepp started to straighten up. With his last ounce of strength, Alex aimed a short, sharp kick at his Adam's apple.

Grunting, the Stasi twin grabbed his injured neck. His face turned red and he sank to his knees. His head hit the floor with a thud. Schlaff ran to him, barking in German and calling out his name again and again. Mauser's rough work shoes twitched against the black floor. A dark stain began spreading over the front of his jeans.

On the huge screen across the room, the Führer shrieked in rage.

Dr. Rauch hurried to Mauser and felt his neck. His eyes glistened like the entrails of a slaughtered animal. He turned to Schlaff and shook his head.

Alex got his first chance to study the cellar. No chairs. The performances put on here were enjoyed by a standing audience.

"Filthy Jew-boy!" Schlaff screamed. "You killed him!"

"You're next, Oskar," Alex said calmly.

Pulling something from his pocket, Schlaff launched himself furiously at Alex. The Taser emitted a debilitating electric shock. He lost control of his muscles and slumped to the floor, his eyes closed. He felt like he had been detached from his body.

A prick—something injected into his neck.

He opened his eyes.

Dr. Rauch was retreating as if Alex were a tranquilized rhino that was just coming to. The start of an erection was visible in the doctor's pants. His heels clicked faintly through his bloodstained overshoes.

"That will tenderize your flesh, Jew-boy," Schlaff yelled from afar.

Alex tried to wiggle his fingers, but they wouldn't move. His feet, either. Nothing moved.

Schlaff's black moccasins were now covered in overshoes, and he had put on a white plastic coverall to protect his expensive clothes. Latex gloves made his hands look like prostheses.

He threw Alex's limp body over his shoulder with surprising ease. Alex's neck refused to obey him, leaving his head hanging loosely. Where was the sick neo-Nazi taking him?

Schlaff dropped him on a white tile floor. A shower stall. Except that there was no drain. His large body was pressed against the glass pane. A set of keys clattered above him, and a swinging metal chain hit the wall. Schlaff was sitting on his heels, locking him into nickel-plated restraints. Alex couldn't feel his body.

The huge screen showed a painting of a young girl with slashes in her flesh and three bearded men with big noses collecting her blood in goblets. Above it was the logo of *Der Stürmer*. Alex's eyes were transfixed by the petrifying image.

Schlaff nimbly picked Alex up, passed a steel chain through the restraints, and pulled it sharply upward. His body rose and stretched until his feet were off the floor and his whole weight was suspended from his wrists. The restraints cut into his flesh like razors. Schlaff grabbed him around the waist and swung him like you swing a child. The chain tightened, and his feet flopped limply against the floor.

The walls were closing in on him, as if he were in a trash compactor. His heart was racing, three beats a second, and his body was trembling uncontrollably. A sharp pain stabbed at his chest and spread to his shoulder and down his left arm. He was covered in cold sweat. His stomach was clenched as tight as a fist.

Gradually his muscles began to respond, and feeling started returning to his legs. He looked up. The chain was attached to a ring in the concrete ceiling. In the shower stall there were no faucets and no showerhead.

Just tiny spray holes.

He screamed as loud as he could.

Oh God, he was in a gas chamber!

Monstrous images rose from the depths of his early years. He was helpless. Something inside threatened to break. His mother screaming in her sleep; the memories that were too much to bear; the terrifying sights that buried his childhood. It was all pouring out, crashing around him, and the pain in his heart was unendurable.

The dungeon of horrors filled with Oskar Schlaff's laughter. His demonic face came closer, the blue butcher's eyes gleaming. "You pissed yourself, Jew-boy!" he gloated maniacally. "And we haven't even started yet."

The warmth in his pants was growing colder.

"You already understand where you are, don't you, Jew-boy?"

Paralyzed with fear, he struggled to steady his convulsive breathing. He felt like a pitchfork had stabbed him in the heart.

But he wasn't dead yet.

Calm down . . . he said to himself. *Just calm down . . . close your eyes and breathe deeply . . . give your heart a chance to slow . . . deep breaths . . . breathe . . . breathe . . .*

His chin slumped to his chest. He opened his eyes. There was something on his shirt.

Yellow.

A Star of David.

"I paid a fortune for this," Schlaff said. "It's an original, from the Kaunas ghetto."

His heart started racing again, and he was taking in too much oxygen. The unbearable pressure in his head returned. *Slowly . . . deep breath . . . keep it steady . . .*

On the screen across the room, hundreds of flags were waving in the wind. A sea of swastikas. Columns of believers caught up in a mob frenzy, eagerly stretching their right arms straight out in a nauseating "Sieg Heil." He looked away. His stomach contracted violently.

He remembered how his father used to wake him up from nightmares. How he would stroke his head and wipe his face, gathering him in his arms and holding him tight until he settled back down. He longed desperately for the protective arms of his late father.

His body was on fire. His eyes filled with tears, and from the ruins of his life emerged a grief like he had never known before. It was a bitter grief for his mother, for the atrocities she had suffered, atrocities he could not shield her from.

He wept for the childhood she never had, for the chronic depression concealed under a thick layer of makeup. He wept for the scraps of dry bread she refused to throw away and chewed on at night. His body shook with tears for the blows she had suffered from the butts of rifles and for the innocent joy that had been buried in a mass grave.

His late mother appeared before him, bent under the weight of survivor's guilt.

The tears were cleansing.

For the first time in his life, he was able to acknowledge his mother without feeling guilt, only compassion and heartache.

The pain in his chest was subsiding. His heart was beating more slowly, and his breathing was calmer and steadier. Even the cramped space was becoming tolerable, though his arms in the restraints above his head were cold and stiff.

Just break free.

Dr. Rauch was picking his nose, his finger in his nostril up to the knuckle.

Schlaff approached, a remote-control device in his hand. "It's a shame you killed the Mausers. We had our game. You should have seen them in authentic striped pajamas, removing bodies from the gas chamber . . ." Schlaff clicked his tongue and then lowered his eyes, contemplating, his eyelids twitching.

"I see you're feeling better," Schlaff said, his eyes sparkling. "Wonderful! We can get started!"

The German pressed a button on the remote.

Something moved.

The folding panels of the aluminum wall on the left slid back quietly along a track to reveal welded-joint steel shelving units. Extending the entire length of the wall, they were loaded with large glass mason jars.

Each jar had a square label with a picture on it.

A face. Dozens of faces.

Alex hurled, covering himself with puke.

The jars contained ashes.

"All your friends are here," Schlaff said, sounding amused.

Alex spit. His chest was on fire and his stomach was convulsing. He tried to count: eight rows; more than a hundred jars . . . maybe a hundred and fifty!

They were all here. All the people who had vanished. Oskar Schlaff the serial killer kept mementos of his victims.

"Nibelungs," Schlaff giggled. "More precisely, grilled Nibelungs. And they're not alone."

The German came closer but still kept some distance. His face twisted at the sight of the puke.

"The media likes to show dramatic pictures of neo-Nazis marching in uniform in Germany or America or wherever. They're not the real Nazis. They're nothing more than stupid kids who have yet to learn how to jerk off! Fucked-up youngsters who do more harm than good. All they do is talk. Talk is easy."

His face became serious. "We act, Jew-boy. We just act. And tonight we are taking a giant leap forward!"

Pointing to the wall, he said, "The bottom row are Jews we hunted here in Germany, weak Jew-boys with long noses—filth that has been trying to corrupt the Aryan nation for hundreds of years.

"Above them are the coloreds, human refuse that streams here from Asia and Africa. The next two rows are the greatest enemies of Christian Europe—Muslims!"

Dr. Rauch lowered his eyes and nodded like a pious congregant listening to a sermon. He stopped rooting around in his orifice.

"In view of the speed with which they are reproducing, polluting Germany and the rest of Europe," Schlaff went on, "we have to work quickly and decisively. The international media only thinks about the next edition, the next news flash, the next issue. No one looks any farther, to the future. The world is simpleminded. It can only see as far as the end of its nose.

"In another ten years, perhaps twenty, Muslims will be the majority in Germany, France, Italy, and Britain. We are cleaning the streets, working quietly and thoroughly. Not counting your Nibelung friends, there are one hundred and twenty-seven jars here—Jews, Muslims, and coloreds that we have cleaned out of Berlin."

Schlaff cleared his throat and pulled on his nose before continuing. "The cathedral in Cologne, the Duomo in Florence, St. Peter's in Rome—they plan to tear them all down to make way for mosques for the hundreds of millions of Muslims who will overrun Europe. Can you tell me that that is not a cancer?"

"Bullshit, Oskar. You're collaborating with the Syrians. If you haven't noticed, they happen to be Muslims."

Schlaff chuckled. "Collaboration with the Syrians is a means to a greater end. We will get to that later. You are showing your ignorance, Jew-boy. The Syrians stay in Syria. The slime we get comes from other places. The swarms from Turkey are the *Exxon Valdez* of the Aryan race!"

"I thought Jews were your problem."

"At the moment—but just for now—there are one hundred and sixty thousand Jews in Germany. There are almost four million Turks! You try to take over the economy; you shove your hands in our pockets and elbow your way up the ladder of the legal system. You are stingy and greedy, but there are not enough of you here that you would be able to seize control. You are a cancer, but an insignificant one. Hodgkin's. There is a treatment for it. Patience, Jew-boy—you will find out about it soon enough.

"You think the world revolves around you. For you, it's a simple equation: World War II equals the Holocaust." Schlaff clicked his tongue. "Do you know what rank was held by Adolf Eichmann, the architect of the final solution?"

Alex remained silent.

"Lieutenant colonel. And how many German soldiers served in Treblinka?"

Alex remained silent.

"Sixteen. Are you getting the picture, Jew-boy? The extermination of the Jews was justified and necessary, but it was merely a footnote in the story of the great war. Are you ready for act two?"

Alex's heart sank.

Schlaff pressed a button on the remote, and the aluminum wall on the right started folding open. Two lights in the ceiling came on, illuminating a pair of stainless-steel doors about two by three feet in size and three feet above the floor.

Refrigeration units. A metal gurney stood beside the doors.

Alex's stomach and throat contracted, but there was nothing left to vomit.

"I imagine you're wondering what the refrigerators are for. Let me show you," Schlaff said, pressing the remote again. A red firebrick wall appeared to the left of the refrigeration units. In the middle was a blackened cast-iron door with a round glass window. Flames leaped behind it.

Oskar was beaming.

"It's a crematorium, Jew-boy. A crematorium!" he said gleefully. "You must admit that I have prepared a warm welcome for you."

A blue vein was throbbing in the Nazi's forehead. He seemed entertained. He stood next to a white apparatus the size of a washing machine and pressed a button. The noise was repugnant. A bone grinder.

Dr. Rauch let out a delayed piggish giggle followed by a snort. It was hard to breathe.

Schlaff held his hands up to the crematorium door, his face glowing with pure delight. "I love to feel the heat on my hands! I can sense the work getting done, the filth being cleaned away. By the way, do you know who is grilling in there right now? She arrived yesterday morning, after a long journey . . ."

Alex turned his head away. His eyes encountered the wall of jars. Across the room the Führer was shrieking on the giant screen, his mustache as big as Rauch's head.

They were burning Jane.

Here.

Right in front of him.

He wanted to scream, but there was no one to hear his pain.

"I didn't have a chance to devote time to her before tonight. Did you know it takes two hours to burn a body?"

The figure 1126C glowed red on the control monitor beside the iron door.

"She'll burn down to about four and a half pounds of ashes. Your jar will be heavier. Which shelf would you like?"

He had had enough of Schlaff's sick games.

"You are witnessing history in the making, Jew-boy. This is not an ordinary cellar. It's a small-scale extermination camp, the first in a chain to be built around the world."

Laughing, he added, "Even McDonald's began with a single branch."

"Why don't you take your medication and go lie down," Alex said.

Schlaff ignored him. "It's a shame the Mauser brothers will no longer be able to do their part for the cause.

"They started out in my kitchen, did you know that? Washing dishes. We knew one another from the Stasi. Those were the days! I saw right away that their place was not in the kitchen but in the slaughterhouse."

"Hey, Oskar," Alex called out. "Have you heard the latest news from Damascus?"

Schlaff froze. "What?"

"We butchered your uncle tonight, on the roof, next to the cage."

Schlaff's expression grew dark. "You . . . you're . . . you are trying to buy time."

"Why not try calling Uncle Alois and find out for yourself. You don't want to miss the funeral. I heard he begged for his life. Just like you begged the boys at the orphanage in Nuremberg before they took turns raping you."

Schlaff's face went red. Beads of sweat glittered on his brow.

"Call Uncle Alois, Oskar, and you'll see that you're all alone in the world again."

Schlaff's arrogant facade shattered. It could be heard throughout the cellar.

"Passover is coming, Oskar. We Jew-boys need blood. Go on, make the call!"

Schlaff pulled his cellphone from his pocket but quickly realized that it was pointless.

"Go outside. You'll get a signal there. Or are you scared to leave me here?"

The German looked distressed. He glanced at the lifeless body of Sepp Mauser.

"You've got my phone, Oskar. I'll do you a favor and tell you where to find the picture of Uncle Alois's dead body."

Schlaff approached him quickly, still holding his phone, and punched Alex on the chin.

His head dropped and salinity spread in his mouth.

Schlaff was standing in front of him; the smile had disappeared.

Alex spat a mixture of saliva and blood in his face. The red goo slid down the German's cheek. Without wiping it away, Schlaff stepped back out of reach.

Dr. Rauch stood frozen at the far end of the cellar, next to the screen. Schlaff unzipped his coverall and took out Alex's phone.

"Curiosity killed the cat, Oskar," Alex said quietly, spitting blood onto the floor.

Schlaff's face fell. He blanched and let out a scream, staring in horror at the image.

Schlaff went to the wall of jars and returned holding an old yellow tin can. On the label were a red stripe, a black stripe, and a skull.

Alex managed to read: ZYKLON B.

"Did you know that this extraordinary product was developed by a Jew? Fritz Haber, his name was. Ironic, no?"

Schlaff opened the can very carefully and held it up to Alex's face. It was half-full of pale crystals a little larger than coarse sea salt.

"I imagine you've been wondering why it's cold down here." He paused dramatically. "When the crystals reach a temperature of twenty-six degrees Celsius, Jews tend to die instantly."

Schlaff pulled open a metal drawer in the gas chamber wall and poured the crystals in. Then he pressed a button, and something started beating.

Alex was paralyzed with fear. He couldn't feel his arms.

"I have turned the heater on. As soon as they're hot enough, the crystals will start to emit hydrogen cyanide, but I'm afraid you won't get to see that," Schlaff said, struggling to smile.

His heart was overflowing. Sounds were growing fainter and receding into the distance.

Something landed heavily and painfully on his face.

A fucking bucket of water.

"Open your eyes!" Schlaff ordered.

He was going to die.

"You have stopped laughing, Jew-boy. Don't worry—by noon you and your British girlfriend will be together again, side by side here on the shelf."

Schlaff pressed a button on the remote and a thick glass door slid closed with a pneumatic whoosh, locking Alex into the gas chamber.

"No!!!" he heard himself scream.

The cell was sealed off.

He could see Schlaff's lips moving, but he could no longer hear his voice. His ears filled with the chilling sounds of his racing heart and labored breathing.

Suddenly, Schlaff's voice blasted at him from behind. Psychopath. A gas chamber with an intercom.

Soon it would start filling with gas.

"There were six of us," Schlaff shouted. "Six doing God's work, what you see here on the shelves." He stepped closer to the glass wall. "You killed the twins," he scolded, "my two finest talents. Now there are four of us left. Only the good doctor and I are here. Guess where the other two are, and what they are carrying in their luggage?"

The inhalers.

Hochstadt-Lancet!

"In just a few hours we will begin to fulfill my revered uncle's last wish. At the age of ninety-nine, he was finally about to hear the first heartbeat of the Fourth Reich!" Schlaff was screeching. Spittle sprayed from his lips.

"Endlösung der Judenfrage Zwei," Schlaff said, his eyes ablaze with fervor. "The Final Solution Two!

"Very soon, six million Jews will die again—but this time, there is no need for concentration camps. You Jew-boys are already concentrated in one place!"

He paused like a seasoned orator, allowing time for his mind-numbing message to sink in.

"I'm going to be dead in a few minutes anyway," Alex said, "so do you mind telling me why Justus ratted us out?"

"Erlichmann, that piece of junk . . ." Schlaff muttered. "Hypnosis," he barked abruptly. "We took him from his bed in the middle of the night. Dr. Rauch drugged him while he was asleep, and we brought him here. When he regained consciousness, Rauch hypnotized him. Justus was a fool—but a genius. He held every detail in his head. Then we brought him out of the trance and drugged him again. He was back at home before dawn. He slept until noon but had no memory of his nighttime adventure."

"How did you find out he was running the Ring for Mossad?"

"You have a lot of questions, Jew-boy," Schlaff chuckled. "By the way, the temperature has already reached eighteen degrees."

"Aren't you going to grant me my last wish? I want to know what happened."

"Very clever, Jew-boy. Justus tried to play games with us—he stopped paying. Did you know he had been giving us money every month for a long time? One day he came home and found a dead pig in his living room with a Star of David branded on its chest. He got the message. I demanded ten times the normal amount, and he paid up like a good boy."

"How did you find out he was working for Mossad?"

"You have to pay for what you did, Jew-boy. You killed the Mauser brothers. They were my bloodhounds! I would point to the garbage in the street and they would go fetch. We had to kill your people where we found them. Abducting a pro can be risky. But all the others were brought here alive."

"You were going to tell me about Sepp."

Schlaff licked his lips. He seemed to be considering his answer.

"Dear departed Sepp had Justus in his sights for quite a while without his ever knowing. One rainy day, Justus went to Grunewald. Sepp was watching. He saw Justus get into a car. Sepp snapped pictures of everyone, including the man in the backseat. I recognized him instantly. I had seen him on TV. It was Reuven Hetz, the head of Mossad. I realized that Justus could be of great service to us. Question time is over, Jew-boy. Twenty-one degrees!"

Luftwaffe bombers flew in formation on the screen behind Schlaff. Cut.

A Panzer factory. Cut.

Children beaming with pleasure. All blue-eyed blonds. Cut.

Hundreds of columns of Wehrmacht soldiers. Sieg Heil! Sieg Heil! Sieg Heil!

A moment of silence fell over the dungeon of horrors. Alex looked at the iron door of the crematorium where Jane was being burned to ashes and was filled with infinite sorrow.

"I see that you are enjoying the films," Schlaff said. "Before you take your last breath, you might benefit from some wisdom from a great man. Listen to what the Führer says in *Mein Kampf*. It is from the chapter entitled 'Race and People.'"

Schlaff goose-stepped across the cellar, his legs straight and his knees locked. Keeping up his maniacal march, he recited the words from memory in the tone of a professor lecturing his students.

"Each animal mates only with one of its own species. The titmouse cohabits only with the titmouse, the finch with the finch, the stork with the stork, the fieldmouse with the fieldmouse, the housemouse with the housemouse, etc."

Schlaff was in the midst of worship.

"Every crossing between two breeds that are not quite equal results in a product that holds an intermediate place between the levels of the two parents. For this reason, it must eventually succumb in any struggle against the higher species!" Spittle sprayed from his lips, and his shrill voice increasingly became an imitation of the Führer's.

Rauch mouthed the text along with him, like a pious member of the flock.

"The stronger must dominate and not mate with the weaker, which would signify the sacrifice of its own higher nature!"

Schlaff turned abruptly to Alex. "Do you understand what the Führer is saying, Jew-boy?"

The gas chamber was getting stuffy.

"Twenty-four degrees!" Schlaff announced like a TV weatherman.

If only he had a hammer, he'd smash the fucking intercom, the glass wall, and Schlaff's skull. "Do you know who thrust the knife into Uncle Alois's heart in Damascus?"

Schlaff went rigid.

"Did Uncle Alois ever tell you how he burned down the Café Trezeguet?"

There was a satanic fire in Schlaff's eyes.

"Roger Trezeguet's son killed Uncle Alois. A Jew-boy. A JEW-BOY!"

Schlaff had apparently toyed with him enough. "Do . . . do

you . . . ha . . . have . . . anything t . . . to say . . . before you d . . . die, Jew-boy?" He looked down at the remote in his hand. The red button had lit up. His finger was already on it.

It was over. There was no way to save himself.

Alex took a final look at the crematorium, where Jane's remains were being burned.

Maybe they'd never had a real chance. Maybe she was right and he'd never really lived, never gotten a taste of the joy of life. It was time to say good-bye to the only person he had left: Daniella.

"You did a nice job down here, Schlaff. A gas chamber, a crematorium, refrigerators for the bodies, shelves for the jars, even a giant screen. But you forgot the most important thing, Oskar—a mirror. So you can look at yourself and see what you really are, not what you imagine in your sick fantasies."

Schlaff snorted contemptuously.

Alex didn't let up. "You hate Jews and you hate Muslims and you hate Justus Erlichmann and Gunter Erlichmann. You hate everyone, everyone who isn't you—everyone who's different from you."

"Shut up, Jew-boy!"

"Did it ever occur to you that what you really hate is yourself?"

Schlaff gave him a patronizing look. "Congratulations, twenty-six degrees! Any last words, Jew-boy?"

He wasn't going to give the scum the pleasure. He had no intention of begging.

"Shut up and press the button."

Oskar Schlaff pressed the red button.

A loud sucking sound horrified Alex. A fucking vacuum pump!

In a minute, death would flow in, replacing the air being pumped out.

Schlaff had no compunctions.

Alex remembered Daniella as a baby. Taking her first steps. The first time she said "dada," and later "I love you." Planting a kiss on his cheek. His Daniella. He tried to force himself to find comfort in the memories.

Naomi quietly crept into his mind, along with their muted life together, devoid of excitement or joy.

Then came Jane, the love of his life; the greatest regret of his life. She was a few feet away, but it was the closest they'd ever come. His heart filled with remorse over the lost women in his life.

A dull pain throbbed behind his eyes. The pressure in his head was mounting. The oxygen was running out.

"You are about to die, Jew-boy!"

The pressure increased. His head was pounding: *bo-boom, bo-boom.* He felt woozy.

He remembered the machine gunner in Leipzig. The pool of blood around his head was getting smaller, being soaked back up. The man rose from the dead, sat up, leaned on his arm, and stood.

And then, as if wiping away a bad dream, he passed his gloved hand over his face, picked up the machine gun, and fired a heavy barrage at the Wehrmacht troops.

"It is time," Schlaff shrieked, bursting the bubble of his thoughts and pointing the remote at the gas chamber. There was a click, and then another, and the glass in front of him turned white.

Something splattered on it.

Red.

Something banged against the glass.

A head.

Schlaff's.

A large red hole had opened in the German's cheek. Blood was pouring out. His face was pressed against the glass door. He collapsed onto the floor, the blood smearing down the glass.

Someone was there.

The pressure behind his eyes was blinding.

A shape.

A gun.

Dr. Rauch threw his hands in the air. Sweat glistened on his upper lip.

Justus Erlichmann was grinning at him. "Do not worry, Doctor. I would never shoot a physician."

Petrified, Rauch slowly lowered his short arms until they were hanging by his sides.

"But I would shoot a veterinarian," Justus added, pulling the trigger twice.

As the bullets entered his chest, Rauch's stunted body was thrown backward into the wall of jars. He reached out to grab hold of a shelf, but his hand hit a jar. The glass container tumbled to the floor and shattered, scattering ashes like flour on the black surface.

A nauseating, bitter odor filled the air.

Rauch's head hit the floor. Blood spread over his pink shirt as his little feet kicked at the pale ashes.

His piglike eyes were still gaping when his heart stopped beating.

Alex was stuck in a tub of tar. Muffled voices in the distance. It was done; he was dead.

The words seemed vaguely familiar.

They were calling his name.

The sound was coming from too far away.

Someone put a hand on his face, caressing him tenderly, speaking softly.

Who was this person? What was he saying?

The gummy tar gradually thinned out.

A cold floor. A black floor.

He opened his eyes.

"Justus?"

"Alex!" Justus cried. "I was afraid I was too late. But I'm here now, and Schlaff is dead. They are all dead. It's over."

It was cold on the floor.

"You passed out," Justus said. "Lack of oxygen."

Alex struggled to sit up, leaning on his elbows, but he had no feeling in his arms. His body burned and throbbed with pain.

Stubble cast a shadow over Justus's pale cheeks. His blue eyes were sunken into dark circles.

"Where have you been hiding?" Alex asked.

"At home."

"No way!"

"There is a secret room between the pantry and the guest bathroom. I built it a long time ago."

"You were in the house?"

"Last night you slept in the pantry cupboard. I was two feet away, on the other side of the wall. You didn't know. You were blocking my exit. I bumped into a table and it made a noise. Perhaps subconsciously I wanted you to find me. You spoke on the phone. Then you got up and searched the house."

"What were you doing there all this time?"

Justus smiled sadly. "Waiting."

"The whole fucking time?"

"I realized that something had gone seriously wrong and I was in danger. So, yes, I abandoned the Ring in the hope that later I would be able to salvage what was left of it. I needed time to find out what had gone wrong. If I was killed, a whole life's work would have been lost."

"What about the blood in the cemetery?"

"I was scared. I felt like I was being watched. When we were in the café together, I thought that perhaps you had brought people with you to kidnap me and bring me to Israel. I decided to go underground. I bought a large syringe at a pharmacy and filled a small soda bottle with my blood. I saw you enter the cemetery. I hid there until I was sure you had found it."

"What made you come here?"

"I followed you."

"The virus is on its way to Israel!" Alex suddenly remembered. "I have to get upstairs and make a call. If we're lucky, the Security Agency will catch Schlaff's couriers in time. They stole the inhalers from the Orchid Farm!"

"Yes, I heard that fool boasting about it before," Justus chuckled.

"What's so funny?"

"The inhalers they have are of value only to asthma sufferers."

"What!?"

"I went to the Orchid Farm the day before I met you in Berlin. As I said, I feared I was in danger, so I decided to switch the virus inhalers with ordinary Ventolin."

"What did you do with the vaccine?"

"I replaced the three inhalers. The ones I left behind contain a strain of methicillin-resistant *Staphylococcus aureus*, commonly known as flesh-eating bacteria. If the couriers used them as they were instructed to, there will be no need to look for them. Very soon they will present themselves at an emergency room with a high fever and an infection that is resistant to antibiotics."

"Where's the virus now?" Alex asked.

"Hidden in a safe place."

"How did they get into the Cube?"

"I have given that a lot of thought. The only answer I can find is that they took a picture of my iris when they brought me here. There are companies that will reproduce the image and print it on a contact lens. I must have given them the entry code under hypnosis."

"I was sure they had killed you and stashed the body somewhere," Alex said. "But this morning it struck me that the whole time you were gone, no one showed up at your house. No maid, no cook, no gardener."

Justus gave him an approving smile. Then his face turned serious. "I realized that they were only going after the Ring, not Mossad. I could not deal with them by myself. You showed me that you were the right man for the job, so I decided to disappear and let you handle it."

"Did you bribe Reuven?"

Justus's expression became grim. "Like me, Reuven sensed that something was wrong, but I did not have any answers for him yet. I thought that perhaps my personal issues with Schlaff were distracting me. Reuven told me that he was obligated to report his suspicions to the prime minister. I could see the wheels turning in his head. He was hungry, so I gave him something to chew on.

"Israeli politicians do not contend with the real problems. Their sole concern is their own survival. A second Holocaust is just a matter of time. I thought that if Reuven were prime minister, he would be able to prevent it."

Justus the idealist had tried to buy himself an Israeli prime minister. A lot of influence for a little money.

Alex said, "It doesn't bother you that Reuven has no principles and no scruples?"

"A person with principles and scruples will not win an election in Israel these days," the German said.

"Why was Schlaff blackmailing you?"

Justus lowered his eyes and shook his head.

"I'm sorry," Alex said, "but I have to know."

"My father was an SS officer, Alois Brunner's deputy at Drancy. When he learned that Germany was planning to exterminate all the Jews in Europe, he defected. Roger Trezeguet, Gerard's father, hid him and brought him to the Resistance.

"Our fortune . . ." Justus paused and pursed his lips, ordering his thoughts.

"Before my father began saving Jewish lives, he did a terrible thing. He took . . . he stole precious gems from a Jewish family. Everyone could see that those who were deported to the East never returned. The family offered him everything they had to save them, and told him where to find the family jewels. They were concealed in the leg of a table that had been confiscated by the Nazis. My father found it in a camp near Drancy where they stored the property they looted from the Jews. In a moment of weakness, he took the jewels for himself. Then, to hide his crime, he arranged for the family to be sent to Auschwitz."

Justus's lower lip was quivering. His expression was somber. "My father confessed to me years ago. He was deeply ashamed. It was a despicable, inhuman act. Two days after the Dresdener family was loaded on the transport, he decided to redeem himself, to defect from the army of the Reich and save as many Jews as he could."

"Who killed him in Davos?"

"Oskar, most likely. I taught him about RC helicopters."

"Who's Rachel Dresdener?"

"You could only know about her if you had read my will," Justus said with a sad smile. "I see that you found a way into my vault at Berghoff Bank." He gave Alex an admiring look before going on. "Almost the entire Dresdener family died in the camp. Only the youngest daughter, Rachel, survived. She is an old woman now, all alone in the world. She lives in Israel, in Kiryat Motzkin. I have been sending her money for many years. She does not know where it comes from.

"After the war, my father sold the jewelry and invested the money in art and real estate. And so the source of my family fortune is a crime, an atrocity."

"What does all that have to do with Oskar Schlaff?"

"After the fall of the Berlin Wall, Oskar discovered that he was the nephew of Alois Brunner. He went to see him in Damascus. Brunner had never lost his hatred for my father. I assume he mentioned his name to Oskar, and Oskar saw the opportunity to extort money from us. We patronized his restaurant for more than twenty years, almost from the day it opened. We came even when no one else did. Oskar was a young man back then, still trying to make his way in life. There were rumors about him. It was said that he worked for the Stasi, that he was an informant. My father helped him, gave him money. That did not stop him from blackmailing us.

"We paid and we kept silent, but we did not know the identity of the blackmailer. We did not know that it was Schlaff, or that he was Brunner's nephew. When I found out, I prepared a letter bomb, but it was his girlfriend who opened it, not him. He knew that it came from me. The rest I heard tonight, together with you."

"Why didn't you just tell the truth? You could have compensated Rachel Dresdener for the jewels and put an end to it all," Alex said.

"My father made me swear to keep his secret as long as he lived." Justus lowered his voice. "Did Gerard die in Syria?"

"Gerard is fighting for his life, but they've managed to stabilize him. The chopper must have landed in Israel by now. He killed Brunner last night in Damascus. He thought he was dying, so he told me most of the story. There was only one moment when he broke down and cried."

"When?"

"When he spoke of you. He loves you. He was sure you were dead. It was hard to hear."

Justus's eyes glistened. He wiped away a tear.

"The bond between us . . ." Justus took a deep breath before going on. "We are more than brothers. When I did not answer the phone, he rushed to Berlin. I know all about the body in the trunk and the grave in the forest."

A shadow passed over Justus's face.

"I am so sorry about the Ring. It was my father's legacy to me. He created it with his own two hands, but I could not . . . so many people have died . . ."

Justus gazed at the wall of jars. His eyes were moist, but his voice was steady. "It is all gone. I am glad that my father is not here to see it."

He attempted a smile. Suddenly he looked different, and not merely because he was not as meticulously groomed as usual.

The aura of German malevolence had faded.

Justus was now German in the same way that Jane was British. Even his German accent no longer grated on Alex's ear; the German language was no longer a badge of dishonor. Alex had heard the phrase "the other Germany" more times than he could count. For the first time, he understood what it meant.

His body still ached from the abuse it had suffered, and he was totally drained. But strangely, his heart felt lighter. The heavy lid that had held his life in check had been lifted.

"Help me up," Alex said.

Justus bent over and held out his arms. Alex clutched them. Clenching his teeth, he pulled himself up and immediately folded over in pain. Justus grasped him securely to keep him from falling. Alex straightened up as best he could and looked Justus in the eye. "You saved my life," he said. "I'll never forget it."

He threw his arms around the German. Justus returned the embrace, careful not to hurt him.

"I also came to find out who informed on the Nibelungs," Justus said, his voice cracking. "It appears that it was me." He shook his head sadly.

Then he went into the toilet.

Doubled up in pain, Alex stumbled to the door of the crematorium and felt the heat. He looked through the thick glass window. Flames; a skeleton; the remains of a human body. The love of his life.

His chest rose and fell heavily. In despair, he wept silently, thinking of the days to come, of the love that wasn't to be, of the chance for happiness disappearing in a column of smoke.

From the direction of the toilet, he heard glass shatter. "*Scheisse...*" Justus spat from behind the closed door.

Alex took a deep breath. In a shaking voice, he asked, "Is everything all right?"

"Yes . . . I broke the mirror," Justus answered.

The black floor was covered with a layer of pale ashes. On the screen, the Führer was shrieking behind a dais and swastikas were waving in the wind. Sepp Mauser lay dead, not far from the body of Dr. Rauch. Oskar Schlaff was sprawled next to the gas chamber, his eyes wide open.

Alex had been through several circles of hell tonight. He had looked death in the eye and made peace with it, but he was desperate to get out of this dungeon of horrors.

What was taking Justus so long?

Alex stood in front of the bathroom door. "Are you coming?"

Silence.

"Justus?"

No answer.

He banged his fist on the door.

Silence.

Alex leaned on the handle. The door was locked.

He looked down at the space between the door and the floor.

A dark pool of blood was spreading toward his feet.

In the Al-Malki district on the western outskirts of Damascus, about a mile and a half from his home, in the basement morgue of Shami Hospital, in the cadaver refrigerator, on a cold stainless-steel slab, lay the naked body of Alois Brunner.

The temperature gauge read four degrees Celsius. He had been there for a long time.

He refuses to die.

AFTERWORD

DAMASCUS, 1985

Alois Brunner, an infamous Nazi war criminal, was born on April 8, 1912. After serving as Adolf Eichmann's second-in-command, he became commandant of the Drancy internment camp near Paris. He is considered personally responsible for the deaths of 125,000 Jews.

After the war, Brunner fled, finding a safe haven in 1954 in Damascus, where he collaborated with the Mukhabarat. He resided alternately in the Hotel Dedeman and in an apartment at 7 Hadad Street in the Abu Rumaneh district.

There is no record of his death, no grave, and no tombstone.

ACKNOWLEDGMENTS

A book of this sort involves a substantial amount of solitary work. I am extremely grateful to Hannah Wood for her excellent editing work and for ironing out the wrinkles in the plot. My heartfelt thanks go out to all those who lent a hand and gave me the benefit of their time and knowledge:

Uri Adoni
Cobi Argov
Amitai Bar Am
Yotam Dagan
Lilach Dor
Nathan Dunevich
Ruthi Dunevich
Shirra Dunevich
Michael Eiser, Berlin
Yuval Golan
Amnon Jackont
Ephraim Karnon
Yaron Merchav
Yifat Niv
Ronen Orr
Ariel Pridan

Tal Ravid Stern
Navit Rosenzweig
Eyal Rosner
Nir Ruttenberg
Giovanni and Francesco Toscano, Bucine

And last, thanks to everyone who asked me during the past three years:
"Well, when?"

Roni Dunevich was born in Tel Aviv in 1961. Before he began his literary career, he was a copywriter, art director, and strategic consultant. His first book featuring Alex Bartal, *Hunted* (not yet translated into English), received the Gold Prize. His second Bartal book, *Unfinished Business* (also not yet translated into English), was serialized in Israel's biggest newspaper. He lives in Israel.